The Beneficiaries

P K Taylor

This is a work of fiction and, except in the case of historical fact, any resemblance to actual persons, living or dead, is purely coincidental.

Published by Whiston Press Publications.
For information: Phone 949 521 0364.

Printed in the United States of America.

Library of Congress Cataloging-in-Publication Data is available from the publisher.

ISBN-10: 0615952364
ISBN-13: 9780615952369

For Mum and Dad.

ONE

"Thank God!" Jeremy Danvers exclaimed when he saw the sign:
Welcome to Tipping
Population 412
Please drive carefully

He was nearly home.

The stone cottages of the remote North Yorkshire village came into view as he screeched around a sharp right hand bend. Relief flooded through him, but it was short-lived. A terrified glance in his rearview mirror confirmed that the black Audi was still there and closing in quickly. Its offside wheels clattered over the cat's eyes in the middle of the road as it moved out to overtake him.

Too desperate to heed caution and too exhausted to care, Jeremy floored the accelerator and swerved violently to the opposite side of the road. He didn't see a deep pothole near the curb until it was too late. The front offside wheel plunged into the hole with a sickening crunch and the rear wheels lost traction. The impact caused the hatchback door to fly open.

"Oh shit, shit, SHIT!" Jeremy screamed as he fought to regain control. Sweat trickled down his sides.

He stole another look in the rear view mirror, but the open hatch door blocked his view. He peered into his side mirror and let out another scream when he saw his backpack topple onto the road. It fell heavily

1

with a dull thump, liberating its contents, and scattering books, papers and oddments of clothing across the narrow country road.

The Audi had to swerve sharply to avoid the jettisoned articles. A hefty book hit the Audi's front grill with a loud "Thwack!" The book ricocheted across the road where it skidded to a halt against the grass verge. The displacement of air as the two cars hurtled by, lifted the pages, snapping them over like the report of a machine gun.

"Come on, come on!" Jeremy screamed at his old battered car as he rocked back and forth in his seat, willing it to go faster. The Audi dipped in and out of view as it tried to overtake him. On the verge of panic, Jeremy took the next bend with too much speed. He careened around the hairpin with his tires squealing and barely missed plunging over the edge into the dark ravine below.

"Oh God help me," Jeremy whimpered as the rear end of the car clipped the guardrail. He cringed when the hatchback door lurched upward and came back down with a thundering bang.

In that instant, he knew he could not outrun the car behind him.

"How the hell did I get into all this shit?" he remonstrated dispiritedly. A wave of nausea washed over him at the thought of the stolen artwork strewn across the road behind him.

"Idiot, idiot, IDIOT!" he shouted, cursing his own stupidity. Hot tears of regret threatened to spill down his cheeks. He hardly dared think about what was going to happen when the man in the black Audi caught up with him. His life was in danger, but going to the police was not an option. It was too late for that.

His only chance would be to somehow get off the road. He reasoned that if he could make the next five or six miles to the small town of Wickham, he might be able to hide amongst the crowds of shoppers and buy some time. It was a Friday, and that meant it was market day. The place would be at its busiest.

A picture of the tented stalls lining the pavement around the cobbled market square flashed through his mind. He knew the town well, and was familiar with its tiny back streets and cobbled lanes. The market town offered a chance of throwing off his pursuer. It was his only option.

* * *

Just as the speeding cars careened out of view, an antique, blue Morris Oxford nosed its way toward the exit of the tiny car park at the village post office. A large puddle filled with thick mud, the bane of any visitor to the store, guarded the exit as if daring anyone to cross it. The puddle was rumored to be more than a foot deep in places. With a sigh of resignation, Barrington Smith drove through with his usual trepidation, emerging on the other side with a liberal amount of mud clinging to the underside of his car. He grumbled loudly about the lousy parking, and heaped the blame for it upon Pearl Wiggins, the proprietor of the post office that also doubled as the general store. When Barrington swung onto the road, he failed to see the abandoned backpack lying in the center of the lane. The Oxford clipped the pack's corner with its nearside front wheel, shunting it toward the curb. The impact, assisted by a timely blast of wind, sent a vortex of papers into the air.

If eighty-two-year old Barrington Smith had looked in his rearview mirror, he would have been shocked to see the cloud of paper behind him. Crouched in the driver's seat, his eyes barely above the level of the steering wheel, he slowly pressed down on the accelerator, bringing the car up to a cruising speed of about twenty-five miles per hour.

Brigadier Dickie Cranshawe Booth, the driver of another car coming from the opposite direction, saw the oncoming vehicles approaching, but he didn't realize how fast they were going until they were almost upon him. At first, his eyes focused on the white car in front. The black car following it was hidden from view. But just as Dickie arrived at the outskirts of the village, the Audi swerved into the middle of the road.

"What the . . .? Jesus Christ!" Dickie Cranshawe Booth yelled as he slammed the brakes of his Range Rover to the floor. He instinctively yanked the steering wheel hard to the left, closing his eyes as he braced for a head-on collision. The car veered sharply, mounting the grass verge on the opposite side of the road to the post office. It screeched to an abrupt halt, stopping just short of the dry-stone wall that separated the road from the field beyond. With his hands still clenched to the steering wheel, and hardly daring to open his eyes, Dickie raised his head to look around, stunned that he was still in one piece. He flinched when he saw a maelstrom of papers flapping wildly all over the road. Befuddled and in shock, he wheeled his head around in the direction of the speeding cars. Disappointed and annoyed, the only vehicle he saw was Barrington's large blue tank of a car moving at a snail's pace down the road.

"What the devil…? Blithering bloody idiots. Going to kill someone," he stammered.

He let his head fall back against the headrest as he fought for composure. His heart hammered at an alarming speed and he could feel sweat moistening the back of his neck. He exhaled loudly and loosened his shirt collar, yanking it from side to side.

Several deep breaths later, once the initial shock receded, a torrent of rage welled up inside him.

"We'll see about this," he muttered. "Speeding maniacs!" Fuming, he kicked open the driver's door in one swift movement, which was impressive for a man of Dickie's corpulence, and stomped to the front of his car to look for signs of damage. He had missed the wall by inches. Relieved, but hopping mad, he turned in the direction of the post office across the road to see if anyone had witnessed the incident.

"Why is there never anyone around when you bloody well need them?" he barked into the emptiness around him.

The post office was usually busy at this time of day, but it was market day in Wickham. Every Friday morning, a good portion of Tipping's four hundred or so inhabitants made their ritual pilgrimage to the street market, happy to escape the confines of their little village.

* * *

Meanwhile, on the outskirts of the town, Jeremy raced along the main road with the Audi close behind.

4

"Oh, thank Christ!" he exclaimed when he saw a church tower in the distance. Wickham was just ahead. He was nearly there. "Not far," he whispered. "Not far now."

In his mind, he pictured the route into town. He knew he had to cross the river into the main car park where he could hide among the other cars, gain some anonymity, and a moment to think. The traffic began to build as he got closer to the town. Only a few cars passed traveling in the opposite direction, but he could see the line of market day traffic backing up ahead about a quarter of a mile in the distance.

The turn into Carmichael's farm was coming up on his left. It was a rutted driveway that snaked its way up to the farmhouse. Jeremy remembered that it wound around the main dwelling, narrowing to little more than a dirt track as it skirted the barns and outbuildings beyond. During the summer holidays, he had spent long hours playing with the two Carmichael boys who were close to his age.

The dirt track continued into the woods behind the farm, eventually leading to a narrow stone bridge, centuries old, spanning the river at the south end of the car park in Wickham. However, he could not be certain that the bridge was wide enough to accommodate a car. It was a thoroughfare used mainly by hikers, but he had no time to think of anything else.

Jeremy swung the car into the lane at the last moment, the rear off-side wheel losing contact with the road. "Oh sweet Jesus!" he exclaimed as he narrowly avoided rolling the car.

When the back wheels regained traction, he pushed down on the accelerator and plunged forward toward the farmhouse, bouncing in and out of the deep ruts in the lane. Sweat dripped from his brow, stinging his eyes. He frantically tried to wipe it away using the back of his arm. A terrified glance into his rear-view mirror revealed an empty lane behind him. "I've dropped him!" Jeremy said aloud.

"The bastard's missed the turn!" He was jubilant for a moment, but he knew he had to get out of sight quickly.

Apart from a dog barking from somewhere deep inside the building, the farmhouse seemed quiet. Thank God, he thought. Jeremy slowed as he rounded the house in case the occupants were around, but sped up as he passed the large barn and sheds. No one was to be seen.

A rickety sign stood at the entrance to the woods marking the way to Wickham. The track was even narrower than he remembered. He used the brakes hesitantly, worried that the car would not get through. His mind raced with indecision. He checked his rearview mirror again—still no sign of the Audi. He ran both hands down his face and resolutely ordered his mind to ignore the possibility of being caught. He had to keep calm. It was too late to turn back to the main road. Resigned, his only choice was to turn onto the track. Jeremy drove with considerably more care as he inched his way toward Wickham.

Overgrown in many places and pitted with mud-filled potholes, the track was not an easy route. He picked his way toward the bridge, cursing as the car jostled and bumped its way along.

Branches of shrubbery scratched the sides of the car and mud cloyed the wheel arches. He fought to maintain focus on his plan of escape, gritting his teeth in grim determination.

Jeremy almost wept with relief when he caught a glimpse of the river through the last of the trees. He came to a halt before leaving the concealment of the dense vegetation. His stomach sank when he leaned forward to reconnoiter the bridge through the filthy windscreen and saw how tight a squeeze it was going to be. At least it's still standing, he thought doubtfully, taking in the crumbling stonework. Fortunately, there was no sign of any hikers making their way across. Satisfied that the black Audi was no longer a threat, he pressed forward. With only inches to spare on either side, he drove over the bridge and into the parking lot. He slid into an empty space between two non-descript cars and turned off the engine.

The stillness magnified the enveloping silence. Jeremy's ears were ringing after hours of driving. He covered his face with both hands, slumped against the steering column and let out a loud sob. He had not slept properly in days, not since he had discovered the truth about the paintings. The sheer weight of exhaustion pressed down on him, about to crush the little resistance he had left. The temptation to rest, just for a few moments, was almost overwhelming, but the stab of fear when he thought again of the man in the Audi made him snap to attention.

Jeremy jerked his head around and made a rapid assessment of the car park. It was busy. Most of the parking spaces were taken. A few people were milling around. Good—safety in numbers. Surely, his pursuer wouldn't try to tackle him in the open like this. He made a quick decision, flung open the driver's door and lunged to the back of the car. He wrenched the hatchback open, and for a moment stood motionless, mouth gaping as he stared into the car in stunned disbelief.

"Oh bloody hell!" he exclaimed. He had hoped there might be something left, but the empty trunk screamed back at him. He felt sick to the pit of his stomach when he saw that he had lost everything: the backpack, the artwork and all the rest of his things were strewn across the road in Tipping.

Overcome by a moment of panic, he slammed the door and sprinted towards the public toilets at the entrance to the car park. He intended to lock himself in a stall until he could think of a plan. Halfway there, he changed his mind. He realized he was acting irrationally. Christ, an imbecilic simpleton could do better than this. He stopped abruptly, spun around and dashed back to the car. With a pained sob, he realized he had to go back to Tipping.

* * *

"Smart move kid," Conrad conceded reluctantly, as he overshot the turn into Carmichael's farm. He pounded the brake and the Audi screeched to a halt fifty yards down the road. When he slammed the car into reverse, Conrad did not see the cyclist behind him until it was too late.

"Jesus! Shit!" he yelled as he saw the cyclist fling himself to the side of the road, the bicycle taking a trajectory in the other direction. Conrad leaped out and rushed to the old guy lying on his side on the grass verge, somewhat dazed, but otherwise in one piece. Conrad guessed he was at least seventy.

"Oh my God! I am so sorry. Are you okay? Here let me help you up."

"Gerroff me, you bloody idiot! You need to look in yer mirror. You could've killed me."

"Look, I really am sorry," Conrad replied, "but I'm kinda desperate. I'm trying to catch up with someone who's stolen something from me. He's driven up that track back there," he said pointing in the direction of the lane leading to Carmichael's farm.

"Ohhh, American are you? Don't get too many in these parts. Not used to the roads, eh?" enquired the old man, his demeanor softening.

"Yes. My name's Conrad Rankin," Conrad replied, extending his hand. The elderly gentleman got to his feet, brushed himself down, and leaned forward to shake Conrad's hand.

"Dennis Whitlock's mi' name."

Conrad removed his wallet from his back pocket, took out several large bills and offered the money to Dennis. "Here—please take this. It should cover any damage to your bike."

"Oh, no. No lad. No need for that. This 'ol bike of mine 'as seen more than a few knocks." He walked to where his bike was lying and pulled it upright. He shook it and bumped its front wheel on the ground a few times before declaring it undamaged.

" 'Ad this here bike fer years now. They don't make 'em like they used to no more."

"You must take this," insisted Conrad, shaken by the thought that he could have seriously injured the man. "It's the least I can do. Are you sure you're all right? Can I give you a ride somewhere?"

Shaking his head before climbing back on his bike, Dennis said, "You know lad, if you step on it, you might just catch up with 'im."

"What do you mean?"

"Well, I reckon he's 'eddin to Wickham."

"What? How do you know that?" asked Conrad.

"Well, it's a bit narrow mind, but I reckon he's goin' to try and cross th' old bridge into town. He's not goin' to drive into a dead end is he? Old Carmichael's takes you right down into Wickham car park. Now if you put your foot down, you can 'ed him off. Carry on down t' main road and take first left at the sign post into town. You'll see signs fer car park."

Conrad caught the general gist of what Dennis had told him. If he moved quickly, there was still a slim a chance he might catch up with the kid and get the artwork back. He thanked Dennis for his help and offered one last apology before running back to his car.

"Starsky and Hutch!" Dennis called after him as Conrad drove back onto the road. "That were one of mi' favorites!"

Conrad arrived in Wickham just moments after Jeremy had concealed himself between two parked cars. After a quick scan of the full parking lot, and seeing no sign of Jeremy, Conrad reversed into the rear yard of Hammond's Bakery, the building closest to the car park. Ignoring the no parking signs, he leaped out of his car without bothering to lock it and sprinted to the corner of the bakery where he had a good vantage point.

He cut a strange figure, crouched in his immaculate attire, so obviously out of place in the rural backwater of Wickham. Dressed in dark-hued Armani, his clothes smacked of expensive taste. In his early thirties, over six feet tall and tanned, the strength of his masculinity defined beneath the fine silk of his sweater, he was a strikingly handsome man. His golden blond, sun streaked hair was fashionably messy and the square set of his jaw lent him a natural, rugged appeal.

Conrad peered across the car park, trying to pick out the white Volkswagen. Where in hell have all these cars come from? It was beyond him why so many people would be in such a small town. He turned his head in the opposite direction toward the general noise in the background and noticed a few stalls set up at the end of the street, attended by hordes of people. Oh, a street market, he guessed, a phenomenon that was entirely foreign to his lifestyle.

He turned his attention back to the car park, and was lucky enough to see Jeremy make his frantic dash toward the toilets. Now where is he going, Conrad wondered, on the verge of running out and grabbing the kid. He watched Jeremy come to an abrupt halt in the middle of the car park, spin around, and sprint back to his car.

"What the . . . what's he doing?" Conrad whispered. Alarm bells started to ring in his brain. He hesitated, unsure about whether to run

9

out and intercept him. Then it dawned on him. "Oh Jeez. He's lost the frigging paintings!" he said aloud. The car chase flashed through his mind. He remembered the hatchback door of Jeremy's car flying open and stuff falling onto the road.

"Oh, fuck." His stomach clenched with the realization that the artwork, centuries old and worth more to him than any possible monetary value, was now scattered in the middle of nowhere. He knew in an instant that the kid was going back to look for them. He turned and raced to his car. He needed to get back to the village, and fast.

TWO

Barrington Smith tuned in to his favorite radio show, *War-time Sing-a-long*, which aired every Friday between 10:00 and 11:00 a.m. as he continued his drive home. The velvet tones of Vera Lynn's, *The White Cliffs of Dover*, filled the airwaves. Barrington smiled, his new dentures visible between his thin lips. Beginning to relax at last, he slumped a little further into his seat. His eyes, once a piercing blue, were dulled with age, and yellowed around the pupils. They took on a glazed-over, glassy appearance as his mind lost focus on the road ahead.

"There'll be blue birds over the white cliffs of Dover," crooned Vera, accompanied by Barrington's raspy tenor.

The words of one of the most popular songs from the Second World War resonated in Barrington's mind, teasing the deep recesses of his memory. Captivated by the melody, he was transported back to D-Day, June 6, 1944. As a sergeant in the 2nd Battalion, East Yorkshire Regiment, a part of the 3rd British Infantry Division, he had landed at Sword Beach in Normandy. Caught in the crossfire from mortar bombs and snipers on the exposed beach, roughly a quarter of his unit had been lost in the first twenty-four hours of combat.

Barrington shifted awkwardly in his seat as the memories flooded back. His shoulders flinched when he recalled the terrific noise of the shelling and gunfire.

"No, I'm not going to think about it, I'm not," he whispered through clenched teeth, slapping his hand on the steering wheel again.

Absorbed in his sad little reverie, Barrington had no recollection of any vehicles speeding through the village when he was questioned later. Nor did he recall seeing anything lying in the road. Why all that paper was stuck behind one of the windscreen wipers of his Morris Oxford was a complete mystery to him.

Ten minutes later, parked at the side of his cramped little cottage less than half a mile from the post office, he shook his head in disgust.

"Government can't even keep the streets clean anymore. Don't know what this country's coming to . . . "

Still grumbling about the government's shortcomings, Barrington shuffled to the front of his car and snatched the litter out from under the windscreen wiper. He balled one piece into a tight wad and was about to do the same to another larger piece, when a thought struck him. He wasn't one to waste anything, not even a few pieces of stray paper as long as they were reasonably clean. The frugal years of rationing after the War had taught him to put everything to good use. Instead of tossing the litter into the dustbin, he carried it through the front parlor and into his kitchen where he placed it on a stack of newspapers by the back door. He would tear them up later for his cat's litter box.

* * *

Nestled high in the hills of North Yorkshire, Tipping commanded a panorama of sweeping vistas stretching as far as the eye could see. The village was a peaceful backwater of chocolate-box prettiness, a little tableau in stone. Most of the homes and shops were clustered around the central village green. *The Three Bees* was the larger of the two pubs in the village, and was located at the far side of the green at the foot of a rather steep climb up to the old 11th century church built by the Normans. Stark in its beauty, it was a historical landmark that added its own quaint charm to the village. The tiny graveyard to the rear of the chapel offered the most majestic views over the surrounding countryside. In the winter when the tourists were gone, it was a quiet, lonely retreat.

Driven by a sense of duty and guilt, Dickie Cranshawe Booth occasionally made an effort to visit the burial ground of some of his ancestors, but he always stopped at the pub first for a bit of sustenance. Fortified by a few pints of *The Bee's* finest ale, he would stagger up the climb, stopping every now and then to catch his breath. By the time he made it to the far end of the graveyard, he would be ready to collapse, panting, onto the bench overlooking the broad sweep of the valleys below. He would inhale deeply, breathing in the crystal air while he sat and watched the cloud shadows racing on the winds, trailing ribbons of shade and brightness across the landscape. For those few moments, in the emptiness and silence, he would feel a sense of solitude and a temporary reprieve from his debt-ridden existence.

Not today though. He was in a hurry. After the incident with the two speeding cars tearing through the village, he toyed with the idea of marching to the post office to ask if anyone had seen anything. He also considered slipping over to *The Three Bees* on the other side of the green facing the road. Lord knows, he needed a drink, but he quickly thought better of it. Celia would be waiting for him. She would be wondering what was keeping him. Besides, he wasn't even meant to be anywhere close to the village at this hour.

The thought of trying to explain to Olivia, his wife, why he was in Tipping at 10 o'clock on a Friday morning instead of being in Wickham, made him wince. No, he would have a discreet word with Barrington when he got the chance. Ask him if he had seen anything.

Dickie hesitated by the wall for another moment, looking around for signs of life. Apart from a few dozen sheep in the field next to his car, the village was empty. A curlew cried in the distance, breaking the silence.

"What are you lot looking at?" he bellowed in the direction of the sheep. Alarmed by the noise made by Dickie's screeching brakes, they had huddled together in the farthest corner of the field, ears pricked, ready to take flight again.

"Omnivorous idiots," he cursed under his breath, venting some of his frustration on the sheep. He considered himself to be a man of significant importance and was entirely unused to being driven off the road by some ignorant lout.

He cast another annoyed glance toward the post office, and as he did so, his attention was drawn for an instant to some kind of baggage strewn against the curb on the other side of the road. He also noted more debris scattered around, a pair of tattered jeans, a few books, and what looked like a shirt. A football lolled in a puddle.

"Humph", he snorted bitterly. "Bloody football hooligans." In Dickie's mind, "football hooligans," a description he bestowed on any-body he disapproved of, and there were many who fit this category, were the root cause of most of modern society's problems. The drivers of the speeding cars were undoubtedly of this ilk. He screwed up his face in distaste.

"Thankless, thoughtless, disrespectful louts," he muttered. "They're all the same, the lot of them—Yobbos!"

He kicked at a wad of papers as he turned and strutted back to his car. He was dimly aware that there were a number of sketches and draw-ings, as well as pages of newspaper. A stray picture of something or other was flapping in defiance on his car seat.

"Ha!" he exclaimed, and with a blast of vengeance, fell into the driver's seat squashing the paper beneath his ample posterior. He ground his backside into the seat for good measure, and with a modicum of satisfaction, drove on.

The departure of the Range Rover revived some of the papers strewn across the road. Several pages became airborne again, making valiant attempts to stay aloft, but the delicate wind offered no assis-tance. A few pieces clung onto the lower branches of trees, but the general mass of paper found a resting place in the thicket and beds of nettles at the edge of the field where the sheep had resumed their mundane grazing. A few rebellious sheets launched themselves on the occasional wisp of wind, but they too eventually surrendered, flutter-ing to the ground in defeat.

One piece of paper, a loner, different, heavier than the rest, remained trapped within a book that protruded from the top of the backpack. Its outer-most edges strained to be free, teased by the rush of air as the

Range Rover drove by. It danced flirtatiously, joyous in its first exposure to sunlight in more than 200 years.

* * *

There was another witness to the two cars racing through the village that morning: Pearl Wiggins, proprietress of the post office and general store.

Tall, pale and fleshy, Pearl Wiggins was a large woman, big-boned, her mother had always said. Pearl preferred to think of herself as curvaceous and well nourished. Heavily trussed in a Platex Girdle, rolls of fat were forced from each end of her corsetry, accentuating an impressive bosom and substantial thighs.

Unnaturally constrained, she held herself in a stiffly upright manner, treading carefully around the post office with slow, concentrated effort. She was not given to sudden movements.

Once considered a moderately *handsome* woman, she was now, at the age of sixty-four, not quite so alluring. Her creamy pallor was maintained by frequent applications from her favorite cosmetic tool, her powder compact. She kept it, along with her Bird Of Paradise, Max Factor lipstick, in the side pocket of the apron she wore for work every day. The striking orange color of her lips was in stark contrast to the chalky whiteness of her skin, so that her lips seemed to precede the rest of her body when she entered a room.

"Like a big preying mantis with luminous lips," was Barrington Smith's caustic description of Pearl.

Coiffed, tight, short curls held in place by a fearsomely strong lacquer, framed her face. An essential part of her routine was her weekly visit for a shampoo and set at Candice's Hair Parlor. The majority of Tipping's female residents over the age of sixty sported a similar hair design, all of them devotees of the village's only salon. The ladies of Tipping held Candice, who had received training at Vidal Sassoon and earned a six-month diploma, in awed esteem. Aside from Pearl's post office, the hairdresser's was the hub of local gossip. Not much went on without Candice finding out about it.

The store had been especially quiet that Friday morning. Mrs. Hardcastle had just left with her usual quarter of boiled ham, so Pearl nipped into the back for a few minutes to put her feet up and have a quick cup of tea. Just as the kettle came to a boil, the bell above the shop door rang.

"Oh, bother." She set the kettle back down on the stove and with a loud sigh, turned and went back into the store.

"Now then Barrington," she said when she saw him standing lamely in front of the post office counter. She was somewhat taken aback to see him in the store again so soon. He generally only came in once a week and he had already been in the day before.

"What can I do for you?" She waited expectantly, wondering "what on earth" he wanted. It was hard not to show any surprise or reveal how thrilled she was to see him again.

He hesitated for another moment, pursing his mouth as if on the brink of saying something, but then with a sudden change of mind, he turned and made his way to the canned vegetables.

I wonder what's got into him, she thought, intrigued by his unusual behavior. She moved to the other side of the store where she had a better vantage point and pretended to be busy with the meat-slicer.

Half concealed behind the machine, she could watch what he was doing without being too obvious. He seemed to be absorbed by the labels on the canned peas, a look of serious concentration on his face. Every now and again, he would rub his chin and shake his head as if he were trying to make up his mind about something. Occasionally, he glanced in her direction, and when she caught him looking, he would quickly dip his head and feign renewed interest in the peas.

What on Earth? Hmm, come to think of it, he's been acting odd for a few weeks now, coming into the store far more often than his usual once a week for his pension and a few bits and pieces. And he's been very quiet, not his usual grumbling self.

She was still pondering these things when, as if seized by a sudden moment of decision, Barrington lifted his head, drew himself up to his full height, and strode purposely toward the counter again. Not wanting to appear over eager, Pearl took her time wiping down the meat slicer before casually making her way to where he stood waiting.

"Well then. What is it you're wanting?" she asked, in what she hoped was an uninterested way. She lifted a hand and gave her curls several soft, little pats.

"Well, it's like this," he began, shifting nervously from foot to foot. His face was red as a beet. He placed both his hands on the counter and seemed to brace himself for what he was about to say.

"It's just that . . ." He cleared his throat and swallowed several times. "I need . . . Well, I need to ask you . . ." he stuttered, a pained expression on his face.

Oh, my dear Lord, Pearl thought. She felt a surge of warmth spread from her head to her toes. She had nursed a secret little flame for Barrington for many years, but she hardly dared imagine that he just might have the same feelings for her. With a touch of desperation, she wondered if it could really be so. Is that why he keeps coming into the store? Is that why he's blushing, because of me? Oh my . . . Pearl leaned forward and turned her head slightly, inviting him to whisper in her ear. Her mouth fell open and her eyes grew misty. "You can tell me Barrington," she whispered breathlessly.

Caught off guard by Pearl's odd behavior, Barrington abandoned any ideas he had about asking her for help getting his pension. The government had issued a new PIN number for his pension account and he was darned if he could remember the damn thing.

He lifted his cap and ran his fingers through the scant hair he had left. Then without warning, he slapped his hand down on the counter and shouted, "One Heinz jam pudding!"

Startled, Pearl jumped backward, her hand against her chest. Her heart was thumping in a way it hadn't done in years.

"Right you are then," and with lightness to her step, she turned to fetch his pudding.

She waited until he had left, and then, with uncharacteristic speed, Pearl rushed through the door at the rear of the store and shot up the stairs to her bedroom window where she could watch him leaving the car park. Half concealed behind the curtains and panting heavily, she peeked out just as he was about to drive through the puddle at the exit.

"Wretched puddle," she muttered. "I'll have to get on the phone again to the town council."

But then she caught a glimpse of the back of Barrington's head, and her puddle problems were quickly dismissed. Now that there Barrington would be quite a catch, she thought. He must have a pretty penny put by, what with him never having got married or having children.

"Pearl Smith," she whispered. Hmm, the Smith part was a little plain for her liking, but she supposed she could get used to it. She tittered to herself, enjoying her daydream, when she was distracted by the loud roar of two cars driving within inches of each other, tearing along the road outside.

"Well, I hope they get stopped by the police!" She turned her head to watch them fly by, when something fell out of the back of one of the cars. An explosion of papers and other articles made her jump back from the window.

"Oh, my goodness!" she exclaimed. "What in the world?"

She was just about to rush outside, when another vehicle coming from the opposite direction, swerved onto the grass verge, almost hitting the stone wall, sending a another blast of papers all over the place.

"Good Heavens above!"

Pearl fell back against the bed. She had come over all dizzy, what with the excitement, and not to mention the exertion of climbing the stairs so quickly. She lay back, fanning her flushed face with both hands.

"Just get my breath back. What a commotion!" She took several deep breaths and willed herself to relax.

After a few minutes, when her heart rate approached normal again, she felt decidedly better. Not wanting to waste another moment, she got up off the bed and made her way back down the stairs as quickly as her corset would allow. She arrived at the roadside just in time to see the Brigadier's Range Rover disappear into the distance. Paper and books were scattered all over the road. She looked around, tut-tutting with disapproval at the mess outside her post office.

"Now who's going to clean this lot up?" She grumbled. Shaking her head in disgust, she bent down to pick up as much as she could before heading back into the shop to get a bin liner.

THREE

Capra Aegagrus Hircus, more commonly known as the domestic goat, is reputed to eat almost anything. Goats have an intensely inquisitive and intelligent nature. They will explore anything new or unfamiliar in their surroundings. The three goats sharing their field opposite the post office in Tipping, with a few dozen sheep, were no exception.

Their morning, so far, had been very exciting indeed. The loud screech of Brigadier Dickie Cranshawe Booth's tires as he narrowly avoided hitting the wall bordering their field startled goat and sheep alike, causing them all to bolt into the furthest corners. The goats being of superior intellect were the first back on the scene to investigate.

If their brains had the capacity to appreciate good fortune, the goats would have been thrilled by the bounty of treasure that fell from the heavens that Friday morning. In front of them, a scattered banquet of papers were delivered in dramatic fashion from Jeremy's car. Most of them lay still and inviting against the wall, but a few others skipped across the grass, blown by the wind, irresistible in the way they flapped and gyrated, beckoning the goats to have a little nibble at the edges.

* * *

The journey back to the village seemed to take forever. Jeremy drove as fast as he dared along the narrow country road, constantly on the look-out for the black Audi. He felt a jolt of adrenaline every time a car came into view, and then a wave of relief when he realized it was a different car. His knuckles showed white as he gripped the steering wheel, pulling it down hard one way and then the other as he veered around each sharp bend in the road. He nearly lost control on several of them, driving dangerously close to the edge. Barriers lined the road along some of the steeper sections, but for the most part, the sides fell away precipitously to the deep valleys below.

He felt sick at the thought of his belongings scattered all over the road in Tipping. "How could I lose them?" he shouted.

Jeremy tormented himself with painful images of the artwork being run over and ruined by every vehicle passing through the village. After everything I've been through, he reflected miserably. How was I to know they were stolen?

Six watercolors by J.M.W. Turner, worth what, thousands, millions, and now I've gone and lost them. Un-fucking-bloody-believable! He wanted to cry.

"Oh Christ, I hope they're still there," he muttered dismally. With grim resignation, he accepted the fact that he had probably lost them. Anyone wandering through the village close to the road would have already seen his backpack and all the papers. His only hope was that one of the locals might have picked them up. He was fairly certain they would keep them for him if they saw his name on any of the papers. His real concern was if a stranger to the village had found them, or if passing cars damaged them. He squeezed his eyes shut for an instant, in a silent prayer. Please, please let me find them.

He screeched to a halt in a lay-by just beyond the post office. After a hair-raising car chase through Tipping, and then all the way to Wickham, he could only hope that he had finally lost the American. Without wasting a moment, Jeremy leaped out onto the road in search of his belongings. As he jogged towards the post office, he noticed his football lolling in the gutter. He felt mildly relieved to see it there, despite the fact that he never played the game. He had inherited the football from an uncle on his mother's side. George Best, and a number of other team members from Manchester United's past, had allegedly signed the ball, but the signatures were faded and indecipherable. Still, it was a conversation piece.

Apart from the football and the squashed remains of his toilet bag, the road looked depressingly empty. He came to a stop outside the post office where he stood by the puddle to look around. With his hands on his hips and breathing heavily from fear and exertion, he slowly scanned the road and the verges to each side. Seeing no sign of the backpack, his heart sank, but a small movement in the thicket across the road caught his eye. He sprinted toward a thick bed of nettles beneath the wall and to his immense relief he recognized his handwriting on several pieces of paper trapped in the undergrowth. Giddy with delight and blinded by the hope that he might yet retrieve the precious Turners, he hurled himself, without thinking, into the nettles, swiping at the papers before they escaped again. Oblivious to the pain inflicted by the stinging flora, he lunged about, this way and that, as a blast of wind caused by a passing car enticed the papers to become airborne again. He let out a yelp of joy as he launched himself into the air to grasp one of the watercolors. He landed heavily, out of breath, with his back against the stone wall.

"Thank God!" he gasped. He held the painting close to his face and with tears in his eyes he kissed it softly and caressed it against his chest.

He heard something clatter onto the top of the wall immediately behind his head. Startled, he swung his head around and was confronted with a pair of tiny hoofs and the flickering tip of a pink tongue, reaching for his hair.

"What the?"

He jumped to his feet and placed both hands on top of the wall. What he saw on the other side made him scream in horror. "Noooooooo!"

In one swift, agile movement, he vaulted into the field, and with a desperate lunge, dove headlong for the goat that was standing with the remains of a half-eaten piece of paper between its prehensile upper lip and tongue.

"Come here you bastard!" He shouted so loud his voice could be heard clear across the road as far as the post office.

* * *

23

When Conrad spotted Jeremy's white Volkswagon in a lay-by at the side of the road, he swung into the car park outside the post office on his right. In his haste, he didn't notice the large puddle at the entrance until it was too late. The Audi plunged into the hole with a sickening crunch.

"Shit!" He hadn't expected a pothole as deep as that. Making a mental note to check the damage later, he pulled up outside the window of the building and exited the car as fast as he could. As he ran towards the road, he heard a loud cry coming from the field opposite. He looked up to see the Danvers kid darting across the field in pursuit of a terrified goat.

Conrad sprinted across the road and stopped short of the wall, trying to fathom what the kid was doing. Unsure of his next move, Conrad made a quick survey of the field and realized what had happened. He could not fail to notice the amount of paper littering the field.

"Oh, hell," he sighed.

A loud bleat drew his attention to a stand of trees at the edge of the field to his right. A small white goat was perched precariously on one of the lower branches of a young Horse-Chestnut tree. Conrad squinted, focusing on what the goat appeared to have in its mouth.

"I just don't believe this," he said, shaking his head in amusement. He looked back at Jeremy who was on all fours, panting in the middle of the field.

"Oh Jeez," Conrad laughed. He climbed over the wall and jogged to where Jeremy had flopped, exhausted onto the ground.

"Heh, kid . . . no, no, it's okay," said Conrad hastily when he saw the horrified expression on Jeremy's face.

Jeremy dropped the painting he had clutched to his chest and scrambled backwards, crab-like on all fours, in the opposite direction. "I haven't got them!" he screamed.

"No, listen. I don't want any trouble." Conrad shouted after him. He held out both palms, fingers splayed in mock surrender "Please, just listen for a minute. I'm Conrad Rankin – Claudia Rankin's son. She was killed in the car crash two weeks ago with Julian Parks." Conrad dropped onto the grass and laid one hand on Jeremy's shoulder. "It's okay. It's okay," he repeated. "Really. I don't want any trouble. I just want to talk to you . . . "

Jeremy's jaw dropped open in stunned disbelief. "You . . . you're not going to shoot me then?" he stuttered with wild, pleading eyes.

"What? God no. I swear I'm not going to harm you," Conrad assured him. "You were one of the last people to see my mother alive. Please, I just need to ask you a few questions."

"I've already told the police everything. I don't know anything about your mother. I saw her once, that's all. I never met her."

"You didn't speak to her?"

"No. She was in the car when Julian Parks came to the gallery. She didn't get out. I only saw her from a distance. I'm telling you: I never met her."

Conrad rubbed his brow. "The police think she was involved in the theft of some major pieces of art. I find that impossible to believe. There must be some mistake." There was a strange desperation in his voice. "My mother was a wealthy woman. She didn't need to resort to crime. It doesn't make sense."

"I–I, don't know anything," Jeremy faltered. "I was only working there for a few weeks. It was a summer job. I–I was just helping out."

Conrad looked Jeremy in the eye, his voice dead serious. "So why didn't you talk to me yesterday when I came into the gallery, and again this morning? Why did you drive off like a mad man if you've got nothing to hide?"

Jeremy opened his mouth to speak, then clamped it shut. He considered Conrad's suave appearance, his stylish, immaculately tailored clothing and the expensive sheen of his face.

"Look, Bryce Edwards-Bernard, the owner of the gallery, told me everything," Conrad continued. "He told me the police think my mother and Julian Parks left some valuable artwork with you at the gallery the day he and my mother were killed in the car crash. They think the artwork was stolen. I know you've denied this to the police, but," he paused for a second, "I think you took them, didn't you?"

Jeremy swallowed hard. His eyes flickered from Conrad's face to the spot in the field where he had dropped the painting.

"I–no. Yes. Oh God." He dropped his head into his hands. "I didn't mean to. I've been such a bloody idiot. It's all such a mess. When I saw

25

you, I panicked. I thought you had been sent to get the paintings back . . . I thought you were going to . . . going to kill me!"

"No, no, "Conrad laughed. He offered Jeremy an encouraging smile. "You've got it all wrong. I flew here from the States to get some closure on my mother's death. I didn't know anything about the artwork until yesterday, not until Bryce Edwards told me. I knew my mother had some interest in art, but she never discussed it with me. I had no idea about the extent of her collections. I was shocked, and I still am." He stroked his chin and frowned. "The police suspect her of making illicit deals on the black market. If that's the case, why haven't they said anything to me about this? "He squeezed his eyes shut for a moment and shook his head. "I don't get it?"

Jeremy felt his throat tighten. His shoulders hunched and he cupped his hands in front of his face. "Oh God. I can't believe I've got myself involved in this. I've been such a fucking idiot." He began to cry.

Conrad jerked his head up in surprise. He didn't expect the kid to break down like this. "Hey, it's okay," he whispered. He gave Jeremy's shoulder a friendly squeeze.

"No, it's not," Jeremy sniveled. His voice was muffled behind his hands.

"I've lost them. They fell out of the back of my car. There's one over there."

He lifted his teary face and pointed in the direction of the little watercolor lying on the grass. "That's the only one I found. I don't know where the rest are. They could be anywhere by now."

"What? How many are we talking about?"

"Six watercolors. Turners."

"Holy shit!" Conrad exclaimed. "Are sure they are the real thing? I mean have you actually checked them out?"

"No, but they must be originals. Why else would Scotland Yard be involved?"

"Well, do you know which Turners we're talking about? How much they're worth?"

"I'm not sure. I haven't had the chance to do any research, but if they are originals, they could be worth thousands, millions maybe."

"What? Jesus. We'd better go and get them." Conrad stood up. "Come on," he beckoned to Jeremy with a wave of his hand.

"I–I don't know," said Jeremy. He lifted his head from his knees and looked up at Conrad with frightened eyes. He wiped his nose with the back of his hand. "I don't know anything about you. How, how do I know I can trust you?"

Conrad fixed Jeremy with his blue-eyed stare. He stood still for a long moment deliberating what he should say. He knew that if there was to be any chance of convincing the kid to trust him, he needed to come across as open, honest and genuine. But given the uniquely privileged circumstances of his background, and the peculiar situation he was in now, it was hard to know how much information to give.

"You don't, not yet," Conrad said eventually, a look of concern in his eyes. "We need to talk." He cast a quick glance across the field. "But we can't afford to waste any time. We need to start looking for the paintings before someone else finds them. Look, let's talk as we look around. Okay?" He offered a hand up to Jeremy. "Come on, we'll figure this out. Things might not be as bad as they seem. There might be a way we can help each other."

"Okay," Jeremy answered with a tiny whimper of a smile. After a moment's hesitation, he grabbed Conrad's hand and let Conrad pull him to his feet.

For a few seconds they stood face to face, hand in hand. They were almost the same height, Conrad, the taller by half an inch. It occurred to Jeremy, in that instant, how much softer the American's eyes were, close-up. From a distance, they seemed a deep shade of blue, piercing, almost hard in their intensity, but now they betrayed a tinge of sadness and vulnerability in their depths.

Encouraged by the American's easy manner and natural charm, Jeremy felt some of his fear slip away. "I'll get it," he said, starting for the painting on the ground. He lifted it gently along its edges with his fingertips and held it out for Conrad to see.

"Nice," said Conrad. It was a little watercolor of a rural scene, a sweeping landscape of rolling hills under a vibrant, stormy sky.

"We'll need to roll it up loosely, like this," said Jeremy, rolling it carefully in his hands. "I haven't got anywhere to put it." He looked down at his checkered shirt and jeans.

"I've got an inside pocket," said Conrad. He held out one side of his lightweight jacket. "I could put it in here."

Jeremy took one step back and held the furled painting against his chest. "I–I don't know," he said hesitantly.

"You can trust me," Conrad coaxed. He smiled and waved Jeremy closer. "Come on, give it to me." When Jeremy did not move, Conrad stepped forward and gently removed the painting from Jeremy's grasp.

Conrad opened his jacket and pushed the watercolor into the inside pocket as far as it would go. He let his jacket fall into place and patted the front of it with one hand. He puffed his cheeks and let out a loud exhalation. "Okay. At least we've found one of them," he said. He nodded toward the stand of trees near the road. "Have you looked over there?" he asked.

"Yeah, but only a quick look."

"Right, well let's check again. I thought I saw a goat with something in its mouth and it looked like paper to me. Come on," he waved Jeremy forward. It's time we talked."

FOUR

"You've heard of United States Steel, right?" Conrad asked, as they walked together side by side.

"Yeah."

"Well, my mother is, I mean, was," he corrected himself, "the daughter of James Henry Poole. He was chief financier of the company back in the early 1900s. My father was Randolph Prescott Rankin Jr., sole heir to a substantial fortune amassed by his own father in the late 1800s."

"Railroads?" asked Jeremy.

"Yeah, right. America's Gilded Age," Conrad said, relieved that he was talking to someone with a reasonable level of intelligence. "Anyway, their marriage made quite a splash in the headlines at the time. Dazzling descriptions of the wedding plastered across the front covers of every society magazine in the country —that kind of thing."

"Really?" said Jeremy. He shot Conrad a glance from the corner of his eye. "Like the Kennedys," he added, awestruck.

"Well not exactly, but yeah, kind of," Conrad laughed. "They had no involvement in politics but they were extremely wealthy. My father was much older than my mother, by sixteen years. I guess I came along as a late surprise. My father was fifty-eight when I was born and my mother forty-two. I think they were shocked more than anything—bewildered. I mean, who in their right mind would want a new born at the age of fifty-eight?" He made a soft snort through his nose and kept his eyes locked on the ground in front of him. His face held a pained expression.

"Why are you telling me all this?" Jeremy asked, a puzzled look on his face.

"Because I want you to believe that I am not involved in any of this . . ." He paused for a moment trying to find the right words. "In this so-called crime . . . and I want you to trust me. But for you to really understand, I need to tell you something of my background, especially about my relationship with my mother. None of what I tell you will make any sense otherwise. Please," he flashed a look at Jeremy. "This won't take long. Just hear me out, okay."

"Okay," Jeremy said with a shrug of his shoulders.

"My father was a workaholic," Conrad continued. "He was obsessed with making even more money, and as far as I know, my mother spent most of her time traveling, or else she was busy organizing some kind of charitable enterprise. I didn't see much of either of them. We were never close.

I don't think my mother really wanted children. I think she saw it as an obligation, producing an heir for the amalgamated fortunes," he said with a wry smile. "Left to her own devices, I'm sure she would have happily settled for a life without kids. As for my father," Conrad swallowed. "I think he tried, but there was never any depth of emotion in him, never any outward displays of affection. He was always distant, reserved, cold, and . . . and he was old." A look of disappointment hung on his face.

Jeremy stooped to examine a loose leaf of paper on the grass.

"Is it yours?" Conrad asked.

"Yes. It's nothing. Some notes," said Jeremy, disappointed, rolling the paper into a tight tube and pushing it into a back pocket.

"Let's carry on to the trees," said Conrad, nodding in their direction. He waited until Jeremy fell back into stride beside him before continuing. "I grew up surrounded by enormous wealth. There was nothing I couldn't have as a child. I suppose I was happy enough, although looking back, I think there were times when I spent too much time on my own. I never had any siblings and very few relatives were around." He shrugged his shoulders. "The only relatives I ever knew were some wizened old aunts on my father's side."

"Where did you grow up?" Jeremy asked. "I mean, where in the States?"

"Boston, mainly. We had homes all over the world, but Boston is where the principal home is. My parents were not exactly the hands on kind. They didn't have much involvement in my day-to-day routine. I had a nanny to do all that. I had very few friends. My family's wealth and status necessitated a measure of isolation from general society, so I spent much of my early childhood on my own. I was tutored at home until I was nine." A note of sadness crept into his voice.

"A nanny?" Jeremy raised an eyebrow. "Were you lonely?"

"Kind of. Sometimes. Although, being alone is very different than being lonely, and believe me, there were many times when I much preferred being on my own. Nanny and my mother used to conspire to import so-called *friends* into the home." He shook his head in disgust. "I can't even begin to tell you how much I hated that."

Jeremy glanced at Conrad. "Why?"

"I never liked any of them. They could never keep their hands off my collections."

"Collections?"

"Yeah, my collections. I suppose that if I did have any sub-conscious emotional neediness as a child, then it was channeled into an overwhelming compulsion to collect material objects." Conrad shrugged his shoulders. "I'm sure any therapist would concur with that," he added with a wry smile.

"What kind of collections? Art?" Jeremy gave Conrad a fleeting quizzical look.

"No, no, not art. I started with die-cast soldiers." Conrad's eyes sparkled at the memory of his early passion. He remembered playing with the soldiers tirelessly, researching and recreating whole battle scenes that took over his bedroom and the entire playroom. From soldiers, he moved on to coins, stamps and die cast cars, to vinyl records, books and military memorabilia. He spent endless hours meticulously cataloguing, ordering, arranging and displaying them, and he would raise the roof if anyone dared to touch them.

He especially loathed other kids invading his room with their meddlesome, dangerous curiosity. They just had to touch everything, especially when he told them not to. He deeply resented having to empty his shelves and hide his favorite things before they arrived. Each of them had the uncanny ability to sniff out the rarest, most valuable pieces. It was like a treasure hunt for them, a great game, made all the more enticing by the way Conrad cried so easily. Most of them found this amusing and never tired of the game, especially when Nanny wasn't around to spoil the fun. One friend in particular, continued to haunt Conrad's memories well into adulthood with a painful persistence.

Thursdays were Claudia's Bridge night, and Neville Brian Prendergast, the son of one of Claudia's bridge partners would be ushered up the stairs to play with Conrad while the adults were busy downstairs. Nanny was usually around to arbitrate, always unfairly, thought Conrad bitterly, if the antics of the two nine-year- olds became too boisterous. Nanny was always on at him about manners and respect.

"Neville is a guest in this house Conrad, and you must treat him as such."

Yeah. Like unwanted vermin, thought Conrad. He nursed a venomous hatred against Neville, who with his pointed, twitching nose and black beady eyes, reminded Conrad of a rat. Black greasy hair slicked back from his forehead made Neville's snout seem even longer. His tapered facial features were in stark contrast to the rest of his short, pear-shaped body, especially his bulbous, backside. The moment they were dismissed by the adults, Neville would scamper up the grand staircase and shoot straight into Conrad's room where he would scuffle about, eyes darting this way and that, prying into every corner and recess until he found what he was after. The hunt and then the destruction of Conrad's collectibles gave Neville enormous satisfaction.

"Show us where you've stashed your stuff Connie-boy", he'd wheeze as he attempted to squeeze under the bed. "I know it's here somewhere you pansy."

"One of these days I'm going to flatten you Neville," Conrad would reply meekly from the open doorway, ready to escape to Nanny. He knew his screams would bring her bustling down the hallway, but invariably Neville would be ready with a wily excuse and a few well-timed, forced tears.

"It was an accident. It wasn't my fault it broke. Conrad fell on it," he'd whimper, the squashed pieces of one of Conrad's toys in his hands. He'd turn big wet doe eyes on Nanny and when she looked away, he'd shoot a look of withering spite at Conrad; a cruel smirk wrapped around his sharp little teeth.

A head-height taller than Conrad and a good deal heavier, Neville was a capricious bully and a well-practiced liar. If his simpering excuses didn't fool Nanny, he'd begin to bawl at the top of his lungs, knowing full well that his mother would be there within seconds to comfort him. Conrad's protestations fell upon deaf ears, dismissed by that traitor Nanny as being a touch over-dramatic. There were times when he loathed Nanny as much as he hated Neville. He was still brooding over Nanny's deficiencies when Jeremy's voice snapped him back to the present.

"So what do you collect now?"

"Oh, all kinds of things, but vintage cars mainly—the very fast ones," Conrad laughed.

They had reached the shade of the trees. Conrad stopped walking and glanced over his shoulder the way they had come. When he met Jeremy's eyes again, his face was serious. "I was packed off to a private boarding school when I was nine. I couldn't wait to leave. I was relieved to get away," said Conrad. He remembered waving goodbye to his mother as she drove away in her Bentley. There had been no sobbing farewell. Such an obvious display of affection would have been achingly embarrassing for both of them. They had parted instead, with a polite, indifferent goodbye. His father had not been present. Conrad couldn't recall the reason why. "I didn't miss them. After boarding school, I went to Princeton. Got my degree and stayed on for an MBA."

"Princeton?" Is that one of the Ivy leagues?"

"Yes. I had a great time there."

"Yeah, I can imagine," Jeremy half-laughed, feeling a prick of envy. He studied Conrad using the corner of his eye as he poked about in the thick mess of vegetation by his feet. It was easy to picture the tall, privileged American at a prestigious school like Princeton. There was something about Conrad's unattended handsomeness, his quiet reserve and his self-deprecating manner that made it impossible not to like him.

He had no doubt that the women at Princeton were drawn to those very qualities like bees to a honey-pot, Jeremy pondered with a stab of jealousy. No such bloody luck for me, he thought sourly. He made a mental comparison of his own unkempt, gangly appearance to the raffish good looks of the American by his side.

"My father died a few years after I left Princeton," said Conrad. He started toward the mass of undergrowth by the wall beyond the trees.

Jeremy's head jerked up as he fell into stride beside Conrad. "Oh, I'm sorry."

Conrad held up a hand. "No, It's okay. It didn't come as a great shock. He had been ill for some time."

"But now your mother's gone as well . . ." Jeremy's voice trailed off. He didn't know what to say, so he said nothing.

"I know," said Conrad, shaking his head slowly. "It hasn't sunk in yet." He frowned and pressed his lips together. He felt a sinking feeling in the pit of his stomach when he considered the loss of both his parents. He was not exactly heartbroken at their death, but the fact that they were gone had left him feeling empty and lost, as if he were in some kind of emotional vacuum. It was this inability to feel true sorrow that bothered him most, that and the peculiar circumstances surrounding his mother's death.

"I don't know what I feel anymore. I guess I'm confused more than anything. I mean, this guy she was seeing, Julian Parks, who was killed in the car crash with her . . ." Conrad paused for a moment trying to find the right words. "Why didn't I know any of this? I honestly didn't think my mother would bother with that kind of thing after my father died. I mean, neither of my parents were the passionate sort."

Thinking back, he could not ever remember witnessing any show of physical fondness between them, although it had never occurred to him that either was unhappy with this situation. Instead, their relationship seemed to be little more than a stiff, stultifying politeness.

"You mean Julian Parks, the art dealer," said Jeremy.

"Right," said Conrad, eyebrows raised. "The art dealer. And that's the other thing I do not get—the art. I knew she liked art and had a few nice pieces, but I had absolutely no idea that she was a major collector, and I'm talking major here, like on a world scale." He glanced at Jeremy and shook his head again. "Truly, I had no idea until her will was read a few days ago. I know it's hard to believe, but I'm telling you the truth. I was beyond shocked when I found out about the extent of her collections." He grimaced and squeezed his eyes shut at the memory.

Conrad fell silent again. His mind drifted to the meeting in the attorney's office. He had assumed that the reading of Claudia's will would be a tedious, perfunctory affair, a predictable afternoon of politeness and boredom.

His father had already left him a sizable estate and he had no reason to believe that as sole heir, he would not be the principal beneficiary of the entire Rankin fortune now that his mother was dead.

Closeted inside a dimly lit, stuffy room and lulled by the secure knowledge that he was about to become even wealthier, Conrad had struggled to maintain rapt attention to the drone of the attorney's voice as the will was read aloud to the small gathering of family and close associates. As the air in the room was slowly sucked out, he drifted in and out of wakefulness, and at times he came dangerously close to falling asleep, his chin dropping to his chest with disconcerting regularity.

"A significant Fauvist collection . . . Andre Derain, Maurice de Vlaminck." A distant sound of alarm bells had started to ring in his mind.

"Appraisal . . . Christies . . . Three million . . ."

As if surfacing from the depths of the deepest ocean, his mind struggled to grasp what he was hearing. The drone went on: "Sisley, Turner—original water colors."

Jolted back to consciousness by the mention of a collection, Conrad shook his head several times, barely able to process what was happening. What? Which artists? What paintings? He was confused.

He was aware of one or two fairly nice pieces dotted around the various properties they owned, but he had never paid much attention to them. He certainly had no idea that Claudia had any real interest in that field. It was as perplexing to him as it was irritating. He was incredulous and furious that she had chosen not to share this with him. Why? The question screamed in his brain. He felt horribly cheated in some way.

His mouth dropped open when he heard the approximate value of her collection. It was too much to take in. A voice within him shouted that it was ridiculous, ludicrous. He would have known about it for God's sake. This cannot be true, he thought as he leaned back in his chair, hands over his mouth.

Conrad looked up at the motionless revolving fan set into the ceiling, his eyes focused on a strand of cobweb dangling from one of the blades. Time seemed to slow to a crawl, suspended almost, while he struggled to get his mind around the whole business. Gradually, tiny flashes of memory illuminated what had been staring him in the face the whole time. His stomach sank as some of the pieces fell into place. He felt a wave of nausea wash over him as he remembered little details from his childhood.

The ghastly painting that hung in the library, the one that had, according to Conrad, an uncanny likeness of Mrs. Prendergast—surely that could not be one of mother's pieces? Yet, thinking back to Claudia's reaction when he had remarked upon its hideous nature, she laughed and hugged him close, which was very peculiar, and whispered that he would adore it one day.

Then there was the monstrosity that claimed a wall in the palatial dining room of their lake house in Upstate New York. He distinctly remembered being shocked to see it on one of his visits during the summer holidays. It was a lurid rendition of some French scene or other, ridiculously out of character for his parents and their ultra-conservatism.

"Jesus. We're not keeping that up are we?" he said in withering response to seeing it for the first time.

"Don't be so quick to judge, Conrad," Randolph had muttered from behind The Wall Street Times. "The Tate Gallery paid thousands for a pile of bricks arranged in a so-called art-form. Around about the time you were born, I seem to remember."

"I'd rather have the bricks than this."

Randolph peered over the top of his newspaper, lifted a finger to his lips and whispered, "Me too, but don't tell your Mother I said that." They laughed over their shared moment of conspiracy.

He did not see the painting again. It disappeared. An innocuous floral sketch that was infinitely kinder to the eye had taken its place. He later found out that it was worth half a million.

The longer Conrad sat staring at the fan, the more some of the clouds obscuring his mother's character slowly receded, revealing a few hazy glimpses of the truth about Claudia. He had always believed that her interests strayed no further than the bridge table and some charity committee or other that she always seemed to be involved in, but now it appeared that she was a collector too. Only it struck him that she had gone about it in a covert, secretive manner for some reason. He knew instinctively that Randolph had been excluded from this aspect of her life. This pleased Conrad immensely, although he could not quite identify why he felt that way.

He rocked back and forth on his chair, a look of deep concentration on his face. A few at the gathering looked at him with frowns of disapproval. He thought again of his mother. Did she miss him now, wherever she was? Had she ever really loved him? There was a part of him that so desperately wanted something more from her that he could not quite touch. There was always something missing, some vital connection that eluded him. Why had she not shared her art with him? She must have known how passionate he would have been about it.

A thought struck him. She had done it deliberately. Engulfed by a wave of self-pity and anger, he let his chair bang forward to the floor on all four legs, startling everyone in the room, sharply interrupting the deadening torpor of the proceedings. He slumped forward, holding his head between his hands. He had felt a shocking, desperate need to cry.

"Are you okay?" Jeremy was staring at him. The sound of his voice broke the spell of Conrad's thoughts.

"What? Yes." Conrad stopped abruptly in his tracks. He looked past Jeremy to some point in the distance. His face was set, on the brink of saying something, but then he faltered and lowered his gaze to the ground.

"What's wrong?" asked Jeremy.

"Apart from some generous donations to various charities, I inherited everything, including her art collections." Conrad raised his head. His face was deadly serious. "She kept her art hidden from me. Collecting was the one passion we might have shared, but she . . ." he paused to weigh his words carefully. "She didn't want that. She froze me out." He kicked at the grass with his shoe.

"Maybe it was because she, well, you know . . ." Jeremy hesitated, not wanting to say the words. "Maybe she didn't want to drag you into something that wasn't legal."

"No. I've told you, she didn't need to resort to crime. She had more goddamned money than she could spend in her whole lifetime. That's bullshit." Conrad's eyes flashed with emotion.

"Well, that's not what the police think," Jeremy countered.

"Is that what you think? What do you know about all this? I've told you about me, now it's your turn."

The faintest flicker of a smile passed across Jeremy's face before he spoke. "Oh, you're not going to fucking believe it," he said bitterly. I am in so much shit. I don't even know where to start."

"Well, why not start at the beginning," Conrad suggested gently. He nodded in the direction of the village. "Is this where you're from?" He waited for Jeremy to respond. "Well, what about your parents? Do they live here? Brothers, sisters?" he asked when Jeremy remained silent.

Jeremy let out a loud snort. "You've hit the nail on the head," he said with derision. "I've lied to my parents and to my whole family for the past three years."

He slumped onto the grass. "I've got to sit down for a few minutes. I'm knackered." His eyes were lined with exhaustion and bore the hollow look of someone who had not slept in days. "We're not going to find the paintings," he moaned. 'I told you: they're gone, disappeared."

"Don't give up," said Conrad. "We haven't looked along the road yet." He looked across the road toward the buildings on the far side.

"What's that place over there? Is it a store? Maybe the owner or the workers saw something? What do you think?"

"Huh? Yeah, maybe," Jeremy answered despondently. "That's the post office. I'll go over in a minute and ask Mrs. Wiggins if she saw anything. She's the woman who runs the place."

Conrad swept both hands through his hair and dropped to Jeremy's side.

"Okay, so tell me how you got involved. I want to know everything."

Jeremy picked at a blade of grass and took a moment to respond. "I never had a great relationship with my parents either," he said eventually. "Hey, look, I'm really sorry about your parents. At least mine are still alive." He dropped his gaze and continued to worry the same blade of grass. "But you're not going to starve without your parents. Me though, I have nothing. My parents are going to cut me off when they find out what I've done." He hung his head and looked as if he were going to cry again. "I don't know what I'm going to do."

"And just what is it that you have done that is so bad?" said Conrad.

"Oh God," Jeremy covered his face with his hands. "I am well and truly fucked."

Conrad placed several soft little pats on Jeremy's back. "Come on. It will be okay," he said. "We're in this together now. You can tell me."

Jeremy sniffed hard. "I–I was never good enough," he began. His voice sounded muffled behind his hands. "My parents are academics, pioneers in biotechnology. They are well known in the scientific world. You can look them up. My dad is Professor Alistair Fletcher Danvers and my mum is Dr. Philippa Wright Danvers." He turned his teary eyes to Conrad and propped his chin on his bent knees.

"Biotechnology," Conrad repeated. "Interesting."

"They expected me to carry on in their footsteps, just like Peter, my older brother. He's the golden boy," he added with sarcasm. "He's six years older than me. He got a first at Cambridge and then went on to get a doctorate in microbiology. He's leading a research team now, something to do with bovine intestines. But me," he tightened his jaw and shook his head in sad resignation. "I'm just one huge fucking disappointment. I always have been." His lower lip trembled and in a torrent of words, his whole sorry, turbid story came flowing out, like a roiling river bursting its banks.

FIVE

The sad truth was that Jeremy had always struggled at school, something no one could understand. Everyone assumed that the son of two great intellects would do well, if not excel, but it very quickly became apparent that this was not going to be the case. Mathematics in particular was his greatest weakness, a failing so grave as to be considered a cardinal sin in the Danvers household.

"A daydreamer," his primary school teachers said. "Inattentive and lacking concentration. Fails to grasp the basic concepts."

At first, his parents blamed his poor academic performance on the teachers and the school. They insisted on special assessments and evaluations and then more testing and reassessment. They pulled strings within their academic circle and recruited experts in child development, but none of it did any good. Their opinions pointed to only one thing, a just below average child. Average. The utterance of this one word was blasphemy.

It did not occur to his parents that Jeremy's averageness was just a natural part of who he was, that he was not made like them. His mother blamed herself. She was convinced that she must have done something wrong during the pregnancy. She must have been exposed to some toxic substance or stood underneath power lines for too long. Maybe she had too many hot baths, or it could have been the crab cakes she had grown to like so much. Perhaps he was starved of oxygen at birth. She agonized endlessly, dissecting every detail of her pregnancy in the hope of unearthing some clue that explained why Jeremy was not clever like the rest of them. All of their rational, logical training and all of their scientific methodology went out the window. They did not and could not accept Jeremy's *situation*.

Something or someone had to be at blame. It was easier to deal with that way. So it was an obvious decision to dismiss the local public schools as hopelessly inadequate, ignoring the fact that Peter had done perfectly well there, and opt to send Jeremy, in his early teens, to Rivington Boarding School For Boys. Its excellent reputation, and the number of pupils who made it to Oxbridge, justified the exorbitant fees. Plus, by packing him off to a boarding school in Derbyshire, they were able to say that they had done all they could for him, while distancing themselves from the shame of his less than stellar academic performance.

If it were not for Jeremy's friendship with Nigel Bryce-Edwards, his time at Rivington would have been unbearable. The only son of a successful fine arts dealer, Nigel was even less popular than Jeremy, and popularity was the paramount requirement for success at a boys' private boarding school. They were both relegated to the rank of unpopular because they looked so un-athletic. Jeremy was tall, lanky and very thin. His fragile, ungainly appearance was accentuated by his wan complexion. He rarely ventured into the sun because he always burned, so his unexercised pallor remained the same throughout the year. He had a kindly face, with inviting warmth in his light brown eyes, but his mousey hair stuck out at all angles and looked as if it had been freshly electrocuted, a burden he attributed with a deep resentment, to his father.

In contrast, Nigel was the short, fat, roly-poly type. He had wide, doe-like eyes, and plump, rosy cheeks. His head was a mass of curls, incongruous and very dark. His aversion to sports of any description made him a natural ally for Jeremy. Together they endured the resourceful cruelties of adolescent teasing. They were routinely persecuted throughout their stay at Rivington. They were nick-named "Piggy and Wiggy."

* * *

"Art? You can do that in your spare time!"

That was his father's withering response when Jeremy first tentatively mentioned an interest in that direction. Having miraculously scraped through his General Certificates of Secondary Education (G.C.S.E.'s), he was about to make his advanced (A) level subject choices.

"But dad, you don't understand. I don't want to do biochemistry. I'm no good at any of the sciences. Art, Fine Art—It's what I'm interested in. Nigel wants to go to the University of York and get a degree in Art History. It's what Nigel's dad . . ."

"Enough of this, Jeremy!" Alistair interrupted sharply. "You can't afford to make the wrong choices at this stage. A good solid foundation of academic subjects is crucial. You don't want to go wasting your time with artsy-fartsy classes like art and drama for Christ's sake! You've got to eventually make a living, and you're not going to do that swooning over a few paintings." He shook his head, laughing, as if it was all a stupid little joke, and then turned his attention back to the computer. "Now go find your mother and see where she's got to with that tea. There's a good lad."

It infuriated Jeremy that his parents dismissed anything unconnected with science as a waste of time and energy. He hated their presumptuous, myopic opinion that anyone involved in the arts must be of lower intelligence. They believed that people only went down that path because they were not capable of doing anything else—at least, that's what it seemed like to Jeremy.

"But Nigel's dad's made a fortune. He's got more money than us!"

He knew this would hit a raw nerve with his father. During the last vacation from school, Nigel had come to stay with the Danvers for a week. His parents dropped him off in spectacular fashion, in a car so fabulously expensive, that it was probably worth more than Alistair could ever hope to save in his lifetime. Parked on the drive next to Alistair's beat up old Ford Escort, it magnified the massive disparity between a fairly comfortable middle class existence and those with serious money. It was like a smack in the face to Alistair, who had repeatedly told Jeremy that selling a few paintings was not a proper job.

No matter how much Jeremy argued or remonstrated, his parents would not agree to let him drop sciences entirely, although they did grudgingly allow him to take history as one of his 'A' level courses, and as far as they were concerned, there was no question that he would be applying to universities to study for a Bachelor of Science degree.

"Now, we don't expect Oxbridge, Jeremy, but there's no harm in applying for Leicester or Manchester. Your father has some excellent connections, and I can give you some work in the labs over the school vacations. That always looks impressive on application forms."

* * *

"But they don't have to know which degree you take," said Nigel, quite matter- of- factly, in answer to Jeremy's lamentations about his parents.

"Are you out of your mind? This isn't funny you know."

"No, really. Your parents don't ever have to know which degree you're taking."

"Oh yeah? And how do you propose I'll get away with taking art history instead of biochemistry, especially when they're footing the bill?"

"It's easy old boy. Once you're eighteen, all communication from the university has to be addressed to you. Any stuff about the finances isn't going to mention the actual degree, and even if you did need the odd signature, you are talking to me—master forger extraordinaire!" He spoke in a very confident way. "I do owe you a massive favor."

For the best part of a year, Jeremy had kept Nigel generously supplied with his mother's discarded mail order catalogues, where the various models for women's undergarments provided the visual stimulation required to satisfy a fifteen-year-old boy's pubertal lust.

"But you'll need someone to intercept the mail when you're not around," Nigel suggested. "Can you think of anyone?"

"Hmm, well there's old Barrington Smith, the odd-job man, stroke gardener. He comes to the house every day like clockwork at two in the afternoon. He picks up the mail from the post box set into the wall at the front of the house and drops it through the letter box in the front door on his way round to the tool shed. He works on my mother's vegetable garden for an hour or so before going to his allotment."

"Well, that's bloody perfect then. He's your man alright!" Nigel exclaimed. "But how are you going to persuade him to say nothing to your parents?"

"I don't think that will be too hard. Barrington and I get on pretty well. I've helped him out a few times. He's hopeless with new technology, so I've shown him how to use a mobile phone and I've set him up with a video recorder, you know, that kind of stuff. He owes me," said Jeremy with a wry smile. "And, "Jeremy raised his index finger to make his point, "he can't stand my father."

"Really?" said Nigel, eyebrows raised in curiosity.

"Yeah. Barrington's an outspoken, proud, stubborn old bugger and he's not afraid to voice his opinion. He knows I've never wanted to follow in my parents' footsteps and he's never been able to understand why they won't let me make my own choices. He has no tolerance for narrow-mindedness, and he's said as much to my father's face—numerous times in fact."

"I bet that went down well," Nigel scoffed.

"Yeah, well, my father's been trying to get rid of him for years. He says Barrington's so old that he's incapable of doing any meaningful work, but my mother thinks it would be too cruel to let him go. She won't budge because the old fellow has been around forever. In fact, I think we inherited him from my grandparents on my mother's side. My father though, hasn't got a benevolent bone in his body. He'd get rid of Barrington in a heartbeat if he had his way, and Barrington knows it. No, it shouldn't be too hard to make a special, secret agreement with Barrington. He'll help me if I ask him; I'm sure of it."

* * *

Under a veil of subterfuge and lies Jeremy attended the University of Roehampton, one of England's lesser-known universities. It was a scientific wilderness according to his parents, but a godsend for Jeremy, who felt a measure of security in knowing that his parents had no connections or influence there. His parents were undoubtedly disappointed with

Roehampton, but they acknowledged that Jeremy was lucky to get into any university. It was, in fact, the only place to make him an offer through the clearing process, but to Jeremy's great delight, Roehampton offered a very respectable art history program. And so it was, three years later, he emerged with a Bachelor of Arts degree in Art History. For the first time in his life he felt he had found something for which he had a real affinity, something he was actually good at. Apart from moments of blind panic at the thought of discovery, he loved every minute of his time there.

*   *   *

"If you can get your hands on a bit of 'dosh', you can come in with me," said Nigel. "Join my little enterprise." His father had promised him a few "nice pieces" to help get him started on his own if he graduated from York with a first class honors degree. The two of them had maintained their friendship despite the physical distance separating them. They had both just finished their final year at their respective universities and were celebrating over a few pints before beginning work in the gallery in Harrogate the next morning.

"You're a lucky sod," said Jeremy, looking at Nigel through a green mist of envious bile. "You've got it made, haven't you?" Compared to his own, generally fraught existence, it sickened him that Nigel had everything so easy.

"And where am I going to get that kind of money then?" He asked, with more than a little impatience. "I'm hardly going to ask my parents for a loan am I? When they find out I've been lying to them for the last three years, they're not exactly going to be leaping for joy are they?"

"Well, at least you've got a job for the summer. My old man's got a soft spot for you," said Nigel, trying to sound encouraging. "You're the first one he thought of when Bruce, his second-in-command, announced he was taking off to the south of France for a month."

Jeremy remained silent. He was sitting with both hands on either side of his head, elbows propped on the bar.

"My old man's going to be spending most of the summer in the gallery in London. He knows I can't cope on my own with Bruce gone as well," Nigel twittered on.

"Yeah, right," Jeremy answered in a forlorn tone. "I've got my graduation ceremony coming up in four weeks. They'll find out the truth then. They'll never forgive me you know. They'll cut me off. They won't be able to bear the humiliation of being lied to for all this time." He swept his hands through his hair, flattening it for an instant before it sprang upright again. He felt worry tremors shiver through his body.

"Oh God, what am I going to do?"

He looked at Nigel and repeated, "What am I going to do?" a little too loudly, so that the couple sitting at the bar next to them gave him an odd look.

"I wouldn't want to be in your shoes old boy," Nigel responded glumly, shaking his head. "Look, you know you can stay with me until you get on your feet. You'll have some money coming in from helping out in the gallery. My dad is bound to ask you to stay on after Bruce gets back."

"Yes, yes I know," Jeremy interjected a little too emphatically, "and I'm really grateful, but I can't sponge off you and your dad forever."

He stared into his glass, a look of concentration on his face. "If I could just show them that I can make a go of a career in fine art, that I can actually make some money from it . . . " He gulped a few mouthfuls of beer, wiping the froth from his mouth with the back of his hand. "If they could see some success, they wouldn't be able to object so much then, would they?" He drank the rest of his pint and promptly ordered another. He felt like drinking himself into oblivion. "My dad is going to go ape-shit."

SIX

"Right then darlings," Bruce, the assistant manager shrilled, as he was about to depart from the gallery. "I think I've covered everything." He wore a worried look and wrung his hands repeatedly.

"Now we've been through the inventory, we've gone over the new acquisitions, and we've checked the orders," he said, reeling off a mental checklist.

"It's okay Bruce. Don't worry about anything. We'll be fine. I've been involved in the business since I was this high," said Nigel confidently, holding his hand about two feet off the floor. And anything we can't handle, we'll call my father, pronto. Now off you go before you miss your flight."

"I know, I know" Bruce replied. "I worry about every little thing. I'm sure there's something I've forgotten. I can just feel it niggling away in the back of my mind. Oh my, I feel a little light headed." He wafted a hand vigorously in front of his face. "It's my nerves you know; they're in tatters. You have no idea how much I need this break."

He pressed a finger between his eyebrows as if staunching a headache. "Oh, I remember what it is. Julian's in town, Nigel, so you can always call on him if you're desperate, without bothering your father in London." He glanced at his wristwatch and exclaimed, "Oh my goodness, look at the time!"

After one more shuffle of the papers on his desk, Bruce took a pink silk handkerchief from the breast pocket of his Ralph Lauren white linen sports jacket and waved it in the air above his head as he pranced toward the door. "Au revoir then boys!" he exclaimed, turning at the doorway to blow them a kiss. "Cote d'Azur, here I come!"

Jeremy walked to one of the two large bay windows at the front of the gallery. He watched in amusement, laughing and shaking his head as Bruce danced across the street with light butterfly steps. Jeremy felt a tingle of happiness to be in the pleasant spa town of Harrogate to the southeast of the Yorkshire Dales, otherwise known as the Antiques and Arts Center of the North. It was a vibrant place, famous for its elegant Victorian and Edwardian architecture, for its teashops, flower festivals, Turkish baths and its international conference center.

"At last," Nigel muttered. "I thought he was never going to leave. Right then, I think it's time for a tea break. You hold the fort here and I'll nip in the back and put the kettle on." He rubbed his hands together and left the room.

"Huh? Right. Two sugars," Jeremy called after him. He turned from the window and wandered through the two large rooms located either side of the double entrance doors where a variety of modern works by local artists were exquisitely displayed. The works were predominantly paintings, but a few sculptures and photographs were discreetly placed about the room. He wondered what his parents would think if they could see him now.

A ghost of a smile touched his lips when he considered how fortunate he was to be working in the most prestigious part of town. The Bryce Edwards Gallery was situated in the stylish Montpelier quarter, in one of Harrogate's most elegant facades. It boasted an opulent exterior and occupied a prime location between Sotheby's Antiques and a quaint bistro overlooking the splendid gardens of Montpelier Hill. He lingered for a moment in front of a pretty little landscape that he instantly recognized as a local beauty spot, then sauntered to the rear of the building where the more valuable works were exhibited. The two high-ceilinged rooms at the back that housed the eighteenth and nineteenth century oils and watercolors by British artists were his favorite part of the gallery. He took his time, examining each piece, as he wandered about the rooms.

"Tea's ready!" Nigel yelled from the office.

"I'm right here," said Jeremy as he walked through the door. Nigel jumped back in surprise.

"Jeez, you startled me creeping around like that. I thought you were still in the front."

"Just having a little wander," Jeremy snickered. "Why are you so jumpy all of a sudden. This place isn't haunted is it?"

"No, you just startled me that's all. I wasn't expecting to see your ugly mug so soon. Here, this one's yours," he laughed, pushing a mug across the desk in Jeremy's direction. He sank into a sumptuous leather office chair and lifted his feet onto the desk.

"Wouldn't it be something if we could afford a place like this for ourselves," Nigel mused. "You know, like starting our own business?"

"Yeah, as if that's ever going to happen."

"Ah, you never know Jez, you never know," Nigel winked at him. "It's all about seizing the right opportunities. You never get anywhere sitting on your arse waiting for good fortune to fall into your lap."

The chime of the bell above the entrance door interrupted them.

"Your turn Jez. I made the tea," said Nigel, with a smug smile across his face.

* * *

The rest of the morning remained mercifully quiet in the gallery, allowing Jeremy ample time to brood about the predicament with his parents. He paced through the rooms deep in thought until he finally stopped in front of a nude painting by the modern British artist, Helen Purdie. He stood with one arm folded across his waist and stroked his chin. The subject matter of the artwork depressed him even more, reminding him of another woefully inadequate part of his life. Girls his own age terrified him and recollections of awkward, past acquaintances made him wince with embarrassment. He acknowledged with a long sigh that he really did need to make more of an effort to address his pitiful sex life. His thoughts were interrupted by a shout from Nigel.

"Just nipping out to grab a sandwich. Do you want anything?"

"Nah. I'm not hungry," Jeremy responded gloomily. He was too worried to eat anything.

"Christ, Jeremy, you need some meat on your bones. I'll bring you a donut or something. Back in a sec!"

Moments later the door swung open again. Expecting to see Nigel darting through the gallery looking for his wallet or something he had forgotten, Jeremy turned to see a tall, distinguished looking man stride through the doorway, holding a fairly substantial, rectangular brown package.

"Good afternoon. Can I help you?" enquired Jeremy.

"Ah. Julian Parks is the name. Is Nigel here?" the man replied, speaking in the Queen's best English. He was dressed in tan slacks and a navy blue, brass buttoned, double-breasted blazer. A silk cravat in a lighter hue of blue was tied waggishly at his neck, lending him a dapper appearance. His dark, wavy hair, dappled with grey was swept back from his forehead and smoothed behind his ears, making him look younger than his fifty-six years.

"Oh, hello Mr. Parks," said Jeremy, surprised. "I'm Jeremy Danvers, Nigel's friend. I'm helping out for a few weeks. Pleased to meet you. He walked toward Julian, hand outstretched.

"Ah, yes. Heard all about you old boy," Julian replied hesitantly, leaning the package against the wall. He held Jeremy's hand in a vice like grip and shook it vigorously, casting a nervous glance out the window.

"Really?" Jeremy responded, a little rush of pleasure running through him. Julian Parks was a well-known arts dealer and personal friend of Nigel's father. Both originally hailing from Yorkshire, the two of them often did business together and periodically collaborated on various collections and exhibitions in the North of England. It was widely known that Julian possessed an impressive private art collection. He was a rich man with a debonair, flamboyant manner. He had a reputation for mixing with the higher echelons of society.

"Ah. Bryce Edwards has spoken very highly of you. Yes, most highly. Trust him explicitly. Nigel's popped out eh?" He looked out the gallery window again. He seemed flustered and clearly in a hurry. Jeremy looked in the same direction as Julian and saw a sleek black sedan with dark tinted windows idling in front of the gallery.

"Blast and damnation! I was hoping to catch hold of him. I need to put this fellow," he said, indicating the package with a nod of his head, into the safe for a few hours. Got a lady friend waiting outside you see and I don't want to cart this around. Rather gets in the way of the cocktails." He let out a loud guffaw and then looked Jeremy in the eye, tapping the side of his nose with his forefinger. "A little business luncheon . . . too valuable to leave in the car," he added in a conspiratorial whisper. He nodded and narrowed his eyes. "Some rather nice pieces I've managed to acquire," he said proudly, "for my lady friend, to be shipped to the States. Tell you what," he said genially. "Do you mind awfully if we nip into the back and pop it in the safe? I've got the combo."

"I wish I could help you Mr. Parks..."

"It's Julian, please," he interrupted, sensing the situation was not going quite as he had anticipated.

"Well, I've been given the strictest of instructions to allow absolutely no one near the safe without Nigel being here. I'm really sorry Mr., I mean, er, Julian, but you can see what a predicament I'm in."

Several loud beeps from a car's horn broke the brief, awkward silence that had descended between them. Julian wheeled around to look outside again and then seemed to reach a hasty decision.

"Hmm. Looks like we'll have to leave the fellow in the store room then. Hide it amongst the other knick-knacks down there. I know I can depend on you, er Jonathon, no, Jeremy wasn't it . . . to keep an eagle eye on this rascal," he said, patting the parcel lightly with one hand. "Lead the way old boy!"

A closed door at the rear of the largest room in the back opened onto a metal skeletal staircase. It led down to a small, dimly lit room that housed new acquisitions waiting to be inspected away from the sun's damaging rays, and other pieces ready to be crated and shipped to various destinations. Julian carefully concealed his package behind the largest crate in a far corner.

"Let's just pop something on it for identification," Julian said as he reached for a roll of masking tape lying on one of the large tables. He ripped off a small piece and stuck it on top of the package. "There we are, that should do it," he said jovially. "Wouldn't want it to get mixed up with the others, would we? Well, thanks again old chap . . . saved my life . . . got to fly . . . back in a few hours." He flashed Jeremy a beaming smile, swept back up the stairs and bounded out of the gallery.

Unable to contain his curiosity, Jeremy darted to the window and peered outside. A chauffeur hopped out of the car and opened the rear door for Julian. Just as he sank into the sumptuous leather seat, an attractive older, blond woman leaned forward to speak, her face lit with laughter. Her elegant poise and expensive attire made it obvious to Jeremy, even from a distance, that she was a well-bred woman of some distinction.

* * *

The afternoon passed quickly with a steady stream of people visiting the gallery. About three hours after he had left for lunch, Nigel telephoned to say he was going to be a "touch late" having met up with some old acquaintances down at the Horse and Jockey. The loud peels of laughter in the background annoyed Jeremy intensely.

"It's been busy over here. I need to ask you about Jul . . . "

"Speak up Jez! Can't hear you with all this noise!" Braying voices and loud music boomed in the background.

"Just get back as soon as you can!" Jeremy shouted into the receiver. He put the phone down sharply, feeling a mixture of envy, irritation and a growing suspicion that Nigel was going to be "nipping out for a sec" on a regular basis. "Lazy sod," he muttered.

Jeremy looked up at the antique clock on the wall opposite the desk and frowned. I wonder what's keeping Julian, he thought idly. He's been gone for more than a few hours. Well, if he's not here by six, I'm out of here. He'll just have to drop by tomorrow if he wants his stuff. It can't be that important. Nigel can take the crap if it is.

* * *

Nigel didn't stagger back to the flat until the early hours of the morning. When Jeremy awoke, he eased open Nigel's bedroom door. From the way Nigel was sprawled spread-eagled face down and fully clothed on his bed, it was obvious that he had spent the whole of the previous evening drinking. Annoyed that he had been left alone in the gallery for the whole afternoon, and piqued because he had missed the fun, Jeremy made no attempt to get ready for work quietly. Instead, he clattered around and deliberately banged the cupboard doors, but the cacophony of snorts and snoring emitted from Nigel's bedroom continued without interruption, making it irritatingly obvious to Jeremy that he was going to be on his own again for the best part of another day.

"Great," he muttered sourly. His resentment towards Nigel went up another notch. He put his feet up on the coffee table in front of the television and sank down into a deep black leather chair, munching his cornflakes. He lifted the remote, turned up the volume and began scrolling through the channels until he found the local news. He half-watched for a while but soon grew bored of the minutiae of small town life. He was about to change the channel when an announcement made him sit bolt upright.

Breaking news: two people dead after a head-on collision on the A1, just outside of Knaresborough in Yorkshire, involving an articulated lorry and a Mercedes. Police have released the name of one of the deceased passengers in the car as Julian Parks, an arts dealer from London. The identity of the other deceased passenger has not yet been released. The driver of the car, chauffeur Carlisle Mannering and the driver of the lorry, Terrence Wainwright from Harrogate, are in critical condition in Harrogate Memorial Hospital.

"Bloody hell!" Jeremy slid his breakfast bowl onto the table, spilling milk over its surface. He jumped to his feet and swept both hands through his hair. "Jesus Christ. Nigel. Get up. You've got to see this!" he shouted. "Nigel!"

* * *

The next week passed in a blur. Nigel's parents caught the earliest flight back to Leeds and Bradford airport where Nigel drove to meet them. The three of them traveled to Harrogate in a state of shock. His mother, unable to come to terms with the news, cried into a handkerchief.

"I can't believe he's dead, I just can't," she kept repeating. Within hours of their arrival, a tide of friends and colleagues flooded the gallery, still too stunned to accept the awful tragedy. Jeremy was kept busy answering the phones that rang incessantly. The identity of Julian's companion in the car was announced later that week, as Claudia Rankin, a wealthy American of some standing. Speculation about the relationship between her and Julian, added to the media frenzy. For the first few days after the accident, news reporters and photographers hovered outside waiting to pounce on anyone entering or leaving the gallery. Jeremy too, was assailed at every opportunity, but the reporters soon left him alone when they realized he was an outsider of no import.

By week's end, Julian's demise was old news and the reporters were gone. The stream of visitors to the gallery gradually slowed and on the first Sunday following the accident, the Bryce- Edwards departed to London for the funeral. Jeremy was left to cope on his own with a skeletal staff comprised of Jack, who did the framing and crating for shipments, old Hughes, who did the books, and Moira, the part-time assistant.

"Don't know how we could get through this without your help Jeremy," said Nigel's father as they were about to leave for London. "You've been an absolute godsend to the gallery, what with everything that's gone on. I can't thank you enough." He gave Jeremy a friendly slap on the back. "Do you think you can stay on for the rest of the summer?"

Jeremy felt hugely relieved to see them all leave. Peace at last and free use of Nigel's flat. The week's traumatic events had left him feeling exhausted and in need of solitude. He was looking forward to being in the gallery on his own. He loved to walk through the gracious rooms and linger in front of each piece of art, drinking in the beauty of them all. The creaks of the old floorboards as he went from room to room seemed to speak to him and calm his frayed nerves. His worries felt more distant and a little less daunting when such lovely things surrounded him.

However, his utopia did not last long. The first of two alarming developments was a phone call from his parents announcing their intention to come and see him in Harrogate the following day.

"We've got bags to discuss Jeremy," his mother said. "We need to make arrangements for your graduation ceremony."

"Ah, yes, right." Jeremy replied. He groaned inwardly as a wave of worry-tremors rushed through his body. He felt nauseous.

The second, and even more alarming incident was the visit on the same morning as the phone call, from the police.

He was sitting behind Bruce's desk going through the mail when two men entered the gallery. As soon as he saw them, Jeremy knew instinctively that they were not there to buy art. The taller of the two, a young man in his late twenties, approached the desk and said in a surprisingly deep voice, "We're looking for Jeremy Danvers." He withdrew his hand from his jacket pocket and held out his police identification, "Detective Collins, and this is Detective Sergeant Maurice Patterson from the Arts and Antiques division of the Metropolitan Police Force- Scotland Yard." He nodded towards his much older colleague, a short, stout man in his mid-fifties. At the mention of his name, Patterson turned his attention away from the print he was studying and looked at Jeremy, who nodded meekly in response.

"We're here to ask you a few questions about Julian Parks. He was here on the afternoon of the nineteenth, the day of his accident?" It was a statement rather than a question.

Oh Jesus, what do they want, thought Jeremy, already feeling guilty of something, although he wasn't sure what. A number of possibilities raced through his head. The package! He had intended to mention it to Nigel's father but the time was never right. He also toyed with telling Nigel, but something in his gut told him not to do so. It was still tucked away in the storeroom. He remembered Julian saying that the package contained some "nice little pieces." He wondered if they were valuable. A terrible, fleeting thought came thundering into his head. What if he kept them? They might be his ticket to success; the stepping-stone he needed to enter the art world. No one would know. He cleared his throat, and fighting to keep the fear out of his voice, managed to say, "Yes, but he wasn't here long."

Patterson moved along the wall of paintings, leaning forward occasionally to read the artists' names. He was about six feet away from the desk when he asked abruptly, "Did he leave anything here?"

Startled by the directness of the question, Jeremy felt the color drain from his face. There was something menacing in Patterson's tone that made him falter. Both men were looking at him. Their hard eyes seemed to see right through him.

"No," he said a little too emphatically. The word seemed to hang in the air.

God, what have I done? Why did I say that? I must be out of my mind! I've just lied to the police! Jeremy screamed inwardly, while trying to maintain an impassive face.

"You do realize," said Collins, "that Mr. Parks is currently under investigation for, now how shall I say this, some business indiscretions."

"I have no idea. What do you mean?"

"Theft, Mr. Danvers. Art theft." Patterson spat out the words.

"What?"

"Yes, Julian Parks has been under suspicion for smuggling a significant piece of art out of the country last year without an export license. It still hasn't been proven, but we have information that he was about to do the same again, only this time we're talking about six paintings."

"Six?"

"Yes, Mr. Danvers. Six very valuable watercolors."

The two men didn't stay long, but it felt like an eternity to Jeremy. They asked more pointed questions about the nature of Julian's visit to the gallery that day, and one lie led to another, so he told them that Julian had called in to get a telephone number from Bruce's desk. They also seemed interested in how long they had been acquaintances and whether Jeremy knew where Julian was going later that afternoon. He was terrified they were going to ask if they could look around the premises. Fortunately, they seemed satisfied with his answers. He surprised himself with his exterior coolness, but inside he felt sick with guilt and worry.

Jeremy's relief when they left was almost palpable. His armpits felt damp and he developed a buzzing, incipient headache. He wanted to run down the stairs to the storeroom and tear open Julian's package, but he resisted acting too quickly. Someone might be watching him through the window and they might surprise him by coming back to the gallery. No, he would have to wait for the right moment, when he was sure he would not be disturbed. It was going to be a long day.

"What do think?" Collins asked Patterson as they strode down the hill back to their car.

"The kid's lying," Patterson was a man of few words. "Have him watched. And get a search warrant"

* * *

Three thousand miles away, across the Atlantic, Conrad Rankin was sitting on a hard, uncomfortable ornate chair in the foyer of the Rankin mansion on the outskirts of Boston. He sat in an awkward upright position, his chin jutting out and his head tilted back against the velvet padding of the chair. He had just returned after the reading of his mother's will.

Slanting rays of sunlight poured in through the decorative glass set in the enormous entrance doors, casting a swath of bright light across the polished marble floor. Conrad watched the dust motes dancing in the warm late afternoon air, breathing in the silence and vastness of the old house. He sat without moving for a long while, thinking about how empty his life had become. He had his collections and more money than he could spend in a lifetime, and yet he was not happy. He had brief moments of enjoyment, but if the truth were known, most of the time he felt unfulfilled, lonely and bored.

On his lap was Claudia's cell phone. It had been returned to him along with her personal affects and luggage. Three messages were left on her phone: two from her attorney, and one from her gentleman *friend*, Julian Parks. The first two, relating to her estate, piqued his interest, but it was the last message that intrigued him the most. From the tone of the man's voice, it was obvious there had been a romantic involvement, a notion that bothered him enormously. Although he couldn't visualize his mother in this way, it was the content of the message that burned his curiosity. He listened to it several times.

"Claudia, everything is taken care of. They're all yours now - our little secret. We'll swing by Bryce Edwards on the way and leave them in the safe for a few hours. I'll pop back later and pick them up. I'll be over at eleven. Have the champers on ice . . . time to celebrate!"

He dropped his gaze and looked down the hall towards the library where the hideous likeness of Mrs. Prendergast was hung. I wonder how many thousands that's worth.

Bryce Edwards . . . is that a person or a place? And what did he leave in the safe? Probably artwork since Parks was an art dealer . . . a secret? Hmmm.

Struck with a sudden decision, he leaped to his feet and ran into his father's office. He lifted the phone and dialed his personal assistant.

"Barbara . . . yes, it's me . . . I want you to do some digging for me. I need you to find a fine arts specialist; the best in this country and quickly . . . "

"What? Yes, as soon as possible. No, I don't care what it costs. I'll forward the contacts you're going to need to access the details of my mother's will, and, I'm going to want her art inventory. I want to know about her latest acquisitions, where she got them and where they are now—every last one of them. I want to know how the art is moved, the export side of things . . . What . . . ? Yes. Yes—exactly. First, though, I want you to find out who or what Bryce Edwards is. It's going to be somewhere near where my mother died. What? Yes, Knaresborough or Harrogate, or maybe York . . . Oh—and get me on a flight to England A-S-A-P to the airport closest to the scene of my mother's accident. Yes . . . yes, and I'll need a car."

SEVEN

Jeremy had always nurtured a deep dislike of wet weather, but on this particular day, it was to be his savior. The heavens opened around four in the afternoon and the rain hadn't stopped when it was time to close the gallery at six o'clock. Jeremy's state of anxiety after the phone call from his parents, followed by the visit from the police rendered him all but useless at work. The rain was a welcome deterrent to most shoppers, and the gallery was nearly dead. With time on his hands, he spent the best part of the day fretting over the mounting number of lies he had told, especially the hideous mistake of not telling the truth to the police. He sat at Bruce's desk and bit his fingernails to the quick, thinking about the hidden package downstairs. Although he was desperate to investigate, he did not dare take the chance until he had closed at the regular time and locked all the doors.

He watched the hands of the antique grandfather clock on the wall opposite Bruce's desk tick by with agonizing slowness. He waited impatiently for the brittle, aged chime to announce six o'clock. At last, it was time to turn off all the lights except for the ones in the window displays, and lock up. With a huge amount of relief and a great deal of trepidation, Jeremy made his way down the staircase at the back of the gallery and entered the storeroom on tip toe, hardly daring to breathe. He was the only one left in the gallery, but he still crept around, terrified that the police might come back unannounced.

Although it remained light until after nine o'clock each evening in the summer, the grayness of the day barely filtered in through the two small windows in the basement storeroom. An ominous gloom filled the room, making Jeremy feel more on edge than he already was. He quickly pulled down the blinds on each window, then went back to the door and turned the key, locking himself inside. After a moment's hesitation, he switched on the lights and blinked as his eyes adjusted to the brightness. He made his way past some wooden crates stacked against the wall and headed toward the far end of the room where several large packages were piled in the corner. With trembling hands he carefully leaned each package against his legs until he found the smallest one with a piece of masking tape attached, concealed at the back. He lifted it and leaned the others back against the wall. He took the package to a large table in the center of the room that was used for crating. He looked toward the door and strained to listen for any sounds. Other than the sound of rain falling heavily from a broken gutter, he could hear nothing.

Jeremy ripped the brown packing paper away from the raw wood crate inside. He carefully pried it apart and discarded the pieces in a large container by the door. Using a large pair of scissors, he snipped the taut plastic sheeting away that enveloped a smaller frame of wood, within which were laid six pieces of art. They were watercolors, all quite small, the largest measuring only about five hundred by four hundred millimeters. He leaned forward to scrutinize the one on top and almost immediately stepped back, bringing his hand to his mouth.

"Oh, sweet mother of pearl!" he gasped. Too stunned to move, he stood paralyzed while his heart hammered against his ribcage.

"Oh, dear God, what now?" he asked aloud. He was still unable to move, but grew increasingly aware of the urgent need to get out of the gallery in a hurry. After several deep breaths, he gathered his courage and stepped forward again. With his hands shaking, he delicately lifted the contents from the package, carefully laying each one on top of the table.

He nearly jumped out of his skin when he heard a loud rapping coming from upstairs at the front of the gallery. Someone was at the entrance. The knocking stopped for a moment and then repeated, only louder.

Dear God—who the hell can that be? It could be the police again, he thought, a wave of panic surging through his veins. Oh Jesus, this lot has my fingerprints all over them! What am I going to do? I can't run without being seen, and now I can't deny knowing anything about all this. He wished he had turned off the lights, but if he did, whoever was at the door would know someone was there. The knocking stopped. Hardly daring to breathe, he stood motionless, silent over the artwork, listening for the slightest sound. Several minutes passed . . . Nothing . . . just the rain falling from the gutter and the distant humming sound of passing cars. It must have been a late customer.

Perspiring heavily, Jeremy slowly exhaled his held breath. With a heightened sense of urgency, he carefully stacked the paintings, rolled them loosely, and secured them with a piece of string. Tapping the light switch as he passed, he darted out of the storeroom and ran up the stairs in twos. When he reached the top, he grabbed his baggy rain jacket and slid the roll of art down the left hand sleeve before pulling the front zipper. He quickly set the alarm, and holding Bruce's large golf umbrella at an angle to shield his upper body from the wind and rain, crept out into the alley at the rear of the gallery. Safely hidden behind the umbrella, he felt confident that no one would notice the odd stiffness of his arm.

As soon as he arrived at the flat, he went straight to the bathroom and locked himself inside. Only then did he dare to make a close examination of the artwork. Sitting on the edge of the bath, he unfurled each sheet of paper and held them, one at a time, under the light. He immediately recognized the unmistakable style. He felt a mixture of exhilaration and fear as his eyes took in the landscapes. He had been taken aback when he saw the first watercolor in the gallery. During the twenty minutes it took him to get to the flat, he agonized over whether they could possibly be authentic originals, but looking at them now and feeling the age of the paper, he felt with near certainty that they were. The police wouldn't have much interest in them if they were just prints or copies. He sat, mesmerized by the possibility that he was holding six original nineteenth century pieces by J. M. W. Turner, the greatest of all Britain's watercolorists.

Jeremy carefully balanced the paintings on his lap and slumped into a sitting position on the bathroom floor. Holding the sides of his head in his hands, he let his chin fall to his chest. What in the name of God, am I going to do now? Why in hell did I lie to the police? I should have just told them Julian had left the package. Oh, Jesus . . . I am so done for. He was filled with terrible remorse. He began to cry softly into his hands, wishing he could undo the entire mess. The fleeting thought of just running away flashed through his mind, but then, he remembered having to meet his parents the following day. He threw his head back in despair, and banged it several times against the wall. How could he face them and pretend everything was okay? He was not sure he could get through such a ghastly ordeal.

Thirty minutes or so later, numb from sitting on the hard bathroom floor for so long, he gathered up the paintings and hauled himself to his feet. He turned off the light and went straight to his bedroom where he rolled up the artwork and hid it inside his wardrobe before launching himself, spread-eagled, on top of the bed. He buried his head in the quilt, exhausted and full of rampant self-loathing.

Torn by indecision and guilt, he spent a wretched, sleepless night fretting over what he was going to do. His mind was in turmoil, swinging from one option to another like a pendulum. By dawn's light, he was still no nearer to a decision. Worn out from his shabby moral evasions, he staggered to the kitchen in the half-light and poured a glass of tap water. After gulping it down, he turned to the cupboard behind him in search of breakfast. He found a few smashed cornflakes in the bottom of an almost empty box and tipped them into a bowl.

While munching on his cereal, the fog in his mind cleared and he knew what he needed to do. Above all else, he had to escape from Harrogate and get away from the gallery. He felt the need to flee to his parents' home in the tiny village of Tipping, deep in the heart of Yorkshire, where he could hide the paintings and lay low for a while. Yes—that is what he would do. He would speak to Mr. Bryce Edwards over the phone and tell him that he needed to attend to a few things at home before travelling to Roehampton for his graduation ceremony. He would meet with his parents that morning, and then he would ask Moira, the part-timer if she could cover for him for the next few days until Bruce returned.

Enlivened by his resolve, Jeremy swept up the few possessions he had brought to Nigel's flat and shot down the single flight of stairs to where his white Volkswagen Golf was parked in his allotted space outside. He opened the hatchback and flung his stuff haphazardly into to the car. Loping back to the flat, taking the stairs in twos, he rushed back inside to get the rest of his belongings and conceal the Turners the best way he could. He placed two of the smaller watercolors between the pages of his largest art book and then rolled the others into two loose bundles and placed them amongst a wad of university papers in a large backpack.

After a shower and a last check around the flat, he felt significantly better knowing that he need not come back to the flat again after he left the gallery later that day. The thought of retreating to his family home in Tipping, far away from the gallery, gave him a feeling of relief and just a little hope. First, though, he had to face his parents.

* * *

Unfortunately, the day turned out to be an absolute nightmare, far worse than he could have imagined. He was forced to endure an excruciating morning in Bettie's tearooms, one of Harrogate's famous landmarks. Thank God, his parents were departing the following afternoon for their annual trip to a science convention in Prague. It meant he would have a few weeks to himself at home, time to sort things out. So, it was in a cloud of guilt, over tea and scones, that he indulged his parents in their efforts to finalize arrangements for his forthcoming graduation ceremony. His mother had been in her usual fine form, going on at length about how wonderful it was to have two sons graduate in the sciences, and then, just to turn the knife, his father brought up the prickly subject about Jeremy's future plans.

"You'll be applying for a Masters then. You might consider Manchester Jeremy; they have a fine faculty . . . " His father's voice droned on.

After what seemed like an eternity, they dropped him off at the gallery, where he could at last agonize about his appalling situation without having to act as if nothing were wrong. His face ached from having to continually force a smile. The pounding headache he had all morning worsened to an incessant, hammering assault on his entire being. An ominous feeling that things were about to spiral out of control kept nagging at the back of his brain. He was not far wrong.

Around two in the afternoon, the doors to the gallery swung open, and to Jeremy's astonishment, in marched Nigel and his father. Scotland Yard's Detective Collins, Detective Sergeant Maurice Patterson and three other constables accompanied the two ashen-faced men. Collins immediately instructed Jeremy to refrain from any conversation with the Bryce Edwards until told to do so, not to answer any phone calls, and to stay seated where he was. He was not to leave the premises under any circumstances, while Patterson escorted both Nigel and his father to the safe in the rear of the gallery. One tall constable with a cold, unsmiling face stood by the door. The others fanned out and systematically searched every room.

Less than an hour had passed when Detective Collins' ringing cell phone interrupted him from scrutinizing papers found in Bryce Edward's office desk. The expression on his face visibly changed when he heard the message. With the phone still to his ear, he signaled with a wave of his hand to Patterson, who was stood by the open safe door.

"Sir . . . Sir . . . Rankin's just landed at Leeds-Bradford airport," Collins said. "He's picked up a car and he's headed in this direction."

"Right." A glimmer of a smile threatened to lift the corners of Patterson's mouth. "This is it. This is our man. Make damned sure they don't lose him. I want to know every move he makes, every piss-stop he takes, and I want to hear about every single person he talks to. Oh, and get me the chief superintendent on the phone," he added. "We're going to need some backup."

"I'm on it sir."

Patterson looked at his watch and frowned. "We'd better finish up and get out of here. Rankin could be here within the hour. I don't want him to know we're onto him- not yet anyway."

* * *

Several hours after their appearance to execute the search warrant, the police made, what seemed to Jeremy, an abrupt departure, citing other pressing business. They left behind a flustered and disgruntled Mr. Bryce Edwards who immediately cornered Jeremy.

"Well, what in hell's name has been going on? They bloody well searched the London gallery and then hauled us back here! You know they're searching Nigel's flat as well don't you? Christ knows what they're going to find in there!" He strode back and forth, pulling both hands through his hair.

"They're telling me they've had some tip off that Julian left some stuff here . . . that he's involved in some kind of black market deal . . . I feel like they're trying to implicate me!" He spat out the last words, growing red in the face. "You were the only one here Jeremy, so I think you've got some bloody explaining to do!"

Reeling from the unexpected shock of hearing that the police were searching the flat, Jeremy could barely contain the feeling of panic that was welling up inside him.

"But I've already told the police everything—twice! He left nothing here . . . he–he was looking for Nigel. Then he went to look for a telephone number from Bruce's desk," he blurted loudly.

"What did he want me for?" asked Nigel who stood wide-eyed at the back of the room.

"That's what I'd bloody well like to know!" his father shouted crossly.

"Well, don't blame any of this on me!" yelled Nigel angrily. "I haven't got any idea what he wanted. What was he meant to have left anyway?"

Visibly shaken, Mr. Bryce Edwards walked over to the desk where Jeremy was sitting and took out a half-empty bottle of Scotch and a shot glass from one of the drawers. Without offering any to Nigel or Jeremy, he swallowed two measures before speaking again, this time in a slightly more controlled manner.

"Seems that Julian's been facilitating the exchange of some *lost* Turner masterpieces. Stuff that's been missing for years." He paused to pour another drink and then continued," It's ever since the Tate launched a website at the end of 2002 in the hope of retrieving missing Turners from across the world. The whole business created a huge renewal of interest in his works—it's been a huge success. I think five hundred or so pieces have turned up from all sorts of sources, mostly from private collections and the odd piece turning up in grannies' attics. Seems that Julian managed to procure some rather valuable pieces."

"What do you mean? If he got the work from a legitimate source . . . I don't see how he could have done anything wrong," interjected Nigel. He looked at his father with wide-eyed innocence.

"Ah, well, seems he's been acting as a go-between for an extremely wealthy client, someone who wanted to remain anonymous—as they always do in the dubious art underworld. Numerous priceless pieces can then sit around, hidden for decades, centuries even. He must have got his hands on some hot little pieces. The real question is: Who gave him the paintings?"

"Well, it doesn't matter does it if he can prove the provenance, and if he bought them legit." countered Nigel.

"Ah, well—that's just it. The problem will undoubtedly lie in the provenance of this untraced art. Most work that goes *missing* doesn't just get lost. It's usually been stolen from the legitimate owner, and as you know, most art theft is perpetrated by international organized crime syndicates. They use the stolen art to trade on a closed black market, for drugs or arms. Just doing business with these low-lifes is highly questionable . . . some very dubious characters involved . . . *very* dubious," he repeated.

"I can't believe Julian would be that foolish," said Nigel.

"I wouldn't have either, but it seems he was smitten with that American woman, Claudia Rankin. Love and lust can drive a man to do unthinkable things, I suppose. Anyway, the police seem to think that she's probably the one who put him up to this."

"But, it doesn't make any sense," Jeremy said. "I thought she was loaded. Why didn't she just wait for some decent stuff to come up at auction and buy legitimately?"

"Impatience probably . . . used to getting everything with a click of her fingers . . . who knows? The subterfuge probably adds a little extra spice to the acquisition."

"But then she'd never be able to show the Turners if they weren't really hers to have."

"Oh come on Jeremy! Don't be so damned naïve," said Mr. Bryce Edwards. "The reward isn't the ability to showcase their collections. The reward for high end art theft is simply to own a tangible piece of beauty . . . to possess it for personal pleasure . . . to know that they have it and it's theirs alone to admire."

Still trying to grasp the magnitude of what he was hearing, Jeremy tentatively asked: "So do the police know which Turners he got hold of? I mean, are we talking really serious money here?"

"God knows . . . You know what the police are like. They only tell you what they want you to hear, but I suppose it has to be a tidy sum, otherwise they wouldn't be so interested, would they?" He paused for a moment. "Hmmm . . . there was that missing Turner, the watercolor of Bamborough Castle that turned up in the late seventies. It had been lost for over a hundred years . . . I think it sold for about three mill. The last really big sale was in 1990, Turner's view of Venice. That one went for over twenty million. Oh, and *The Blue Rigi*, of course, last year—that went for nearly six mill."

Jeremy gasped and shrank into the leather swivel office chair. He wrung his hands as he digested the information. He felt sick to his stomach, and his head throbbed more painfully than ever.

Mr. Bryce Edwards looked first at Nigel and then at Jeremy before continuing. He swallowed more of the Scotch, and then, in a deeper, serious tone, he said, "There's something else that worries me about this business though." He paused for a moment, thinking about what he had to say. Jeremy and Nigel looked up simultaneously.

"It's something Patterson, the Scotland Yard copper hinted at."

"What?"

"Well, when he was leaving he told me to watch my back. You know what that means don't you!" he shouted.

I—I've no idea," stammered Nigel, trying to grasp what his father was saying.

"That we might be in some sort of danger!"

At this, Nigel gasped and Jeremy nearly fell off the chair.

"What do you mean, in danger?" demanded Jeremy.

"I think he meant that whoever supplied Julian with the Turners is probably going to have a shot at getting them back again before they have a chance to resurface," Mr. Bryce Edwards answered. "I mean—why wouldn't they? News travels fast. They'll have a good idea that they're still out there somewhere. If the police think they were dropped off here, then so does everyone else. Oh Christ. All I bloody well need now is for some gun-wielding member of the mafia shooting up the gallery and putting a hole through the back of my head!"

At that moment, Mr. Bryce Edward's cell phone rang, making all three of them jump. "Yes!" He snapped into the phone. "Oh, Jean, it's you . . . yes, yes, I'm sorry." His voice faded as he walked towards his office in the rear of the gallery to take the call from his wife.

"Jesus Jeremy. I can't believe all this shit," whispered Nigel as soon as his father left the room. This was the first time he and Jeremy had been alone since the arrival of the police to execute the search warrant.

"You know you can trust me Jerry, old boy," he continued in a conspiratorial whisper. "Where have you put the paintings? Did Julian leave any instructions?"

"What? I can't believe you're asking me that!" seethed Jeremy through clenched teeth. He leaned closer to Nigel so he wouldn't be overheard. "He didn't bloody well leave anything here. It was you he wanted to see . . . why was that Nigel? Don't tell me you're involved in any of this."

"Oh, no . . . no . . . You're not going to fucking well try and involve me," Nigel said defensively.

Growing red in the face with anger, Jeremy spat out, "I never bargained for any of this drama. In fact—I've had enough. I . . . I need a few days to myself," he faltered. Then quickly added, "I've been here on my own for ages . . . and seeing as you and your dad are back sooner than you expected . . . I—I need a break Nigel."

"Yes, but–but . . . oh come on Jez—I was only ragging you. Of course, I believe you. I was joking, really old boy. Look, I thought we could have a few drinkies down at the Horse and Jockey tonight . . . have a bit of a laugh. Christ, we both need to let our hair down, you know . . . get caught up on stuff," protested Nigel." You can't just leg it out of here on my first night back!"

"No, I mean it Nigel. There are things I need to get sorted out at home . . . my–my parents were here this morning you know . . . it was a damned nightmare"

"Oh Shit, really?"

"Yes, I need to get out of here. You have no idea what it's been like having to deal with the police and taking all this crap. I've had enough!" Jeremy wailed.

EIGHT

Jeremy left Nigel and his father in the office, bickering about whether Moira, their part-timer, might fill in a few extra hours until Bruce returned to the gallery. He could hear Nigel whining, obviously alarmed at the thought of having to put in a full days work now that Jeremy was not going to be around to cover for his trysts to the pub each afternoon.

Just as Jeremy was about to leave, the electronic beep signaling the opening of the entrance door sounded, and in walked a tall, blond, immaculately groomed man in his early thirties. His presence seemed to permeate the room as he stood by the door for a moment, calmly surveying the gallery. He eventually turned to Jeremy who stood frozen near the desk.

"Good afternoon," he said, confidently. "Is the owner, a Mr. Bryce Edwards here?"

Stunned for a moment by a flash of recognition and then a stab of fear, Jeremy falteringly replied, "Er . . . yes . . . I think he's in the back . . . in his office. I, uh . . . perhaps I can help you?"

"No, It's Bryce Edwards I need to see. It's important. I've come a long way," Conrad answered firmly.

"I'll, uh, just see if he's available then," Jeremy stammered, unnerved by the American accent and the nagging feeling that the stranger seemed familiar somehow. He had seen that face before somewhere—those intense blue eyes . . . the air of refinement.

Jeremy turned and left the room. He squeezed his eyes shut for a second as if this would force the fog over his memory to lift, but he could not quite place where he had encountered the American before. He walked to the rear of the gallery and gently knocked on the office door.

"Come in!" Bryce Edwards bellowed.

Jeremy poked his head round the door. "I'm leaving now. Thanks for everything. I'll be in touch after my graduation. Oh, and there's someone here to see you. He didn't give his name, but I, uh . . . I think it's important."

"What's it about?" Bryce Edwards snapped.

"I don't know, but I think you should see him. He says he's come a long way. He's American."

"Oh God, what now? Okay, okay. Show him in." Bryce Edwards put his fingertips to his temples and worked the skin in slow circles. "And it better be important after the day I've had."

Jeremy ushered Conrad into Bryce Edward's office and then made for the exit. He was about to step outside when he realized he had forgotten his jacket.

"Oh, bloody hell," Jeremy muttered, and reluctantly went back inside.

He did not want to disturb Bryce Edwards again, so he crept about on tiptoe. He could hear the muted tones of conversation as he passed the office. He had not intended to eavesdrop, but the urge to hover for a few seconds outside the door was irresistible. He pressed his ear against the door and held his breath. He caught the tale end of a sentence spoken by the American: " . . . something left here by Julian Parks. I think it belongs to me now."

Jeremy felt a nauseating jolt of alarm. He lifted his hands to his face. Dear God. This American—he must have been sent to get the Turners back. It was just like the Scotland Yard coppers had warned. He looks like a man used to getting his way; like someone unafraid to use violence. Jesus Christ, I've got to get out of here.

He reeled backwards and stumbled in a panic toward the rear exit. He flew out of the building and raced to his car, which he deliberately left at the top of Montpelier, several hundred meters from the gallery.

In a panic, he dropped the keys twice before managing to insert the correct one into the ignition. Fumbling with the controls, Jeremy cried out when he saw the petrol sign illuminated on his dashboard. "Oh Shit, it's empty!"

He pulled into the first petrol station he came to on West Park Street. As he filled the tank, he tapped his foot nervously against the garage forecourt. It seemed to take forever. He cast terrified glances up and down the road, cursing the trickling flow of petrol. "Come on, come on!" he muttered, urging the pump to work faster.

* * *

From the raised voices and general state of disarray in the gallery's office, Conrad realized he had caught Bryce Edwards at an awkward moment. The man had clearly been surprised, shocked even when Conrad had introduced himself and explained the reason for his visit. However, after managing to gain some composure, Bryce Edwards offered Conrad his condolences on the death of his mother. Then, without pause, he insisted that he was completely unaware of any relationship, business or otherwise, between Julian and Conrad's mother. And, as far as he was concerned, knew absolutely nothing about any package that had supposedly been left at the gallery. He told Conrad that neither he nor his son, Nigel, whom he had at first neglected to introduce, were even in Harrogate at the time of Julian's visit. Jeremy Danvers, had been the only one there, and if Conrad wanted more information then he would have to go to the police, whom it seemed, were taking close interest in the whole affair.

"They think something fishy has been going on," said Bryce Edwards, collapsing into the leather office chair. He reached into his jacket pocket and brought out a large handkerchief to mop the perspiration from his face. "In fact, they were here less than an hour ago. Turned the bloody place upside down looking for the stuff!" exclaimed Bryce Edwards, growing angry again.

"You'll have to excuse me Mr. Bryce Edwards . . ."

"It's Bernard . . . Oh, and please take a seat," he said offering Conrad a comfortable armchair in the corner of the room. He signaled to Nigel, who looked as if he had seen a ghost, and with an exaggerated nod of his head indicating the office door, said, "Nigel, perhaps we could offer Mr. Rankin something to drink. Tea—coffee? Not quite up to American standards of course," he proffered apologetically.

"Nothing for me, thank you," said Conrad.

"I'll have one Nigel, there's a good lad," said Bryce Edwards, eager to be alone with the tall American.

Conrad waited until Nigel left the room before continuing. "Mr. uh . . . Bernard, I'm not sure that I understand what's going on here . . . I . . . why are the police involved?"

"Ah, well, I can only tell you the little I know . . . don't suppose it can do any harm . . . I'll be damned if I understand any of this myself."

* * *

Conrad drove away from the gallery with a sinking feeling that he might be getting involved in something he had not expected. He was beginning to feel uneasy about the whole situation. What in hell's name had his mother been up to? The idea of her being involved in some underhanded scheme was almost too much to take in, and yet . . . there was the niggling doubt that had been planted in the back of his brain when he listened to the last phone conversation between his mother and Parks. "Our little secret," Parks had said.

Turning onto West Park Street, the A61, a busy main road running through the center of Harrogate, Conrad tried to recollect the questions the police had asked him when he had arrived two weeks previously, to identify Claudia. They had not seemed to be suspicious of anything at the time, and they hadn't asked anything that was out of the ordinary on such a morbid occasion. But then he doubted if he would have noticed anything odd anyway. He was in too much shock over his mother's untimely death and too stunned by the revelations of her clandestine affair with Parks.

His instincts warned him to drop the notion of digging further. He certainly did not want any trouble with the police, and even the thought of being caught up in the dubious underworld of art theft, was perturbing at best. But he felt consumed by a burning curiosity to find out more.

Dog-tired after the long flight from the States followed by the drive from the airport to Harrogate, he was in dire need of a shower and a bed. Fighting to stay alert in the heavy traffic, he decided to make his way to the Crown Hotel where his assistant had made a reservation, and get some sleep. He would think about his options after some rest.

He was driving cautiously, peering ahead, looking at the street signs. when he saw the gallery's young assistant, Jeremy Danvers, standing at the pumps in a petrol station on the opposite side of the road. The kid was not hard to miss with that terrible hair, thought Conrad. What a stroke of luck!

With renewed energy, Conrad swung the car around at the next set of lights and drove quickly back to the garage. He recalled the look of terror on the kid's face when Conrad had walked into the gallery a short while ago. Instinct told him that the kid probably knew a lot more than he was letting on. Conrad reasoned that it would not do any harm to talk to him.

He pulled into the garage just as Jeremy was struggling to replace the filler cap on a beat up old white Volkswagon Golf.

"Excuse me. Mr. Danvers!" he shouted as he stepped out of his sleek, black Audi saloon, leaving the engine idling and the driver's door ajar.

Jeremy turned his head. His face looked tired and drawn as if he had too many late nights. At first, he stood motionless, but then his jaw dropped open and a look of recognition followed by horror spread across his face. He dropped the filler cap and leaped straight into the car, ignoring Conrad's call.

"Hey, hold up a minute!" Conrad ran over to the car before Jeremy had the chance to pull the driver's door shut. Resting both his arms casually across the top of the driver's door, Conrad leaned forward and said, "I think you forgot something dude. Drive off now and you're going to lose your gas cap. It's still loose."

Torn between gunning the accelerator and trying to appear unperturbed, Jeremy gulped before replying meekly," Er . . . yes. Thanks."

"You look like you're in a hurry. I've just been with Bryce Edwards . . . it seems you and I need to talk."

"Talk? With Me!" exclaimed Jeremy, unable to keep the fear out of his voice.

A puzzled look flashed across Conrad's face before he continued. "Look, this isn't a good place to talk. Let's go get a drink where it's more comfortable."

"No. No," Jeremy interrupted a little too loudly. "I can't. I haven't got the time right now . . . I . . . uh . . . have got to be somewhere . . . er . . . an appointment," he stammered, pulling feebly at the drivers door.

Conrad maintained his grip on the car door and replied in a cool tone. "Well, this shouldn't take long. I think you have some information about something that belongs to me—something Julian Parks left at the gallery." He looked directly into Jeremy's eyes as he said this: "I've come a long way to speak to you."

Thrown off guard by the piercing scrutiny of the American's icy, blue stare, Jeremy faltered before managing to stammer, "I haven't got any idea what you're talking about. He didn't leave anything with me. I–I've already told the police this . . . and . . . and Mr. Bryce Edwards." He thought about the paintings stashed in the back of the car, terrified his eyes would betray him.

"S-sorry, I can't help you. I've really got to get going," he said, pulling more forcibly at the door.

"Now look, kid," said Conrad, narrowing his eyes. He thought a little monetary enticement might help loosen the kid's tongue. He held onto the door with one hand and he reached inside his jacket with the other. "I know what you've told the police and Bryce Edwards, but I'm sure I can offer you something to help you . . . ah . . . remember what really happened. Let me introdu . . . "

Without listening to the rest of the sentence, Jeremy yanked the driver's door shut, slammed the car into gear, and sped out of the garage, tires screeching.

Narrowly avoiding several collisions, he tore out of Harrogate as fast as his aging Volkswagon could go. Too tired and fraught to be entirely rational, and dogged by a terrible sense of foreboding, Jeremy was convinced he was dealing with some hardened criminal sent by some even darker underworld syndicate to retrieve the Turners. When he saw the American reach inside his jacket, he panicked, thinking that he was about to have a gun pushed into his face.

Instead of heading north towards Ripon on the A61, Jeremy took a right turn as soon as he could and then looped around on the back roads to eventually head south, in the opposite direction to Tipping. Terrified in case he was being followed, he could not take the risk of heading home just yet. He quickly calculated that he would be better off trying to disappear in a busy place, until he was sure it was safe to go home.

So, with fearful glances in his rear view mirror, he headed south along the A1 to the large, populous city of Leeds. It was time to call in a favor from one of his few chums from Rivington. He was pretty sure Charlie Butterworth would be only too pleased to accommodate an old friend who turned up, especially if he arrived on the doorstep with enough beer for the night. Yes, he would doss down at Charlie's, and if his hangover were not too crippling, he would make his way to Tipping the following morning. Emboldened by this new plan, he sped into the city, weaving his way this way and that through the busy shopping streets on a long circuitous route. By the time he reached Charlie's, he was certain that no one had followed him.

Conrad had not expected the kid to drive off like that. He took a few half-hearted steps in the direction of the speeding car, but realized it was too late to stop him. With his eyes still trained on the back of the retreating Volkswagon as it disappeared into the rush-hour traffic, Conrad exhaled loudly, uncertain about what to do next. After a few moments, he made his way back to the rented Audi he had left idling at the end of the garage forecourt. "Jeez. I need some sleep," he whispered aloud.

Only when he reached the hotel and began gathering his belongings did he take notice of the open road map on the passenger seat. Bryce Edwards had mentioned that Jeremy was headed home for a while. Conrad remembered that it was definitely somewhere in Yorkshire, but the name of the place eluded him. He leaned over and picked up the map, trying to recollect the name of the town, or was it a village? Despite his weariness, Conrad poured over the map, hoping that a few of the place names would trigger his memory. He located Harrogate with his finger and then began to trace the roads radiating outwards into the heart of North Yorkshire. He quietly read out the names of various settlements.

"Ripon . . . Leyburn . . . Askrigg . . . High Shaw . . . Tubbs . . . Ti . . . Wait a minute . . . Tip . . . Tipping! That's it! Tipping."

He peered at a tiny, isolated dot on the map, in the middle of the Yorkshire Dales to the North West of Harrogate. It looked as if there were one road into the village and one road out. Ha! Bingo! He felt a thrill of pleasure with this last piece of good fortune. There was still a small chance; a long shot, that this trip was not going to be a waste of time after all. Conrad smiled. It should not be too hard to find the kid in such a tiny place—should it?

Conrad slept fitfully, waking at four in the morning still feeling tired. He tried to go back to sleep, but his mind was too restless. He lay in bed for another hour churning over the unexpected turn of events, his mind in conflict over what to do. He finally gave in to the time difference and got up, showered, and ordered an early breakfast.

At a little after seven in the morning he set off on what he hoped would be a leisurely drive through some of Yorkshire's finest country-side. His spirits lifted considerably when he felt the warmth of the June air on his face.

He followed the busy A61 to the pleasant market town of Ripon and then turned onto the smaller A6108 that wound its way across flat terrain towards the Moors. At first, he did not pay a great deal of attention to his surroundings. He was too preoccupied with how he was going to go about locating Jeremy once he reached Tipping. But when he turned west onto the 684 towards Hawes, he could not help but notice the dramatic change in the landscape. He was so busy taking in the lush slopes of the surrounding countryside that he nearly missed the battered road sign on his left indicating the road to Craggsdale Moor. He pulled onto the side of the road to study the map. He traced the route with his finger and looked ahead up the narrow, steep road in front of him. As far as he could tell, Tipping lay close to the top of the moor. A sign indicating hairpin bends with gradients up to 20 percent stood on sentry at the side of the cattle grid that spanned the entrance to the road. Well, thank God, it isn't winter, he thought. He shuddered to think how treacherous the road would be under a foot of snow and ice.

He opened the driver's door window a crack to let in the warmth of the morning, and set off again for the top of the Moors. He gradually weaved his way higher and higher, changing down into his lowest gears for the steeper sections. He saw only one other car cautiously making its way down from the opposite direction. Apart from that one intrusion, he felt a growing sense of exhilaration as he cast quick glances across the panorama that was unfolding beneath him. Unable to resist, he stopped to take in the magnificence of his surroundings. He pulled over into a lay-by and stepped out onto the edge of the road. With an easy stride, he stepped across the barrier and took a few steps towards the precipitous ledge.

The warmth of the sun beckoned him to tilt his face toward the sky. He closed his eyes and filled his lungs with deep breaths of the crystal air. Apart from the gentle whisper of the wind and the distant cry of a bird, it was silent and still. There was a special clarity in the air, a sense of space and airiness. When he opened his eyes, he was entranced by the breathtaking views, made all the sweeter by the profusion of wild flowers that speckled the lower slopes.

His reverie was rudely interrupted by the incongruous loud noise of a car engine laboring up the hill. With a disappointed sigh, Conrad turned to look at the intruder who had shattered his moment of peace. As the white car swung into view, Conrad stood rooted to the spot, too incredulous to move. His jaw dropped open in disbelief. It was the kid, Jeremy Danvers, in the old white Volkswagon Golf. Fucking unbelievable.

Once over his initial shock, Conrad leaped over the barrier and dove into his Audi. Shoving the gear into first, he shot back onto the road and set off in pursuit. The kid had definitely seen him. There was no mistaking the look of abject horror written across his face.

* * *

Pearl Wiggins and three elderly members of Tipping's Rambling Association stood with their noses pressed against the post office window. The ladies were dressed in their sensible hiking gear: woolen socks up to their knees to deter ankle- biting insects, loose fitting pants to facilitate the climbing of stiles, quilted, fleece-lined jackets, tightly zippered to their chins in case of any lingering morning chills, and robust walking boots for the rugged terrain they were about to traverse. Three miles was about their limit, but they always exaggerated the distance. They each held a long, whittled stick to assist on uphill sections, and to fend off any would-be attackers. However, Audrey Ormerod, the self-appointed group leader, displayed her importance by having a ski pole, much to the others' envy, instead of a stick. It was a part of their ritual to call in at Pearl's post office to stock up on provisions before setting off on one of their treks.

"Isn't that Alistair's boy, Jeremy?" said Audrey, squinting through her enormous, goggle-like glasses. "What on earth is he doing with that goat?"

"And who's that with him?" wondered Pearl aloud. "That tall chap with the blond hair."

"Well, he's not from round here, that's for sure," said Irma Hepplethwaite. At age seventy-four, she was the youngest of the three ramblers.

"He's very handsome."

"Hmmm…" Their four heads nodded in unison, as they pressed a little closer to the window.

"What do you think they're up to?" asked Pearl.

The ladies watched as the two men wandered back and forth across the field. Every now and again, one of them stooped to pick something up. They made their way to the trees, and sat down on the grass. They appeared to have a heated conversation. Occasionally, Jeremy would gesticulate with his hands in a dramatic manner, and then he would dip and shake his head.

"Move your head, Irma! I can't see," said Audrey, bobbing up and down on her tiptoes. All four ladies were now squashed behind the counter near the meat slicer where they had a better vantage point.

"What are they doing now?" asked Madge, the shortest of the ladies.

"They're chasing another goat!" exclaimed Irma who was weaving her head this way and that to get a better view.

"Let me see!" cried Pearl, pushing all three of them out of the way.

"Oh, oh . . . Wait a minute . . . "

"What?" The other three cried in unison.

"Huh!" Pearl drew a sharp intake of breath. "They're coming this way!"

Hurriedly, Pearl shot behind her station at the meat slicer, while the other three ladies shuffled to the other side of the counter and pretended to be looking at the deli meats.

The little bell above the door rang as Jeremy entered. He stopped abruptly in the half-open doorway as soon as he saw the crowd inside. The ladies all turned to look at him at the same time, but it was Audrey who pounced first.

"Why, it's young Jeremy Danvers isn't it? My, haven't you grown?"

"Ah . . . uh . . . yes . . . good morning ladies," he replied. The last people he wanted to see were Audrey Ormerod and her gossiping brood of ramblers. He was hoping to catch Pearl alone and ask her, in a roundabout fashion, without arousing any suspicion, whether she had seen anything fall onto the road, in particular, his backpack. He grimaced slightly, and took a step backward, half-turning to make a quick escape, but it was too late. In a rapid pincer movement, the ladies encircled him, denying him any hope of a polite retreat.

NINE

"Dickie darling, where have you been? I've been getting worried about you!" shouted Celia from the top of the steps leading to a handsome carved doorway with fluted columns. The house behind her, named *Horton Grange* was built in the grand manner, with large expansive windows and scrolled pediments. Ivy climbed over the mellow bricks reaching up to the eaves.

A buxom woman in her mid- forties, Celia was the much younger, second wife, and now widow, of the late Fergus Hartnell, the local veterinarian who was still fondly remembered by his fellow countrymen for miles around. His skills and courteous manner had not been lost on Dickie Cranshawe Booth, who, in more affluent times had relied on Fergus to attend to his shooting dogs and his wife's beloved horses.

Smiling broadly, Celia bounced down the steps onto the graveled driveway, pulling a cashmere wrap around her shoulders. She arrived at Dickie's car in time to throw her strong arms around his neck as he hauled himself, grumbling loudly, out of the driver's seat.

"I've had the most dreadful morning! Been to see this fool of a bank manager and then some bloody football hooligans nearly ran me off the road! Nearly killed me! Impudent young devils!"

"Oh, my poor Dickie," cooed Celia, stroking his head. "Come inside and tell me all about it and Celia will make you feel better." She giggled a little as she grabbed his hand and pulled him toward the house.

"What's that?" she asked as a piece of paper that had been stuck to the damp crotch of Dickie's trousers, fluttered to the ground. She bent down and picked it up. "Oh, it's lovely, Dickie. Where on earth did you get this?" she asked, holding it out for Dickie to see.

"Let me see that," said Dickie snatching it out of her hand.

It was a beautifully executed little watercolor, a landscape, not very big, but delightful just the same.

"Is there a signature? I can't see it without my specs," said Celia.

"Oh, throw the damn thing away… It's nothing; it's just a piece of rubbish that blew in off the road. There was litter all over the road in the village. Probably fell off the back of a lorry . . . filthy . . . don't know where it's been." He tossed it carelessly back into his car where it landed unceremoniously on the edge of the passenger seat.

"Don't be a silly, she said, smiling at Dickie, her lover for the past eight months. "Come on, my cuddle bunny, let's go in and I'll pour you a drink." She pressed her body into his and rubbed her cheek against his chest. "Hurry, I'm dying for you," she whispered, throwing him a smoldering look.

After a frantic coupling in one of the guestrooms, Dickie rolled off the bed and staggered to the bathroom with barely enough strength in his legs to carry him. He put both his hands on the lip of the washbasin and leaned his weight against it. The woman is an absolute tigress, he thought, fighting for breath—an insatiable appetite. He was mildly alarmed that their bedroom antics should leave him so winded. He had been putting off his annual physical for too long. He was, nevertheless, exceedingly pleased with his surprising virility. After thirty years of marriage to Olivia, a tightly conservative woman, *correct* at all times, especially in the bedroom, he thought sourly. It was as if his suppressed manhood had been given a new lease on life. Still panting, he ran the cold-water tap and splashed water on his face. With his eyes squeezed shut, he groped for a towel from the rail beside the sink. He slowly patted his face dry. Feeling somewhat recovered, he leaned in toward the mirror above the washbasin and stretched his neck from side to side, turning his head this way and that, trying to squint at his profile.

He still had a good head of hair, although considerably thinner than it used to be, but not bad for a man of sixty-four. It had a gingerish hue. His mother had proudly insisted on referring to its color as strawberry blond, but he much preferred the more manly description of *russet*. His face was broad and fleshy, with drooping jowls and a neatly trimmed moustache that hovered above his upper lip. Tufts of grey hair protruded from his ears. Disturbed by the increasing number of lines etched into the skin on the sides of his eyes, he leaned into the mirror more closely and pulled his temples back with his fingers. Hmm . . . not too bad. Still a handsome devil. He stepped back a few paces to get a better view of his nakedness. Turning to one side to see his profile, he grimaced when he saw the expanse of his paunch, hanging depressingly closer to his groin every week. He grabbed hold of both sides of his stomach and stretched his *love handles* to the sides of his body. He sucked in his gut, inflated his chest, and flexed his buttocks. Hmmm . . . you could do with losing a few pounds, Dickie old boy. He made a mental pledge to take the dogs out more often.

"Dickie, whatever *are* you doing in there? I'm pining for you," Celia called in a smoky tone from the bedroom. "We've got ages yet darling . . . "

* * *

Dickie didn't get back home until after one in the afternoon. He had to drive faster than he liked because he didn't dare be late for lunch. Olivia hated tardiness. She was waiting for him in the study of their seventeenth-century manor house, with a pinched expression on her face.

"Oh, there you are . . . at last," she said, emphasizing the last two words. Millie's been waiting on the arugula; it goes soggy if it's out too long." She got up from behind the desk where she had been looking through a mound of unpaid bills and walked past him. "We're eating in the conservatory, dear."

"Right-ho. I'll just clean up a little and be right there," said Dickie a little too brightly, so that she turned to look at him with more than a hint of suspicion.

"You have actually been to the bank, haven't you? You've surely not put it off again?" she asked in an accusatory tone. Her small, bright eyes narrowed with disapproval.

"Of course I have dear. I'll go through it all in a moment. I'll be right with you. Tell Millie to serve. Oh, and pour me a drink would you darling; just a little snifter to keep me going."

Olivia made her way to the sun-filled conservatory overlooking the splendid gardens at the rear of the house. It was crammed with expensive antique furniture and littered with valuable knickknacks. In the summer, it was her favorite room, with the sun blazing through the tall arched glass windows, and a view beyond of the lush green lawns bordered by pristine flowerbeds.

Lying almost comatose in a pool of sunshine were two aging golden Labradors. The elder of the two managed to open one eye as Olivia rattled around in the drinks cabinet. By the time she had settled into a deep armchair in front of the large cocktail table, the dog had already lost its battle with sleep. A loud chorus of heavy breathing filled the room. The distant ticking of a grandfather clock off in the foyer drifted in through the doorway, adding to the peaceful ambience of the balmy afternoon.

Olivia pulled deeply on her cigarette, narrowing her eyes as the smoke trickled from her lips. With her head laid back against the chintz-covered armchair, she pondered their dire financial situation. She stiffened as she thought about how wealthy the family had once been. It was hard to believe that the Cranshawe Booths, created Lords of the manor of Wickham in 1554, then Knights in 1610, and baronets in 1621 had once held around twenty-eight thousand acres of land in Yorkshire. And look at us now she thought with a great deal of bitterness, down to a paltry few hundred acres of parkland and the kind of house that eats money.

She again inhaled deeply, holding her breath for as long as she could before slowly exhaling two curling tendrils of smoke from her nostrils. Through half-closed eyes, she watched the smoke dissipate into the warm room, gently wafted by the breeze coming in from the open French doors.

The third daughter of Henry Fotheringham, Viscount of Pembroke, Olivia had known no other life than one of privilege and entitlement.

Although her forbears had been forced to sell off substantial portions of their estate rather than face financial ruin, the family had continued to live in relative luxury. But the creditors could only be put off for so long. Catastrophic loss of income from land coupled with burgeoning costs eventually resulted in bankruptcy. The greatest casualty of all was the destruction of Hesketh Hall, the primary residence of the Fotheringhams for centuries. Like so many other ruinously costly stately homes, it eventually succumbed to the ball and chain.

As a young girl, Olivia dreamed of marrying a Duke, or at the very least, an Earl. However, by the time she reached the age of thirty, having failed to meet her *prince charming*, she supposed that marriage to Baronet Richard Cranshawe Booth was not an unreasonable match for the mature third daughter of a bankrupt Viscount. Nonetheless, it was still hard not to feel thoroughly disappointed, since a baronet was the lowest rank of inherited titles.

Invented by James 1, baronetcies were created for the sole purpose of selling the titles to fund his Irish wars. Although the title could be handed down from generation to generation within a family like a peerage, a baronet enjoyed none of the privileges of peers, a fact never lost on Olivia. If the title of *Lady* were not before her name, she would never have persevered in her marriage with Dickie.

She realized early on in their marriage that he was unable to provide her with a sustainable bank account. He quickly proved himself to be just as bad as all the other Cranshawe Booths before him. Generation after generation of reckless spendthrift Cranshawe Booths, and their steadfast, complacent neglect, had resulted in mindboggling debt. And now, their own stately manor home, Booth Hall, was just about falling down on its last wood-wormed legs. Dickie, typical of his kind: prep-school, Eton, Oxford, and then the army, was ill prepared to survive the demise of his inheritance. While she reluctantly conceded that she couldn't apportion all the blame for the steady decline of the British aristocracy on his shoulders alone, she could not forgive his feckless mismanagement of the remaining estate and the ridiculous schemes he had tried in futile attempts to raise money. Tears began to prick the back of her eyes as she contemplated losing everything. She was simply not equipped to live the life of a commoner.

Olivia abruptly stood up and made her way back over to the drinks cabinet. It just won't do, she thought. It's too beastly to think about. She poured a large measure of Famous Grouse Whisky and downed it in one straight gulp just as Dickie entered the room.

"Hah! Started without me I see." He was about to give her a peck on the cheek, but thought better of it when he saw the look of disdain written across her face.

"Well? She asked in a clipped manner. "What did he say?" She was referring to Dickie's appointment with the bank manager.

"Ah. Well . . . yes . . . that," he began awkwardly, interrupted by the rattle of a serving trolley being pushed into the room by a woman of indeterminate old age. Crouched over the handle with her head at an odd angle, Millie, their kitchen help, shuffled to the ornate cocktail table with excruciating slowness. With trembling hands she transferred the contents of the serving trolley to the table and announced, "luncheon is served ma'am."

Jolted back to consciousness by the sound of the serving trolley, the two dogs raised themselves to a sitting position with surprising speed. Fully alert, and drooling long strings of elastic saliva onto the marble floor, they sat with their eyes trained on the neatly cut cucumber and salmon sandwiches, arranged in the manner insisted upon by Olivia, on the exquisite Wedgewood china. A small salad dish containing shredded lettuce and thinly -sliced tomatoes was set to one side of the tray.

Dickie eyed the sandwiches with despair before turning to grab his drink from the cabinet behind him. He swallowed the Scotch with relish and promptly refilled his glass tumbler, fully aware that it was going to be his only real sustenance before dinner at seven. He craved a large pork pie and chips with lashings of gravy, the type of food that Olivia thoroughly disapproved.

"You're not exactly starving are you Dickie? You could stop eating for two months and you'd still be no slimmer than a walrus," was her withering response when he had once touched on the subject of their luncheon menu.

Olivia was a tall, long-limbed woman of astonishing thinness. Her hair was immaculately coiled into a tight chignon protected by a Hermes scarf whenever she ventured outdoors. Tight-lipped and *correct* at all times, she was nothing if not conservative. She had never ridden on a public bus or used a public lavatory. She had never eaten a take-out and had only ever had sex on a bed with the lights off. Her fashion aspirations strayed no further than a knitted twin-set, a practical, below the knee tweed skirt, regardless of the summer temperatures, and a green quilted hunting jacket. A string of pearls, supposedly once worn by Queen Anne, lent her a certain refinement and also disguised her aging neck. In Olivia's eyes, impeccable grooming was a sign of good breeding. Sloppiness was something she could not tolerate. She liked everything to be neat, in order, and in its place.

"That's all. Thank you Millie," she said shrilly, with a touch of haughtiness. Can't even get decent servants these days, she thought miserably. She waited until the old woman left the room before turning on Dickie.

"Well?" she demanded impatiently.

"No luck, I'm afraid." He took another liberal drink from his tumbler before continuing. "The house is so costly, I told him. Bills so high, taxes hitting the roof, capital almost gone. Can't get over how young the fellow was; thought he was a trainee at first," shaking his head, "quite extraordinary."

"So is the bank going to extend the loan or not?" She asked in an exasperated tone.

"Ah, well, yes, for a short time, a few months or so, but he did suggest, no, I shall rephrase that: he demanded we do some, ah, cost-cutting. Trim the expenditure, that sort of thing."

"What do you mean?" she asked wide- eyed, blinking rapidly.

"He said we need to do away with some of our major expenses." The words tumbled from his mouth as if he couldn't wait to get the subject over fast enough. He continued before he lost his nerve.

"He was very brusque; one of those social agitators. I don't care for him at all," said Dickie indignantly. "He suggested firing Millie; getting rid of Wilfred, and cook . . . and . . . and, well, damned near all the staff! I'm so sorry dear. I know its frightfully bad form," he said, hanging his head, "not the sort of thing one likes to hear."

Olivia sank back into her chair, clearly aghast. She could not have looked more shocked had she just been informed that she was pregnant with triplets.

"Get rid of them?" she muttered blankly. "But how could I possibly cope? Wilfred's already doing two jobs—butler and gardener! And he only has casual help for the gardens in the summer. He knows we've already opened the west wing to visitors doesn't he? And you must have told him how we've had to accommodate guests? You did tell him all this, didn't you, Dickie? You surely told him that I can't possibly survive without help," she asked beseechingly. An expression of pure misery was written across her face. Her lips quivered in an effort to keep from bursting into tears.

"Yes, yes, of course, dear. He's well aware of all that, but the fellow is insisting that we economize even further."

"But I've already got rid of the horses, and, and . . . we're down to two cars . . . And no chauffeur! Oh . . . this is all so embarrassing."

"There's no arguing with the man. In fact, I'd say he got quite snippy with me. Accused me of having an astonishing ability to bury my head in the sand when it comes to finances. Made me out to be a bloody ostrich!"

He sighed ponderously before continuing. "I told him it was imperative that one maintains the hierarchies of wealth and rank, to set an example to those beneath us . . . that it is ones duty to preserve ones inheritance."

He took another long draught from his drink, emptying the glass. "And do you know what he said to that? He had the nerve to say: 'Sir Richard, there are those who might describe the aristocracy of today as being somewhat redundant and a drain on the country's resources. I don't think that you quite appreciate how appalling your situation has become. You need to come to terms with the fact that you are broke, quite penniless in fact.'"

The spider veins on Dickie's cheeks were pulsing with indignation. "Next thing we know, he'll be inciting the masses to riot and revolution, that sort of thing."

"Oh, I am quite sure he harbors a great deal of social envy," Olivia agreed. "He sounds absolutely beastly. He has no idea how utterly repellant it is to have strangers invade your home. I can't quite believe that we've had to resort to a B and B in the West wing. Mummy would have had a fit had she still been alive!" She cast Dickie an agonizing glance.

"Look, not to worry, my precious. Dickie will think of something, he always does," he said soothingly. Thankfully, the Scotch had started to take affect. The sharp edges of the morning's distasteful business seemed a little fuzzy, not nearly so bad as they were a few hours ago in the bank.

"Time to sell off the Wedgewood, I think," he muttered, studying the bottom of his empty glass.

At this, Olivia let out a sob that she hastily stifled with a silk, monogrammed handkerchief. It would not do to let the servants hear.

TEN

While the ladies assailed Jeremy inside the post office, Conrad went back to his car with the painting Jeremy recovered from the bed of nettles on the far side of the road. He took off his jacket, sat in the driver's seat, and placed the artwork on his lap. There was no obvious signature, but he thought it was ably executed, dramatic, yet detailed. He liked it. He gently rubbed his fingers along its edges, feeling the weight and age of the paper. He sensed that it was old. He closed his eyes and lifted it towards his face. He inhaled deeply, breathing in the paper's aged aroma. The smell reminded him that old paintings needed to be protected from the sun, disturbing his reverie. He looked quickly about him before walking to the back of the car. He opened his trunk and placed the artwork in the middle of some paperwork on the top of his clothes inside a small traveling case. His eyes lingered on the case as a sickening thought came into his head. "Oh shit," he whispered. He had put his fingerprints all over the watercolor.

He debated going into the post office, but decided against it. Instead, he examined the bumper on the front of his car. It was scraped at the bottom, but did not appear to be damaged. He looked at the large puddle at the entrance to the car park and wondered how it could be left like that. It was ridiculous. A glance around the rest of the pot-holed parking area confirmed that the place was not in the best state of repair.

Conrad turned to look at the façade of the building in front of him. Even before he noticed the date of 1872 chiseled into the stone pediment across the top of the entrance, he could sense that the place was old. His eyes drifted to the stone mullioned windows on the upper story and the grey slate roof tiles. The walls were freighted with a wild profusion of scented wisteria and ivy, lending an air of general charm to the place. A peeling sign hung a little askew across the top of one large window on the ground floor that read: "Tipping Post Office and General Store." Underneath, off to one side, in much smaller script was: "Proprietors: Arthur and Pearl Wiggins."

Drawn by the sound of running water, he strolled to the side of the old building. He turned onto a quiet, narrow path, flanked to one side by a low stone wall, beyond which, a coursing brook flowed, winding its way around the perimeter of the village. He picked his way along the path, side-stepping the muddier sections until he reached a narrow footbridge that spanned the stream. Conrad stopped and leaned against the wall to look down at the torrent of water underneath. A group of Mallard ducks was floating serenely on the far side of the stream, but as soon as they saw him, they turned against the current and began to paddle furiously, quacking loudly, in his direction.

Amused, he watched them for a while before glancing upstream, where he could just see one corner of the cropped village green in the distance. Freshly mown that morning, the earthy scent of cut grass hung heavy in the warm air. He closed his eyes for a moment and inhaled the sweetness around him. The faint drone of bees carried on a calm breeze made him feel relaxed and sleepy. He stood very still with his hands placed on top of the wall, and listened to the ever-changing cadences of the water as it rushed by.

A gentle rustle came from the post office wall when an occasional puff of warm wind stirred the magnificent wisteria blooms. The stress of the last few days seemed to fall away from Conrad's shoulders. The place had a tangible sense of peace, something he had not felt for a long time. Slowly, after several minutes, he opened his eyes and thought about walking back to his car. He wished he had time to linger by the stream. It was such an idyllic little spot. But he was conscious of the need to see if Jeremy had any luck in the post office.

As he pushed himself away from the wall, he felt a loose slab of stone beneath one hand. Curious, he looked down and pressed on one edge of the slab, making it tilt at an angle that revealed a small hollow underneath. At one time it was probably filled with smaller stones. Harsh winters and the resultant freeze-thaw had probably weakened the wall in places and worn away small sections. He lifted his hand from the stone and let it fall back in place. A nice little hidey-hole, he thought idly. He mulled over his situation as he walked back to the post office.

He smiled when he thought about the confession Jeremy had blurted out in the field. The kid was a nervous wreck, caught up in a mesh of preposterous lies. Once he convinced the kid that he was not a conniving, petty thief out to line his own pockets; that he was a man of considerable means, more than able to survive without resorting to crime, Jeremy's whole sad, sorry tale came pouring out, as if the floodgates holding back the truth had finally burst under the weight of carrying the burden of guilt for so long. Conrad had listened patiently, patting Jeremy's shoulder in a display of concern, fighting the urge to laugh out loud when Jeremy revealed how he had thought Conrad was a gun-wielding, violent member of some dark, criminal outfit sent to get the Turners back.

On the surface, the two of them had nothing in common. Their appearance, background, and present circumstances could not be further apart. But there was something about Jeremy's obvious loneliness and isolation, and the fractured relationship he had with his parents that evoked some sympathy from Conrad. He shook his head as he walked, well aware of how ridiculous the scenario must seem to an outsider. What a bizarre twist of fate it was to cross paths with the likes of a frightened, hapless young student, here of all places, in the middle of nowhere.

Conrad knew he should walk away and be done with the whole affair. The situation was fraught with peril, and it would be stupid and reckless to get involved, but he felt a growing compulsion to find out more. He could not ignore the unmistakable buzz of excitement he always felt when he was this close to any object that other collectors might covet.

Six original Turners—How could he turn his back on them now, when they were here, so tantalizingly close, almost at his fingertips? For all he knew, they could be rightfully his. What if his mother had acquired them legally? It was probably going to be damned hard to prove now that Julian Parks was dead. Shit. And there was the possibility that the Turners were stolen. What then? They would have to be returned to the rightful owners and Conrad would likely never see them again, a scenario that made his stomach sink. And if he did find them first, could he really give them up? He was not sure. He would think about that later.

As Conrad approached the front of the building, a group of elderly ladies dressed in hiking apparel filed out of the post office grumbling loudly.

"She's a secretive one, that Pearl Wiggins."

"Hmmph! Well, she's always been one to keep everything tight to her chest. Anyone would think we don't know how to mind our own business!"

"Oh, Uh-ahem. Good morning!" shrilled the tallest of the three women when she saw Conrad.

Conrad stepped back to allow the ladies to pass, trying not to stare at the woman's glasses. They had to be the biggest spectacles he had ever seen a person wearing. Her eyes looked enormous behind the thick magnifying lenses. They gave her a giant insect-like appearance.

"Good morning ladies," he answered, smiling down at them.

"Ooh," the three ladies made a collective gasp.

"Now I'd recognize an American accent anywhere," beamed the bespectacled lady. "I have a nephew who's married to a girl from Lake Winnipesaukee. That's in New Hampshire, you know. They have a lovely house, well, I say house; it's really a cabin . . . not a small one mind, quite spacious really; very rustic, right on the lake. I've never been you know, but the photographs he sends me are just . . . "

"Yes, I know it," Conrad interjected. "It is a beautiful place. I'm from Boston, in Massachusetts, not too far away from the lake. Well, if you'll excuse me Ladies," he said in an apologetic, but firm tone as he turned toward the door. "Have a good day."

"Oh, but . . . " The Rambler's' disappointment in the brevity of the conversation was palpable. Their eyes were trained on Conrad's back as he reached for the door handle.

"Huh!" The ladies inhaled simultaneously when Conrad hesitated for a moment, as if something had just occurred to him. He turned away from the door and strode purposely back towards them.

"Actually, perhaps you ladies could help me. I need a place to stay; somewhere close by . . . a few nights . . . can you recommend anywhere?"

They were thrilled beyond measure to be of assistance. The three of them shuffled around him in tight formation.

"You could try the pub in the village: The Three Bees!" Irma Hepplethwaite burst out.

"No, no, Irma. This gentleman wants something better than that," said Audrey, taking command. She had noticed his expensive clothes and car.

A small voice came from a short lady buried beneath a large hat with earflaps. "Rose-Hill cottage by the church is very homely."

"That won't do at all!" said Audrey in a bossy manner. She thought for a moment and then exclaimed, "I know! I know the very place! Booth Hall! That's the ticket!"

"Oh, yes!" they all agreed heartily.

"Sir Richard Cranshawe Booth and Lady Cranshawe Booth you know," said Audrey with an air of authority.

"Ah, right," replied Conrad hesitantly. He wasn't quite sure how to respond. "Sir who?"

* * *

Jeremy was angry when he left the post office. Cursing under his breath, he strode over to the Audi where he could see one of Conrad's legs sticking out from the driver's door. As Jeremy approached, Conrad lifted an index finger to indicate he would be one minute. He was talking on his cell phone.

"Well?" asked Conrad when he had finished the call he had put through to his personal assistant, asking her to check on the merits of Booth Hall. "What did she say?"

"Mrs. Wiggins picked up a load of stuff from the road, but she won't give it to me—not yet anyway."

"What do you mean, she won't give it back?" Conrad's voice betrayed a hint of irritation when he spoke. "What about the Turners? Did she mention anything?"

Jeremy shook his head. "No, she wouldn't tell me what she picked up. She didn't mention any paintings. She started on at me about how I shouldn't have been driving so fast through the village, that I could have killed someone . . . you have no idea what she's like. She went on and on . . . and then she asked who you were . . . I didn't tell her, of course . . . I just said you were a . . . well, an acquaintance." He kicked at a small stone in frustration. "She said she's thrown it all into her dustbin and she'll have a look through it when she's good and ready and not a minute before. She said the wait will do me good—teach me a lesson for driving like a maniac.

"So we don't know whether she's got them or not then, do we?" said Conrad with growing impatience. He got out of the car and turned to look at the front of the post office.

"It's no use you asking her," said Jeremy, reading Conrad's mind. "She won't budge, and if you mention anything about the artwork, you'll just make her suspicious. She'll go running straight to the police."

Conrad shook his head. "I can't believe this! How long is she going to keep you waiting?"

"I have no idea. Knowing her it could be days, weeks—who knows?"

"You've got to be kidding me," Conrad replied. He was barely able to contain his frustration. "Did you ask her if she saw anyone else around when your stuff fell out of the car?"

"Uh, well, that's the other problem," said Jeremy meekly.

"Oh, jeez, what else can go wrong?"

"Well, she mentioned that old Barrington Smith had been in, but I'm not worried about him. I know him pretty well; he does some work at my parents' house. He'll be in the pub tonight," he said, nodding in the direction of the Three Bees. "I can talk to him later."

"So what's the problem then?"

"Right, well." Jeremy looked across at the field and then back to Conrad before continuing. "She saw two other people. One was Brigadier Dickie Cranshawe Booth. He stopped by the wall for something. She's not sure what he was up to, but she definitely saw him driving off."

"Wait a minute. Is this, er, Lord Cranshawe Booth of Booth Hall?"

"Right," said Jeremy. "How do you know that?" he asked with a puzzled look on his face.

"It seems I'm staying there tonight. A few of the local ladies recommended the place. Did she see him pick anything up?"

"No. But I didn't want to ask her too much. It's not a good idea to make the likes of Pearl Wiggins too suspicious, and you need to watch every word you say to the ladies you talked to. They're the worst gossips you're ever likely to meet. Once they get wind of anything, the whole village will know about it . . . Actually, make that the whole of Yorkshire," he added glumly.

"Yes, well, I kinda guessed that. You know if I'm staying at Booth Hall for the next few nights, I'll be able to ask this Cranshawe guy a few questions . . . discreetly, I mean. You'll have to fill me in on what you know about him. Do you think he could be a problem?"

Jeremy laughed aloud, and rolled his eyes heavenward in response. "You have no idea what you're in for!"

"Oh, great," Conrad said despondently. "So—who was the other person she saw?"

"Well, this isn't good. It was one of the local teenagers, playing hooky from school. She thinks she saw him grab something off the road. When she yelled at him, he ran off."

"Oh, shit. Do you know him?"

"No, but I'd recognize him if I saw him. She thinks it was a kid called Kevin Ogden. I've never spoken to him, but I know his family. Put it this way, they're not the type you'd want for your in-laws." Jeremy laughed nervously and attempted to flatten his hair with both hands. "It's a Friday, so he'll probably be at the village disco tonight, so we . . . "

With mounting impatience, Conrad interrupted and said, "Look, we can't afford to wait around. The longer we leave it, the less chance we have of finding the paintings. We've got to move quickly before they disappear." He dipped his head in thought for a moment and then abruptly looked up.

"Where does she keep her trash? You'll have to look through it right now."

"What!" exclaimed Jeremy, "You must be joking? Not in broad daylight. She's bound to see me from any room in this place," he said indicating the post office with a flick of his head. She'll have the police straight over and then we're really done for."

Conrad looked Jeremy squarely in the face and said with a hint of amusement, "Then you'll have to come back tonight when it's dark, won't you? And," he continued, leaning close to Jeremy's ear, "You'll have to go to the disco as well, and talk to the kid."

"Oh God—I don't know if I can do this," Jeremy added.

"Yes you can. You'll be okay if you do everything I tell you. Calm down and pull yourself together. This is going to work. Believe me. Now—what time is the disco?"

"I'm not sure, probably around 7:30 or 8:00. It's just for the local kids so it won't be on too late."

"And what time does it get dark?"

"Uh, about 9:00, 9:30."

"Right. So here's the plan," said Conrad. "You're going to go home now, to your parent's house, and act as if everything is normal. You're just home for a visit, right? If the police find you, and they probably will . . . " He cast a furtive glance over his shoulder. "Stick to what you have already told them. As far you are concerned, Julian Parks left nothing at the gallery. And if the police ask about me, you tell them I wanted to talk to you because you were one of the last people to see my mother and I wanted some kind of closure."

"Right."

"And if the police stop me, then I'm going to say the same thing: I wanted to find out if you had seen my mother. I'm going to deny having anything to do with the artwork, which is the truth. I won't tell them anything about what you've told me. I don't want to be implicated in anyway. Is that understood?" Jeremy nodded meekly.

"Right. So I'm going to talk to Cranshawe Booth at Booth Hall, and you're going to go to the disco and question the kid. Then we'll meet somewhere. Let me think where . . . "

"We could meet at my house; my parents are away, so we won't be disturbed."

"God, no," said Conrad. "I can't possibly be seen going into your house. The police will jump to all sorts of conclusions. No. It's far better to meet on neutral ground. Is there a bar in the village?"

"You mean a pub? There are two," said Jeremy.

"Right. So which one?"

"The Three Bees. It's on the Green at the bottom of the hill that leads to the church. You can't miss it."

"Okay," said Conrad. "We'll meet there – 9 o'clock. I'll make sure I'm there a little earlier so we don't walk in together. You get there on the dot. Just stroll in, exchange a few words – it will look odd if we ignore each other. Have a quick chat, tell me what you managed to find out, all very casual, and then we split up, leave separately and meet again an hour later, at 10 o clock behind the post office. I'll keep a lookout for you as you search through Mrs. Wiggins's bins. Oh—and bring a flashlight."

"But what if someone is watching us? What if the police are here?"

"Good point. We'll need a signal," said Conrad. "Some sort of sign that we're okay to talk." His forehead creased in concentration. "You've got a wrist watch, right?"

"Uh, yeah."

"Well, if you think everything is good and it's safe to meet, then wear one. But if at any time you feel something's going wrong, then you take it off, right? And the same goes for me. If you see me wearing a watch, then I'm confident we'll be okay, but keep your eye on it, because if something happens inside that pub that makes me feel nervous, the meeting is off."

"But how will I get in touch with you if I can't speak to you in the pub and we can't meet behind the post office?"

"I'll have to leave a message for you. "His eye flickered to the side of the post office. "When you were inside the building, I wandered up the path over there, the one next to the stream. There's a loose stone right on the top of the footbridge, in the middle, almost dead center, and there's a hollow underneath. If anything goes wrong tonight, I'll leave a message for you under that stone, but if I'm being followed or I can't get there, check again tomorrow or the next day. Keep looking, because it'll be the only way I can make contact with you. But for Christ's sake, be absolutely sure no one sees you. If these paintings are so important, and if the police have any suspicions about you, they're going to be all over this place, if they aren't already."

Jeremy's eyes grew wide with fear. "What?" His head swiveled in all directions. "Where? Do you see anyone?"

"Don't look around," Conrad hissed. "Act normal. You haven't done anything wrong – remember. Stay calm. Don't draw attention to yourself."

"Yes. You're right . . . you're right. I'm sorry." Jeremy's chin dropped to his chest. "So what do you get out of all this? You're taking a big risk trying to help me," he said without looking up.

"We're going to find the paintings and I'm going to keep them until I can prove my mother didn't steal them. It might not be that easy though, and it will take time. You won't be able to say anything. I've given this some thought and I'm prepared to offer you an incentive . . . "

"What?" Jeremy's jaw dropped open. "What do you mean?"

"$200,000 if we find the art and another $300,000 in two years time when you have proved you can keep your mouth shut."

Jeremy's mouth opened and shut, but no words came out.

"If we can find them before the police do, then you need never be implicated in any of this. The police will never see your fingerprints. They will have no proof that you ever laid eyes on them. But you have to keep your mouth shut forever, and I mean forever. The police are going to do their best to make you believe that I'm an untrustworthy, unscrupulous, collector driven by obsession and greed, and that my mother was just the same, and I admit there is an element of truth in that. I am obsessive, and I will spend a great deal of money and go to great lengths to acquire a particular piece, but I have never crossed the line between right and wrong Jeremy, not once. I swear to you that it has never crossed my mind, not even for an instant, to gain something by illegal means. Collecting is a game, an exciting, irresistible game to me. But it wouldn't be the same if I cheated. I'd get no satisfaction from that. I'm offering you a way out of this mess."

"But what if they really are stolen?" the words crept out of Jeremy's mouth.

"Then I will have to think of a way to give them back." The words came out with little conviction.

ELEVEN

Pearl ducked behind the deli counter when the tall blond man looked toward the store. It would not do to be caught watching. She did not want him to think she was the nosey sort. However, unable to contain her curiosity, Pearl crept behind the shelves of canned goods until she reached the edge of the large window at the front of the store. With her back flattened against the wall, she slowly craned her neck to peek at the two men talking outside.

Something very odd was going on; she could feel it in her bones. She was dying to know more about the tall stranger and what he was doing in these remote parts with the likes of Jeremy Danvers. Thank goodness, she had shooed Audrey and the ramblers out of the post office when Jeremy had come in asking about his belongings.

"The less Audrey Ormerod knows the better," Pearl muttered sourly. "Always has to know everybody's business, that one."

She watched a while longer until the stranger drove off alone in his car. She had a moment of panic when it looked as if Jeremy was about to come into the post office again, but he seemed to change his mind and set off down the road and eventually disappeared from view.

Without wasting a second, Pearl flew across the store to the door at the back. Breathing heavily, she scurried down the dark hallway and into the tiny kitchen in the rear. She quickly unlocked the back door that led to a small walled garden and hurried to the large dustbin that stood against a rickety tool shed in one corner.

After rooting through the contents of the bin, Pearl collapsed into her old wing-backed chair by the fireplace in the parlor. Exhausted from a morning of unaccustomed activity, she lifted her legs onto the poof and sat back to revive herself with a strong cup of Yorkshire tea.

"Lord, what a morning!" she exclaimed, wiping a crumb of a Mr. Kipling's Almond Slice off her chin. What with Barrington's attentions and all that sweeping up outside and then rummaging through the garbage . . . I can't lift another finger, she thought. No energy these days. I just need a little rest. She laid her head back against the chair and closed her eyes. "Just forty winks old girl," she said aloud. With her arms folded across her ample bosom, she tried to empty her mind, but she was far too agitated to relax. Her thoughts kept creeping back to the morning's strange turn of events. She really wanted to daydream about Barrington and romantic possibilities, but other prickly, worrisome thoughts kept popping, un-invited, into her head. She shuffled about in her chair and tried to shake off the unwelcome intrusions, but it was no good. Unable to settle, she opened her eyes and grumbled into the empty room.

"Well how was I to know it was all Jeremy's stuff? I'd have kept it all for him, if I had known."

With a pang of guilt, she glanced at the watercolor she had picked up from the road and hung on the wall opposite the fireplace. It was a lovely little scene, a local beauty spot where she and Arthur occasionally picnicked in their younger days. Admittedly, the style of the painting was a touch dramatic for her taste, but she recognized the location immediately and thought Arthur might have liked it. He always favored a nice landscape, she thought fondly. Mind you though, it wasn't easy trying to get it to fit into one of those old frames. She had to do some trimming and snipping with the kitchen scissors. Well, it's too late now . . . how was I to know it was Jeremy's? I can't very well give it back to him in this state now can I? Anyway, he shouldn't have been driving through the village like that, she thought, trying to console herself . . . and he should have shut the car doors properly. None of this is my fault. It's all his own doing. She shrugged and took another bite of cake, followed by a long sip of tea. Her eyes wandered over to the watercolor again. Hmmm . . . I'd best not mention it to him . . . he probably won't even miss it.

Pearl did not know what she expected to find amongst the things she had thrown into the dustbin, but she was disappointed that she had not found one thing, apart from the watercolor, that was remotely interesting. There were a few books about art and history as well as some clothes and toiletries. She had put the lot into carrier bags and then bundled them away in the cupboard under the stairs. Hmm . . . odd about all those art books though . . . I thought everyone in the family were scientists. Oh well . . .

She finished her tea and placed her cup and saucer onto the small table next to her chair. Reaching down with one hand into the backpack on the floor at her side, she lifted out a large notebook and dropped it on her lap. She flipped through the pages of hand-written script, but saw nothing that caught her eye. It was all stuff about art and history.

Deflated, she put the notebook down and reached back inside the bag. This time she retrieved a wad of papers. Most of them appeared to be printed text about art history, nothing of interest. She rummaged in the bottom of the bag and pulled out a roll of papers tied loosely with string. With renewed interest, she unfurled two little watercolors, one of which was instantly recognizable as *Cowsgill Craggs*, a local outcrop of rocks not too far away from Tipping. The other painting was a vista across a lake with some hills in the background. It too seemed familiar, but she could not quite place the location.

Pearl closed her eyes and tried to conjure up an image of where she had seen the view before, but gave up when nothing sprang to mind. She ran her fingers across the outline of the lake, and tried to make out the figures in the foreground. Not a bad painting, she conceded, although she did not care much for the style. It was all too hazy and indistinct for her liking, but at least he had made an attempt. She thought it odd that she had no idea the lad had an interest in art. He had never mentioned it before. Ah well, it just goes to show, you can never judge a book by its cover, she mused.

With a loud sigh, Pearl lowered the papers onto her lap and let her head fall back against the chair. She looked up at the incongruous cheap print of Penzance in Cornwall above the mantelpiece. Dull and faded with age, hung slightly askew, the washed out picture stared forlornly from its chipped frame. Now there's a right lovely painting she thought, recalling the occasion when she and Arthur had bought it on their honeymoon. The picture was a masterpiece in Pearl's eyes. She looked from her picture of Penzance to Jeremy's watercolor hung on the opposite wall, comparing the two. She let her gaze settle on Jeremy's painting and decided that it really wasn't up to much. Oh, he'll never miss it. He won't even know it's gone. He'll most likely pop back in tomorrow, she reasoned, feeling much better about everything. I'll give him the rest of his things then.

She settled back in her chair and closed her eyes again. She dozed for a few minutes, but the weight of memories in that little room were at times too heavy to bear. Her eyes strayed to a framed photograph on top of the dresser across the room. It was a picture of Arthur taken shortly before he died. Tears pricked the back of Pearl's eyes, as they always did, when she thought of him. She could not help it. She had loved him despite everything that had happened.

He died of a heart attack, alone in the back parlor—the very one where Pearl was sitting, while he was watching television. Pearl could never forget that night; it was so clearly imprinted in her mind.

"Why did you leave me Arthur?" she whispered into the empty room.

She had gone to bed first as usual. She liked to have a bit of peace to read a nice, romantic novel. "Mills and Boons" were her favorites. Arthur was more than happy with this arrangement. She knew that the moment he heard the creak of the top stair, he would whip out his paper, check on the horses and then he would watch "Match of the Day" with a few Newcastle Browns for company.

"Night luv," she had called from the top of the stairs.

"Night Pearl," he had answered. Those were the last words they had spoken to each other. She recalled waking up with a start, groping instinctively for the small clock on her bedside cabinet. It was after two in the morning.

"Arthur?" she whispered, reaching across to his side of the bed. She patted her hand on the cold, empty space, wondering where he was. Not unduly alarmed, she pulled herself upright against the headboard and strained to listen for sounds coming from the bathroom across the landing. Hearing nothing, she reluctantly heaved herself out of bed, pulled on her dressing gown and made her way across the landing to the top of the stairs. "He's likely fallen asleep in front of the television," she muttered.

Pearl cautiously made her way down the stairs, tut-tut ting as she went. Close to the bottom, she could hear the high-pitched noise of the television signaling the end of the day's broadcasting. The lights were still on, and as she entered the cozy little living room at the rear of the store, she could see Arthur's legs stretched out in front of him, the newspaper open across his chest.

She felt a mild flutter of fear. He wasn't snoring like he usually did. He was so quiet. She walked over to his chair and gently shook his leg.

"Arthur. Wake up luv. It's gone two in the morning. Come up to bed." She leaned closer. "Arthur," she said, close to his face. "Arthur! ARTHUR!" She shook him hard by the shoulders, cold fear closing like a vice around her heart.

"ARTHUR!" she screamed.

Fumbling at his neck and then his wrist, she felt hopelessly for a pulse. She shouted and cried at the same time as she shook him. "Arthur, wake up. Arthur, wake up! It's me, Pearl! WAKE UP!"

She grew angry then, despair flooding over her. She beat on his chest, fists flailing as she tried to pound life back into him, but she knew he was gone. She knew her Arthur was dead.

It took her such a long time to get over his death. They had never had children, much to their regret. Pearl knew she would have made a fine mother, none better, but it just never happened for them. So, it had been just the two of them for all that time. Forty-one years they were married. After he was gone, she noticed a particular silence that filled the house. It reminded her of a shade of grey—a really dark grey.

After closing the store at 5:00 p.m. each afternoon, she wandered around the house, pausing here and there, touching things gently and re-arranging one or two objects. She hovered in each doorway, watching the light enter the windows and stretch over the furniture and floors, lying down over the empty chairs, cold and silent as a held breath. As daylight took its leave, she settled in her high-winged chair by the fireplace in the tiny parlor with its worn carpet and tired drapes. Here, alone, sitting in the glow of the fire and the warm shaded lamps, with her milky tea and digestive biscuit, she sat and stared at Arthur's empty chair.

When it was quite dark, Pearl walked again from room to room, lingering occasionally, looking around and drawing curtains. When at last, the day slipped away and the peace of the house was at its deepest, she slowly climbed the stairs to her bedroom, pausing for a moment at the top to catch her breath. Through her bedroom window she could see how the wind moved the branches of the trees outside; beyond them she could see the lights of the village twinkling in the darkness. If she pressed her head close to the pane, she could sometimes feel the wind pushing against it. Each night before she got into bed, she opened the wardrobe and ran her fingers slowly along Arthur's jackets. She stood silent, hardly daring to breathe, as she fingered one sleeve after another. Then she reached up and gently, very gently lifted a lapel to her cheek and whispered, "Oh, Arthur."

His gambling habit swallowed up the little they had saved, and they were forced to mortgage the store to pay off the ensuing debts. Apart from the bit of money she had after cashing in her Premium Bonds, she was left with almost nothing, except perhaps her dignity.

Pearl struggled on in the post office, well beyond the time she hoped to retire. She pretended to everyone that she carried on through choice; that she really did not want to give up something that had shaped her life for forty-one years.

"It's what Arthur would have wanted. He'd hate for me to leave just yet." It was just a little harmless, face-saving white lie.

"You should get out a bit more Pearl. You and Arthur have worked all your lives here. You'll have a fair bit of cash saved up won't you? It's time to see the world. What are you waiting for? If you don't spend a bit now, who are going to leave it all to—the Dog's Home?" That's what they all said to her. If only they knew.

Over the years, her little post office and store made less and less money. She could not hope to compete with the big supermarket in Wickham. She still had her regulars, and passing tourist trade during the summers was always handy. But it was only a matter of time before she could no longer make ends meet, especially with all the new government changes to the Royal Mail. Pearl knew that the old system was finished and the closure of the smaller, less profitable, rural post offices was imminent. She would hang on as long as she could, but as far as she was concerned, the writing was on the wall. Her only hope was to remarry.

Her eyes popped open with that last thought. The corners of her mouth lifted into a smile as she ran an idea through her head. *I could take Jeremy's things to Barrington's house and then Barrington can give it back to Jeremy when he goes to do his odd jobs at the Danvers' place. Hmm, yes, that should work nicely, very nicely indeed.* Pearl rubbed her hands together and chuckled. The prospect of seeing Barrington again made her feel a lot better. She put her head back, closed her eyes and played the scenario over in her mind. *I'll go later on . . . after closing.* Seconds later, the bell above the door to the post office rang.

"Oh, bother!" She heaved herself forward. "Never a minute to miself," she grumbled. *Well, up you get Pearl old girl; time to get back to work.*

She took the two watercolors and inserted them between the pages of the book. The rest of the papers she stuffed inside the backpack on the chair. After a few quick adjustments to her corset and a liberal coating of fresh lipstick, she made her way slowly into the store.

* * *

"Oh, mornin' George," said Pearl with a hint of surprise. She eyed the tall stranger standing beside the constable and patted her curls before continuing. "What brings you in here? Is it a nice bit of ham you're after?"

After a moment's hesitation, George Barlow, Tipping's local police Constable, cleared his throat and said, "No, not this morning Pearl. We're here on official business."

"Oh," she replied, a million thoughts racing through her brain. A sinking feeling that their visit might in some way be connected to Jeremy was forming in her mind. With a great deal of effort, she forced her luminous lips into a rigid smile and asked, "How can I help you then?"

Normally she would have moved closer to the counter when a customer made an enquiry. This time she remained rooted to the spot. She eyed the tall stranger nervously, wondering what their "official business" might be. A little knot of fear tightened in her stomach. She thought about the watercolor hanging on the wall in her parlor and prayed that they were here for something else entirely. She wasn't used to hearing George speak with such an authoritative tone.

"This is Detective Collins from Scotland Yard. He'd like to ask you a few questions, Pearl."

* * *

The ramblers were still grumbling about Pearl when they turned into the lane bordering the field opposite the post office. They were too busy talking, and were headed the wrong way to see the village constable and plain-clothes detective enter the post office from the other direction. Their chatter continued until the lane wound its way around the top end of the field where the gradient increased sufficiently to make Audrey shout a command to the others. "Time for a breather! We'll have ten minutes for refreshments." Grateful for the chance to take off their rucksacks, the ladies sank onto the grass verge for a rest.

"Phew, it's quite warm out, isn't it?" said Irma. She took off her jacket and used it to sit on. She shuffled back so that she could lean against the wall. The other two flopped down next to her.

"Yes, it's a lovely day alright," said Audrey in response. "It's a pity Jean couldn't join us, but her bunions are playing up."

"Hmmm," chorused the others.

They each took a sip from their water bottles and leaned back against the wall with their eyes closed, sunning their faces.

"Hmm. This is lovely," said the voice beneath the earflaps. "My mother always swore by chamomile mixed with burdock leaves for bunions . . . OH!" She shrieked as a pair of hooves clattered on the top of the wall behind her.

Mildly alarmed and curious at the same time, the ladies roused themselves from their resting spot and turned to peep over the wall. A scruffy white goat stood on the opposite side of the stone wall. As soon as it saw the ladies, the goat bleated loudly as it tried to scale the wall again. Another goat stood to one side, about ten feet away from the wall, munching contentedly on what looked like a large piece of paper.

"What on earth is that creature eating?" asked Audrey.

As the ladies turned to look at the goat, their attention was diverted by the activity outside the post office. Irma Hepplethwaite was the first to notice.

"Ooooh, look!" she shouted, pointing towards the post office in the distance. Isn't that George's patrol car outside Pearls?"

"Oh, yes . . . So it is," replied Audrey. "Quickly, hand me the binoculars. Hurry!"

"What's going on? Can you see anything? What's happening?"

"Wait a minute . . . I can't see anything . . . Oh! . . . He's coming out . . . No, wait!'

"What? Let me see Audrey," demanded Irma, making a grab for the binoculars. "You'll not be able to see properly because of your glasses."

"Get off Irma," said Audrey sternly. She propped her elbows up on the wall and pressed the lenses of the binoculars to her glasses. "There, you see. I've got the hang of it now. Oh! There's someone else with him! I've never seen him before . . . Huh! They're walking across the road . . . get down! They're climbing over the wall into the field!"

At Audrey's command, the ladies ducked back down out of view. They huddled together, shoulders touching, with their backs against the wall.

"That does it," whispered Audrey. "There's definitely something going on. It must be something to do with the Danvers boy and that American. I'll bet Pearl Wiggins knows something about this. I just know it!"

"I think you're right Audrey," said Irma in agreement. "Didn't the Danvers boy ask Pearl whether she'd found something of his in the road? Maybe he's lost something valuable. What do you think, Audrey?"

Audrey's eyes narrowed in concentration as she replayed their visit to the post office through her mind.

"What I'd like to know is why the police are involved?" she spoke aloud. The others leaned in close waiting for her opinion. After a few moments, she announced in an authoritative tone, "Well, whatever's going on, we're going to find out about it. Jeremy and that friend of his were looking for something all right, and now George is as well. I wonder who that man is who's with him? Hmm . . . You know, I think there's something in this field that everyone's looking for. Up we get, NOW!" she ordered. Keep your heads down and make sure you're not seen. The first thing we're going to do is get hold of whatever that goat has been chewing on . . . looks like paper to me . . . and then we're going to walk around the other side of this field and see if we can spot anything," said Audrey, struggling to her feet. "Well, come on then! What are you waiting for? We've got to hurry before George finds whatever it is before we do!"

They got up as fast as they could and donned their rucksacks. Exhilarated by their unexpected mission, they set about their business with astonishing speed.

"Then I think we'll pay that Pearl Wiggins another visit," panted Audrey.

* * *

Pearl nearly died on the spot when the plain-clothes detective asked her whether she knew anything about Jeremy's lost belongings. As soon as he mentioned the word "painting," she felt her eyes dart toward the door leading to the parlor in the back of the building. The image of the little watercolor hanging on the wall opposite the fireplace burned in her mind. She was terrified her eyes would betray her guilt. Her heart began to hammer so loudly that she was certain they would be able to hear it. Her corset felt unbearably tight and her legs shook so much that she was afraid they were about to buckle beneath her.

Sensing her alarm, George Barlow, Tipping's local constable, whom she had known for the best part of twenty years, explained in a gentler, familiar tone that the police suspected that Jeremy Danvers had come into the procession of some very, very valuable paintings. He said there was no need to get into details about how and why Jeremy had them. It was probably all quite innocent, but they didn't belong to Jeremy and it was imperative that the artwork be located as soon as possible. He went on to say that he had received several reports that a white car—Jeremy's car, had been driven at dangerously high speeds through the area that morning and the rear door of his car was open. Allegedly, some things fell out of the back, and he and Detective Collins were there to ask whether she had seen anything fall onto the road and whether she or anyone else had picked anything up. They were especially eager to ask whether Pearl had noticed any paintings amongst the things she might have picked up. Pearl's assistance and cooperation in this matter, would be greatly appreciated, he added.

Still rooted to the spot, Pearl managed to stammer, "How, how much are these, these paintings worth?

George looked at Detective Collins who then answered in a quiet, confidential manner, "They could be worth millions Mrs. Wiggins."

Pearl's mouth fell open. All she could think about was the watercolor she had snipped around the edges with the kitchen scissors. Worth millions! Her mind screamed. She felt the color drain from her face as she broke into a cold sweat. She was on the verge of fainting and had to grip the edge of the counter in front of her.

"Are you alright Pearl?" enquired George, a look of concern on his face.

"Oh, yes . . . yes . . . just a little flustered . . . what with all this commotion," replied Pearl. "It's been a busy mornin alright," she said slowly, summoning up the willpower to gain some composure and think about what she was going to do. One thing was certain: she wasn't about to tell them anything about the watercolor in the parlor. She did not want to go to jail for vandalizing a painting worth millions of pounds.

"Well now, it just so happens . . . " A plan had begun to take root in her brain. Stalling for time, she said, "He should never have been driving so fast through the village. These young-uns never take any notice of speed limits. I risk my life every time I cross that road, George. I've been telling you for years that there should be a zebra crossing there. Audrey and Irma Hepplethwaite were within a whisker of their lives only last Sunday when . . . "

"Yes, yes Pearl. I'll certainly be having words with young Danvers when I see him, but what's important just at this minute is whether you saw anything fall onto the road."

"Time is of the essence," Mrs. Wiggins, added Detective Collins with a hint of impatience. "We know that Mr. Danvers came in here less than thirty minutes ago. What did he want? Did you hand any of his things to him? We need to . . . "

"I most certainly did not," said Pearl firmly. "I told him I'd give him his things in my own time, when I'm good and ready. He needs teaching a lesson that one . . . driving like a maniac . . . I said to him I'd be having words with his father when he next comes by."

Both George and the detective raised their eyebrows and stepped forward closer to the counter.

"So you have his things Mrs. Wiggins," said Detective Collins, optimistically.

"Oh, yes. It so happens that I do," she said, deliberately telling them as little as possible so that they would have to coax it out of her.

"So, where is it now Mrs. Wiggins?" asked the detective politely.

"I've got it all put away under mi stairs . . . for safe-keeping like." She stopped talking then and looked at the two policemen who were anxiously waiting for her to mention the artwork. Just as the detective was about to open his mouth to ask, Pearl said," Well, I expect you'll be wanting me to fetch it then."

Detective Collins looked at his colleague with palpable relief.

"We'll give you a hand with it Pearl," said George, stepping in her direction.

"Oh! No, no George, thank you," replied Pearl a little too quickly. She couldn't let them anywhere near the parlor. Rapidly thinking of an excuse, she whispered just loud enough so that Detective Collins could hear as well, "I've got mi Johns drying in the back," she said, coyly. "I'll just nip in on my own. I'll be back in a jiffy."

"Underwear," George whispered to the detective when Pearl had disappeared through the door at the back of the store. "She's drying her underwear. Probably not something we'd want to see," he quipped.

The detective's eyebrows shot up in alarm at the image of Mrs. Wiggins's voluminous underwear. He shuddered and looked out the window.

As soon as the door closed behind her, Pearl scurried down the hall and into the parlor where she had left Jeremy's backpack on her wing-backed chair in front of the fireplace. She quickly turned the pack upside down and emptied its contents onto the floor.

"Dear Lord, have mercy upon me," she muttered as she rummaged through the notebooks and papers. She had already made the decision that it would be wise to conceal all three watercolors from the police and confess to nothing. She reasoned that if none of the artwork turned up in Jeremy's things, then the police were less likely to pay her any attention. She was going to stick with her plan to take them to Barrington's. Right now though, she needed to get rid of George and that detective before they discovered what she had done to the watercolor. On her hands and knees, on the verge of panic, she lifted first one book and then another, shaking each one to free any loose papers trapped between the pages.

"Oh, sweet-mother-of-pearl! There they are," she whispered. With trembling hands and several audible sighs of relief, she hid the paintings under the chair and put everything else back into the pack. She grabbed hold of the chair arm and struggled back to her feet. She stood still for a moment to get her breath back, then bustled into the dimly lit hallway where she stopped by the cupboard under the stairs to retrieve the carrier bags full of Jeremy's other belongings.

"Here we are then," she announced, panting heavily when she re-entered the store. "There's a backpack and some other things that I've put into some bags for you," she added, trying to sound helpful.

Detective Collins pulled the backpack across the counter and loosened the drawstrings to take a look inside while George made a thorough search of the carrier bags. He shook his head when the detective looked across at him. "Nothing," he said.

"Have you looked through any of this, Mrs. Wiggins," asked Detective Collins?"

Pearl pressed her lips into a thin line of disapproval and looked at the detective in what she hoped was a suitably offended expression. "I should think not, Mr. uh, I mean Inspector. I'm not the sort to go rooting through other peoples' things." She folded her arms, lifted her chin in indignation and breathed out loudly through her nose.

"It's Detective, Mrs. Wiggins," he said, re-iterating his rank. He stopped what he was doing for a moment and looked directly into Pearl's eyes. He spoke in a flat, serious tone. "I take it then, that you have no knowledge of the missing artwork?"

For the briefest of moments, Pearl hesitated before answering. With her arms still folded under her bosom, she crossed her fingers, swallowed a few times and then said a little too loudly, "Well, if I did I would have told you so, wouldn't I?" It was only a little white lie. For starters, she wasn't to know the pictures were so valuable. How was she to know they were missing masterpieces? When she snipped the watercolor, she thought it was just a piece of discarded junk that had fallen onto the road outside. It was only later that she discovered it belonged to Jeremy. No, I will not feel guilty. I did my neighborly duty and picked up the mess. There's not many who'd have gone to the trouble of cleaning up the street now is there?

The policemen stayed a while longer, asking her to relate everything that had happened that morning. The detective appeared to be very interested in the other people she had seen in or around the post office. He stood to Pearl's left, in front of the greetings cards. He blocked her view out the big glass-plated window as he made notes in a slim black pocket book. Every now and then he looked up from his notebook and looked directly at Pearl, as if he had not quite heard what she said. Sometimes, he asked the same question twice, which made Pearl feel increasingly uncomfortable. When he asked her about why Jeremy had come into the post office, she averted her eyes—a movement that did not go un-noticed by the detective, and addressed her answer to George instead.

Pearl did not like Detective Collins one bit. She considered him too young to be a detective. Too young, too slick and too direct, and, of more import, he was not a local man. His posh southern accent made her even more uncomfortable.

"If what you're after isn't in the bags, then you'll most likely find it in the field over there," she said, nodding toward the other side of the road. "There were papers everywhere when I first went out, a right mess all over the place and in front of my post office. I knew I'd have to clear it all up myself. Leave it to the council and nothing will ever get done, just like that puddle out there. It's been there for years Inspector, er, Sergeant. I've been on the phone to the council I don't know how many times and all they do is give me the same old excuses," she ranted. Pearl was still complaining when the two policemen left the post office and crossed the road to the field.

Carefully hidden from view behind the greetings cards, Pearl watched them search the field. She was disturbed briefly by Mrs. Timmins who popped in for her usual sliced loaf and quarter of gumdrops. Pearl quickly dispensed of her, announcing that she had come on with a dreadful headache and was in too much pain to hold a conversation. Mrs. Timmons left with a disappointed look on her face. She missed the usual update on all the local gossip.

As soon as she felt the coast was clear, Pearl hung the closed sign on the front door. Ten minutes later, freshly powdered and rouged, her lips a fiery orange, she slipped out of the back door pulling her plaid shopping bag on wheels behind her.

TWELVE

Detective Sergeant Maurice Patterson of the Arts and Antiques division of the Metropolitan Police, and Constable Lawrence Walker, a solid, dependable sort on loan from North Yorkshire's headquarters, sat waiting opposite the Danvers' house in an unmarked car. They were parked in the shadow of an enormous Yew. Its gnarled branches spread majestically across the width of the narrow country lane, offering a canopy of cool shade from the mid-June sun. Warm breaths of air, laden with the smells and sounds of summer, wafted through the car's open windows, making it difficult to stay awake.

"I've got another call to make," said Patterson, stifling a yawn. "Keep your eyes peeled and let me know when the young bugger turns up."

Barely 5 feet 8½ inches in his stocking feet, Patterson was a short, generously proportioned man, borderline overweight with a little extra padding around his midriff. A wide, round face made him appear more corpulent than he really was, but his untoned physique gave a clear indication that he was one who avoided exercise.

Although he would not be considered handsome, he was not unattractive either. His thinning, grey hair had an appealing, permanent mussed-up look, as if he perpetually stood in the wind. His large, wrinkled face was like that of a kindly old bulldog with a weathered exterior and big soulful eyes.

Nearly thirty years in the police force had exposed him to the full spectrum of humanity, from the lowest scum of society, to decent, upstanding and innocent victims of crime. A disproportionate amount of time spent with the former had left him bitter and frustrated. It sickened him that despite the best efforts of the law, so many scoundrels got away with their wrongdoings.

Dragged up by his mother on a council estate in north east London, his father having abandoned them soon after his birth, Patterson could empathize to some degree, with the poor sods like him, who were born into nothing and were forced to fight for every rung on the ladder toward a better life. He could forgive the occasional indiscretion and their odd brush with the law. He did not condone, but he was able understand some of the forces that drove a person to crime. He was not a man of unbending high principle. His values had been shaped from a lifetime of experience.

"Got any more of those mints?" Patterson asked when he got off the phone. "I need something to keep me awake. I haven't slept properly for days."

Constable Walker pushed a hand into his trouser pocket and extracted the remains of a roll of mints. "Here you go," he said, and flicked the top mint into Patterson's palm. "So how long have you been on the case, Sarge?" Walker asked.

"Too bloody long," said Patterson, looking mildly irritated.

"Arts and Antiquities—that's a very narrow field," Walker remarked. "How did you get into it?" Patterson exhaled loudly. He was tired and in a bad mood.

"I drifted into it. I spent my first ten years in the Metropolitan Police in the East End, dealing with violent assault and robbery, but then I got lucky and was posted to Hampstead, one of those nice, posh suburbs of London. Do you know Hampstead, Walker?" Walker shook his head.

"Nah."

"Well, you've got to have a wallet as deep as a diamond mine to live there. Big houses packed with nice pieces of art and expensive toys," said Patterson with mild distaste. "Burglary of course, is the major crime, but there has been a massive increase in art theft over the last twenty years. I went from dealing with mindless thugs and drug addicts to chasing down devious, conniving art thieves. They're the worst kind of villain, Walker. I hate those smug bastards—every single one of them. The general public has got no idea about the enormity of art crime."

"Oh, I can believe it," Walker interjected. "It's the only kind of serious crime that seems to be almost . . . " He paused in an effort to formulate the correct words. " . . . socially acceptable, isn't it? I think art crime is considered to be high class and in some ways prestigious, almost like a gentleman's crime. I mean, just look at the Hollywood movies and how they glamorize the art thief."

"Exactly," Patterson agreed. "Your average John Doe thinks it is all a romantic game; some glamorous "Thomas Crown Affair" affecting the lives of only a few silly rich people. But the sad, sordid reality is that the exchange of stolen art is a worldwide, multi-million dollar business; the fourth largest form of organized crime in the world, funding some of the shittiest operations you can imagine." Patterson shook his head in disgust.

"Really? It's that bad?"

"Oh yes. It's universal and it's getting worse. Most art thieves are associated with large, often international, organized crime syndicates. They use stolen art to trade on a closed black market to fund all sorts of crimes like drugs, arms and terrorism. Art is a relatively easy commodity to move around, and it's not that hard to get hold of."

"Right," said Walker nodding his head. "I heard about a case where the thieves stole stuff in broad daylight, right under everyone's noses. They walked into a museum, whipped a painting off the wall and walked straight out with it."

"Yeah, that actually happened, although security is a lot better now than it used to be. With new technology, the bigger museums have some pretty impressive systems in place, but it's the smaller, privately owned museums and galleries that are still a problem. They don't have the same kind of funding you see," said Patterson. "But there are other ways art disappears. Take a country at war for example. That's where most of the really important stuff disappears. Cultural desecration, looting . . . " His words trailed off.

"Hmm, I hadn't thought about that side of things, " Walker said.

"What really pisses me off though," Patterson continued, "is that most art criminals are never apprehended, and in the rare cases where are brought to trial, they nearly always get off very lightly. Did you read about the recent case of the French waiter who stole more than 200 artifacts worth $1.4 billion from over 170 museums across Europe?"

"Yeah, I read something about that in the paper. Didn't he stash it all in his mother's house and then she destroyed most of it when she realized the police were onto him?"

"Yes, that's the one. The selfish sod didn't even take it for the money. He just wanted to possess the art for his own satisfaction. And do you know what he got in the end, after stealing $1.4 billion? Twenty-six months."

"Twenty-six months?" Walker asked incredulously. "Is that all?"

"Yes. It's pathetic. It makes my blood boil to think about it. Talk about a screwed up system of justice." Patterson's jaw tightened. "It's the spoiled rich bastards I hate the most though, the trophy hunters who steal for the fun of it. They have nothing else to do with their time. They steal art for the buzz of being in possession of something no one else has. They hang on to the art, hide it away and most of it never resurfaces again. I can't even put into words how much I despise that kind of selfishness."

"So, do you collect art yourself?" asked Walker, trying to lighten the subject.

"No I bloody well do not," was Patterson's scathing response. "I don't give a rat's arse about a few strokes of paint on a canvas. It's all pointless, frivolous overindulgence, as far as I'm concerned." He turned to look at Walker's surprised face. "Yeah, I know. It's not exactly what you expected is it?"

"I'm surprised," said Walker, baffled. "I took it for granted that you would be an avid arts enthusiast."

"Well, I'm not," Patterson said bluntly. "I'm in this game for other reasons. Nothing gives me more satisfaction than nailing those smug bastards." His eyes glittered with barely suppressed rage. "It's the challenge and the hunt you see, the fitting together of all the pieces of a puzzle.

Tenacity and perseverance are my greatest strengths, oh, and patience. I am relentless, Walker. If it takes months, a year or a decade, I never give up. The look in their eyes when I finally have them backed into a corner. That's the prize at the end that makes it all worthwhile."

Walker did not respond, unsure of what to say. Patterson sat staring straight ahead through the windscreen, a tic moving in his jaw. An awkward silence filled the car.

"I retire next year," Patterson said. "I've done my thirty years. I've had a few good offers for work in the private sector, arts recovery and security, but I need to go out on a high. If I can pull off this one last case . . . " He seemed to be talking more to himself than to Walker. "It'll make all the difference, the difference between a good offer and a lucrative offer. Bargaining power, Walker, bargaining power."

Walker arched his eyebrows and sucked in his breath before he spoke.

"Another mint, Sarge?" he asked amiably, trying to snap Patterson out of his despondent mood. "We're down to the last two."

Patterson held out a hand without saying anything. A minute of silence passed between them. "Right then, I'd better bring you up to date with the case before our laddo turns up. Art crime is not as straightforward as it may seem. It can be . . . " he paused for a second, "complicated."

* * *

Patterson spent the next ten minutes explaining the intricacies of the case. Five months before, at the beginning of 2005, rumors about the discovery of six missing watercolors painted by J.M.W. Turner, an artist considered to be Britain's greatest watercolorist, began to circulate throughout the art world, generating huge excitement amongst academics and collectors alike. The paintings, part of a collection known as *The Yorkshire Collection*, had vanished nearly two hundred years before. Of all the watercolors and drawings Turner had produced, those from his visits to Yorkshire were widely acclaimed by experts as amongst his finest.

Naturally, the projected value of the missing art encouraged a number of claimants to step forward. Longman's Publishers immediately claimed ownership with documented proof that they had originally sponsored the work. It was well known that Turner was a regular visitor to his friend and patron, Walter Fawkes, who was a descendant of Guy Fawkes of Farnley Hall in Yorkshire between 1810 and 1825. During this period, it appeared that the Reverend Thomas Dunham Whitaker, through the publishers, Longman, had commissioned Turner to produce 120 watercolors. Later, they would be engraved to illustrate a proposed *General History of the County of York*. However, the project was abandoned on Whitaker's death, in 1821. According to an entry in one of the journals kept by Turner as he traveled throughout Europe, only 29 of the paintings were completed, of which 23 were documented. The remaining six paintings promptly disappeared, blipped off the scholarly radar, widely believed to have been lost for good.

Such disappearance of art was not unusual. As the Reverend Whitaker lay dying of consumption, Turner must have known that the *Yorkshire project* was unlikely to survive the demise of his patron. What likely happened was that the last six pieces he finished passed directly from his easel into private hands. Over the years, the paintings probably changed owners several times and eventually the thought that that dusty picture of Aunt Beatrice's could really be a Rubens-or a Turner, or a fancy whatever, slowly faded from the minds of the heirs.

Occasionally, such pieces eventually made a slow ascent back through the art market, into the public arena. Some might even become a star turn at a Christie's sale, but many fell prey to the foraging art dealer whose interests strayed little further than a fat paycheck from an unscrupulous collector.

The moment Patterson heard from one of his most reliable sources that the watercolors were about to resurface, he knew he had to act quickly to prevent them from falling into the wrong hands. His priority was to ensure they did not leave the country before the courts settled all claims to ownership.

Longman's case was certainly legitimate. But so was Lord Whitcomb's claim. He was a direct descendant of William Fawkes. Whitcomb argued that before leaving Yorkshire, Turner had bequeathed the paintings to the family. He pointed to several entries in journals kept by Lady Fawkes between 1823 and 1825, indicating the presence of the art in Farnley

Hall at that time. In 1871, a fire decimated the hall and it was believed that the paintings had been destroyed.

However, an elderly lady living in Wimbledon claimed to have bought six unsigned watercolors that fit the description of the missing Yorkshire landscapes from an arts dealer for five hundred pounds in 1959. She alleged that two years later, the paintings, along with other personal items, were stolen from her home.

Nothing further was heard about the work until January of 2005, when rumor began to circulate of their possible discovery in the dark attic of a large private house in York. That they might eventually come to auction after the various claims were settled, caused a venerable buzz of anticipation among collectors all over the world, but according to Patterson's mole, clandestine moves were afoot to prevent the paintings from ever reaching the public arena.

Under British law, the Department of Culture, Media and Sport (DCMS) would temporarily restrict the export of the Turners on the grounds that they were of outstanding aesthetic importance or of outstanding significance for the study of Turner's later works, thus allowing time for a British institution or individual to raise enough money to keep the work in the U.K. But Patterson discovered that before the DCMS had time to act, the artwork was about to be smuggled out of the country to one of the civil law countries of Europe, such as Switzerland where a *good faith and protection law* was in place. Once there, the purchaser could say he or she bought the work of art in good faith, and unless proved otherwise, they would be entitled to keep it, even if it had been stolen in the past.

Patterson's gut instinct was to look for a rich patron, someone keeping a low profile in the background, working through a middleman. His first move in this type of case was to go straight to the auction house records to see which collectors had been buying works by the same artist. Once identified, they would be the first on Patterson's list of suspects, and Claudia Rankin, a name already well known to him, a collector of Turners works since the early 1990's, was at the top of that list.

Her name first appeared on the *missing art* radar back in 1994, shortly after two Turner paintings, *Shade and Darkness* and *Light and Color*, worth

50 million pounds were stolen from the Tate while on loan to the Frankfurt museum. After passing through several hands, the paintings were eventually retrieved by the Tate after they reportedly paid 3.5 million pounds to the German authorities that supposedly used the money to pay a chain of informants. The culprits who stole the paintings were never formally identified, but some interesting names were revealed, including the likely instigator of the theft—Arkan, the Serbian warlord. Another name that popped up, by virtue of her already impressive collection of Turners, was that of Claudia Rankin, an extremely wealthy American connoisseur of the arts. Although her name was only a peripheral whisper, it was still enough for Interpol to attach a permanent red asterisk on the cover of her file.

Patterson was elated when Claudia Rankin set foot on English soil three weeks before, at the end of May. Within a few days of her arrival, Patterson's investigation revealed that Julian Parks, a respected arts dealer, had acquired six paintings of unknown origin, for an undisclosed amount of money. It was a matter of trying to catch either one of them in possession of the artwork.

Yet no one had bargained for the untimely death of both Parks and Claudia Rankin. It came as a bitter blow, just as Patterson was about to close the net. When news of the car accident on the road to Knaresborough, just outside of Harrogate, reached Scotland Yard, Patterson knew that he had to act with the utmost urgency if there were to be any chance of retrieving the paintings. He was convinced that the Turners were still close by. He could almost smell them, they were that close, and yet they had somehow managed to slip away, right from under his nose.

Patterson was convinced the Danvers boy had something to do with their disappearance, but he was damned if he could figure out what possible connection the kid had with the Rankins. There was no obvious link between them, no hint of a motive for the kid to be involved. And then there was the re-appearance of Conrad Rankin in England. That was no coincidence—it couldn't be. Rankin had to be Patterson's man, but so far he did not have one shred of evidence.

Something about the case did not smell right, something that Patterson could not quite put his finger on. Things were not going the way he liked. At the back of Patterson's mind, a little tremor of doubt, a feeling that he was losing control of a situation for the first time in his thirty years on the job, was eating away at him. The case was beginning to give him indigestion.

A city boy through and through, Patterson felt his stomach sink when he realized his quest was about to lead him to the rural purgatory of Yorkshire. However, he conceded that the scene was fitting in a way. After all, the missing work was a part of Turner's *Yorkshire Collection*. It was an odd coincidence that the paintings were returning to their place of origin. Perhaps fate was playing its hand, but he quickly dismissed it as a fanciful notion. He was not comfortable with fuzzy-grey, superstitious nonsense. In truth, he did not give a flying squirrel about where the Turners eventually ended up, so long as it was not on the wall of one of that spoiled bastard's mansions. He had never met Conrad Rankin, but he already knew he was not going to like him.

* * *

"Sir. He's here!" Walker announced, tapping Patterson on the arm. Jeremy's white car was approaching slowly from the opposite direction.

Patterson jumped in his seat, alert within seconds. He rubbed his face with one hand and leaned forward to peer through the windscreen.

"Let him pull onto the drive and then move in after him. Don't give him a chance to enter the house. I want to see what he's got in that car first."

As soon as Jeremy began to turn off the lane, Walker turned the ignition and made ready to swing onto the Danvers' drive.

"Christ, I hope the idiot's still got the stuff in his car," said Patterson without much confidence. "Something tells me we're going to find bugger all."

They swung onto the graveled drive and came to a screeching halt just as Jeremy stepped out of his car.

"Step away from the car!" Patterson called out as he jumped out of the unmarked vehicle.

Jeremy shrank back in wide-eyed alarm, a look of unmistakable horror written across his face.

Patterson strode toward him and held out his warrant card. "You know who I am Jeremy, Detective Sergeant Patterson, Scotland Yard, and this is Detective Constable Walker from Harrogate CID."

Walker flashed his warrant card and then without saying a word, moved between Jeremy and the house.

"We have reason to believe that you have stolen articles either on your person or in the car. We have the power under the Police and Evidence Act to search you and the car. The search will be recorded and you may request a copy from police headquarters in Harrogate. Is that understood?" Patterson looked at Jeremy with hard, impassive eyes.

Jeremy opened his mouth to reply, but no sound came out. He swallowed hard as Patterson took a step closer.

"Do you understand?" Patterson repeated.

Jeremy swiveled his head to look at Walker, then turned back to face Patterson. His eyes were stretched wide with fear. He finally spoke in a thin dry whisper. "Yes, yes, but I haven't got anything. I–I don't know what you're talking about."

"Oh, I think you do," said Patterson. "Step away from the car and hold your hands out to the side. And I'll take those keys," he said indicating the car keys in Jeremy's hand. He motioned to Walker with the wave of a finger. "Constable Walker will search you."

"You left the Bryce Edwards gallery in Harrogate around 5:00 p.m. yesterday. Where have you been between then and now?" Patterson looked Jeremy straight in the eye as he spoke, unsmiling.

Jeremy tried to keep his hands from shaking as Walker patted him down. "Leeds and then here," he said, his voice trembling.

"Why Leeds?"

"I–I went to see a friend."

"Who?"

"Charlie Butterworth. He's a friend from school."

"How long did you stay?"

"I just stayed the night."

"Then where did you go?"

"I came straight here."

"How long are you staying?"

"I–I . . . just for the weekend."

Walker stepped back and shook his head. "Just his wallet, Sir," he said, handing it to Patterson. Patterson leafed through the wallet and nodded towards the car. "Open the hatchback door," he said to Jeremy.

Patterson and Walker followed Jeremy to the back of the car and waited until the rear door swung open. Walker leaned forward and removed the few items that were there: a battered looking toiletry bag, a football and a few loose pieces of paper covered in handwriting.

"Do these belong to you?" asked Walker. Jeremy nodded lamely.

"Not much stuff for a weekend away," Patterson commented. "No change of clothes?" He looked at Jeremy through narrowed, suspicious eyes.

"No, well I–I" Jeremy stammered, his thoughts racing.

"Let me help you out a little, shall I," said Patterson sarcastically. "We've got several reports of a vehicle matching this description," he nodded towards Jeremy's car, "driving at reckless speed through the village at around ten this morning. Two witnesses confirm they saw a black Audi in close pursuit and," he paused to let this information sink in, "they also saw something fall out of the back of the car in front. Ring any bells?"

Jeremy stared back at him slack-jawed, stunned with the lurching knowledge that Patterson knew a lot more than he was letting on. A rush of fear coursed through his veins turning his legs to jelly, as if they might buckle beneath him at any second.

"I've already told you, I don't know anything about any stolen art!" Jeremy blurted out. "I thought he was going to kill me!"

"Who?"

"The American, Conrad Rankin. I got it all wrong though." Jeremy's shoulders slumped and he looked down at his feet. "He just wanted to ask me about his mother."

Patterson remained silent for a moment then said in a calmly, "I think you've got some talking to do lad. Should we do it inside or should we go down to the station?"

Jeremy's eyes flickered to the house. "Here," he said quickly.

Settled at the table in the kitchen, Jeremy told Patterson and Walker a carefully edited version of the whole story from the moment Conrad Rankin set foot in the gallery, to the car chase that morning. He insisted again that Julian Parks had left nothing at the gallery. He told them how Bryce Edwards had scared him into thinking that someone from the criminal world might make an attempt to retrieve the paintings and how he thought that Conrad Rankin was the man sent to get them.

He admitted that when he was speeding through the village some of his things fell out into the road, and that he talked to Conrad in the field, but he made no mention of the lies he had told to his parents. And, he did not breathe a word of the secret agreement he had made with Conrad. When he finished his tale, he swore again, in dramatic fashion, that he had no knowledge of the missing artwork.

"I was only helping out for the summer, and now all this, this drama has happened. It's got nothing to do with me. Everyone thinks I've got the paintings, but I haven't!" He almost screamed the last words. He threw Patterson a helpless look. "I just need to have a few days to myself. That's why I came here. I've had enough. I can't take anymore."

Patterson glanced at Walker, unable to disguise the look of disappointment on his face. "Take down the details," he said to Walker with a long exasperated sigh. "Names, times, the lot."

"You do understand the penalties for lying to the police, don't you," he said sternly. "And if you have knowingly handled stolen goods . . . You'll face jail time for that," he added.

When Jeremy answered with a quavering, "I know, but I haven't done anything wrong," Patterson shook his head wearily, stood up and pulled a cell phone out of his pocket. He stabbed at the keys and walked out of the room with the phone to his ear.

"Fucking shit," he cursed under his breath.

* * *

An hour later, Detective Sergeant Maurice Patterson, Detective Collins, and Constables Lawrence Walker and George Barlow, gathered around a wooden table outside of Tipping's fish and chip shop, Hilda's Plaice, to discuss the day's progress.

"You'll not find a better piece of haddock, Sir," said Local Constable Barlow between mouthfuls. "She's got a secret recipe for the batter— been in the family for generations."

"Not bad, Constable, not bad at all," replied Patterson, nodding in agreement as he tucked into his food with relish.

"So, it looks like we've hit a dead end then, Sergeant," said Constable Barlow.

Patterson swallowed the last of his chips. He balled his greasy chip wrappers into a tight wad and threw them into the bin a few feet from the table.

"Not at all, Constable," he said. "I think there's a good chance the paintings are still in this village." He smiled faintly and added, "Somewhere."

"Well, if they're still here sir, I'll soon know about it. There's not much that goes on here that I don't know about. I know this place like the back of my hand, an' all that lives here."

Patterson made brief eye contact with Detective Collins, his Scotland Yard colleague, and gave him a meaningful look. He then turned to the local constable and said, "Well then, this is where we are going to have to depend upon you Constable Barlow. As you say, your local knowledge of the vicinity and the people who live here may well prove to be invaluable to our investigation. When you're finished here, I'd like you to talk to uh . . . what's his name . . . the local kid?

"Kevin Ogden, sir," replied Barlow.

"Find out if he picked anything up from the road . . . see if he saw anything that might be useful. And then there's the old chap— Barrington Smith. Have a word with him as well."

"I'm on it right now, sir," he said, already standing and straightening his jacket. The thought of being a crucial part of such an important investigation, gave him a huge thrill. Nothing this significant or exciting had happened in Tipping since the Royal family had passed through on their way to Harrogate in 1975. "I'll be off then," he said, puffing out his chest. "You can rely on me sir. I'll be in touch the moment I have something."

As soon as the local constable was out of earshot, Patterson turned to the others and said, "That should keep him busy for a while. Our local constable doesn't need to know everything. How long has he been stationed here?"

"Fifteen years. He did a brief stint in Harrogate CID and that's about it," said Collins.

"Hmmm," said Patterson thoughtfully. "More than long enough to get attached to these people. He doesn't need to know too much." Both Collins and Walker nodded in agreement.

Detective Collins lowered his voice and said, "Still nothing on Danvers then?"

Patterson shook his head. "No. The kid's clean and there was nothing in his car, so we still haven't got one thing on him—not enough to bring him in anyway. But I'm telling you, the kid was scared shitless. There's something he's not telling us."

"Do you still think Parks gave him the paintings?"

"I think Parks was too nervous to carry them around and so planned to drop them off at the gallery until he was ready to move them. I don't think he expected to find our boy Danvers on his own there. No, I think it was Nigel Bryce Edward's he expected to see, but then again, there might have been some collusion between all three of them. Anyway, I'm convinced Parks still left them at the gallery and for some reason, Danvers bolted with the paintings." He shook his head as he spoke," It's a pity our man lost him on the way out of Harrogate. The kid's had a window of time to pass them on, or get rid of them"

"Do you think there's a chance he's still got them?"

"I'm not sure Tom. I'm not sure," he said creasing his forehead as he thought. There's got to be some connection between him and Rankin; something we're missing." He tapped his fingers against the top of the wooden table, and stroked the stubble that was beginning to form on his chin. "Nah, you know what? I think the daft idiot's lost them—let them fall out of the back of his car . . . and now half of this bloody village has got their hands on them. Jesus Christ! What a fuck up!"

He looked across the Green at the pub called *The Three Bees* as a group of hikers arrived, looking hot and in need of a drink. All the tables outside were taken, so they filed inside, chatting loudly, through a narrow doorway at the front of the pub that was flanked by two hanging baskets. A riot of color from the baskets and the wooden planters arranged around the pub's perimeter, gave the place the look of a picture postcard.

"Shit, it's getting busy. We're running out of time." Patterson sighed heavily and turned to Constable Walker. "I've got you and two of your men for another," he looked at his watch, "thirty six hours. Make damn sure those two don't lose sight of Danvers and Rankin. For the time I've got you, I need this surveillance to be airtight. That means I want to know every move Danvers and Rankin make and every Tom, Dick or Harry they talk to, is that understood?"

"Yes, sir. Fields and Evans are both good men. I can vouch for the two of them. They won't let you down sir. Evans followed Rankin to Booth Hall where he's booked for the night. There's only the one road in regular use, in and out of the property, the rest are nothing more than mud tracks, but are still passable. I've got Evans watching the road."

"Hmm. Yes, well, it's the best we can do. It's impossible to watch every inch of the place."

"And Fields is watching the kid. Danvers hasn't left the house since you last saw him, sir. His car's still parked outside."

"Good, good."

Patterson turned to Collins. "So nothing turned up at the post office? What's your gut feeling about the Wiggins woman?"

"As nervous as hell. My gut tells me she's hiding something. I think she knows a lot more than she told us."

"Is that right?" said Patterson. His eyes narrowed as he absorbed this news. He thought for a moment and then turned again to Walker.

"You need to get over there," he said, nodding in the direction of the post office. "Find out what time she closes up and then watch her like a hawk. I want to know the minute she leaves the building."

"Right. I'm on it sir," said Walker as he shoveled a handful of chips into his mouth. "I'll get straight over there."

"So, we've also got nothing on Bryce Edwards and his son, Nigel. Both squeaky clean it seems," Patterson said. "Hmm, we're missing something, Tom. Something doesn't feel right." He strummed his fingers on the wooden bench again and thought for a moment. "I want you to do some more digging into Nigel Bryce Edwards. Find out what he's been up to since leaving, where was it, York University? And I want to know about his relationship with Parks. I want to know every move the two of them have made over the last two or three years. Then I think it's time we paid Rankin a visit—have a little chat with him. He's at Booth Hall—Cranshawe Booth's place. What've we got on Cranshawe?"

"Not much. Titled, old school, and up to his ears in debt. I don't see him connected with any of this. Do you?"

"No, Tom, I don't. I think it's coincidental that Cranshawe, Cranshawe Booth . . . Christ, what kind of name is that?" he asked. "Brigadier Richard Cranshawe Booth happened to be driving through the village at the same time as Danvers," he said, reading from a small notebook he had extracted from his pocket. He may well have picked something up off the road . . . We need to question him about that. But I can't see any connection between him and Rankin."

"Hmm, but then why would Rankin be staying at Booth Hall?"

"Coincidence—Rankin's got to stay somewhere, and something tells me that the local B and B isn't going to be good enough for the likes of our man."

Patterson stood up and put the notebook back into his trouser pocket. "Let's get a move on," he said, inclining his head towards their parked car. "I'm getting a bad feeling about all this. Over my dead body are those paintings going to leave this village."

Collins got up and fell into stride next to Patterson.

"We'll head over to the constabulary building while Barlow's out of the way. I've got some calls to make while you get into the operating systems and find out about Bryce Edwards and Parks. Then we'll go to Booth Hall and question Cranshawe Booth if he's around—see if he saw anything. I want you with me when I talk to Rankin though. I want to know what you make of him. He's our man all right, but we need to catch him red-handed. We've got nothing concrete on him yet —piss all in fact, so I don't want any more cock-ups. If Rankin gives us the slip, he'll have his hands on the Turners before we know it, and it'll be the last anyone sees of them. I want to nail that bastard before he leaves the country.

THIRTEEN

Conrad brought his car to a halt outside an enormous pair of wrought iron gates, beyond which, loomed a commanding house at the end of a long tree-lined drive. It stood on a raised knoll, surrounded by lush green parkland that contrasted sharply with the stark grey moors behind it. He recalled the description of Booth Hall given to him over the phone by his assistant, as she read verbatim from information on the internet: "a stunning Jacobean Manor House, straight from the pages of Jane Austen's romantic England."

"Hmm," Conrad pondered aloud. The place reminded him more of the bleakness described in a Charlotte Bronte novel. He imagined that Mr. Rochester's Thornfield Hall in Jane Eyre looked something like this. His brooding thoughts were confirmed when a huge shadow cast by a somber bank of clouds building to the west, slowly shrouded the building, giving it an eerie, desolate look. A small sign, half hidden by tall weeds growing at the side of the lane, pointed to the Hall's public entrance, 100 yards away.

The hot summer's day had been glorious, but now it looked as if a storm was brewing on the horizon. A sudden blast of wind shook the leaves of the massive elms that stood majestically on each side of the stone gateposts, prompting Conrad to close the car windows and press on to the hall.

His initial impression of Booth Hall was re-affirmed when he saw the condition of the drive. The road was in a terrible state of neglect, the surface torn up in places and pockmarked by deep craters of muddy water. He half-considered turning the car around and heading back to the village to find somewhere else to stay, but then decided he did not have enough time. He needed to lock himself inside a hotel bedroom and examine his mother's inventories of her collections. He had bought the information with him on a flash drive so he could look through it on his lap-top during the flight over. He could not recall any Turners amongst her impressive British collection, but then, he had not been looking for them. However, now that it seemed she was a chief suspect in a dubious Turner transaction, he could barely wait to take another look.

He also needed to seize an opportunity to speak with the Hall's owner, Brigadier Cranshawe Booth, and without raising too much suspicion, ask whether the Brigadier had picked anything up from the road outside Tipping's post office that morning. Just how he was going to do this, he had no idea, but he was determined to think of something.

The bumpy, arduous ride was spent dodging the potholes and large stones that poked up from the road's surface. Despite being in a hurry, he was forced to drive at a snail's pace with his eyes glued to the road for most of the way. He rattled over several cattle grids and twice he had to stomp on the brakes to avoid hitting sheep that suddenly darted across the road in front of him. By the time he pulled into a large stone court-yard at the rear of the hall where several others cars were parked, he felt exhausted, as if he had been running for miles.

"Thank God," he muttered, when he finally turned off the engine. He got out of the car and flexed his shoulders backwards and forwards, rubbing the back of his neck at the same time. He was looking forward to lying down, undisturbed, on a soft bed in a nice quiet room where he would have a few minutes to think carefully about this whole business. He looked around the courtyard.

He was struck by the quietness. Apart from a few parked cars and the loud cawing of rooks high up in the boughs of the towering oaks and beeches that sheltered one of the wings of the Manor House, no signs of life were evident. He noticed that the long line of stables he had passed on the way in, were empty, and as he looked around, he detected a general air of neglect. The loose scaffolding that was erected across the back of the house looked as if it had been abandoned long ago and from where he stood, Conrad could see that the roof and guttering were in a sad state of repair. Damn! This was not what he had expected. He had envisioned Booth Hall to be considerably grander than this, but it was obvious that the implied prosperity on the Internet was illusory. God knows he needed some luxury after flying three thousand miles and then chasing Jeremy Danvers half way across Yorkshire. He looked at his watch with the futile hope that he might still have enough time to find somewhere else to stay, but he already knew it was too late. "Shit!" he exclaimed angrily.

Resigned, he cast a glance around the courtyard wondering if he had missed a sign for the entrance. The buildings that lined two sides of the yard appeared to be derelict. A rusty iron pump hung over an old stone water trough against a wall in the far corner, and he noticed thick tufts of grass growing between the cobbles on the ground. Frustrated, he ran a hand through his hair and was about to get back into the Audi, when he heard a loud rattling noise coming towards him from the direction of the house. An elderly man, well into his seventies, Conrad guessed, dressed in a faded tweed jacket and long gum boots appeared from behind the stables pushing a wheel barrow full of twigs.

'Ha! Thank God,' thought Conrad. He was beginning to think the place was uninhabited.

"Hello," he called as he strode over. "Good afternoon. Am I in the right place to check in?" Conrad enquired politely. The man looked up in surprise, not expecting to see anyone in the courtyard. He hesitated for a moment and then dropped the handles of the wheelbarrow as Conrad approached. Nodding his head in greeting, the corners of the man's mouth lifted into a cautious smile, but he made no attempt to speak.

"Uh— hello. Good afternoon," repeated Conrad. How are you?"

"Oh middlin', lad, just middlin," the old man said at last. He took off his frayed cap and wiped his brow with the back of his jacket sleeve.

"Uh, right, good," replied Conrad uncertainly. "Well, I'm not sure if I'm in the right place, but I'm staying the night here, and I'm looking for reception to check in," Conrad said hopefully.

"EH?" the old man bellowed, cupping a hand to his ear. He was obviously hard of hearing. He put his cap back on and moved closer to Conrad so that he was only a foot or so away.

"Guests, where do they check in? Conrad shouted in the man's face, feeling unnerved by the close proximity.

"Tha's stayin' 'ere then?"

"Yes, yes!" Conrad replied trying to keep the frustration out of his voice. "Where do I check in?" he shouted even louder.

"Tha's not from these parts are thee? I can always tell you know," the old man shouted back, tapping the side of his head with his index finger. "I've got a good ear for accents . . . Scotland, I'll wager!"

This is appalling, Conrad screamed inwardly.

"Ah, no. I'm from the United States."

"Eh? You'll 'ave to speak up young man. I can't 'ere a thing with those blasted birds squawking like that." He threw an angry glance towards the trees at the side of the house.

"Mrs. Flint used to make Rook pies in the old days you know. She was one of the 'ousekeepers. They used to 'ave two of 'em and I used to 'ave two full time gardeners to 'elp me out. There wasn't a blade of grass out of place in them days."

The old man's features seemed to soften and a light came into his eyes as though he were talking more to himself than to Conrad.

"But I'll tell thee summat," he continued in a conspiratorial whisper, "This place isn't what it used to be, not since the war. I've been among this lot all mi life and I'm tellin' thee that since the war nothin's been the same."

Which war? The Boer War, perhaps, thought Conrad. His patience was wearing thin.

"The old house was different then. Six servants there were, and everything just so, all tidy like." The old man shook his head despondently. "Things 'ave been even worse since master Dickie took over," he continued. "Ad to let go of most of the staff—down to the bare bones now. Everythin's gone down hill since Mr. Carruthers passed away. He were the butler you know. They never replaced him and now I 'ave to double up on . . . "

"Really? That's a great pity," said Conrad interrupting the old man's rambling. "But I don't have a lot of time. Where can I check in? Please!" He almost screamed the last word.

"Oh, right you are then," replied the old man, a little startled, as if he had heard the question for the first time. He pointed toward a heavy pair of wooden doors at the top of a short flight of stone steps at the rear of the house.

"I think you'll find what yer after over there."

"Thank you," replied Conrad, remembering to talk loudly.

"Now, afore ye go, young man, I've got summat else to tell thee . . ."

In no mood to share any more confidences, Conrad pointed histrionically to his watch and bade the old man a final goodbye. He turned sharply on his heels and almost broke into a run as he headed towards the Manor House. He flew up the steps and pushed open the heavy door. An ominous rumble of thunder sounded overhead as he entered the dark interior.

The diminishing afternoon light followed him into a large dimly lit room. Taking a few moments to let his eyes adjust to the gloom, he quickly surmised the room was empty. Disappointed, Conrad walked towards a high wooden counter that ran along part of the far wall, on top of which lay a large ledger and a neat stack of color brochures describing Booth Hall and its history. At one side of the counter was a brass buzzer that he assumed was there to summon someone from inside the house. He pressed it a couple of times and then turned to look around while he waited.

To the right of the room was an arched doorway that looked as if it led into the interior of the house where a much smaller door was recessed into the wall behind the counter, partially concealed by heavy, red velvet drapery. Two enormous overstuffed chairs placed across from each other at the ends of a rectangular, ornate cocktail table, dominated the middle of the room, but his eyes were drawn to the various stuffed animal heads that were affixed to the walls. There were deer and foxes and what he thought were weasels dotted about. A ferret with a surprised look on its face, as if it had turned at the very moment of its death, stood lifeless on top of a long book-case that lined the wall to his left.

The flickering light cast from the wrought iron wall sconces glinted on the animals' glassy eyes, giving the unnerving impression that they were not quite dead. Conrad hunched his shoulders. Ugh, creepy, he thought. With a grimace, he averted his eyes and turned to look up at the high ceiling instead, which he noticed was heavily patterned with crests and hunting motifs. The cornices were particularly interesting, but the feeble lighting made it difficult to appreciate the carved details.

With an impatient sigh, he looked down at the counter again and pressed the buzzer with force for a lot longer than was polite. Where in God's name is everyone, he thought crossly. How can this place possibly survive if there isn't anyone to greet the clients? He thought about what the old man outside had told him concerning the demise of the hall, and loss of staff. Well, no wonder. He waited a few more minutes.

"Oh, for Christ's sake!" He leaned forward across the counter, toward the small door behind the drape and listened for any signs of life. Nothing. "Oh, come on" he groaned. With mounting frustration, he pressed the buzzer three more times in quick succession.

As he strained to listen for the slightest sound, he thought he heard some muffled noises coming from deep inside the house. After a few moments, he was sure he could discern the approach of shuffling footsteps. Aha. At last! He felt like shouting for joy.

After a seemingly interminably long time, a tiny white-haired old woman emerged from behind the recessed door and hobbled to the counter. Barely able to see over the top, she said, "How can I help you sir?"

Somewhat taken aback—he wasn't expecting to be greeted by someone who appeared to be at least eighty, dressed in an old fashioned parlor maid's uniform. He stumbled on his words. "Oh, er . . . right. I believe I have a reservation for two nights. My assistant made the booking a few hours ago. He made a mental note to call her as soon as he got the chance and tell her exactly what he thought of Booth Hall. "Conrad Rankin's the name."

"Now then," the elderly woman said. "Let me see." She opened the large leather-bound ledger on top of the counter and flipped open the page where a long, silver bookmark had been placed. Peering through a pair of wire-rimmed spectacles, she ran an arthritic finger down the column of names. "Hmmm," she wheezed as she leaned myopically close to the page. "Mr. Rankin. Here it is. Oh, yes, you'll be very pleased. The Daffodil Room." She smiled up at him.

Conrad was perturbed by the advanced age of the staff he had encountered thus far, as well as the apparent lack of modern technology to handle the check-in procedure. He had expected a computer at the very least. He thought it might be wise to check on some of the finer details of his accommodation to see if any other surprises awaited him.

"En-suite—right?" he asked lamely. Something in the back of his mind told him that *The Daffodil Room* was not going to come anywhere close to the standards of the Ritz.

"No, no it's not sir," she said shaking her head, "but there is a bathroom on that floor," she added brightly, as if this information should please him immensely.

"You young 'uns," she wheezed. "When I was a girl, all we had were outdoor lavvies. The water used to freeze in 'em in the winter . . . "

Conrad stared at her, stunned. "No en-suite?" This was beyond intolerable.

"Well, do you have anything else? Something with a bathroom," he asked helplessly. This was not going well.

"Oh no, sir. We're in the middle of some . . . well, some uh . . . renovations, and all the best rooms are booked, although there is the . . . " she stopped short of finishing her sentence and shook her head. "No, never mind," she trailed off.

Conrad immediately leaped on her hesitation and asked imploringly, "Do you mean there is something?"

"Well . . . there is the East Wing" she whispered cautiously, but there's not many who would want to stay there."

"Does it have its own bathroom?" he asked tersely. He was tired, in a hurry and needed solitude to think about the day's events. What could possibly be so terrible about the East Wing to put him off?

"It is what you might call deluxe, sir with its own bathroom. It's one of the original rooms of the house, built at the same time as the Pele tower. Now in case you don't know—that's a medieval fortified tower," she added importantly. "Steeped in history. But . . ." she hesitated, "the East Wing is, well, it's . . . 'Aunted!"

Conrad wanted to laugh aloud at this revelation, but he managed to remain silent. A ghost. Jesus, he thought, what next? This is utterly ridiculous. He would much rather be spooked by the specter of Booth Hall than share a toilet with someone. The thought of a shared bathroom was incomprehensible, an impossibility. Nothing and no one was ever going to convince him otherwise. He had enjoyed his own suite of rooms since he was two days old—anything else was not an option.

"I think the East Wing will be fine, thank you," he said politely, stifling a laugh.

"It's the *Grey Lady* you know. "Happened centuries ago . . . Baroness Montague . . . hung herself after being jilted by her lover . . . with a rope of pearls. She was found 'anging from the four poster bed . . . the very same one you'll be sleeping in." She narrowed her eyes waiting for Conrad's response.

"I'll take the room," he said firmly, reaching into a back pocket for his wallet. Do you take American Express?"

"Well, if you're sure." She bent down and reached into a drawer beneath the counter top to heft out another enormous leather-bound book. "If you could sign just here," she said opening the book to the appropriate page and pushing it towards him. She placed a fountain pen in its center and tapped the page with a gnarled finger.

There was something vaguely irritating about the archaic proceedings, perhaps because he was so used to first class service, but there was a quirky quaintness about the whole business that amused him. He supposed it attracted the kind of tourist that wanted to feel the age of the place and experience a piece of tangible history.

"And will you be taking tea with Sir Richard and Lady Cranshawe Booth?"

"Tea?" he asked, looking up from the register.

"Yes, at four o'clock, every second Friday in the summer months, Sir Richard and her Ladyship avail themselves to have high tea with the commo . . . Er, with the guests, she corrected herself. She was about to say *commoners,* but thought better of it. "For an additional cost, of course. It's not every day one gets to converse with the aristocracy," she added haughtily.

"Really?" Conrad tried to stifle a laugh, but he was secretly delighted. He had not imagined getting the opportunity to come face to face with Cranshawe Booth as soon as this. "Yes, of course," he replied. He looked at his watch and asked, "Let's see, how long have I got?" It was three forty.

"You've a few minutes yet, sir. I'll just finish up here and then I'll show you to your room. Wilfred can fetch your bags."

"Oh no. Really—I can bring my own bags in. I've only got the one," he said hurriedly. He thought about the Turner concealed in his luggage.

"Hmmph," she said disapprovingly. She bowed her head slightly and said, "As you wish, sir."

"Oh, and one more thing. I'll be needing somewhere to eat, probably around 7:30," Conrad said. He checked his watch again and made a mental calculation of how much time he had.

"I was thinking of venturing into the village. The Three Bees has been recommended."

"Oh yes, you'll be wanting to go to the Three Bees at the bottom of the 'ill leading up to the church. They 'ave the best Yorkshire Puddin' for miles around you know," She licked her lips. "That and their meat and tater pie with gravy. Although, mi personal favrit is the steak and kidney puddin. I always like it with . . . "

"Ah, yes, yes," Conrad interrupted. "It sounds perfect. I'm sure I'll uh—find something on the menu. If you could make that reservation for me . . . "

FOURTEEN

Thank God, he had insisted on carrying his own bag to his room. Wilfred, he later found out, was the deaf old man he had spoken to in the courtyard. Instead, the old woman from reception was his escort.

"Mrs. Cavendish is mi name, but you can call me Millie if you need anything," she said obligingly as they passed through the arched doorway that led into a darkened corridor at the rear of the reception room.

"I spend most of mi time in the kitchen, but now I 'ave to sometimes 'andle the reception as well, 'specially when it gets busy."

"These are some of master Dickie's ancestors," she informed Conrad, raising a finger to point at the paintings lining the walls. She stopped in front of a large portrait of a dark-haired, portly man and said, "This one's Walter Cranshawe. He bought this 'ouse in 1688, after his career at court in the service of King James II. He's the one that brought the young French gardener with 'im; Guillame Beaufort, a pupil of Le Notre at Versailles, to plan a fashionable garden here at the Hall." Conrad nodded his head, genuinely interested in the history and somewhat surprised by Mrs. Cavendish's memory for details.

"He's the one that jilted her," she added, giving Conrad a knowing look. "Baroness Montague . . . that's why she did away with 'erself . . . because of the gardener."

"Ah, yes," said Conrad, bringing to mind what she had told him earlier about the *Grey Lady*.

"Now if you follow me, I'll show you a portrait of the baroness herself."

With slow shuffling steps, she continued down the corridor ahead of Conrad until they reached another doorway that led to a heavy wooden staircase. Conrad noticed the thickness of the treads and how they were worn and warped in places. "Is this the oldest part of the house?"

"It is sir. These stairs are made from solid slabs of elm, cut down from this very estate. Here we are—Baroness Montague." She stopped in front of a gilt framed oil painting.

Conrad looked at his watch again, conscious that he really needed to get moving, but he could not resist a quick look at the infamous *Grey Lady*. He was not sure what he had expected the Baroness to look like, but he had hoped to see at least one feature that set her apart; perhaps a certain look in her eye, or an aura of sadness about her. But to Conrad's disappointment, the baroness was indistinguishable from all the other well rounded, fleshy women so often portrayed in the generic portraits of the 17th century. She was sitting upright in a chair, well trussed in satin and lace with two white poodles at her feet. Conrad leaned closer to the painting and peered at her dark eyes, hoping they might reveal some emotion, but they stared back empty, and lifeless.

"Hmm, so why is she referred to as the "*Grey Lady*?""

"Well it seems that's all she ever wears now she's dead—a grey silk dress over a crinoline . . . and I can vouch for that myself sir," she added.

Conrad raised an eyebrow and turned to look at Ms. Cavendish who, sensing his curiosity, immediately whispered: "I've seen her twice on these very stairs."

He wanted to laugh aloud again. There was something very endearing about Ms. Cavendish and her almost childlike attempts to frighten him.

"Ms. Cavendish," he said warmly.

"Oh, you can call me Millie, Mr. Rankin."

"Alright then . . . Millie. When I have a little more time, perhaps tomorrow morning, I would very much like to hear about Booth Hall and its occupants, but right now, I've really got to hurry if I'm going to make it for high tea." He looked pointedly at his watch.

"Of course, of course, young man," she said, already climbing the stairs. "You're quite right; it won't do to be late. If there's one thing Lady Cranshawe Booth can't abide – it's tardiness."

Five minutes later, relieved to be on his own, Conrad flopped down onto the large four- poster bed in the Montague Suite in the east wing. He put his hands behind his head, exhaled loudly and glanced around the room. It was much as he had expected, high ceilinged with heavy oak paneled walls, and floorboards that creaked with every footstep. The lace-canopied bed was a grand affair, high off the ground with ruched bedding from top to bottom. Most of the furniture in the room looked as if it were antique, including two delightful little upright chairs, possibly French 18th century, placed either side of the escritoire, which, under different circumstances, Conrad would be looking at through a collector's eye.

It felt wonderful to grab a few minutes to relax and unwind before facing the Brigadier and his wife downstairs. Mrs. Cavendish had given him directions to the drawing room, warning him that anything beyond the red ropes was strictly out of bounds and that he should under no circumstances stray from those areas of the house designated as open to the public. "Her Ladyship is very particular about the family's privacy," she had added.

Her statement reminded him about what Jeremy told him concerning the Cranshawe Booths. "You'd think they were royalty, the way they go about the place —full of airs and graces."

This information amused Conrad. He was used to mixing in elite social circles, so the thought of meeting the likes of the Cranshawe Booths did not worry him one bit. In fact, he was quite looking forward to it.

He easily surmised that all was not well at Booth Hall. It was obvious that the Cranshawe Booths had fallen on hard times, but he was well aware that their type would be the last to admit it. He had met plenty of individuals just like them, poor as church mice, but by virtue of their blue blood and claims to superior lineage, still considered themselves to be above the rest of general society.

He could forgive the vague eccentricity of the British aristocracy and their obsession with class. But he could not abide anyone who harbored unmerited ideas of superiority; individuals who went about with false pretensions of grandeur as if they were in some way entitled to live a certain lifestyle without actually earning that right. It was that sort of ingrained snobbery, so prevalent among the ranks of the British peerage that he detested. It sounded as if the Cranshawe Booths were afflicted with the same lofty opinion of themselves. He too had been born into money, and had inherited a vast fortune, but never once did he consider himself to be a snob. He was wholly conscious of how hard his father, and his father before him had worked. Conrad was a firm believer in meritocracy. He wanted more than anything to make something of himself to prove that he could be resourceful and successful in his own right.

Well then, we'll see how quickly the Cranshawe Booths attempt to disguise their smug attitude when they find out how much money I have. It always gave him enormous satisfaction to see how quickly people courted his company when they realized his worth. He loved the power his money gave him, and he had no qualms about using its influence whenever it suited him.

His introduction to the Cranshawe Booths was probably going to be no exception. They would soon be fawning at his feet. He was under no illusions, however, as to the insincerity of any bonhomie forged between them. He knew that he could be the richest man in the world, but being an American with a comparatively short lineage and, more importantly, a person of means without a title, meant that underneath the veneer of friendship, the likes of the Cranshawe Booths, would always have the same nostril wrinkling contempt for him.

A loud clap of thunder snapped him from his reverie causing him to turn his head toward the two large mullioned windows that afforded a view across the estate to the rear of the Hall. From his vantage point on the bed he could see dark sheets of rain sweeping across the rim of moorland in the distance. "Hell!" he said aloud. He rolled off the bed and walked to the window. This weather was going to seriously hamper the plan for Jeremy to sneak into Pearl Wiggin's backyard and search her dustbins. The prospect of keeping a lookout in the pouring rain was not something he relished.

Conrad's thoughts were interrupted by another rumble of thunder. He climbed back onto the bed and reached for his laptop. He knew that he should check through his mother's art inventories, but he didn't have time if he were to be punctual for high tea in the drawing room. He would have to do it later, after he made contact with Cranshawe Booth. He checked his watch again, placed the laptop on the bedside table and got up from the bed. He took his wash bag from his traveling case and headed into the large, antiquated bathroom. He thought about how ridiculous it was that not all the rooms had their own bathroom. Jeez, we all want to experience a slice of history, but that was taking it a bit too far.

A large, ornate sink, in the shape of an open clamshell, occupied the far end of the room. A hairbrush and comb set with ivory handles and a dainty hand mirror were neatly displayed on top of the vanity next to the sink.

"Yep, definitely not the Ritz," he said to himself. "Ah well . . . "

He looked into the huge gilt mirror above the sink, turned on the faucet and splashed water on his face. Well, at least there is running hot water, something to be thankful for. Although he wanted a shower, that too would have to wait until later. He groped for a towel hanging by the sink and pulled it to his face. With the towel still pressed against his chin, he walked back to the bedroom and looked for a temporary hiding place for the Turner. His eyes wandered across the room in search of possibilities.

The tiny safety deposit box concealed behind one of the wooden wall panels was too small, and the drawers in the desk were too obvious. The best place was probably the top of the canopy above the bed. At least it was above his eye level, and since it was over six feet high, it would likely be out of sight for most people.

The decision made, he dropped the towel onto the bed, flipped open the top of his case and carefully took out the Turner. Standing on his tip-toes, he could just about reach high enough to slide the painting onto the top of the canopy. He walked back to the door to check that it could not be seen by anyone entering the room. Satisfied that it was safely out of sight, he raked both hands through his hair, made one last check in front of the mirror, and made his way down to the drawing room for high tea.

* * *

"Time to meet the peasants!" bellowed Dickie good-humoredly as he strode across the bedroom. "What do you think?"

He had changed out of the clothes he had been wearing that morning and donned a pair of flannels with a lightweight, double-breasted, navy sports jacket. He held out a selection of silk cravats in his hand.

Olivia, who was adjusting her pearls in front of the mirror at her dressing table, threw him a withering look. She absolutely deplored any involvement in her husband's hair-brained schemes to raise money. This was not what she had hoped for when she married him. Her mind screamed in indignation. It was all so . . . so . . . so beneath her.

"I hardly think your neck apparel will come under scrutiny," she answered caustically. "They'll be too busy gawking at all our private possessions." She emphasized the word *private*.

"Now then, dear, we've been over this many times. You have to agree that opening parts of the house to the public is an absolute money-spinner—draws the tourists like flies. In fact, I believe we've got quite a gathering this afternoon," he said, trying to sound encouraging. "Three Americans, I believe. And you know what that means," he said rubbing his hands together vigorously. "It means bags of dosh for the souvenirs."

Olivia rolled her eyes heavenward. "Oh, this is beyond intolerable. I cannot do this Dickie. I can't! Daddy will be turning in his grave." She lifted a monogrammed handkerchief and dabbed her nose. "It is insufferable to have strangers wandering through the house, and those loud, gushing Americans—it's unbearable!"

"Those loud Americans," Dickie said, as he walked over to the dressing table, "are our bread and butter." He draped the cravats across one shoulder and placed his hands on the back of Olivia's chair. He leaned forward over her shoulders and looked at her reflection in the mirror.

"Those rich Americans are prepared to pay handsomely for their slice of culture, and we, my dear, are going to provide it for them. You are going to put on your best social smile and think about your title. Your part in this endeavor is crucial to the preservation of our inheritance. Booth Hall deserves to stay standing, Olivia. It is a Herculean task, I know, but we are the guardians of this place and we must do everything in our power to keep things going for the next generation."

Taken aback by the unusual resolve in her husband's voice, Olivia stared back, speechless and solemn faced, with her lips pinched into a thin line. He straightened and gave her a gentle pat of encouragement on one shoulder. He felt quite proud of his little speech.

"Right then, I think I'll go with the blue stripe," he said, pulling the cravats from his shoulder. Emboldened by Olivia's lack of venomous retort, he puffed out his chest and marched back towards his dressing room.

"Better hurry dear," he called. "Sun's nearly over the yardarm. Don't want to be late!"

FIFTEEN

Conrad arrived just after the clock above the mantelpiece in the drawing room chimed four. He wavered by the door for a moment and made a quick survey of the room. It was quite full, with about nine other people spread out on various seats.

His attention was immediately drawn to a corpulent, ruddy faced man, dressed neat and dapper in a blue blazer and tan slacks who was speaking in an authoritative, braying voice in the far corner of the room. Ah, that must be the Brigadier: Sir Richard Cranshawe Booth.

"This chair is quite unique. It is upholstered from the cloak worn by Charles I when he faced his executioner in 1649."

Every pair of eyes in the room gazed in rapt awe, hanging onto Dickie's every word, apart from a thin, stern looking woman who was perched, motionless, on the end of a chair by the fireplace. She sat stiffly upright with her head turned toward one of the large mullioned windows. She was obviously uninterested in Dickie's speech. She looked as if she had heard it a thousand times before. The glazed look in her eyes betrayed her boredom. Dressed in sumptuous tweed with two strands of pearls around her neck, her legs folded neatly to one side, hands placed one on top of the other in her lap, and a look of disdain written across her face; Conrad surmised that she had to be the Brigadier's wife. She reminded him of a bony, fragile bird that had not been fed properly.

"And this rather perky little object," Cranshawe Booth continued, pointing to a small wooden box on a shelf behind the chair, "was carved out of the very block upon which King Charles laid his neck, prior to his head being severed by the executioner's axe." He waved his hand across the top of the box in a practiced fashion and then stood aside to let the audience have a better view.

"Ahhhh." came the collective gasp from around the room.

"That is awesome!" boomed a loud Texas drawl from across the room. A tall thickset man with a Stetson resting on his lap turned to an overly tanned, buxom woman at his side.

"Mary Lou did you hear that? A real, gen-u-ine piece of history. Hot-diggety-dog! Wait 'till I tell the folks back home." He made a loud "whoop" and slapped both hands on his thighs. His wife, sharing his delight, shouted, "Oh, they'll be tickled pink! Are we allowed to take pictures? A group shot of us all would be just dandy," she added.

"Well, I rather think that . . . " Dickie shot a quick look at his wife. Her face remained frozen except for an almost imperceptible widening of her eyes. They conveyed an unmistakable look of alarm. In very timely fashion, she reached for a small brass bell that was on top of a small table at her side and rang it with unusual vigor.

"Time for tea!" she shrilled.

"Ah, saved by the bell," Dickie quipped, thankful for the diversion from what could have been an incredibly awkward situation. He knew how agonizing it was for Olivia to endure these social gatherings with the public, but having photographs taken with them as well, was beyond her limits, simply out of the question. He puffed out his cheeks and blew a sigh of relief.

"Time for a little sustenance I think," he announced jovially, rubbing his hands together. He was starving. His clandestine meeting with Celia had sapped him of energy, and the meager lunch he shared with Olivia was barely enough to feed a mouse. The effects of the Scotch he consumed at lunch had worn off, and his empty stomach grumbled in complaint. He strode to the fireplace and took a seat next to his wife. He crossed his legs and looked towards the door in anticipation of the food's arrival. His eye immediately caught sight of a tall blond, impeccably dressed, dashingly handsome young man standing in the doorway.

"Ah, we have another guest, he announced jovially. "Do please come in. There are plenty of seats," he said, sweeping his hand across the room. "You're just in time for tea."

Seizing the opportunity to introduce himself, Conrad strode confidently toward Dickie with an outstretched hand. "Thank you. I'm Conrad Rankin. I'm pleased to meet you, Sir Richard."

Conrad's boldness caught Dickie by surprise. Most visitors, unsure of the proper social etiquette in the presence of a member of Britain's upper class, generally displayed a nervous deference in his company, so he was quite startled when this young stranger had the nerve to seize his hand in such a vigorous handshake.

"Ah . . . didn't quite catch the name old boy," said Dickie slowly. The name seemed to ring a bell in the deep recesses of is brain, but he could not recollect where he had heard it. His eyes swept across the young man in front of him, taking in the expensive attire and the impressive watch.

"Rankin, did you say? Hmm . . . Rankin, Rankin." He repeated the name slowly, eyes narrowed in concentration. He tapped the fingers of his right hand against his chin.

"That's right," said Conrad, turning towards Olivia. He inclined his head in a polite bow.

"How do you do, my Lady? What a delightful home you have. The leather wall coverings in the foyer—are they Cordovan? I haven't had the chance to take a close look at them, but I'd say from a glance that they look very similar to the ones acquired by mother on one of her visits to Spain."

He knew from the way her eyebrows arched upward that he had struck the right chord. He surmised that impeccable manners, a little namedropping and a hint or two about his wealth, without being too gauche, would be sufficient to chip away at her social barrier. The taut skin around her mouth seemed to relax a little and a tiny glimmer of curiosity shone for a brief moment in her eyes. He noticed her eyes linger briefly on his Armani shirt.

"Really? Well, I'm sure that my husband, Sir Richard, can arrange for you to take a closer look Mr. Rankin. After tea perhaps," she said, enunciating her words in polished Queen's English. She had obviously noted his American accent.

"And what brings you to this part of the world, Mr. Rankin? A spot of business perhaps," enquired Dickie.

"Business of sorts," Conrad replied. He lowered his eyes and hesitated before continuing. "I'm in Yorkshire to tie up a few loose ends following the death of my mother. She was killed in a car accident outside of Knaresborough a few weeks ago."

"Dear God!" Dickie bellowed. "Rankin! That's it! Knew I'd heard the name before. Yes, it's all coming back to me. Dreadful business . . . plastered all over the news." He remembered the accounts of the Rankin woman's enormous wealth. Well, well. Could be a stroke of good luck to have her son stay here; it might be a relationship worth fostering—certainly no harm in a little courteous banter. These thoughts raced through Dickie's mind.

"I'll get Wilfred to fetch you a chair. You must sit by us. I absolutely insist. Where *is* that fellow when I need him?" he bellowed.

The sound of a serving trolley rattling across the uneven wooden floor announced the arrival of the afternoon tea.

"Ah, here he is!" Dickie announced. "Wilfred, fetch this gentleman a chair would you. Over here by the fireplace," he instructed, pointing vaguely to the empty space by the side of his own seat.

Conrad turned his head to look in Wilfred's direction. The transformation from the scruffy old gardener he had met outside in the courtyard to the starched appearance of the butler before him was quite astonishing. Wilfred's thin hair was swept back and slicked to the sides of his head in a severe middle part, while his freshly shaved chin was held in an awkwardly upright manner, forced into a locked position by the high, stiff white collar of his uniform. Seemingly oblivious to Dickie's request, he continued to push the laden trolley toward the middle of the room. The fine china teacups, saucers and plates clinked and rattled, drawing everyone's attention.

"Wilfred!" Dickie shouted. "WILFRED!"

Startled to hear his name, Wilfred came to an abrupt halt, sending the side plates on the top tier of the trolley teetering towards its edge.

A collective gasp echoed around the room when one of them fell to the ground with a loud clatter. It fell onto its side and rolled several feet until it came to a standstill, miraculously unharmed, beneath the Texan's chair.

"Whoa!" The Texan boomed from his seat by the window. He reached down and gingerly lifted the plate from the floor beneath his chair. "That was close. Nearly a tidy hole in your bank account Duchess, uh . . . I mean my lady . . . uh."

A sharp dig to the ribs from his wife interrupted him.

"It's my ladyship,' she hissed loudly.

"Actually, it's my lady," interrupted a stout, middle-aged, matronly woman. She was sitting on a chaise long on the other side of the room.

"The wife of a baronet is addressed as 'lady' prefixed to their surnames only, but they can, indeed, be called 'my lady.'" She lifted her chin importantly and glanced around to see whether anyone else had heard her. She was gratified to see that most eyes in the room were looking in her direction. A retired history teacher in a private all-girl boarding school for the best part of thirty years, Margaret Pendleton spent her time and her savings visiting Britain's stately homes. Booth Hall was a poor relative compared to some of the finer homes she had stayed in, but the appeal of its resident ghost was too enticing to give the place a miss.

"Well, thank you kindly for the correction, ma'am. I'm mighty grateful. Well, like I was saying, your uh, my lady," he continued, turning in his chair to face Olivia. "It looks like mighty fine china to me. Probably worth a tidy part of one of my oilfields," he quipped, laughing at his own humor.

"And a baronet, such as Sir Richard," interrupted Ms. Pendleton again, "is never addressed as 'my lord.' One has to be a member of the peerage for that." She paused for a brief moment and looked around the room. Satisfied that she had everyone's attention, she raised her voice even more and said with great authority, "A baronet's style of address is quite distinct from that of a peer. In Sir Richard's case, it is Sir Richard Cranshawe Booth of Wickham, as opposed to Richard, Lord Wickham."

Silence. The tension in the room rose palpably. Dickie's face reddened, and a small muscle in his cheek began to throb with indignation.

Olivia managed to maintain perfect composure, her social smile barely shifted, but Conrad knew from the way her shoulders stiffened, that she was mortified by Ms. Pendleton's tactless remarks. The public in general had no idea about the pecking order among the British aristocracy. Having attention brought to the Cranshawe Booth's lowly precedence in the hierarchy, was quite shocking. However, for Conrad, it provided a marvelous opportunity to curry some favor with the Cranshawe Booths. Before Ms. Pendleton had the chance to say another word, he diverted everyone's attention by striding across the room to the Texan.

"Here, please let me take that for you," he said, indicating the plate. "I think this belongs over here." He turned to Wilfred who was standing, rooted to the spot in the middle of the room, and placed the plate back on top of the serving trolley.

"Here we are, no harm done, and please, don't bother with the chair; I can just grab this one." He lifted a small, silk-upholstered chair from its place by the bookshelf and carried it over to the empty space at Dickie's side. At that moment, Mrs. Cavendish shuffled through the doorway pushing another serving trolley laden with the afternoon's refreshments.

"Well, I'm famished. It must be this fresh country air," said Conrad conversationally.

"Quite so," answered Dickie, a look of relief on his face.

A pleasant buzz of conversation filled the room as Wilfred and Millie circulated among the guests serving Earl Grey and a selection of finely cut sandwiches, crusts removed, and delectable fresh cream pastries delivered that afternoon from Hammond's bakery in Wickham. The topics of conversation remained innocuous enough, confined mainly to a discussion on the merits of The National Trust, the largest private society devoted to heritage preservation in the United Kingdom, and the English Heritage, the government run equivalent. Several loud exclamations from the Texan and his wife, who were unable to contain their effusive admiration for all things old and historic, drew stern looks of disapproval from Olivia. She abhorred brashness of any kind. Whoops and hollers should be confined to sporting events only; used anywhere else, especially at high tea with a baronet and his wife, was in her eyes, an obvious indicator of poor breeding. She almost choked on a tiny slice of *mille feuille* when she saw how the Texan stab at his food, as if he were wielding a dagger rather than a delicate, polished, silver dessert fork. Bad table manners simply appalled her. She lifted her chin a little higher and by some miracle, managed to maintain perfect composure when Mary Lou asked if she were ever resentful of having people visit the house.

Eager for the ordeal to be over, she discreetly lifted the edge of her blouse sleeve with one finger and glanced at the slim gold Cartier watch on her wrist, an heirloom left by a distant relative. Dear God, it's only 4:30, she thought, wincing inwardly at the anticipation of another half hour of torture. Determined to avoid having to answer any more embarrassing questions from the guests, she turned to Dickie who was engaged in conversation with the young, blond American about the history of the Hall, a subject she knew her husband would be all too delighted to discuss. She watched the two of them as Dickie described some of the more interesting features of the hall, and was pleasantly surprised by the young man's correct social etiquette. His responses were courteous, yet incisive and confident. She had not expected such good manners and intelligence from someone so young, and from an American too. How refreshing, she pondered, and he was undeniably handsome. Yes, there was something mildly interesting about him that piqued her curiosity.

"A sad reflection of the times,'" lamented Dickie. "Most visitors nowadays, especially the youth, are more interested in anecdotes and gossip about the occupying family, than the architecture or art. People don't come to see the treasures anymore; they just want to hear the stories."

"Your housekeeper, Mrs. Cavendish," Conrad nodded towards Millie as he spoke, "mentioned your resident ghost."

"Ah, yes, the *Grey Lady*. I suppose we should be thankful for her. You cannot beat a good haunting. Draws the tourists in like flies to a dung heap. The number of visitors to the Hall has damned well nearly trebled since her recent flurry of activity."

"Recent flurry?"

"Not a peep out of the Baroness for the best part of four centuries and then, by jingo, out of the blue, there have been six sightings in the space of two years. Quite remarkable—seen her myself, you know. Up in the East Wing. Scared me half to death. Set the old ticker pounding, I can tell you," Dickie said, patting his chest vigorously.

"Has the *Grey Lady* been seen elsewhere in the house apart from the East Wing, Sir Richard?" enquired Ms. Pendleton who had been eavesdropping on Dickie's conversation with Conrad. "And is there a particular time of night when she appears?"

Secretly delighted that Ms. Pendleton had asked the question loudly enough so that most people could hear, Dickie seized the opportunity to address the whole room. He excused himself to Conrad and Olivia, then stood up and walked over to a small painting hung on a wall by the bookcase on the far side of the room.

"Over here," he announced loudly, "is a portrait of the *Grey Lady* herself, painted in 1698." Everyone in the room turned to look in his direction.

He then proceeded to engage a rapt audience, regaling them with stories, vastly exaggerated, of Booth Hall's greatest attraction. Dickie's delivery was masterful, full of witty anecdotes and a good sprinkling of supernatural drama. It was well rehearsed and pitched with just the right enthusiasm to captivate everyone's attention. All of his guests were secretly enthralled with the idea of a chance encounter with the deceased Baroness Montague.

Away from the others, in their chairs by the fireplace, Olivia and Conrad were obliged to converse with each other. Olivia began by offering her condolences to Conrad. Without shifting position, she inclined her head to one side and whispered discreetly, "I'm terribly sorry to hear about your mother Mr. Rankin. It must have come as a dreadful shock. Were you close?"

"I barely knew her," he replied bluntly. "It will probably be the biggest regret of my life." He looked her at her directly, catching her off guard. "Do you have any children?"

"No, Mr. Rankin." She stared back at him. For the briefest moment, he saw a deep sadness in her eyes. She swallowed before whispering,

"My greatest regret." She lowered her gaze and looked away toward the window.

Conrad knew instinctively, that for a fleeting instant, he had stepped across the invisible barrier that existed between them. It seemed almost natural then to reveal a little about himself. He gave her a brief insight into his upbringing, painting for her a picture of privilege and wealth, a background to which she could easily relate.

When she turned to look at him, the hardness in her face had vanished and was replaced by an unmistakable flash of emotion in her green eyes. She was about to say something when Wilfred appeared at her side.

"Ahem." He bent from the waist and whispered into her ear. "There are two policemen at the entrance my lady." He remembered to address her in the manner she insisted upon when guests were present. "They are asking to speak to Master Dick . . . er, I mean sir Richard."

"What on earth for?"

"They declined to say, my lady."

"Well, you'd better show them into the library. Tell them Sir Richard will be with them momentarily."

SIXTEEN

Wilfred invited the two policemen into the library, making a good show of pretense that he was hard of hearing.

"Nice place," muttered Detective Tom Collins once they were left alone. He strode over to one of the bookcases that lined three of the four walls and peered at the titles of the books. On the outer wall, a pair of narrow mullioned windows framed by heavy damask draperies graced either side of an unlit fireplace. A dim, grey light filtered through them, painting the room a dull monochrome. The air in the room belonged to a previous century, stale and lifeless with a heavy aroma of furniture polish. Heavy drops of rain pattered against the panes, adding to the somber atmosphere.

Detective Sergeant Patterson remained in the middle of the room for a moment, sniffing the air. "Christ, it smells old in here. When does this place date back to?"

"Huh? Not sure: Sixteen, seventeen hundreds, I think," mumbled Collins, lifting his head from the book he was leafing through.

Patterson took a quick glance around and wandered over to the large reading desk in one corner. Without touching anything, he let his eyes roam across the top of the desk to a pile of neatly stacked "Horse and Hound" magazines. He hated anything even remotely equine. He made a dismissive snort and turned his attention to a shallow drawer underneath the desk. He pulled on it tentatively and was pleasantly surprised when it slid open. Inside were some loose papers, mostly unpaid bills from the look of them. He was about to lift one up and take a closer look, when he heard loud footsteps approaching. He quickly pushed the drawer shut and walked back to the front of the desk just as a tall, portly man with a ruddy complexion, burst through the door.

"Now then gentleman, what can I do for you?" Brigadier Cranshawe Booth asked. His accent was gratingly posh.

"Brigadier Cranshawe Booth?" enquired Patterson.

"That's correct," the Brigadier replied cautiously, slipping both his hands into the pockets of his sports jacket in an attempt to appear casual and unconcerned.

"I am Detective Sergeant Maurice Patterson from the Metropolitan Police, and this," he nodded towards his colleague, "is Detective Tom Collins." They both held out their identification. The Brigadier stiffened immediately. His eyes widened and his eyebrows arched upward.

"Really? Now what brings Scotland Yard to these parts?" he asked, surprised.

Without telling Cranshawe Booth too much, Patterson explained that they had been on the trail of someone who was possibly involved in a recent art theft from a gallery in Harrogate. It was known that the suspect had driven through Tipping around 10:00 a.m., and it had been reported that several items had fallen out of the car as it passed through the village. Naturally, the police were interested in talking with anyone who had been in the vicinity. They were especially interested in retrieving the things that had fallen from the car.

A look of alarm flashed briefly in the Brigadier's eyes. He took his hands out of his pockets and looked nervously toward the door, as if he feared their conversation might be overheard.

"Why don't we take a seat over here by the desk?" he said quickly, steering them to the other side of the room. "Can I offer you gentlemen a drink?" he asked as he strode over to the bookcase behind the desk and opened a cabinet that was concealed behind a row of books.

"Secret stash," he winked at them. He reached inside the cabinet and produced three crystal tumblers and a half empty bottle of Old Grouse.

Patterson and Collins looked at each other. A silent exchange passed between them before they sat down in front of the desk. The Brigadier's sudden nervousness had not gone unnoticed.

"Not at the moment, thank you," said Patterson. His expression remained blank.

"Ah, not whilst on duty, eh?"

The Brigadier poured himself a generous measure of neat Scotch and then walked to the large leather chair behind the desk.

After a quick gulp, he leaned back in the chair and brought the fingertips of both hands together to form a pyramid. "Art theft, eh? Hmm. I take it that one would be safe to assume that something rather valuable must have been taken for Scotland Yard to be involved," he said ponderously . . . "Or could it be that the suspect might lead you to a far bigger cache?"

"Mrs. Wiggins from the post office said that she saw your car driving through the village at about 10:00 a.m. this morning," Patterson said flatly. He was not going to be drawn into conversation about the case.

"Ten o'clock this morning, eh? Ah yes," the Brigadier responded with a nervous smile. He took another gulp of the Scotch. His eyes flickered toward the door again. "Yes," he paused for an instant, "That's right," he continued, his mind racing. "Nearly had a head on collision. Some idiot coming the other way overtook another car and nearly drove straight into me. Next thing I know, I'm driving through a maelstrom of loose paper. Litter all over the road. Looked like something had fallen off the back of a lorry."

"And did you stop, sir?" asked Collins politely.

"Yes, I did. Nearly hit the bloody wall!" His face began to redden. "I was temporarily blinded by papers all over the windshield. I could have been killed!"

"Can you give a description of the cars?"

"One black, one white, I think. No idea of the make for either. All I can say is that the white one was in front. It was a smallish car, and it was the black one that nearly hit me. Both driving at breakneck speed I might add."

"What did you do when you stopped?" Patterson looked the Brigadier in the eye.

"Well, I checked my car for damage and I looked around to see if anyone had seen what had happened. There was no one around, so I simply got back in the car and drove off."

"Did you look at any of the papers or anything else that was in the road?"

"No, I did not. As far as I was concerned, it was just rubbish. It looked like a lot of newspapers and general litter to me. It never occurred to me that it might have fallen from either car."

"So you picked nothing up?"

"Absolutely not."

"What about the paper on your windshield?"

"I ripped it off and tossed it to the ground. I'm not about to go rummaging through garbage at the side of the road, am I," he said indignantly.

"Did you see anyone else nearby?"

"No, as I've already said, there was no one around."

Patterson exchanged a glance with Collins. "Is there anything else you can remember about the incident, anything you think might be of importance?"

"Can't think of anything," replied the Brigadier in a measured tone. He shook his head. "No, I can't say that I recall anything else."

"Right then. I think that's about all, Sir Richard," said Patterson getting up from his seat. "At least for now," he added. He looked at Collins and said, "Collins here can take a few details down later if you've no objection. It's standard procedure to get a verbal statement from anyone who was in the vicinity."

"Do you mean here at the house?" asked the Brigadier uncertainly. Both Collins and the Brigadier got up from their seats at the same time.

"Yes. It will save you the bother of having to come into a police station. First, though, I believe you have a Mr. Conrad Rankin as one of your hotel guests. We would like a quick word with him. We could talk to him in here if it doesn't inconvenience you," said Patterson. He flashed the Brigadier a quick smile. "Rankin?" The Brigadier sounded surprised.

"Yes, I've just met the fellow." He was about to say something else but then seemed to think the better of it.

"Right," he said, making his way toward the door. "I'll have Wilfred fetch him for you. How long do you expect this business to take? We're in the middle of high tea you see, for our guests. I'll have to jolly them along if I'm needed in the next fifteen minutes or so," he said as he looked down at his watch.

"I'm sure we won't be too long, but please don't hurry your guests. We'll let your butler know when Detective Collins is ready for you," said Patterson in a tone that indicated there was really no other option.

Instead of going straight back to the drawing room to relieve Olivia from the torture of having to host high tea on her own, Dickie sped down the hall in the opposite direction, pausing once when he thought he heard the sound of footsteps. He stood still and listened. Nothing. He turned his head and looked back down the corridor. Satisfied that the coast was clear, he continued on tiptoe until he reached a display case containing two 17th century muskets. He darted to one side of the cabinet and pressed his back up against the wood paneled wall. Hurriedly, feeling with his fingertips, he located two notches on either side of the panel, and then, with a sharp thrust from his ample bottom, the panel swung open to reveal a hidden passageway. After one last, hasty look around, Dickie ducked down and stepped backwards unseen, into the concealed opening.

Crouched uncomfortably in the cramped, dark passage, he frantically patted the pockets of his blazer in search of his cigarette lighter. Bent in such an awkward position, he had to squirm around in order to fit a hand inside his jacket that was stretched tight, almost to bursting point across his chest. He could feel the dampened armpits of his shirt chafing against his skin, adding to a mounting discomfort. Just as his knees were about to give way, he managed to wrench the lighter free. "Thank God. Damned, confounded thing," he muttered. He flicked it several times, cursing every loud click. When it burst into flame, it illuminated a narrow, low-ceilinged passageway that stretched about twenty feet before opening into a small oblong room.

He scurried forward as quietly as possible, bent double, holding the lighter in front of him. When he reached the oak paneled room at the end of the passageway, he straightened up as far as he could. He was two inches taller than the height of the ceiling. He reached for an old oil lantern that was hanging from a row of pegs on one of the walls. He placed it on a small wooden table and after several feverish attempts with his lighter in the stale, musty air of the chamber, the wick finally lit, casting a pool of flickering light so feeble, it barely lit the corners of the room.

There was little in the chamber apart from the table, two chairs and a small wooden cabinet pushed up against one of the walls. On top of the cabinet was a white coiffed wig, a mirror with a long ivory handle and several pots of white face powder and rouge. Hanging on the wall in the darkness, hidden in Dickie's shadow, was a grey silk dress and crinoline.

Eight feet by sixteen, the room had been used as a former hiding place for fugitive Cavaliers during the Civil Wars of the 17th century. It was not uncommon for the castles and country houses of England to have some precaution in the event of an unwelcome surprise, such as a secret means of concealment or escape that could be used at a moment's notice. Hiding places known as *priest holes* were built into many of the principal Roman Catholic houses during the reign of Queen Elizabeth 1 when stringent anti-Catholic penal laws were in force. Persecuted priests could seek refuge, and sacred vessels, vestments and altar furniture could be stored in secret. Later, during the civil wars, the *priest holes* were mainly used to store arms and ammunition, and also for concealing adherents of the luckless House of Stuart.

Booth Hall's secret chamber had its own share of tales to tell. A favorite story of Dickie's was that of Captain James Fitz-Waller, a gallant Cavalier captain, who, after narrowly escaping from the battlefield of Marston Moor in 1644, sped homeward with some of Cromwell's soldiers on his heels. His wife, a lady of great courage, had barely concealed him in the secret hiding place when the enemy arrived to search the house. Finding his horse still saddled, they concluded that the rider was hiding somewhere in the house. They searched the premises minutely for four days, but left empty handed. Fitz-Waller managed to survive to live another day, but thanks only to one of his devoted servants, who at great personal risk, paid nocturnal visits to bring him food and water.

At the moment, Fitz-Waller's exploits were the furthest thing from Dickie's mind. Adrenaline coursed through his body as he fought to control the muddle of thoughts that swept through his brain. He had been completely caught off guard when the police asked him about his whereabouts that morning. Before he managed to stammer any kind of response, his mind had been swirling with the terrifying thought that if he was not careful Olivia was going to find out about Celia. His first instinct was to lie to the police and tell them, as he had told Olivia, that he had been in Wickham all morning, but then the Wiggins woman from the post office had already told them she saw him driving through the village. If Olivia found out he was anywhere near Tipping, which is in the opposite direction from Booth Hall, he knew he would be in for one of her grand inquisitions. Dear God. His life would not be worth living if Olivia found out about Celia. She would skin him alive, leave what was left to the wolves, and then take off with the remains of her trust fund. And the artwork, that scrap of paper he had discarded as a piece of worthless litter—the painting that Celia had seen.

What if it turned out to be what the police were looking for? No, surely not. The chance of it being a piece of valuable art was simply ridiculous. The odds were absurd. And he had sat on it. No, there was no point mentioning it to the police. It would only encourage them to dig further. He would have been forced out to the garages to fetch it from his car. The longer they were on the premises, the more likely they were to come into contact with Olivia. No, it was a far better idea to get rid of them as soon as possible. Given a choice, he would have preferred to give them a statement at the police station. That way, Olivia need never know about it. But he had been put on the spot and practically forced by that Scotland Yard fellow to do it here. And what did they want with young Rankin? What connection did he have to this whole business? Well, there was only one thing for it—he was jolly well going to find out.

Conscious of the fact that he had very little time, Dickie flung his blazer onto the table and crept as quickly as he could to the wall at the back of the room. He dropped to his knees, each one cracking loudly, and then, without making another sound, slid onto the floor on his stomach. For the second time that day, he felt winded, out of shape, and alarmed at the way his heart was pounding. Again, he made a mental note to stop putting off his annual physical.

He took a long, deep breath and willed himself to calm down. Very slowly and very carefully, he lifted a small, hinged flap from the bottom of the paneling and pressed his ear to the opening. On the other side of the flap was a space of about six inches that separated the chamber from what appeared to be a heating vent at the bottom of one of the book-lined walls in the library. As he let out his breath in one long, silent exhalation, he settled in to eavesdrop on the conversation that was taking place on the other side of the wall.

SEVENTEEN

Conrad's reaction was one of trepidation mixed with relief when he was told that the police wished to speak with him. He was surprised they had waited this long. He had half expected them to arrive at his hotel yesterday evening, but perhaps it was better this way. He had been given enough time to get information from Jeremy and to discover that Parks had left the Turners at the gallery after all. Nonetheless, he was still no nearer to an explanation of his mother's involvement. Perhaps this talk with the police would provide some answers. But first, he needed clear his mind and decide how he was going to play this.

As he followed Wilfred to the library, he contemplated how much he should say. He was well aware that the police had probably been watching him since his arrival in England, so he had to be prepared for the fact that they already knew he had been into the gallery in Harrogate and spoken to Jeremy. Denying any of this would be a mistake and it would only cast suspicion on himself.

He decided to hold off on the whole truth and say nothing about Jeremy 's confession or the Turner concealed on the top of the four poster bed in his room until he had a better idea of where the police were going with the case. His best course of action for now would be to play innocent and tell them that the reason for his visit was purely personal. He had come for some kind of closure on his mother's death, which was true in part, and speaking to Jeremy, who was possibly one of the last people to see her alive, was a part of that journey. He reasoned that he would need to be cautious about what he said concerning Jeremy, because it was likely that the police had already spoken to Jeremy first. The police were bound to have questioned Jeremy about why Conrad had wanted to see him, and although he had prepped Jeremy on what to say, he knew that the kid was a frightened, emotional wreck and could not be entirely dependable. He was acutely conscious of the fact that he was taking a huge risk in relying on Jeremy to keep his mouth shut.

When Conrad entered the library, the shorter and older of the two policemen was sitting behind a large desk in the far corner of the room. His tie was not quite straight, as if he had pulled it from side to side trying to loosen it from his neck. The dark circles under his eyes and the weathered look of his face suggested too many hours on the job and not enough sleep. He did not create a formidable first impression.

However, Conrad was under no illusions about the importance of this first meeting. As soon as the man behind the desk introduced himself as Detective Sergeant Patterson of the Arts and Antiques division of the Metropolitan Police, and his colleague as Detective Collins, also from the Met., Conrad knew that he was not dealing with some local, two-bit, inexperienced constables. Scotland Yard meant serious business. Although, Patterson looked like a harmless old bulldog, and Collins a slick city boy, better suited as a banker than a policeman, Conrad was well aware that appearances could be deceptive.

Patterson was the first to speak, half rising from his chair as Conrad walked into the room. He offered Conrad a seat in front of the desk, while Detective Collins remained standing by one of the book-lined walls in a position where Conrad, once seated, did not quite have a full view of him. It was an arrangement that was unnerving and undoubtedly intentional.

"I think you probably know what this is about, Mr. Rankin," said Patterson with a forced smile, "so we can keep this brief and get straight to the point. First of all, I'd like to extend our condolences about your mother. It was a shocking accident."

"Thank you," Conrad replied with a smile and courteous nod at Collins and then Patterson. He sat down, crossed his legs casually and waited for Patterson to continue.

"Our business here is twofold. We're interviewing anyone who was in the village of Tipping this morning around 10:00 a.m. following an incident there. And this incident is also part of a much wider investigation concerning the disappearance of some artwork." His face was expressionless, but his eyes were hard and unsmiling. Conrad quickly revised his initial impression of Detective Sergeant Patterson. His outward demeanor was genial enough, but Conrad sensed a hidden danger in that soft exterior.

"Ah—right," said Conrad, thinking quickly. They obviously knew all about him, so there was no point denying chasing Jeremy through the village that morning.

"I take it you won't mind answering a few questions," said Patterson.

"Not at all," Conrad replied. His mind was working overtime. He reminded himself to stay calm and come across as open and candid with nothing to hide.

"How much is this art worth?" he asked innocently.

Patterson took his time to answer. He leaned back in his chair and considered Conrad through narrowed eyes. "They're worth a great deal—valuable enough for a passionate collector to go to any lengths to acquire them."

"I take it you know of J.M.W. Turner," said Collins. "Have you ever heard of his "Yorkshire Collection"?"

"Yes, of course I've heard of Turner, but I'm not familiar with his Yorkshire Collection. Why?"

Collins gave a carefully edited account of the missing art.

Fear fluttered for a moment in Conrad's belly. He could feel a dangerous undercurrent in the conversation.

"This sounds serious," he said smiling, trying not to look too concerned. "Do I need an attorney?"

"I don't know Mr. Rankin. Do you think you need one?" was Patterson's blunt reply.

"No, no," Conrad laughed quietly. He looked from Patterson to Collins and back again. "There's no need. I'm afraid there's really not much I can tell you. So far, my visit has been disappointing."

"Really?" said Patterson. "And why is that?"

Conrad raised his blue eyes to meet Patterson's hard stare. He knew he had to speak with ease, that Patterson was watching his face like a hawk, waiting for any sign of weakness. It was critical to give just enough information, anything that could be verified, without saying too much and digging himself into a hole.

He paused, trying to find appropriate words to convey the nature of his visit to Yorkshire. "I came because of my mother," he began. He told them of his need to find out more about what she had been doing in the days leading up to her death. Shocked and angry by the media's insinuations of her affair with the art dealer Julian Parks, he felt compelled to ask a few questions and talk to the people who saw her last.

"So the first place I went was the Bryce-Edwards Gallery in Harrogate."

"Why the Bryce-Edwards Gallery?" asked Patterson.

"Because of the message left on my mother's cell phone," replied Conrad, smoothly.

"Ah, yes, the cell phone," said Patterson in a measured tone.

In that instant, it occurred to Conrad that it was perhaps just a little too fortuitous that the phone had been returned to him. Wouldn't the police have kept the phone for evidence if they truly suspected her of some wrongdoing? He wondered then if the message had been used as a bait, to lure him to England and lead them to the missing art. He was aware of Patterson asking another question but another, far more disturbing thought struck him. What if the police thought he had been in collusion with his mother right from the start?

"And did you find any answers there?" asked Patterson.

"Ah no," Conrad hesitated for a moment. He rubbed his forehead, trying to clear his thoughts. Patterson sat still waiting for Conrad's response.

"It was disappointing. I spoke to Bryce Edwards, but he was in London at the time my mother was in Harrogate. He never saw her."

Without taking his eyes from Conrad's face, Patterson leaned back in his chair and crossed his legs.

"Let's just go back to the message left on your mother's cell phone for a minute," interjected Collins from across the room. He slid the book he had been leafing through back in its place on the shelf, and walked casually over to the other chair in front of the desk.

"Can you recall the entire content of the message, Mr. Rankin?"

"Yes. It was from Julian Parks. He left a message to say that he had left something for my mother in the safe at Bryce-Edwards. He referred to it as their 'little secret.'"

"A secret?" Collins's eyes widened. "Does that mean anything to you, Mr. Rankin?"

"I had no clue at all when I first heard the message. I knew my mother dabbled in art, but I had no idea that her collections were so extensive—absolutely no idea. I was shocked and I still am," he said truthfully. "Bryce-Edwards filled me in on all the details. He told me about the Turners and how the police suspect that Parks acquired them illegally on behalf of my mother, but I have no knowledge of any of this. My mother didn't need to resort to crime Detective Sergeant. I refuse to believe it. She was wealthy enough to buy anything she wanted, and besides which, she didn't have it in her to do anything illegal. I mean why would she? Bryce Edwards said much the same thing about Parks. He had no clue there was anything going on between Parks and my mother and he can't believe that Parks would do anything outside of the law. He said that it's totally out of character for him." He shrugged his shoulders and continued. "Apparently, the only person in the gallery when Parks called round before the accident, was Jeremy Danvers, a friend of Bryce-Edward's son who was helping out in the gallery for a few weeks."

"Did you speak to Danvers in the gallery?"

"Briefly, but only for a moment when I arrived. By the time I finished talking to Bryce-Edwards, he had already left."

"And did you see him again?"

"Yes, by sheer coincidence, outside a gas station. I was heading for my hotel, The Crown, when I saw him on the other side of the road. I drove over. I didn't see any harm in talking to him, but as soon he saw me, the kid freaked out. He drove off before I could ask him anything. He was clearly terrified when he saw me."

"Any idea why?"

"Not at the time, but I do now."

"Ah, we'll get to that in a minute. So how did you come into contact with him again?"

"After he drove off, I checked in at the hotel for the night. I left this morning, early, around 7:00 a.m. I couldn't sleep—jet lag. It was a beautiful morning, so I decided to drive to the scene of the accident. I needed to go back there. I'm not sure why." He sighed and looked down at his hands. "And then I took a drive through the Dales."

"Yes," said Collins sympathetically. "We understand. It's been a difficult time for you." He exchanged a quick look with Patterson before continuing.

"So how did you come into contact with Danvers again?" he coaxed gently.

"On the road to Craggsdale Moor. I pulled into a lay-by to look at the view. I couldn't believe it when I saw Danvers coming up the hill behind me. Incredible! I mean, what were the chances of that?" He paused, waiting for their reaction.

"Yes, quite a stroke of luck," said Patterson. He gave Conrad a thin smile of encouragement.

"I waved for him to stop, but the kid floored the accelerator and took off up the hill. I suppose I should have just left it at that, but he clearly had some reason to run from me. It was obvious he was hiding something. I thought he would slow down if he saw me behind him, but well," he laughed and held both hands up in mock surrender, "I guess I was wrong about that. I know, I know. I shouldn't have followed him. I don't know what I was thinking. It was stupid of me."

"Yes, well the constabulary in Tipping received more than one report about two speeding cars this morning, Mr. Rankin. Luckily for you, the people who complained were unable to see the registration plate numbers, otherwise you would be charged with driving at excessive speed and probably a few more misdemeanors on top of that," said Patterson. "You could have caused serious injury to others and to yourself."

Conrad shook his head slowly from side to side. "I know. I'm sorry. I've been under a lot of strain. I lost my father four years ago and now my mother. There's not much family left, no siblings, no one close. I just feel, well, I feel confused. This whole business, this Julian Parks thing with my mother, and these allegations of some kind of subterfuge – I just can't get my head around it. I cannot believe my mother would get herself involved in something like this." He brought both hands up to his head and dragged them down the sides of his face with a loud sigh. "I don't know what to think anymore."

"As you drove through Tipping, did you see anything fall from Danver's car?" Patterson asked undeterred.

"Yes, the rear door of his car flew open and some stuff fell out. Something hit my front fender, but I don't know what it was."

"Whereabouts were you when the things fell out? Were you through the village? Any landmarks that you can remember?"

"No, I'm not sure. Things happened too fast. It was in the village. There were some buildings on one side of the road."

"So some articles fell out of the car Jeremy Danvers was driving. What happened next?"

"I followed him towards a town a few miles away. Wickham, I think. I lost him for about fifteen, maybe twenty minutes on the way, and then I found him again in the town, in a large parking lot near the street market."

"Hmm. In a large parking lot in the town center? Whereabouts did you lose sight of him?"

"Jeez, I'm not sure—he turned down a small farm road just outside of the village. An old guy . . . he told me his name, but I can't remember it. Hmm, it'll come back to me in a minute. Well, this old guy told me that the farm road led straight into the central parking lot in Wickham and that I'd be better off taking the main road, following the signs for parking and heading him off."

Patterson scribbled something down in the folder and then asked, "So was he in the car when you spotted him in the car park?"

"No. I'm not sure what he was doing. I saw him sprint toward the bathrooms, but then he stopped halfway and ran back to his car. He leaped straight in and drove back to Tipping. I followed him, but this time I hung back out of sight. When I reached the village, he was already out of his car. I found him sitting in a field opposite the post office."

"Sitting in a field?" Collins asked, puzzled. "What was he doing?"

"He had his head in his hands and he was crying. He tried to run off again as soon as he saw me. The kid thought I was some kind of villain out to kill him!" Conrad laughed and shook his head. "He thought the mafia or some crime syndicate sent me to force a confession out of him about the Turners, and then kill him before he could give any information to the police. Bryce Edwards is the one who put that ridiculous idea into his head. The kid swears blind that Parks left nothing at the gallery and he never saw my mother. He's running because he thinks the police are convinced he's lying. The kid's a wreck—scared to death."

"You sound as if you think Danvers is telling the truth."

"The kid knows nothing. You're barking up the wrong tree if you think he's got anything to do with this."

"So why the panic to find the stuff that fell out of his car?" asked Patterson.

Conrad shrugged. "Who knows? To find his license maybe, or his college papers, whatever. I don't know. He was freaking out about finding all his notes and bits of paper. A little strange, I suppose, but then the kid's an oddball. I helped pick up a few things for him, notes, a few clippings, that kind of thing. But no paintings and definitely no Turners."

"But why even bother helping him?" Collins asked. Conrad shrugged his shoulders.

"I don't know. I guess I felt sorry for him."

Patterson leaned back in his chair, interlocked the fingers of both hands and brought them up to his mouth. He tapped his hands gently against his lips. Collins looked on steadily, giving nothing away.

"Hmm. So how were things left between the two of you?"

"What do you mean?"

"Will there be any further contact?"

"No," said Conrad emphatically. A puzzled look crossed his face.

"Why should there be?"

Patterson didn't reply straight away. He glanced down at the folder in front of him and appeared to read for a moment. Without lifting his head to look at Conrad, he said, "I believe you too, have a passion for collecting Mr. Rankin." It was a statement rather than a question.

"Ah, let's see here," he continued, reading from the folder. "Impressive coin and stamp collections and you own a car museum in Plymouth, Massachusetts, with over forty vintage cars." He raised his head and looked at Conrad through narrowed eyes. "That's quite a collection," he said.

"Yes, it is. I see the police have done their homework," said Conrad with a weak smile. He could feel the atmosphere in the room deteriorating rapidly. The implication in Patterson's voice was obvious. There was the hidden insinuation that he, like his mother, might go to any lengths to add to a collection.

"What else do you collect Mr. Rankin?"

"Books, maps, furniture, porcelain, armor, one or two rare pieces of Hollywood memorabilia."

"But no art."

"No."

"So, let me just get this straight," said Patterson. "Your mother amassed a fortune in art and you didn't know about it."

"No, I didn't say that. I knew she had some very valuable pieces, but I wasn't aware of the extent of her collections."

"Now, why am I having a difficult time believing that? Patterson's eyes were cold and hard. "And you don't collect fine art yourself?"

Conrad's jaw tightened. Anger flashed for a second in his eyes. When he spoke, his voice was tinged with resentment.

"My father never cared much for art. In fact, I'd say he hated most of the pieces my mother had on display. I think he tolerated them to keep the peace. I hated them too." He paused for a moment and took a deep breath. "She didn't share much about herself. We weren't close. I can honestly say that I barely knew her."

Patterson studied Conrad's face in silence.

"Will that be all?" Conrad asked.

Paterson glanced at Collins, gave him a curt nod and said, "Yes, I think that's it for now Mr. Rankin. Do you have a number where we can reach you if something comes up? Ah, Tom here will take it down." He motioned to Collins who was already reaching inside his jacket for a notebook.

"How long will you be staying in Yorkshire?" Collins asked.

"A few days probably. Tonight, possibly tomorrow. I don't have any firm plans. As I'm sure you already know, I fly back to Boston on Monday," Conrad said with renewed humor. He gave his cell phone number to Collins, then stood up and turned toward the door.

"My card," said Patterson, handing it to Conrad. "Call me if anything comes up. Any time of day."

"Thank you, I will." Conrad smiled and pocketed the card. "And good luck. I hope you find them."

EIGHTEEN

Conrad's first inclination was to dash back to his room, grab the painting and hide it as far away as possible from the Montague suite in the East Wing, but he decided it was more prudent to remain calm and walk in a leisurely manner back to the drawing room to see if high tea was still in progress. It was safer to wait until the police had left before finding a better place to stash the Turner. He needed to quell the knot of fear that was rising in his stomach, and act as if nothing were wrong.

Patterson had made no hint that the police were about to search the premises, so he reasoned there was still time to try and corner Cranshawe Booth about the events that happened outside the post office that morning. A little monetary enticement should be enough to lure Cranshawe Booth into a private conversation. An offer to purchase a few of Booth Hall's antiques was likely to appeal to a near bankrupt Baronet, especially if that offer was generous.

He did not walk straight into the room, but paused in the doorway and took a look around. As far as he could see, all the other guests were still there, but he was disappointed that Cranshawe Booth was nowhere to be seen. Lady Cranshawe Booth had apparently been abandoned to entertain on her own, and judging by the strained expression on her face, she was not pleased. Ms. Pendleton, who was talking loudly about the merits of other stately homes she had recently visited, had her trapped beside the fireplace. Olivia's feigned interest in Ms. Pendleton's dialogue was achieved by the occasional raising of an eyebrow or by a demure nod of her head, but the pain Conrad saw in her eyes when she looked up was unmistakable. Her breeding and impeccable manners made it impossible to escape. It was a matter of putting on a brave face, grinning and bearing it, and enduring the agony until five o'clock on the dot.

"Ah, Mr. Rankin!" Olivia announced as soon as she saw him, not quite able to disguise her relief. "You've come back to us. Do let Wilfred pour you a fresh cup of tea, and you simply must have a pastry. I absolutely insist."

She turned to Ms. Pendleton and smiled apologetically. "If you'll excuse me, I really ought to do the rounds and see to my other guests. It has been a pleasure to speak with you." Olivia uncrossed her legs and walked briskly across the room to where Conrad was standing by the door. She seemed genuinely pleased to see him.

"Wilfred," she called. "WILFRED!" She motioned with a wave of her fingers, to the butler who was standing at attention by the serving trolley. "Tea for Mr. Rankin, please."

She turned to Conrad and quietly said , "I trust the police were not harbingers of bad news Mr. Rankin?"

"No, no. Just a minor misunderstanding," he paused, "about the circumstances surrounding my mother's death. There are a few," he hesitated, "ah, loose ends."

"I see." She looked into his eyes and raised her eyebrows expectantly in the hope he would say more, but he remained silent, unwilling to be drawn on the subject.

"Well," she replied through a thin smile, "I can vouch for the Mille Feuille, a most delicate pastry, as light as a feather – my favorite." She averted her eyes and waved vaguely in the direction of the serving trolley. Scrumptious," she added, trying to sound jolly and light-hearted, but Conrad noticed the catch of disappointment in her voice.

He turned to look at her and was about to apologize for sounding so mysterious when she glanced at her wristwatch and exclaimed, "Goodness, its nearly five already!" "How time flies. Well, I'm afraid I shall have to excuse myself." She inclined her head towards him and, "It's been a pleasure to meet you Mr. Rankin. Good afternoon."

"The pleasure is all mine." Conrad smiled down at her. "Although, I'm going to delay you a little longer. I have a confession to make. I'm not here solely for leisure. I had hoped to meet with your husband in private, to discuss a little—ah . . . 'business'."

"Regarding what exactly?" she asked with a look of surprise.

"Let's just say I have an appreciation for the finer things in life, particularly the rarities of this world. He lowered his voice and leaned toward her, as if he were sharing a secret. "I suspect Booth Hall has a few treasures of its own – the Cordovan leather panels for instance. I'd love the chance to persuade you and your husband to part with them."

A look of disappointment spread across her face.

"Ah, you too," she said wearily. "I should have guessed." She straightened her shoulders and sighed. "Well, Sir Richard is a busy man, but there's a possibility he might find some free time tomorrow. I'll let him know of your interest and Wilfred can inform you later if my husband has an opening." Her tone was clipped, and any trace of the warmth he had detected in their earlier conversation had vanished.

"Now I really must call this gathering to an end," she said, turning away from him. She walked into the center of the room, cleared her throat and announced in a practiced fashion: "Thank you all for coming this afternoon. It's been a delight, as always. Please do enjoy the rest of your stay at Booth Hall and hopefully you will visit us again soon." She paused for a moment, forced a smile, and swept out of the room.

Conrad watched her fragile figure retreat toward a pair of heavy, oak-paneled doors at the end of a long hallway. A thick red rope held between two steel stanchions cordoned off the doors. In the middle of the rope, a sign hung that read: "PRIVATE". He could tell by the way she stalked away from the drawing room with her shoulders rigid and her fists clenched, that he had upset her. He had obviously touched upon a very sensitive subject, and her reaction suggested that things were far worse at Booth Hall than he had imagined. He smiled. Good. The harder up they are, the better for me. He thought about the little escritoire in his room and imagined it in a nook of the study in his Manhattan apartment. Yes, it would go very nicely.

He watched as she unhooked one end of the rope, stepped through to the other side and then re-hooked the clip. She unlatched one of the doors and leaned against it with her shoulder, using her body weight to push it open. With a loud creak, as if it were objecting to performing the task, it opened just wide enough to afford Conrad a brief glimpse of a baby grand piano and an arrangement of fine furnishings in the brightly lit room beyond. Intrigued by the private sections of the Hall and curious to know what lay within them, Conrad could not resist stealing a glance, but he was forced to look away when Olivia turned to push the door shut. He did not want to be caught staring after her, but there was the briefest of moments, a split second when their gaze met, and even though they were at a distance, he thought he could discern tears in her eyes. In that instant, he felt sorry for her, and for some unfathomable reason it bothered him that he had made her cry. A surprising realization struck him—he actually quite liked Olivia Cranshawe Booth.

"Humph! The pastries served at Chatsworth are far superior. Have you visited Derbyshire yet, Mr. Rankin?" A loud voice barked at his side, startling him.

"Ah, Ms. Pendleton," he said, reeling around to face her. "I didn't see you. I'm sorry. Where, did you say?"

"Derbyshire. Much underrated you know, but in my opinion, it is home to some of the finest Halls in this country, and, I might add, the most spectacular scenery. Take the Peak District for example . . . "

"I'm so sorry Ms. Pendleton," Conrad said quickly, interrupting her. "I would love to continue this conversation, but," he glanced at his wristwatch, "I'm going to have to go up to my room. I'm expecting a phone call you see—in the next few minutes, so if you'll excuse me." He turned and walked briskly down the hallway before she had time to respond.

He passed the library on his right and turned into another hallway lined with dark portraits. He hurried on past a large faded tapestry and a glass topped display case containing some interesting Civil War relics, but he did not dare linger in case Ms. Pendleton was following behind. He did not stop until he reached a suit of armor set to one side of the wide sweeping staircase in the capacious entrance foyer. With a backward glance over his shoulder, he was relieved to see that the hallway behind him was empty. Ms. Pendleton must have gone back into the drawing room to harangue some other hapless victim.

Conrad leaned back against the stair banister and breathed a quiet sigh of relief. He felt exhausted. Weary from jet lag and tense after being questioned by the police, he needed to get back to his room, remove the Turner from the canopy of his bed, and hide it somewhere else in the Hall. And he needed to do it quickly. It was just a question of where. Conrad strained his ears to listen for the sound of someone coming, but apart from the ticking of a grandfather clock by the door and some muffled clinking from deep within the recesses of the building, all was quiet.

Several rooms led off the foyer; only two of them open for public viewing. One was a small reading room, dark and poky with deep sofas and an unlit fire in a big stone fireplace. Antique wall sconces with fringed puce shades hung on the walls. A selection of magazines was fanned out on several coffee tables – *Yorkshire Life* and *Fox and Hounds*. Conrad imagined the room with a roaring fire and warm lights, cozy and inviting, but in the gloom of this late afternoon, it seemed cold and dreary. A stag's head mounted above the fireplace added to the general lack of appeal. Conrad could feel its eyes on him, fixed and cold.

He shuddered and moved down the hallway to an elegant dining room cordoned off by a thick red rope held between two gold stanchions. The two carved oak doors were propped open, allowing visitors a full view of the interior. The center of the room was dominated by an expansive, highly polished table laden with what appeared to be fine china. He entered the room and lifted a side plate to examine the markings on the back – Royal Doulton. "Nice, very nice," he whispered, and carefully placed the plate back into its setting.

He looked from one side of the room to the other and slowly made his way to the solitary window framed by heavy chintz curtains. It looked out onto the gardens at the rear of the Hall, offering a view of verdant lawn and overflowing flowerbeds. He took a quick peek through the window. Although the rain had stopped, the sky remained heavy and grey. A small gap in the blanket of clouds allowed a swath of sunshine to spill over the landscape. For a brief moment the gardens shone and sparkled as if exposed to the flash from a camera. But the burst of light was gone within seconds, and the gloom returned even darker than before.

Conrad hated the rain, it depressed him. With a sigh, he turned away from the window and walked to the large ornately carved dresser against the wall to his right. He looked inside the cupboards at the bottom and pulled open several drawers containing various pieces of dinnerware and napkins. Most of the drawers were only half full with plenty of room at the back to hide the painting if he rolled it up. It was just a matter of sneaking back down from his room and hiding it in the drawer without being seen.

He stood up to leave, but could not help noticing the magnificent oil painting depicting what he supposed was a typical English country scene, above the fireplace on the opposite side of the room. It looked tarnished and in need of restoration. He wondered whether it was valuable. He racked his brain for the names of renowned English landscape artists, and to his frustration, he could only come up with two: Constable and Gainsborough. This gaping hole in his education bothered him enormously. It was a void he intended to fill as soon as he had the time.

Still mulling over his lack of art knowledge, he crept out of the dining room into the entrance foyer and quickly made his way up to his room in the east wing. Barely pausing for breath, he lifted the Turner from its hiding place, rolled it up carefully and placed it inside his shirt, down one side against his waist so it was not conspicuous. He then darted back down the stairs and into the dining room where he hurriedly concealed the painting between a pile of cloth napkins at the back of a drawer in the large dresser. In his haste, he did not notice the figure lurking in the dark shadow beneath the stairs.

NINETEEN

Dickie tapped the keyboard with one hyper-extended finger at a time and spelled out the name T-u-r-n-e-r.

"What *are* you doing?" Olivia snapped as she walked into the study catching Dickie by surprise. Startled, he leaped up in his chair and stammered, "Ah, Olivia darling! You surprised me dear. I was just coming to find you."

"Yes, it looks like it!" she snorted sarcastically. "Where *have* you been? Wilfred's been looking all over for you. And what on *earth* did the police want?"

"Ah, one minute dear. I'll just close this thing down." He stabbed at a few random keys until the computer screen went blank. "There, I think that'll do it," he muttered. He hovered in an awkward position behind the desk, halfway between standing and sitting. Both hands were spread on the edge of the desk, supporting the weight of his body.

"Well, what did they want?" she demanded "It was Rankin they were after," he said, thinking fast. "They wanted to know when he checked in and how long he was staying—that sort of thing. Something about speeding through the village I think," he said vaguely.

"Well, they certainly kept you long enough," she said suspiciously. "Speeding? Is that all?"

"Well, that and some other business about his mother's accident. They were interested in the Hall, so I gave them a little lesson in history," he said with a nervous smile.

"I see," she said in a caustic, disapproving voice, in a way that meant she did not *see* at all. "He did not mention a word of it to me when he returned for tea."

She rubbed both her temples with extended fingers and announced, "Well, I need to lie down. I've got a splitting headache. It's been a frightful afternoon . . . " She paused for effect. ". . . having to cope on my own. He—Mr. Rankin, seems to have an eye for our Cordovan leather paneling, and no doubt, anything else of value he can get his hands on. He wants to meet you in private to discuss a 'little business,' whatever that entails. His words, not mine. I said you would let him know this evening, one way or the other."

"Ah, really. Well, well," said Dickie with renewed interest.

"Right," she snapped, clearly angry with him. "Well I can't stand here another minute. I've got to get off my feet before I collapse."

She threw him a withering look and made to leave the room, but stopped as another thought came into her head. "Oh yes. I knew there was something else. Wilfred says the boiler's acting up again." She waited for Dickie to respond, but he remained silent, glued to his spot behind the desk. "God only knows how we're going to pay for the repairs. I suppose you'll flog off my jewelry next, what little there is left." She fingered the necklace around her neck. "I'm quite sure Mr. Rankin would be interested; he couldn't take his eyes off my pearls." She narrowed her eyes and looked at Dickie in disgust. "Right then. I'm leaving. Tell Millie not to wake me for dinner. I think it's one of my migraines." She turned and stalked out of the room with short little stabbing strides.

Dickie's thoughts swung between momentary elation when he heard about Conrad Rankin's interest in some of the Hall's antiquities, to deep despair when Olivia mentioned the boiler. As soon as Olivia left the room, he collapsed into the chair and swept both hands through his hair.

"Whatever bloody next," he swore under his breath. He felt sick to the pit of his stomach at the thought of how much it was going to cost to replace the boiler. They could barely afford the next week's food bill let alone maintain the upkeep of a house that literally ate money. God knows, he thought sadly, how hard I have tried to save this place.

He walked to the window and looked out on the rain-swept land-scape, tracing the long sweeping drive that was once lined with ancient elms, to a point where it disappeared into the drizzle. A painful knot of sadness wrenched at his gut when he recalled the day his father announced that the elms were too far gone with disease and would have to be felled. The day the first tree was hacked to the ground, it was as if the death toll for the Hall had sounded.

His mind drifted back to the cost-saving measures and schemes his father had invented to try to raise cash and save the Hall. From the seminars he had organized in the stables when they still had the horses, to the training sessions in the drawing room. The Land Rover conventions in the courtyard, the wedding receptions, and even an art festival one year—all of them to no avail. When Dickie inherited the estate, he was faced with crippling, almost insurmountable debt. He had few other options. He had already taken advantage of government subsidies, grants and tax exemptions. He was forced to sell off most of the land. Unfortunately, soaring costs, particularly escalating energy costs, drove him to consider measures that were even more stringent. The temptation to sell off the remainder of the Hall's contents had been almost overwhelming. But in a last ditch effort to save the estate, as an absolute last resort, he came up with a ridiculous, but ingenious plan to attract visitors and their cash.

Nothing drew in the crowds better than a resident ghost, especially one that was as accommodating as the late Baroness Montague. With a recent flurry of up to thrice yearly sightings, the Baroness, or the *Grey Lady*, by virtue of her shimmering grey crinoline, was fast becoming one of northern England's most active specters.

Interest in Booth hall doubled and then trebled after the first few apparitions. To accommodate the rush of visitors eager to hear about the haunting, part of the Hall was opened for public access. This included bed and breakfast accommodations, a small souvenir shop, and the opportunity to have high tea on a bi-monthly basis with Sir Richard and his wife. Although the extra revenue brought in by the *Grey Lady* was lucrative, it was like a small drop in the ocean when compared to the enormity of debts and expenses.

The influx of tourist dollars bought only a temporary reprieve, enough to stave off the creditors for a few more months. The inevitable was just around the corner. Dickie knew that it was only a matter of time before he ran out of options and, rather than be faced with bankruptcy, he would be forced to bequeath everything he owned to the National Trust.

There was some small recompense in that. At least they could still continue to live in a tiny section of the hall, but they would be nothing more than custodians, "common renters" as Olivia so eloquently put it. And, as part of the bargain, they would be required to guarantee public access to literally the whole estate, the very thing that Olivia abhorred the most. And their heritage! The bloodline. What of those things? There were no children—only Booth Hall. It was everything. He shook his head in despair. He leaned forward with his elbow against the window and looked down at his feet. He stood motionless for several minutes, lost in deep thought. All of a sudden, he balled his hand into a fist and hit it against the pane of glass.

"Booth Hall is everything I have, and I'll be damned if I go down without a fight!" he hissed through clenched teeth. He vowed there and then, that he would take a shotgun to his head rather than face the embarrassment and humiliation of being a washed-up failure.

"Desperate times require desperate measures," he whispered to himself.

A fledgling plan had begun to take root at the back of his mind. It was a dirty, loathsome train of thought that pricked painfully at his conscience, but he had run out of ideas. He told himself that it was too late to hide behind pride and morals. He kept thinking about the conversation he had overheard between the police and Conrad Rankin. The notion that some art work, worth millions possibly, priceless even, might still be lying by the roadside within a few miles of where he was now standing, was simply incredulous.

He had nearly died right on the spot when he realized the drawing he had wrenched from Celia's hands and tossed into the front of his car might be one of the Turners they were seeking. He had told Patterson and Collins that he had not picked anything up from the road, which was the truth. The drawing had quite simply wafted itself into his car. A slight omission admittedly, but not exactly a crime.

When he overheard the price tag of the artwork, his first impulse was to dash out to the garages and find the drawing in his car, but he reasoned that it would be a foolish risk to take while the police were still on the premises. Instead, he managed to restrain his impatience and decided to remain with his ear up against the grate, and listen in to the rest of what Conrad Rankin had to say.

Rankin did a good job in portraying himself to the police as a self deprecating, honest individual, still in mourning, who had perhaps over-stepped the mark in his pursuit of Jeremy Danvers as a way of finding some closure to the death of his poor, deceased mother, but Dickie was not fooled for one minute. He knew a liar and a braggart when he saw one. He disliked Rankin from the moment he set eyes on him. It was the way he had the nerve to strut across the drawing room without a proper introduction and then shake hands as if they were fast friends. The young upstart, throwing his money around, trying to buy his way into society.

The police had not witnessed how perilously close Rankin had been driving behind Jeremy Danvers, or how fast the two cars had been going. Thinking back to the incident that morning, it was obvious to Dickie that Rankin was trying to force Danvers off the road, to stop the boy from getting away. Very peculiar behavior for a man who just wanted a "chat" about his poor, deceased mother. No, thought Dickie, I am not buying any of it. He decided there was a lot more to Conrad Rankin than met the eye. As far as Dickie was concerned, Rankin's real agenda was getting hold of the Turners by using the death of his mother as a ruse to hide behind. It was a convenient excuse for some of his recent "lack of judgement." Dickie thought it was obvious that the Turners had to be a lot more valuable than the police cared to divulge. And now Rankin wants an audience with me to talk business. Well, how very interesting—most fortuitous. It was as if the dear Lord were at last smiling down upon him and had delivered a timely glimmer of hope. Don't screw up now, Dickie old boy. Handled properly, this whole business might be the miracle you've been praying for.

He turned away from the window and walked over to the fireplace. The unlit, empty hearth stared back at him, cold, black and lifeless; a bleak reminder that it was going to be an impossible winter without the boiler. He stood for several minutes, staring into the empty hearth, dissecting what Rankin had said to the police.

He could not imagine what a local youth like Jeremy Danvers had to do with all this. Dickie did not actually know the young fellow, but he was on nodding terms with the boy's mother, Philippa Danvers who was chairwoman of Tipping's Local Heritage Committee. He seemed to remember her being introduced to him when he attended some local function or other to grant permission for hikers to cross a portion of his land. Quite a strapping filly if he remembered correctly. She was mildly attractive in a masculine sort of way. Not really his type. He preferred a more nubile, fleshy kind of woman. For a brief moment, his mind strayed to an image of Celia's wholesome figure, which caused a comforting surge of warmth to his groin, but he was not in the mood to think of his mistress. He shook his head vigorously and turned his thoughts back to the conversation he had overheard between the police and Rankin.

He remembered that Rankin had said that he helped the boy pick up some things from the field opposite the post office, but he had insisted to the police that the Turners were nowhere to be seen.

"My left foot!" said Dickie aloud. He did not believe Rankin for one second. If anyone other than the Danvers boy had the chance of finding the Turners, then it was Rankin. But where could he have stashed them? It was unlikely he would still have them in his car. Nobody could be that stupid. So where else? Maybe Danvers has them. But no, if Rankin wanted them so much then he would not want them out of his sight, which meant there was a good chance he still had them, perhaps hidden in his room.

He felt a tingle of excitement mixed with fear, in anticipation of what he was about to do next. Since Olivia was safely out of the way with her migraine, and the police were off the premises, he was going to sneak out to the car, retrieve the painting, and hide the precious little beauty in the priest hole. If his instincts told him the work had the feel of authenticity, he would put off meeting Rankin until the following morning. Instead, he would wait until Rankin left the Hall later that evening for dinner, and then search his room. If he were lucky enough to find more of the artwork, his plan was to confront Rankin in the morning with the discovery and threaten to tell the police.

Without doubt, he was taking an enormous gamble. Everything depended upon how far Rankin was prepared to go to get his hands on the Turners. But if his guess was correct, then the two of them might be able to come to a little private, mutual—*arrangement*. He did not care why Rankin wanted the Turners. He really did not give a damn. But from what he had gleaned from the conversation between Rankin and the police, and from what he read about Claudia Rankin in the newspapers, it was quite clear that Conrad Rankin could easily afford to part with some of his vast fortune to pay for Dickie to keep his mouth shut. The word *blackmail* popped into Dickie's mind, but he pushed the vulgar thought to one side. He resolutely refused to allow himself to think of the legal or moral implications of his plan. If he did, he would never be able to go through with it. He told himself that this was not a seedy arrangement conducted by some desperate criminal. This was more of a gentleman's agreement, a little business enterprise from which they both stood to benefit. Quite how he was going to approach Rankin, he had no idea. He would think about that later.

He glanced up at the clock over the mantelpiece and strode over to the desk where he picked up the phone and dialed the kitchen, hoping to catch Millie still cleaning up after high tea. He waited several moments, cursing under his breath, when someone finally picked up at the other end "Millie? MILLIE?" he said angrily." Yes, yes, it's me. Mr. Rankin, our American guest, has he made arrangements to go out for dinner this evening?" He tapped his fingers impatiently against the surface of the desk, waiting for her response.

"Uh-huh . . . uh-huh. Excellent! The Three Bees, eh? What time is his reservation? What was that? 8 o'clock. Good, good. Oh, and Millie, if there are any of those little pastries left, the ones with the icing, you can pop them into the study for me. Just leave them on the desk . . . NO! No, it's quite all right. No need to disturb her ladyship. Thank you Millie."

He replaced the telephone receiver and then rubbed his hands together vigorously.

"Well, time for action Dickie old boy," he said to himself. He took a deep breath, puffed out his chest and strode confidently toward the door. On tiptoe, he crept past the bedrooms, down the main staircase, through the entrance hall, down the main hall and out through a small door tucked away at the rear of the building leading to the garages.

TWENTY

Instead of taking the direct route, Pearl turned left outside the post office and walked straight down the main road to Cherry Lane where Barrington lived. She took the winding, circuitous path through the quieter parts of the village, hoping she would not be seen. She walked as fast as she could so that her pace was almost a march. Every now and then, when she reached the corner of a building or the concealment of a large tree, she stopped for a few moments to catch her breath and check the path behind to make sure she was not being followed.

After the visit from George, the village constable and that smug young detective from Scotland Yard, her first instinct was to rip the artwork to shreds and burn it on the fire in her parlor, but something pricked at the back of her conscience. She just could not bring herself to destroy something so valuable. Instead, over another soothing cup of tea, she decided on a different plan. She would return the pieces to Jeremy using Barrington to do it unwittingly for her, and, if all went well, she would be finished with the whole affair.

Her plan was straightforward. She would ask Barrington to deliver a package to Jeremy when he next went to tend to the Danvers' garden. If Barrington asked any awkward questions, she would tell him that Barry Boswell, the local postman had dropped the package off at her post office because it was too large to fit in the Danvers' little mail box set in the wall outside their house. Pearl had a standing arrangement with many of the villagers whereby she would hold on to packages that could not be delivered in the ordinary way, thus sparing them the inconvenience of driving all the way to the main post office in Wickham.

She would tell Barrington that when Jeremy called in at the post office that morning, she had forgotten to give him the package, so it would be a great favor to her if Barrington could drop it off and save her the bother. She did not think for one minute that he would take a peek inside the brown paper she used to wrap the work. There was no reason for him to do so, and even if he did, he would have no clue of its value. Besides, Barrington could barely see beyond the end of his nose. It was a wonder he was still allowed to drive.

The only real difficulty with her plan was getting to Barrington's without being seen. The last thing she wanted was to come face to face with nosey neighbors who would be dying to know why she was not in the post office. The thought of being bombarded with their endless prying questions nearly put her off stepping through the door; but she had no alternative. She was terrified the police might pay her a second visit with a search warrant and catch her red-handed with the missing art. And she knew what would happen then. She would be thrown in jail for Lord knows how long. She cringed when she thought of what she had done to the painting. And why on Earth did she lie to the police? May the Lord have mercy on her soul.

The sooner she got rid of the painting, the better. Let Jeremy deal with it. If he asked how the painting was damaged, she would deny knowing anything about it. If he was in as much trouble as it appeared, then he ought to be jolly grateful for getting any of the work back at all.

No matter how hard she tried, she could not get her head around the idea of Jeremy being caught up in something as serious as major art theft. It just did not ring true about what she knew about him. She had known the lad since he was in nappies for goodness sake. That boy did not have a mean bone in his body. The police had it all wrong. There must be some terrible mistake.

She recalled the occasion years ago, when that young boy, no more than ten years old, had come into her post office with a ten-pound note in his outstretched hand, asking if anyone had lost some money. He said he had found it wedged behind the empty milk bottles on the step outside. As far as Pearl was concerned, any other young whippersnapper would have pocketed the money or spent it on sweets, but not young Jeremy. She had given him a bag of Licorice-Allsorts as a reward, and a free sherbet every time he visited the store. She did not give two hoots about what that hoity-toity detective said about him. In Pearl's mind, Jeremy Danvers was a good honest boy.

By the time Pearl reached the alleyway behind the fish and chip shop, she was beginning to have second thoughts about her plan. She was tempted to throw the art into the stream and be done with it. She so wanted to turn around and scurry back to the store before anyone discovered she had hung up the closed sign. Getting to Barrington's without running into half of the village residents was proving to be far from easy.

She already had a close encounter with Candice from the beauty parlor. Bumping into her, of all people, would have been fatal. The entire village would have known within the hour that Pearl Wiggins had done something she had not done in a lifetime – closed the post office early. There would have been no escape from the bombardment of questions for days afterwards until every person in the village knew her business. Candice was particularly skilled in wheedling out even the most private information. It was fortunate for Pearl that a delivery van pulled up outside of Evan's pie shop just as Candice came teetering around the corner in her high heels. She must have nipped out on an errand between perms. Just in time, Pearl darted behind the van and waited in a crouched position until she heard the bell above the pie shop door signal that Candice had gone inside. As soon as she was sure the coast was clear, Pearl straightened her clothes, grabbed hold of the shopping bag and set off down the street again. She almost broke into a trot in an effort to reach the bins behind the chip shop before she saw anyone else.

Convinced the police were waiting for her around every corner, Pearl's heart skipped several beats when the rear door of the chip shop opened suddenly and Charlie Fenwick walked out for a quick smoke. He was one of the local lads who did a bit of part time work in the chippie. On the verge of panic, Pearl pretended not to see him and rushed past with her head down. The wheels of her shopping trolley made a terrific noise as they clattered over the cobblestones, but she did not look back until she reached Matlock's Haberdashery at the end of the alleyway.

Thankful for a chance to rest, Pearl shrank into a pool of shade at the end of the passageway. She leaned against the cool wall keeping one hand firmly on the handle of her shopping bag while frantically fanning her hot face with the other. Panting heavily, she kept her eyes fixed on the alleyway behind her, expecting someone to step out at any moment. But to her immense relief, the only sign of life was the noise of a few wasps buzzing about in the window box across the alley. A bead of perspiration trickled down her back. She pulled at the front of her blouse and wafted it back and forth to create a draught between her considerable cleavage.

In an effort to calm down and let her heart rate return to normal, Pearl stood in the shadows for another minute or so. She was well aware that she needed to hurry up and get out of sight, but she could not turn up on Barrington's doorstep looking a mess, all flustered and perspiring. With shaking hands, she fished out a powder compact from a small pocket on the front of the shopping bag, flipped it open and holding the tiny mirror at arm's length, made a quick appraisal of her appearance. After a few hasty repairs to her makeup, a dab of lipstick and a dusting of powder, she stepped out of the shade and crept around the corner of the Haberdashery, out past the children's playground and into Cherry Lane where Barrington lived at number 14. Apart from Irene Tattershall's Poodle barking at her from the upstairs window of number 6, Pearl was confident she had slipped by unnoticed.

* * *

Barrington was surprised when he heard someone knocking on his front door. He was a chaste, fastidious old bachelor who rarely had visitors. He was even more surprised when he opened the door and saw who was standing on his doorstep.

"Now then Barrington," said Pearl, brightly. "I have something here that I want you to pass on to young Jeremy Danvers when you next go over to his house."

She nodded at the tartan shopping bag on wheels by her side, waiting for Barrington to say something, but he remained silent, wide-eyed, rooted to the spot with his jaw dropped open.

"Well, I'll bring it in for you then shall I," she said, eager to get in off the street. After a quick glance up and down the lane to make sure no one else was around, Pearl stepped straight from the street into the tiny living room. Barrington shrank against the wall as Pearl brushed by him. By the time he staggered forward to shout his protest, Pearl was already making herself at home, plumping up the pillows of the threadbare sofa that was set against the back wall facing the window.

"What the . . . Now look 'ere," he stammered. "You can't come barging in when I've got . . . "

"Well, I hope you don't treat all your guests like this Barrington Smith," Pearl interrupted. "I'm here to ask you for a favor. I've a package here," she said, pointing at the shopping bag. "I forgot to give it to Jeremy when he came into the post office this morning. It's important he gets it right a . . . er well what I mean is . . . I thought you could drop it off when you next go round."

"What package? Why the 'eck can't you take it round yerself?" He lifted both hands in the air. "Or why doesn't that postman, what's-is name, Barry summat, why can't you give it to 'im to deliver?"

"Because. Well, because," she hesitated, caught off guard by the unexpected fuss he was making. "Because Barry's finished his rounds for today and its very important this gets to the right place," she said firmly. "Now aren't you going to shut that door and offer me a cup of tea?"

"Important? What the 'ecks going on woman?" Barrington shouted across the room. He shut the door with an angry push and shuffled towards Pearl.

"I'll not be able to say one word until I've had that cup of tea. I've come the long way round you know," she said, fanning her face again. "I'm spitting feathers and my feet are killing me." She bent forward to rub the back of her calves.

"But the lad's at university!"

"No he's not," she said quickly. "He's back in Tipping. He came into the store earlier on and he's . . . " Pearl hesitated, trying to find the right words. "Well, he's in some sort of, well what I mean is . . . " She looked around the room in exasperation. This was not going the way she expected. She looked up at Barrington who was standing with both hands folded across his chest waiting for an explanation.

"Oh Lord," she said with a loud sigh of resignation. She glanced out the window at the softness of the late afternoon and pondered how much she should tell him.

"Well," she said, "what I mean to say is that some things fell out of the back of his car as he was driving through the village this morning and . . . " She paused for a moment to think. ". . . and I happened to pick some of it up." She lifted her chin and nodded as if to confirm that she had done the right thing. "And now I want you to give it back to him," she added matter-of-factly. She looked away and pretended to pick at some fluff on the front of her blouse.

Confused, Barrington shook his head trying to make some sense of what on God's Green Earth Pearl Wiggins was trying to tell him. In exasperation, he bellowed, "Well why the 'eck can't you give it to him yerself?"

Barrington had always been a cantankerous so and so, but she had not expected him to be this prickly about doing one little favor for her. She was hoping he would be delighted to see her, but then she reasoned that men were strange creatures even at the best of times. He had been on his own for so long, he was probably feeling awkward about enter- taining a woman in his front parlor. But she had no doubts that he was secretly thrilled to have her there. He just needed a little gentle coaxing to admit it, that's all.

"Because it's complicated," she replied softly. "And it's just easier for you to do it."

She reached for the shopping bag, pulled it close to her legs and pat- ted the top with hyper-extended fingers. "What I've got is in here." She narrowed her eyes and continued in a whisper, "It seems the lad is in a spot of bother with the police. It's all a dreadful mistake if you ask me. That lad's not a criminal." She pressed her lips into a thin line and slowly shook her head from side to side. "I'm sure he'll explain it all if you ask him about it. For now though, you need to get this back to him safely.

He'll likely be fretting over it. Now, are you putting the kettle on or am I going to have to make the tea myself?" She folded her arms under her bosom and shot him an impatient look.

"Well?" she added. She shuffled her bottom further back on the settee and made another attempt to plump up the pillows. "Oh! What on earth have you got behind these cushions?" Her face screwed up in disapproval. "There's something behind here that's sticking straight into my spine!" she exclaimed.

She sat forward and reached behind the cushion.

"What's this? What the . . . " She rummaged behind her back and extracted several cans of stewed prunes. She held one up for Barrington to see and then swiveled in her seat to take a look underneath the settee.

"Wait a minute, I can't see from here," she muttered, struggling to her feet. She pulled the sofa away from the wall to reveal a stack of canned food crammed behind.

"Dear Lord," she gasped. You've got enough here to feed an army!"

"It's got nothing to do with you Pearl Wiggins," Barrington snapped. He snatched the cans of prunes off the seat and held them against his chest as he nudged the sofa back into place with his legs.

"It's none of your business what I choose to keep in mi own house!" "There's no 'arm in keeping a little put by in case of an emergency. You never know when there'll be another war!" he shouted, red in the face.

"But the war's been over for more than sixty years Barrington!"

Pearl clicked her tongue in disapproval as she surveyed the general disarray of Barrington's cottage. Piles of boxes and even more cans were stashed in each corner. Not an inch of surface of two side tables could be seen underneath the mass of old newspapers and books that were piled haphazardly on top. A battered old chair at the side of the fireplace facing the front door was lifted off one of its legs by the mound of papers and other objects that were stuffed underneath. Long tendrils of cobwebs trailed from the ceiling in the corners of the room, and the window looked as if it had not been cleaned for at least a decade.

"Oh dear, dear me," she said under her breath. It was a home that showed all the signs of a man living on his own for far too long. "This place looks like it hasn't seen a duster since 1945," she muttered, shaking her head slowly.

The wall behind the settee was covered with Barrington's reminders of the war. Rows of prints of wartime cartoons and military pictures, faded, dusty and curled at the edges, were stuck up next to a collection of framed photographs of people whose stern faces and clothing clearly dated them back to the first half of the previous century. On top of a small bookcase in the far corner of the room lay Barrington's war medals, proudly displayed in open silk-lined boxes so they were visible to anyone coming through the front door. The France and Germany Star, awarded to all who fought between June 6, 1944 and May 8, 1945, was set forward from the others, half in its box as if it had been recently lifted out and put back in a hurry. The weight of memories was almost palpable.

The cramped little parlor with its threadbare furniture and dusty memorabilia reinforced Pearl's conviction that Barrington was in dire need of a good woman to look after him. There was no doubt in Pearl's mind that with a little patience and a gentle approach, Barrington would soon succumb to her feminine charms.

She cast an appraising eye about the room to decide which pieces of furniture she would keep. She imagined how her glass-door cabinet would look against the wall at the side of the fireplace. The place was certainly no palace, but with a little elbow grease and the application of her outstanding housekeeping skills, a transformation was not beyond the realm of possibility.

Pearl's scrutiny was interrupted by Barrington's feeble, almost comical attempts to kick at a can of diced carrots that had escaped from its hiding place beneath the settee. To avoid bending down to retrieve it, Barrington tried to roll the can back into place with his foot, but he was hampered by a combination of diminishing eyesight and poor balance. After several swipes, he gave up and collapsed breathless onto the arm of the settee.

"Here let me help you lo . . . " She stopped mid-sentence and brought a hand up to her mouth. She wanted to giggle. She had almost said the word *love*. A surge of warmth brought a blush to her cheeks.

"Now don't go bothering tidying up; I'll get that for you."

With surprising agility for a woman of her size and age, not to mention the constraints of her corset, she bustled across the floor to Barrington's aid, sending the can back into its place beneath the settee with an impressive flick of her left ankle. Before he had the chance to mouth a string of profanities, Barrington was steered by a firm grasp of his elbow and shoved unceremoniously onto the sofa seat. He did not care one bit for being forcibly manhandled in his own home.

"Now you just sit down right here," Pearl ordered in her, no nonsense, mother hen, I am in command of the post office voice, "and I'll fetch the tea. I'll be back in a jiffy."

"But I don't want any bloody tea!" he shouted, pulling himself back on his feet. He almost fell back down again when he heard Pearl scream from the kitchen ten seconds later.

"What the 'ells goin' on," Barrington said when he reached the kitchen door.

He looked first at Pearl, who was standing against the back wall with her hands held up to her face, and then over at the kitchen sink, which was filled to overflowing with the unwashed debris of several meals. A massive tabby cat was busy licking at the remains of congealed bacon and sausage.

She lowered a shaking hand and pointed to the other side of the kitchen and said in a small voice, "That . . . "

"Ernie, you devil!" bellowed Barrington from the doorway. "Come 'ere you rascal."

He walked over to the sink, lifted the cat up and carried it to the back door. 'You're a little tinker, aren't you," he whispered fondly into its ear. "It's all this commotion. He's not used to it," Barrington said, shooting Pearl a withering look. "We like our peace and quiet don't we Ernie? Are you ready for a bit of dinner Ern?" He stroked the cat's back and gently placed its four paws onto the worn vinyl floor. Ernie arched upward and rubbed against Barrington's legs, a loud rumbling purr rose up from his furry ribcage.

Much like Barrington, the cat was getting on in years, losing its hair and going bald in places. Ernie was the latest in a long line of cats with the same name. They were named after his best friend, Ernie Bradshaw, who was killed in action during the first of the D- Day landings.

"No, no. Not the cat," said Pearl trembling. "That!" She walked over to Ernie's litter tray by the back door and bent down for a closer look.

"Oh my God!" she gasped, unable to tear her eyes away from the litter tray.

"Those . . . those, torn bits of paper . . . " she stammered. Both hands flew back up to the sides of her face again. She turned and looked up wide-eyed at Barrington. "Where on earth did you get it from," she paused and then continued—"The paper!"

"Eh?" Barrington replied.

He walked over to Pearl and peered over her shoulder at the contents of Ernie's litter tray. He had been in the middle of cleaning it out and lining it with strips of paper when Pearl appeared on his doorstep, unannounced. The remains of a sheet of paper with a little landscape painted on it lay by the side of the cat's tray.

"What are you talking about woman?" He looked at her as if she were barking mad. He reached for the painting next to the tray. He then turned to a wad of newspapers stacked underneath a cabinet near the sink and took hold of a piece of paper on the top.

"Do you mean these," he said waving the papers in front of Pearl's face. Their edges were torn and looked as if they had had been crumpled and then flattened out again. "I found 'em stuck under the windscreen wiper of mi car this mornin'. Litter all over the place these days—a damned disgrace. Anyway, I don't let anything go to waste. Mi old mam taught me that when there was rationing to be reckoned with. Ernie's not too fussy about what he does his business on. Are you Ern?" he said, turning to the cat.

Pearl took the remains of one of the paintings from his hands and carefully turned it the right way round. She studied it for a moment. An almost inaudible gasp escaped from her mouth as her bottom jaw dropped open.

"You'd better fetch me a chair Barrington," she whispered. "I've come over all light headed."

A few minutes later, after listening to Pearl's confession and her description of the day's events, Barrington answered with, "By 'eck, I think I'll put that kettle on after all."

They sat opposite one another at a tiny table squeezed into a corner of the kitchen. Barrington squinted through the thick lenses of his reading glasses at the four pieces of art that were spread across the top of the table.

"Ard to believe they're worth so much," he muttered. He bent his head closer to the watercolor Pearl had snipped and said, "How do you know they're the real thing? I mean they could be any old rubbish. They don't look any good to me."

He lifted his head and peered over the top of his glasses at Pearl who sniffled and fidgeted with a handkerchief in her hands.

"I'm only telling you what that detective told me – that one from Scotland Yard. 'They might be worth millions.' His very words," she said, sticking out her chin and nodding to emphasize her point. "And now look what we've gone and done to them," she added. She dabbed both her eyes with the corner of the handkerchief and blew her nose loudly.

"We'll be going to jail, you and me, for destroying priceless work," she said, stifling a sob.

She did not intend to tell Barrington anything, but when he showed her the remains of the painting he was about to shred for the cat's litter tray, she nearly fainted on the spot. She recognized the style of the work immediately, and was so taken aback that she blurted out everything that had happened, including her own confession about snipping the edges of the watercolor. The words just came tumbling out.

"Jail!" yelled Barrington. He pointed across the table and shook his finger at Pearl. "Me! I've done nothin' wrong! 'Ow the 'eck was I to know it was some precious paintin'! It's you who's goin' to prison, for takin' summat out of someone else's bag and then choppin' it up!"

"But I didn't know what it was either!" Pearl wailed. "Until the police said they fell out of Jeremy Danvers' car! I never in a million years thought I'd find some precious art just lying there on the road. If anyone's going to prison, it'll be that lad. And if you go and say anything to the police, then you'll be the one responsible for putting him there—you just mark my words, Barrington Smith!" She slapped the table with one hand to make her point.

Barrington drew back in his chair. He pulled the reading glasses onto the top of his head and began to stroke the stubble on his chin, thinking about what Pearl had just said.

"Hmm. What I can't figure out is what the lad was doing with these pictures anyway. How the 'eck did he come by 'em? I mean he couldn't have just walked into some fancy museum and stolen them, could he?"

"Well, there's only one way to find out, isn't there?" said Pearl. "We . . . I mean you, have to go over there and hear what he has to say. The sooner we get this stuff off our hands the better. Tell him we found it like this," she said, nodding towards the artwork. "He needn't know any different."

"The lad's always been a good 'un you know," said Barrington. "He's 'elped me more than a few times you know. Got me one of those cell-u-lar phones," he said slowly, pronouncing each syllable. "One of those mobiles, yer can carry round in yer pocket. I think I'll put that kettle on now. My brain works better over a cup of Yorkshire. I need to run a few things over in mi mind."

He stood up from the table and lifted a dented old kettle to the tap. "There's another thing mi mam used to tell me," he said, with his back to Pearl. "'Never look a gift horse in the mouth', she used to say, mean-ing, don't pass up an opportunity when it comes yer way." He placed the kettle on the front ring of the cook top and reached up to a small shelf above the cooker, feeling for the box of matches.

"Where are the blessed things," he muttered. "Oh . . . got 'em. Little buggers are always trying to 'ide from me." It took a number of matches and several attempts for Barrington to get the gas ring lit, but he eventu-ally managed to put the kettle on for tea. Pearl was tempted to get up and help him, but she sat tight and tried to make some sense out of what he had just said.

"Now—what was I saying?" Barrington asked as he sat back down in his chair. "Ah right" he said slowly. "I've come to a decision." He narrowed his eyes and leaned across the table toward Pearl. "We 'ave a special arrangement, Jeremy and me," he said. "I 'elp him and he 'elps me." He tapped the side of his nose with an index finger. Pearl looked at him suspiciously, not sure of what he was saying.

"G-o on . . . " she said.

"What I mean to say Pearl Wiggins, is that if I agree to 'elp you, then it's only right that you 'elp me isn't it?"

"Yes . . . I suppose so," she said cautiously. "Just what have you got in mind?"

"Well, if I tell thee summat, you've got to keep it to yerself, right?"

"Right," said Pearl, mystified. She leaned in closer.

"You've to swear to keep this to yerself . . ."

"Yes, yes," she urged, trying to keep the impatience out of her voice.

Barrington brought a finger to his lips and whispered, "Well, it's like this— I've got a problem with mi' PIN number."

"Oh, is that all?" Pearl answered, disappointed. "Why didn't you say? You're not the only one you know."

The old pension book, used by over 5 million pensioners in the U.K. had finally been abolished a few months before in April 2005 and had been replaced by a new, more efficient automated system, expected to save the Government over four million pounds. All pensioners had been encouraged to open up a bank account or a post office card account so their pensions could be paid direct.

"I 'aven't been able to get mi money for weeks now," Barrington complained. "I blame it all on the bloody government for sending out them new fangled cards to replace the pension book. How on earth am I meant to remember a PIN number at my time of life?"

"So, have you gone and forgotten it?"

"I got a letter in the mail warnin' in big red letters about not writing the number down or telling it to a single sole, but I ignored it."

"Right," said Pearl slowly. "So what's the problem?"

"Well, I copied the four digits down separately on the back of some photographs hung in the front room, but now I've gone and forgotten the order of the numbers. I've read through 'em countless times - 5371," he whispered. "And I've re-jiggled them this way and that, but no matter which way I key the damn things in, they just don't want to work."

They were interrupted by a loud rap on the front door that made them jump in their seats.

"Now who the 'ell can that be at this time of day?" Barrington asked.

He started to get up from his chair, but Pearl grabbed his arm and pulled him back down.

"What are you doing," she hissed. "You can't answer the door when we've got all this stuff here. She nodded at the artwork. "It could be the police! Keep quiet and don't do anything. They'll be gone in a minute."

"No, they'll see my car. They'll know I'm in."

Another loud rap on the door sent Pearl into a panic. She leaped from the chair and grabbed her shopping bag. "I can't be caught in here! I've got to get back to the post off . . . "

"Barrington!" A loud voice came from the front of the cottage. "Are you in there? Is everything all right?"

"Dear God! It's George Barlow!" Pearl exclaimed. Both hands flew up to her face. "What are we going to do?"

She ran to the back door and then to the table again. "The stuff! Quick, we've got to hide it!"

"Barrington. Barrington. Are you there? It's George." The village constable rapped on the front door again and then walked to the front window. He pressed his face to the window and brought both hands up to the pane to squint inside. He rapped lightly on the window and called out, "Barrington. It's George. I need to have a quick word with you."

"Huh!" Pearl threw Barrington a desperate look and lunged across the table making a grab for the artwork. "Where can I put it?" With the papers pressed against her chest, she ran to the cooker, then to the back door and to the table again. "Where can I put it, where?" She looked around the room frantically.

Barrington stood rooted to the spot, his head swiveling this way and that, trying to think of a good hiding place.

"Give 'em 'ere!" he hissed as Pearl bumped into him in the middle of the kitchen floor. "Stick 'em with these," he said, indicating the stack of newspapers by the door. "He'll never see 'em here." He grabbed the papers from Pearl and hurriedly shoved them under the pile.

"Quick, get out before he comes round the back! Get yer bag."
Barrington opened the back door and gave Pearl a push, launching her
into his tiny garden at the rear of the cottage. "You might 'ave to yank on
it a bit—the gate," he said, pointing with a shaking finger to the wooden
gate set into the wall. "Eight o'clock. I'll meet you in The Bees." He
slammed the door shut and shuffled toward the front door of the cottage. "On mi' way George," he called out. "Just finishin' up on the lav!"

TWENTY ONE

Late afternoon, particularly in the summer, was Audrey Ormerod's favorite time of day. At 4 o'clock on the dot, she put the kettle on, brewed herself a nice cup of tea and then settled down in the big armchair by the window in the back room of her two up, two down cottage to read the newspaper. Occasionally, on hot days like this one, when it was warm enough to go outside without a cardigan, she lifted the sash window and let a little fresh air waft across the room as she read. Routine was her comfort, and she deeply resented any occurrence that prevented her from being home by 3:55pm.

She sat down heavily with the newspaper in her lap, hitched her hiking trousers midway up her calves and gingerly lowered both feet into a bowl of warm water mixed with Epsom Salts. It was sheer bliss to get those hiking boots off. Warm weather made her feet swell and wreaked havoc on her corns. She wiggled her toes and smiled. With a loud sigh, she sank back into the chair and closed her eyes. It had been a long day and a very interesting one too. Audrey's thoughts drifted to the strange events of the afternoon.

She wondered what George Barlow could have been looking for in the field opposite the post office. And who was that suited young fellow with him? And why had the two of them gone inside in the post office before they started their search? She distinctly remembered overhearing Jeremy Danvers tell Pearl he had lost something, so perhaps the search was connected to him. And what about that friend of Jeremy Danvers, the dashing American? What was his part, if any, in all of this?

It was all so intriguing, made all the more mysterious by the unusual disappearance of Pearl Wiggins later that afternoon.

Audrey's forehead creased in concentration. When she and the other ramblers failed to find anything of interest around the perimeter of the field, they made a beeline back to the post office to ask Pearl if she knew what was going on. To their astonishment when they got there, the door was locked and a closed sign was hung up in the window— very peculiar indeed. If Audrey's memory served her right, she could recollect only three occasions when Pearl had closed the post office before 5:00 p.m. The first occasion was years ago when Pearl had a spell in hospital due to a *woman's complaint*. The second was the week following Arthur's death, when the post office was closed for a week. And the third time was when Pearl had some mysterious business to attend to at the central post office in Harrogate. It bothered Audrey to this day that she had not managed to unearth the exact details of what Pearl had been up to on that occasion, but it was rumored that Pearl was in some sort of financial trouble.

The shrill ring of the telephone interrupted her thoughts. Her eyes snapped open. "Who the heck can that be?" she grumbled loudly. She turned to look at the phone on the side table by her chair. She considered not bothering to answer it, but then decided she might just be able to reach it without taking her feet out of the water.

"Audrey? AUDREY? Is that you? It's Irene, Irene Tattershall."

"Of course it's me!" scolded Audrey into the telephone receiver.

"Who else do you think it is? There's only me that lives here. And there's no need to announce who you are every time you call. We've known each other for over seventy years. I think I know your voice by now, Irene." Audrey rolled her eyes to the ceiling. "And this better be important because you know very well that 4:00 p.m. to 6:00 p.m. is my newspaper and crossword time." She reached for the cup of tea on the windowsill and took a quick sip.

Undaunted by Audrey's stern tone, Irene announced: "You'll never guess who I just saw. And . . . " she paused for effect . . . "leaving Barrington Smith's by the back door no less!"

"Huh? What? Who?" Audrey spluttered. She almost choked on her tea. The newspaper fell to the floor as she pulled herself to the edge of the seat.

"You—will—never—guess," said Irene, stringing out the words for extra effect.

"Who? Stop teasing me, Irene, and tell me." There was a silence on the other end of the phone. "WHO?" Audrey demanded.

"Pearl Wiggins!" Irene answered triumphantly.

"Pearl Wiggins!" Audrey repeated incredulously. "Are you sure?"

"Of course I'm sure. It was Pearl Wiggins all right—the very one. And that's not all . . . "

"What do you mean?" Audrey gasped. She put her tea down and pressed the telephone receiver closer to her ear. "Go on then, I'm listening," she said in a hushed tone.

"Well, I heard Freddie barking upstairs, so I had a quick look out the window and who do I happen to see, but Pearl Wiggins hurrying down the lane like her skirts were on fire. She was acting very strangely, if you ask me. She kept looking over her shoulder as if someone were following her."

"Really?" Audrey said slowly. "Go on . . . "

"Anyway, I saw her knock on Barrington's door, someone opened it and she stepped right in and she didn't come out again for another fifty-three minutes!"

"Fifty-three minutes. Well, well . . . " said Audrey, her mind racing. "This is very interesting Irene, very interesting indeed."

"Wait—there's more. Seeing as it was time for Freddie's walk, I thought I'd take him in the field round the back of Barrington's, and just as I was coming around the corner I saw Pearl come flying out of the back door like she'd seen a ghost. She was in a right flap."

"HUH?" Audrey sucked in her breath. "Did she see you?"

"No. I heard Barrington call after her and I managed to duck behind the old shed at the back of his house and . . . "

"Wait! What did he say?" Audrey interrupted.

"Who?"

"Barrington, of course! Who do you think?"

"Oh, right. I think he said something like "I'll meet you in The Bees at 8 o'clock.""

"Well, well, well," said Audrey elated. She clapped a hand over her mouth in delight. This was news indeed. Nothing this interesting had happened for decades. How marvelous. She needed to get on the phone to Madge and Irma straight away and formulate a plan of action.

"But I haven't told you the best bit yet," Irene giggled into the phone. Guess who else called at Barrington's?"

"What? There was someone else? Who, what . . .?" Audrey stuttered, bursting with curiosity.

"Guess who?" Irene taunted.

"I can't. I can't guess. Tell me, Irene! Now!"

"Well, just before Pearl comes flying out the back, someone else arrives at the front door. I'm guessing that's why Pearl was in such a rush to leave."

"Who? WHO?"

"The police!" There was a moment's silence. "It was George Barlow!"

"What? George Barlow? Really?" Audrey leaped to her feet in excitement, sending the bowl flying. Water splashed all over the carpet. "Oh bugger!" she exclaimed. "No, no not you, Irene. Go on, what did George Barlow want? How long did he stay?"

"I've no idea what he was doing there. He didn't stay long—about 15 minutes I'd say, and then he drove off towards the main road in his patrol car. I'll tell you this though: Audrey, there's definitely something odd going on—I can just sense it. What do you think we should do?"

Audrey thought for a moment before answering.

"Have you told anyone else about this Irene?" Audrey asked cautiously.

"No. Of course not. You're the first one I thought to call," Irene answered.

"Well, listen to me," said Audrey, taking command. "Do not say a word to anyone. Not one single soul until I've had a chance to think this through. There's something very peculiar going on in this village, and the fewer that know about this for now, the better," she said, thinking fast.

"Hmm. So Pearl's meeting Barrington in The Bees at eight," Audrey said more to herself than Irene. "And who else goes to The Bees every Friday evening if he's not working?"

"George, George Barlow!" shrieked Irene in excitement.

"Exactly," replied Audrey.

"Right! It's time to rally the girls together. I'm going to call an emergency meeting in The Bees at 7 o'clock sharp, so we're in place before they arrive. I'll call Madge and Irma, and you call Jean. Tell her to get herself and her bunions down to The Bees—no excuses. Tell her I said we have urgent business to discuss. Now remember Irene, not one word. I'm counting on you to keep this top secret until I say otherwise. Oh, and only one dry sherry tonight. We need to stay sharp. I've got a feeling we've got a busy night ahead of us."

TWENTY TWO

The Village Hall was situated at the north end of the Green, opposite the Three Bees, on the corner of the lane leading up to the church. It was originally a church school, built from local stone in 1855, largely due to the efforts of the Reverend James Hardwick, on land donated by the Duke of Leeds. The original building had been little more than one large room with a fireplace and a platform in one corner. But over the years, several small outbuildings had been added to include a small kitchen and separate toilets for males and females.

Unfortunately, in the 1950's, due to overcrowding and lack of funding for repairs, the school was forced to close. Henceforth, the children were bussed to the larger schools in the market town of Wickham, and the church donated the building to the village of Tipping to be used as a Village Hall. Fund raising and contributions from the church and parishioners helped pay for basic maintenance and a few improvements, but it wasn't until early 1994, following a successful application to the Yorkshire Rural Community Council, that the Village Hall Trustees were delighted to announce that the much needed renovation and extension of the existing hall would be able to commence.

The Hall became a central part of village life, offering a meeting place for many diverse groups. The Brownies, Girl Guides, Cubs, Boy Scouts, The Mother's Union, Book Clubs, Bring and Buy Sales, the Annual Farmer's Ball, line-dancing, Toddlers and a Youth Club, all used the Hall on a regular basis. It was also the village meeting place for Parish

Council meetings and was used as the polling station during local and national elections. Most recently, since the appointment of a relatively young and forward-thinking vicar whose hair was long enough to reach beyond the top of his collar, and Audrey Ormerod could testify to having seen it tied into a pony tail on more than one occasion; the Hall was transformed from a peaceful function room, to an ear-pounding disco for the local teens, twice a month on a Friday, during the summer.

The noise coming from inside the Village Hall on this particular Friday evening alternated between a loud booming cacophony of sound each time one of the double entrance doors at the front of the building opened, to a muffled pulsating throb as the door shut again. Tight knots of vivid, lissome, scantily dressed teenage girls occupied the car park outside the Hall. A pride of male youths were lolling on the grass in the middle of the Green, their lit cigarette ends flickering like fireflies in the diminishing light. They collapsed in fits of raucous laughter every time one of them directed a loud taunt toward the huddled groups of girls.

From his vantage point on a bench outside the chip shop on the opposite side of the Green, Jeremy looked forlornly at the Hall and contemplated the torture of having to venture inside to find Kevin Ogden, the kid who was spotted by the road near the post office that morning. The prospect filled him with dread, mainly because it brought back too many painful memories of his own, awkward adolescence. He cringed at the memory of his futile attempts to fit in with the local kids his age. He recalled how he had spent some of the most embarrassing moments of his life hovering in the dim corners of the room, trying to look cool and indifferent, but secretly agonizing over whether he dared make a move to join the others on the dance floor. A tall lanky, un-athletic frame coupled with unfashionable frizzy hair, contributed to an acute lack of self-confidence. Drawing attention to himself had been his worst nightmare, and it still was, because it invoked the risk of being laughed at.

Jeremy looked down at the chips in the wrapper spread out on his lap. He shoveled a handful into his mouth and pondered how he might make his approach to a loathsome fifteen-year-old, known to most of the villagers for his part in causing a stampede of prize Heifers by setting off firecrackers during last year's village fair. Jeremy was on a mission to find out whether the kid had found anything, or seen anyone else pick something up from the road earlier on.

Oh God, Jeremy thought. He swallowed his last mouthful of chips. At the age of twenty-two, he felt ancient, bone weary and exhausted. The day had been interminably long, fraught with fear and uncertainty, but at least he had made up his mind about one thing: to put his trust in Conrad Rankin, at least for the time being. His decision was based partly on gut instinct. He felt comfortable with the American. He liked him. Conrad Rankin was immediately engaging, and he seemed to empathize with Jeremy's diabolical situation. The other reason for his decision was because he could not face the alternative of making a confession to the police.

When Detective Sergeant Patterson turned up at Jeremy's parents house so unexpectedly earlier that afternoon, Jeremy was convinced that the game was finally up. He was certain that he was about to be arrested and hauled into custody for lying to the police, concealing evidence, conspiracy, maybe theft, and Lord knows what else they had to throw at him. He was dangerously close to breaking down and blurting out a whole confession. God knows it might have been easier, but when they failed to find anything incriminating on him or in the car, they allowed him to go free. Patterson gave him a menacing warning about the importance of co-operating with the police, but that was all. It was astonishing.

The moment Patterson's car turned out of the drive in the direction of the village, Jeremy shot into the house and ran up the stairs to his parent's bedroom at the front. Hidden discreetly behind the curtains, he watched until the car eventually disappeared from view. He stayed for several minutes and scanned the lane in both directions. When he felt certain no one was about, he sprinted back down the stairs, out the back door and into the shed in the back garden where the bikes were kept.

Jeremy was tired and in dire need of a shower, but he had to act quickly. The library in Wickham closed at 5:00 p.m., and by the time he got there on his bike, using the back roads to avoid detection, he would not be left with a great deal of time. His mission was twofold: to use the library's Internet to find out as much as he could about the

Turners, and to dig up information about the Rankin family of Boston, Massachusetts—especially Claudia Rankin and her son, Conrad.

His cell phone vibrating in his jeans pocket interrupted his thoughts. He lifted it out and scowled when he saw who was calling. It was Nigel—again. It was the fourth time he had called that day.

I wonder what the hell he wants. He probably wants to whine about how much work he has to do on his own in the gallery. Lazy bastard. Jeremy got to his feet and stuffed the phone back into his pocket without taking the call. Nigel was the last person he wanted to speak to at that moment.

Jeremy thought fleetingly about turning around and heading home to await his fate, but deep down he knew this was not an option. The only chance he had of escaping jail time was to go along with the deal Conrad Rankin had offered to him.

With a loud sigh of resignation, Jeremy threw the empty chip wrapper into the bin next to the bench and turned in the direction of the Village Hall. He pushed his hands into his jeans pockets and set off across the Green, silently cursing Nigel, the gallery, Julian Parks, Conrad Rankin—the bloody lot of them.

He was about fifty yards from the car park outside the Hall when the crowd of youths scattered across the Green in an explosion of loud guffaws. One of them had shaken a can of soda and was charging around with it trying to spray the others. It was as if a meteor had landed in the middle of the group causing them to erupt in all directions. One of them, a short wiry kid with jeans about three sizes too big hanging half way down his backside, broke away from the pack in a fit of hysterical laughter. He ran in Jeremy's direction pursued by a chubby kid who was wielding the soda can. When Jeremy saw the two of them, his jaw dropped. The kid in front was Kevin Ogden. What a marvelous stroke of luck.

"Hey, kid!" Jeremy shouted, setting off in a jog. His immediate thought was that if he could corner the kid outside, then he would be spared the ordeal of having to face him in front of all the other crass, arrogant youths inside the disco.

"Hey, Kevin. Hang on a minute. I need a quick word."

"Huh? What?" Ogden's head wheeled around. He came to an abrupt halt and turned to watch Jeremy approach through narrowed, suspicious eyes. He pulled at the cap that had fallen back on his head, adjusting the peak so it stuck out sideways over his left ear.

Jeremy stopped a few feet away, in the middle of the Green. In a casual, almost indifferent tone, as if the question he was about to ask carried no real importance, he said: "Oh, I'm glad I saw you. It's Kevin Ogden isn't it? I'm Jeremy Danvers. I live here, or well I used to, before university that is. Hawthorn House on Rose-hill Lane," he added.

"Yer what?" Ogden replied, a vacant look on his pimply face.

"Someone said they saw you near the post office this morning, around ten, half ten," Jeremy continued. "Some stuff fell out of my car and I'm asking everyone who was around whether they saw anything and whether they picked any of it up. It's my college papers you see. Exam stuff, that kind of thing."

"Oh right," Ogden replied, obviously relieved he was not in any kind of trouble. "Nah, like I told the local cop, I didn't see anythin' except . . . "

"Hey, Kev! Are you comin' or what?" A loud shout came from the front of the Hall.

"'Ang on a minute!" he bellowed back.

"Been caught nicking fags again, have yer?" another voice called out, followed by loud snickering and laughter.

"The local cop?" Jeremy asked, puzzled. It took a moment for him to register this information. "Do you mean George Barlow?" he said. "What did he want?"

"He wanted to know why I wasn't in school. I told him I'd got up late and was on my way to the bus stop," Ogden replied unconvincingly. "It was that Fatty Wiggins, er, I mean her from the post office that'd told him she'd seen me hangin' around outside."

"Right," said Jeremy slowly. "Was that all he wanted?"

"Nah. He wanted to know if I'd found any of your stuff on the road." Ogden hesitated for a moment. He looked down at the ground, kicked the grass and then threw Jeremy a calculating look before continuing. "And he said you'd be giving out a reward."

"A reward," said Jeremy, caught off guard. "Oh he did, did he?"

"Yeah, that's right."

"So you found something then," asked Jeremy hopefully.

"Nah, but I saw who did."

"Who?"

"What's it worth to yer?"

"You what?" said Jeremy, struggling to keep from sounding frustrated. He had a strong suspicion the kid was playing him. Jeremy clenched his fists and took a step towards Ogden. He felt like throttling him.

"Ten quid and I'll tell yer who's got yer stuff."

"Ten quid! Tell me first and then I'll think about it," Jeremy countered.

"No chance! Who do yer take me for? Some dumb arse?" He began to back off towards the Hall.

"No, wait a minute," said Jeremy through clenched teeth. He stuffed a hand into his pocket and pulled out a five-pound note. "Here, take this," he said offering the fiver to Ogden. "It's all I've got. Take it or leave it."

Ogden stepped forward and snatched the money from Jeremy's outstretched hand. He gave the note a cursory glance and then shot off in the direction of the Hall where his friends were still waiting. He called over his shoulder, "Fatty Wiggins has got yer stuff. I saw her puttin' it in a bin liner."

Well, at least the kid had not seen anyone else near the post office, but the news that the local police were involved was not what Jeremy wanted to hear. He wondered whether Pearl Wiggins had turned the paintings in after he had spoken to her that morning. Or perhaps she just stuffed everything straight into a bin liner without looking through it. If that were the case, then all his things, including the paintings, were still in Pearl Wiggins's dustbin. Conrad was right. They needed to look through her trash, and if the paintings were not there, he would have to ask about them to her face. He did not look forward to this prospect. Pearl Wiggins was someone he took extra care to avoid if at all possible. He knew she had a soft spot for him, ever since he turned in Mrs. Hardcastle's lost ten-pound note all those years ago, but he still dreaded being drawn into conversation with her. She was insufferably nosey and bombarded him with endless questions about how he was doing, and where he was living, and what he was up to, and how were his parents and what about that nice brother of his. Her questions went on and on. If she did still have the paintings, how was he going to persuade her not to go to the police with them? It was all too complicated.

Jeremy let out a hopeless sigh and checked the time on his watch. It was a few minutes after 8:30 p.m., still thirty minutes before his rendezvous with Conrad. He looked at the pub on the other side of the road and felt a nervous flutter in his stomach. He considered walking back to the bench outside the chip shop and waiting there for a few more minutes, but then thought the better of it. If he went into the pub, he could have a few pints before meeting Conrad. God knows he needed a drink.

TWENTY THREE

"Rankin's just left the Hall, Sarge. It looks like he's heading for the village, over," Detective Constable Evans spoke into his radio.

"Right. Stay with him and let me know the second he stops that car," replied Patterson. "And for Christ's sake don't lose him."

Patterson leaned back in his chair and yelled toward the tiny room at the back of the constabulary building. "Tom!"

Detective Tom Collins stood up from the desk where he had been working on the computer and walked to the open doorway. "Yes, Sarge?"

"Our man's on the move," said Patterson, grabbing his jacket from the back of the chair. He motioned to Collins to follow him. "He's heading this way. Get your stuff. You can tell me what you've got when we get in the car. I want to be in place before he gets here."

The two of them flew out a side door leading to the small car park at the rear of the building. "Head onto the main road and park in that lane before the post office. We should be able to see everything that's coming from there."

"Evans, are you still on him?" Patterson barked into his radio from the passenger seat.

"Yeah, he's heading your way."

"Good. Stay with him."

Detective Collins parked the dark blue Rover at the side of the lane, tucked away behind a thick hedgerow. They pulled just far enough forward to afford a view of traffic as it approached the village from the east. Patterson lowered his window and felt the warm evening air.

"Ah, that feels good," he said. "Some bloody fresh air at last."

He breathed in the heavy scent of warm earth and honeysuckle. A light wind rustled the branches of the oak trees on the other side of the lane, gently nudging the long fingers of shadow as they stretched across the car. The landscape was bathed in a soft violet as the evening light began to fade. Patterson turned to Detective Collins.

"So, bring me up to date Tom. Anything else on Julian Parks?"

"I'm not sure—maybe. I checked the airlines and Parks had a return ticket booked to Geneva at the end of the month. Claudia Rankin was booked on a flight to Boston on the day after the accident, but I found out she has property in Switzerland, on Lake Lucerne. It looks like you were right. Parks was going to move the Turners to Switzerland before the D.C.M.S. could place an export restriction on the them."

"Hmm . . . But why would Parks wait so long to move them? Why wait until the end of the month? It doesn't make sense. He'd be putting himself at huge risk trying to keep them hidden for that length of time," said Patterson, rubbing the stubble on his chin. "What about Nigel Bryce Edwards, did you manage to rake up anything on him?"

"Nothing much. No record—squeaky clean. Just finished his art history degree at York, works on and off for his old man, mainly in the gallery in Harrogate and occasionally down to London. But what might be of interest is the time he spent in Florence last year. It was part of his art course—five months abroad, January to May. It seems that Julian Parks was in Florence for most of March and," he paused, "so was Claudia Rankin."

"Really?" said Patterson. "Now that is interesting."

"And then six months ago in December, all three of them were in London at the same time. It was when Turner's, *Blue Rigi*, came up for auction at Christies. Remember how it went for a record price—five point eight million pounds to an anonymous buyer?"

"Y-e-s," Patterson replied slowly.

"Well an export stop was slapped on it immediately, and it's still in place actually, until—let me see . . . " He flicked through a folder on his lap. "Until July 22nd. The Tate is still trying to raise the money to match the price."

"And Parks was at Christie's at the time of the bidding?" asked Patterson.

"Yes, and so were Nigel Bryce Edwards and his father. It might all mean nothing, but I don't know. There might have been something going on between Parks and the kid. It would confirm your suspicion that it was Nigel who Parks wanted to see when he dropped the Turners off at the gallery. Or it could be that Parks and Claudia Rankin were using the kid as an innocent front to move the work."

"Hmm. I want you to check the airlines again. See if our laddo, Nigel, has any flights booked. I wouldn't mind betting he's on a flight to somewhere in Europe this month. Oh, and check on his father as well while you're at it – you never know."

Their conversation was interrupted by Detective Fields on Patterson's radio. "Sarge, Danvers is outside the chip shop. He's looking nervous. Keeps looking at his watch. Over."

"Right. Keep him in sight, but stay back. Do not let him see you. I want to know the minute he moves, and use your cell phone from now on."

"Roger. Over."

"Right Tom, it looks like our two boys are going to meet," said Patterson, straightening up and rubbing his hands together. He checked his watch. "Rankin should be here soon. Keep your eyes peeled." He leaned forward to get a better look through the windscreen.

"Sarge! Walker here." Patterson's radio crackled into life again. "Pearl Wiggins has left the post office. She's heading toward the Green. Over."

"Keep a close eye on her, Walker. We're all in place. Rankin is on the move and heading this way. Evans is on his tail. Danvers is outside the chip shop by the Green. Fields is watching him. Is she carrying anything?"

"Yeah, she's got a bag—a big hand-bag."

"Don't take your eyes off that bag, Walker."

"It looks like she's heading for The Bees, Sarge."

"Right, keep her in sight until she goes in. Do not follow her. Repeat—do not go in that pub. Hang back and stay out of sight. I don't want Danvers to see you. He knows who you are and I don't want him scared off. Go round the back of the building and wait by the back entrance. Have you got that?"

"Got it, Sarge. She's taking her time . . . Keeps looking over her shoulder . . . She'll be a few minutes yet. Over."

Collins and Patterson remained still in their seats as Conrad's black Audi approached. They watched as it turned off the main road and headed toward the Green, followed a few moments later by a dark blue sedan.

"Sarge, he's pulled up outside the pub," Constable Evans whispered into his cell phone "He's left the car . . . yep, he's going inside."

"Right. Move in after him and don't take your eyes off him, especially if he leaves to take a piss," replied Patterson. "Our local man, Barlow's already in there, said Patterson. "He's in plain clothes, supposedly off duty, but don't acknowledge him. I don't want anyone in there to know who you are. Pearl Wiggins is heading for the pub as well. She should be there any minute. Walker will be watching the back entrance. Watch them like a hawk, Evans. This could be our one chance to nail them. Don't blow it. Over."

* * *

The Three Bees was at its busiest when the schools were closed for the holidays, from the middle of July until the beginning of September. With plenty of old world charm, as well as a selection of fine ales, the pub attracted enough tourist trade during the summer months to see it through the long, quiet days of winter. Apart from expanding the former stables into a dining room and modernizing the kitchen, little had changed in the pub since it was built in 1745

The floors still had the original stone flagging. After centuries of use, they were uneven and worn smooth in places. The original wooden beams, decorated with horseshoes and old plates, ran the full length of the low ceilings. An enormous fireplace with a display of blackened cooking pots hanging from the mantle, dominated one end of the lounge. In the winter, the cooking pots were removed and a roaring fire filled the hearth. The dim lighting, yellow as candlelight, although it was in fact electric, gave the lounge a warm, cozy, ambience.

Conrad walked toward the pub's entrance with long, confident strides. He had changed into a pair of jeans and a smart striped Versace shirt, rolled up at the sleeves to expose an expensive Rolex. His blond hair was smoothed back in a rakish fashion, falling in soft waves behind his ears.

A group of young girls, teenagers, was between him and the entrance, and just as he became aware that they were staring at him, one of them pointed and said something, which set them off in paroxysms of laughter.

"Ah, if you'll excuse me ladies," he said, undeterred. The group immediately grew quiet and parted to let him through. He could feel their eyes on him.

"Oh, are you from America?" asked one of them. A tall attractive girl with a cloud of dark curls swayed toward him. She laughed and showed her pretty teeth. The others giggled.

"Yes, ma'am," he said without stopping. He tried not to smile.

The strong smell of smoke hit him as soon as he stepped through the door, making his eyes smart and giving him a renewed appreciation of the recent smoking bans imposed across much of the U.S. Surprised by how crowded the place was, he hovered by the door for a moment to get his bearings, peering through the foggy atmosphere toward the packed bar area. A sea of heads swiveled in his direction.

"Yoo hoo!" A shrill voice rang out above the general din. "Mr. Rankin! Over here, yoo hoo, Mr. Rankin."

Conrad had heard that voice before. Without turning his head, he could see out of the corner of his eye, the lady ramblers he had encountered outside the post office earlier that day, congregated around a table by the fireplace. He pretended not to notice them and made a beeline for an empty seat tucked into one corner of the bar.

"Ah, I wouldn't sit there if I was you," a female voice said next to him. It took Conrad a moment to realize the sentence was being applied to him.

He turned and looked into a pair of striking green eyes, framed by long thick lashes.

"Oh and why's that?"

"It's reserved. For one of the locals."

"Really? There's no where else to sit."

"Well, you could risk it, but I have to warn you that it's considered a capital offence in these parts. You could be shunned by the entire village and taken to the pillory and pelted with rotten fruit," she laughed. A strand of golden brown hair fell across her shoulder.

"I'm surprised it's so busy in here. Is it always like this?"

"It can get packed in the summer, although," she looked around the lounge, "it does seem particularly busy tonight. Hmm, a lot of locals are here, unusual for a Friday," she said, looking puzzled.

"But seriously," she turned back to look at him and offered an easy, infectious smile. "Some of our locals are very particular about where they sit and one of them has this stool every Friday evening for exactly one hour and fifteen minutes. He'll be here in a few minutes."

Conrad watched her lightly glossed lips as she spoke, enamored by the languorous sound of her voice, accented by the softest trace of Yorkshire. Her perfume was like a warm breeze. She was younger than him, mid twenties he guessed, dressed in a white sleeveless top with romantic ruffles around the neck, and a pair of dark, tight denim jeans. A little pendant of a starfish dangled loosely from her neck, tantalizingly close to the hint of cleavage above the top button of her blouse. He felt an urge to look down and take in the whole of her, but he lifted his eyes to meet her amused gaze. He sensed an immediate pull of attraction.

"Ah, well I'm not staying. I've got a dinner reservation. Do I give my name here?"

"You can give your name in here or you can go straight over to the dining area." She pointed to a door where waiters were passing in and out. "It's over in the back."

"You said 'our'. Does that mean you're a local too? You don't sound as if you're from around here."

"My father owns this place." She nodded to the end of the bar where a rosy faced, portly man with a frosting of thin grey hair, was pulling a pint.

"I'm here for two weeks, a vacation. I don't live here anymore; haven't done for years. I grew up with my mother in the south, hence the posh accent."

"Ah," he said comprehending.

"And you," she tilted her wine glass in Conrad's direction, "are most definitely not from around here." She took a sip from her drink. "Where in the States?"

"Boston, New York, mainly New York. And you? Where do you live now?"

"New York," she laughed. "Mainly," she added.

Conrad's eyebrows shot up in surprise. He leaned towards her, about to ask whereabouts in the city, when one of the bartenders interrupted their conversation.

"What can I get for you squire?"

Conrad was briefly tempted to ask the brunette whether she had already eaten and if not, invite her to dine with him. She was attractive, confident and intriguing, certainly his type, and under different circumstances, probably worth getting to know better, but there could be no distractions tonight. He needed to eat, and he had to be ready and alert for when Jeremy showed up.

"Nothing for me, but another glass of wine for the lady, thank you" he replied straightening up and stepping away from the stool. "I have a dinner reservation. Eight o'clock."

"Ah, the dining room is through the back sir," said the bartender indicating the far side of the lounge with a gesture of his hand. "If you give your name to the waitress, she'll get you seated."

Conrad glanced at his watch, 7:56, and then looked at the woman beside him. "I'm going to have to go," he said apologetically, "I'm on a tight schedule. It's been nice meeting you." He offered her his hand and said, "I'm Conrad, and you are?"

"Madeleine, but everyone calls me Maddie," she said, placing her warm hand in his palm. "It's been nice meeting you too, and thank you for the drink."

He squeezed her hand gently and ran his thumb across her fingers. He looked from her eyes to her lips and back to her smiling eyes again.

"Perhaps you'll be here tomorrow evening?" he asked.

She smiled to reveal a perfect set of teeth. "Perhaps."

Conrad let her hand slip slowly from his and turned away from the bar. He sidled around the edge of the crowded lounge to a room at the back where a waitress led him to a small table in one corner. He seated himself, facing the doorway so he could see who was coming in and out of the dining room. If he leaned to his right, he had a partial view of the bar and beyond that, an occasional glimpse through the crowd, to the front entrance of the pub. Satisfied with his vantage point, he smiled and picked up the menu. Excellent, he thought. Now food. He was starving.

TWENTY FOUR

Barrington Smith shuffled into the Three Bees at eight on the dot. Instead of going straight to the bar as usual, he hovered in the doorway and looked around. The place was busier than usual. He was looking for Pearl Wiggins, but saw no sign of her.

"Not like her to be late," Barrington grumbled. He peered through the crowd at the bar, but didn't expect to see her. She never sat at the bar. She preferred the tables near the fireplace. He let his gaze drift in that direction only to see a horrifying site. Audrey Ormerod, Irma Hepplethwaite, Irene Tattershall, Madge Hopkins and Jean Wilson, the dreaded ramblers, were sitting in a tight huddle. They stared at him with their jaws dropped open.

Now what the 'eck are them lot doing in 'ere on a Friday night—my night, he thought, feeling annoyed. Tuesdays is their night. "Nosey buggers," he mumbled under his breath. He chose to visit the pub on a Friday because most of the locals avoided the pub on weekends during the summer when it was overrun with tourists. Friday was always the busiest; a sure bet that he would be safe from the likes of Audrey Ormerod or anyone else he did not care to see. He looked away in disgust, deliberately ignoring them as he headed for his reserved stool at the end of the bar. His day had been lousy so far and now it was worse than ever.

"Good evening Mr. Smith. How are you this fine evening?" asked Maddie. She pulled the bar stool out for him.

"Oh, middlin'lass. Just middlin."

"Bad day?"

"The worst. And I reckon it's not going to get any better," Barrington moaned, inclining his head towards the fireplace. Madeleine glanced in that direction.

"Oh dear, someone you don't want to see?"

"You could say that."

He held on to the back of the stool with both hands and steadied himself before stepping to the side and hoisting one leg onto the seat. He paused for a moment, grabbed hold of the edge of the bar, and in one concentrated effort, pulled himself onto the seat. It was not easy getting up on that stool, but he resolutely refused to sit on a chair at one of the tables. If he could not meet the challenge of getting up on a stool, then as far as he was concerned, he might as well be put out to pasture.

"Here we are then Barrington, your usual," boomed Jim Hargreaves, proprietor of the pub as he placed a pint of dark ale on the bar-top. "Cheers."

"Cheers," replied Barrington without much enthusiasm. He held the glass up to eye level and examined the head of froth, as was his ritual, then took a long sip before placing the pint back down on the bar. "A terrible day," he muttered to no one in particular.

It dawned on him that afternoon, after he had taken another peek at the paintings that it might be in his best interest to hang on to them for a little while longer. If the police, or whoever owned the paintings, wanted them badly enough, then there might be a nice little reward for them. One of the paintings was torn on one side. He had done that when he was tearing up paper for Ernie's kitty litter. Pearl had cut another around the edges, but the remaining two were in good shape, apart from some mud on one of them. He reckoned that could easily be fixed by one of the experts. It seemed to him that if he played his cards right, not only would he be able to bargain with Pearl to sort out his pension woes, but he might also come into an appreciable amount of money. He had read about massive rewards for this kind of thing and he did not feel one bit guilty about trying to make a bob or two if given the chance. It was not as if any lives were in danger; it was just a few silly little pictures that in his eyes were not worth the paper they were painted on. It was all a rich man's game, played by people with more money than sense. He had struggled all his life to make ends meet, so why should he care about a few pieces of frivolous trivia?

Barrington was dimly aware of Maddie, the pub owner's daughter at his side, but he was not in the mood for idle chitchat. She asked him a few questions about this and that and he gave her the shortest answers he could think of until she eventually gave up trying to talk to him. He was relieved when she finally left the bar with a parting: "Well, you take care, Mr. Smith. Have a good evening."

He touched the peak of his cap in response, took another long swig of his beer and returned to his brooding thoughts. He could not figure out what Jeremy was doing with valuable art work in the first place, but there was one thing he knew for sure: that lad was a good 'un and nothing and nobody was going to convince him otherwise. There had to be a good explanation as to why the lad had got himself into some bother, but until he heard the story from Jeremy himself, he wasn't going to say a thing to the police or to anyone else. And he was going to have to make sure, God help him, that Pearl kept her mouth shut too—not something that would be easy to do. She was not exactly the sort to keep quiet about anything.

He felt a sharp tap on his back and turned to see Pearl, nervous, dressed in a vibrant floral frock, her lips a vivid orange, standing with the handles of a large hand bag over one arm.

"You're late," Barrington snapped, unsmiling. "You'd best sit up 'ere," he said pointing to the empty stool beside him. "There's no where else to sit."

"What about by the fireplace? That's where I always sit," Pearl shot back. "I can't abide these stools. Let me just look if there's a table," she said, craning her neck to get a better view of the lounge.

"Oh, dear God!" A hand flew up to her mouth as she wheeled back around to face Barrington. "It's Audrey Ormerod! What's she doing in here on a Friday?" she hissed. "If she catches sight of us together, she'll know there's something going on. I'd best just squeeze in here out of the way." Her voice trailed off as she pushed her way between Barrington and the vacant stool next to him. "They can't see me now," she said, stealing a quick glance over his shoulder. "Oh crumbs, they're all here. What are we going to do?"

"Oh bugger them," Barrington rapped impatiently. "Let 'em think what they like. Now listen, you and I 'ave got important business to discuss, so you'd best get yourself onto this 'ere stool before it's snapped up by someone else."

Pearl looked dubiously at the stool, not sure if her corset, which was feeling tighter than ever after several Almond Slices, was going to allow sufficient maneuverability for her to climb up onto it. In desperation, she ducked up and down on her tiptoes, swiveling her head this way and that, hoping to spot a vacant seat at one of the tables.

"We could try looking outside," she said hopelessly.

"Sit down woman! We 'aven't got time to mess about. Oh no, Audrey Ormerod's makin' a beeline for us right now!" he said in alarm, throwing a sideways nod in the direction of the fireplace. "You need to calm down and listen to what I 'ave to say." He touched a finger to his nose and winked. "I've got it all figured out."

"What!" exclaimed Pearl "She's coming this way? What are we going to say?" she asked. "I think she's got wind there's something going on. That's why they're all in the pub."

"Then you'd best think of something to throw her and her pack off the scent, and you'd best be quick about it, because she's about ten feet away."

Pearl's eyes darted towards Audrey and then to the other ramblers before settling back on Barrington. "There's only one kind of thing that'll throw 'em off," she whispered, half to herself.

"Listen," said Barrington. He glanced fiercely at Audrey approaching, and then continued in a hurry. "This is what we're goin' to do. We're goin' to say nothing; not one word until we've 'ad a chance to speak with the lad. If you say anything to any of them friends of yours, especially them ramblers, they'll go running straight to the police and then I'm telling yer—you've 'ad it. You'll be going straight to jail. But if you listen to me and do as I tell you, everything is goin' to work out just fine." He leaned in close to her and whispered, "You and me are goin' to 'ang on to them paintings until we know the whole story, right? There'll be a reward put out for 'em and if you can keep your mouth shut for long enough, you and me are goin' to claim it," he finished with a note of triumph. Pearl gasped and stepped back a pace, just as Audrey arrived at her side.

"Now then Pearl, Barrington," Audrey threw them both a beaming smile. "Now, if I didn't know any better, I'd say the two of you are in cahoots about something," she laughed, wagging her finger at them as if they were two naughty school kids caught in the act of some childish prank. "Come on then, share the secret."

"Well, it looks like you've caught us red handed Audrey," said Pearl choosing her words carefully. She gave Barrington a flicker of a look and then continued. "We didn't expect to see you and the ladies in here on a Friday night,' she made a little sheepish laugh, so I suppose we might as well tell them our little secret then shall we Barrington?' She looked Barrington straight in the eye and added, "My love."

"Eh?"

"About you and me," she said widening her eyes to try and convey the hidden meaning behind her words. She flashed him an exasperated smile and then turned to Audrey. "Barrington and I are . . . well, we're," she paused trying to formulate the appropriate words. "Well we're, we're stepping out together," she finished in a rush.

"Eh?" Barrington nearly fell backwards off his stool.

"What?" Audrey gasped audibly. "You and Barrington. Stepping out," she repeated incredulously.

"That's right." Pearl threw Barrington a radiant smile and sidled up close to him. "Me and Barrington." Audrey looked from Barrington to Pearl and then back to Barrington, her jaw dropped open in disbelief.

"Well," she sucked in a breath and laughed, an indelicate, choking sound. She threw a quick wide-eyed glance at the ramblers who were goggling in her direction and then turned to face Barrington. "This is very unexpected," she said. "And how long has this been going on then?"

Barrington opened his mouth to say something, but then clamped it tight shut again. He looked helplessly at Pearl, pursed his lips, puffed out his cheeks and emitted a loud exhalation before stammering, "I, er, well, its er, been . . . "

"Two days." Pearl answered for him. "We're still getting better acquainted. Now, if you'll excuse us Audrey," she said firmly, "we'd like a little private time together if you don't mind."

Caught off guard, and too stunned to object, Audrey beat a hasty retreat back to her table by the fireplace. "You will *never* guess what I just found out," she announced in a whisper to the group. Simultaneously, the six ramblers leaned forwards across the table, forming a tight huddle. "You are *not* going to believe this, but . . . " She then proceeded to tell them, with a little added embellishment here and there, about the latest scandal to rock the village.

TWENTY FIVE

Jeremy walked toward the pub with his head down. To keep his hands from shaking, he jammed them into the front pockets of his jeans. He purposely took his time in an effort to look casual and unconcerned, but inside he felt as if he were on the verge of a nervous breakdown. The fact that the Scotland Yard coppers had widened their net and drafted the help of George Barlow, the local constable, made him even more nervous. They were probably watching him, concealed somewhere close by. Behind a darkened window perhaps, or in one of the cars parked nearby. The urge to peek over a shoulder to see if someone were on his tail was almost overwhelming, but he knew that he had to appear normal and unworried as if he had nothing to hide. The plan to make brief, casual contact with Conrad in the pub this evening no longer seemed like such a good idea. His throat felt as dry as pumice.

The pub appeared to be exceptionally busy with people overflowing from the inside of the building to the tables and benches outside in the beer garden. A small knot of hikers, still in their walking gear, stood next to the door, pints in their hands, talking loudly above the general noise level of the crowd. Jeremy sidled around them and slipped through the entrance, hoping that no one had noticed him. Once inside, he cast a nervous look around the lounge area and strode purposely toward the bar, as if he were not looking for anyone in particular. Fighting a growing urge to vomit, he jostled his way through the crowd and squeezed into a tight space at the bar and promptly ordered a pint of bitter. He downed it in several loud gulps and signaled to the barman for another. Pressed in by strangers on both sides, partially hidden from view, he felt marginally better.

Buoyed by the effect of the alcohol, he propped his elbows on the bar, smiled at the folk next to him, and cast a furtive glance around the room. His eyes were drawn to the ladies from the Tipping Ramblers Association who sat at a table by the fireplace, each of them staring straight at him, eyes on stalks, as if they had just seen a ghost walk in. With the futile hope that it was not him they were gazing at, he snapped his head in the other direction, only to be horrified at the sight of George Barlow, in plain clothes looking straight at him from a table set back under one of the windows. Jeremy raised his chin and lifted his pint an inch off the bar to acknowledge Barlow's presence before fixing his eyes on the mirror behind the bar as his mind scrambled to regain composure.

"Oh shit," he muttered. He had not expected the Ramblers to be in *The Bees* on a Friday, and George Barlow was just about the last person he wanted to see. "Shit," he repeated.

The mirror afforded him a surreptitious view of the other people in the lounge. Most of them were obvious tourists passing through, or hikers staying the night before pressing on to another location the next day. A few other locals were scattered about, but none of them seemed to have much interest in him. One or two nodded in his direction, or lifted their pints in recognition, but thankfully, not one of them came over to engage in idle conversation. Feeling more relaxed, Jeremy finished the rest of his pint, ordered a neat Scotch and swiveled his head in the direction of the corridor leading to the toilets. He noticed a man with a short haircut, dressed in formal pants and shirt, watching him from a table near the corridor. When their eyes met, the stranger looked down at his newspaper, seemingly engrossed in the back page. Shocked, Jeremy spun back around to face the bar, his heart about to leap out of his chest. Police—he was sure of it. His hand flew to the cheap Timex on his wrist. He fumbled with the strap, in a frantic effort to get it off before Conrad made an appearance.

He nearly jumped out of his skin when a familiar voice whispered in his ear. "Now then Jeremy." He wheeled around to face Pearl Wiggins who stood close to his side holding a small glass of sherry in one hand. A large rectangular handbag was draped over her other arm.

"I think you and me need to have a little chat," she said quietly, gripping his arm in a surprisingly firm hold. The shock of her sudden appearance, coupled with the overpowering fragrance of her perfume rendered him speechless. "I've a spot over there with Barrington," she said, throwing a sideways nod toward the end of the bar. Jeremy's eyes darted in Barrington's direction. The old man nodded and touched the end of his cap when their eyes met. All Jeremy could manage was a weak smile and a raise of his eyebrows.

"Oh, Mrs. er, Wiggins, hello," he finally managed to stammer with a half laugh. "You made me jump." He held a hand over his chest where his heart was hammering at an alarming speed. "What was that you said?" he asked innocently.

Pearl inched forward a notch, her eyes flitting across the faces of the people standing next to them. Then she leaned in close and whispered, "The police have been asking about you. They came into the post office this morning, just after you'd been in. They think you had hold of something that didn't belong to you and that it fell out of your car outside my post office." She paused and looked him in the eye.

"What? I–I don't know what you're talking about," Jeremy stammered. "I–I . . ."

"Oh I think you do," she interjected. "Me and Barrington know all about what's gone missing, so there's no use denying it." She glanced again at the people standing at the bar and lowered her voice so that it was barely audible and whispered, "We know where they are."

Jeremy stared at her opened mouthed, caught off guard by this revelation. "You know where what is?" he asked testing her.

"The paintings," she breathed, barely moving her lips. "Grab your drink and come over here with us," she said indicating the end of the bar where Barrington sat waiting. "We have a lot to talk about."

"Where are they? How many have you got?" Jeremy asked, as soon as he had helped haul Pearl onto the stool next to Barrington and swallowed his Scotch down in one gulp. "Why didn't you give them straight to the police?"

"Whoa, hold up a minute. Before we tell you anything else, I think you've got some explaining to do first," said Barrington. He leaned towards Jeremy and pointed at him with a shaking finger. "Let's just get one thing straight 'ere lad. Me and Mrs. Wiggins aren't the kind that goes about breaking the law, and we can't abide those that do. Now, we've known you for a long time and we can't believe you've got it in you to steal anything, but if we find out you did, then make no mistake lad—we're goin' straight to the police! So," he looked at Jeremy square in the eye and added, "You'd better start talking this very minute." He drummed his finger on the bar top to make his point. "Now what the 'eck's been goin' on?"

Jeremy stood paralyzed, the cogs of his brain working in slow motion as he tried to decide what to do. They had the paintings, or at least some of them. This changed everything. Relieved beyond measure about no longer having to search Pearl's bins, the problem was how to get the artwork off the two of them without involving the police and without jeopardizing his agreement with Conrad. His eyes flickered to the clock above the bar—8:45 p.m. He had fifteen minutes before Conrad was due to arrive. Barrington was tapping his fingers on the bar impatiently while Pearl stared at him intently. The two of them were waiting for him to say something.

"I uh . . . " he stammered. "I . . . Oh God." He dropped his head to his chest and whimpered. "I promised I wouldn't say anything. I–I don't know what to do. The police are here. They're watching every move I make. They've been following me. Don't look now, but that man near the corridor to the toilets, the one in a white shirt with the newspaper. Him," he flicked his head to indicate a table on the other side of the lounge. Both Pearl's and Barrington's eyes darted towards the man Jeremy described.

"Don't look, I said!" Jeremy hissed. "And George Barlow – he's here as well!"

"George Barlow?" asked Pearl, "Where?"

"By the window. But don't look. You'll make him suspicious if we're all gawking at him."

"Oh, forget 'im. He's harmless enough. Now why not start at the beginning lad?" coaxed Barrington.

"It's best you get it all off your chest," said Pearl. "You never know; we might just be able to help you."

Jeremy looked from one to the other with big doe eyes. A feeling of hopeless resignation and bitter shame washed over him as he began. "I'm in so much trouble." His bottom lip trembled. "I've been so stupid. You can't breathe a word of this to my parents—not one word." He looked at them beseechingly. "I'll tell them the truth eventually, but not now. I can't face it yet."

"Can't face what lad?" asked Barrington puzzled.

Jeremy sighed. "Well, it's about university; I've been lying to them about, about . . . " he swallowed.

"Go on," said Pearl softly. "You can tell us."

"About everything," Barrington added.

Jeremy poured out the whole sad sorry story about his parent's disappointment in him at school; the lies about his art degree; the stress over his upcoming graduation ceremony, and his stupid, idiot lie to the police when they asked him if Julian Parks had left anything at the gallery.

"I don't know why I didn't tell them. I mean, I didn't even know what was in the package at that point." He shook his head solemnly. "By the time I discovered the paintings, I guess I thought it was too late to come clean. They would think I was trying to cover something up—that I was in on it. I mean, they would never believe anyone could be that stupid, would they?" He sighed again. "I didn't want to have my life dissected by the police. They'd end up finding out about my art degree and then my parents would be bound to find out . . . it was all too much. I wasn't thinking straight. I panicked and drove here thinking that I could lie low for a while and figure out what to do."

"Eee by gum. You're up to your neck aren't you lad?" said Barrington glumly. "How many paintings did you say there were?"

"Six watercolors. Turners. You know J.M.W. Turner, known as Britain's greatest watercolorist. He's really famous. The paintings are part of his *Yorkshire Collection*."

"How do you know they're the real thing?"

"I don't know for sure, but I'm pretty certain they are. They're probably worth a mint."

"We've only got four of 'em."

"Four? I found one of them in the field opposite the post office, so where's the other one?"

"You know, I've been thinking that maybe we should just leave 'em somewhere for the police to find, anonymous like," suggested Barrington, ignoring the last question. "That way we can wash our 'ands of 'em and you'll be let off the 'ook."

"No! No, we can't do that," said Jeremy louder than he had intended. "My fingerprints are all over them."

"They're goin' to be more lenient with you if they get them back you know. Better than you getting' caught red-handed with 'em," said Barrington.

"No!" It was Pearl's turn to object. "They'd expect them back in good condition wouldn't they?" she said widening her eyes at Barrington. "You know what I mean," she said pointedly.

"What?" Jeremy asked. His head swiveled back and forth between the two of them. "What do you mean? Has something happened to them?"

Pearl immediately averted her eyes, pretending to examine the contents of her glass, whilst Barrington fiddled with a beer mat on the counter.

"They're not damaged are they?" Jeremy could feel his stomach sink.

"Only a bit—not much. I had no idea they were valuable. I mean, how could I?" Pearl said defensively. "And I certainly didn't know you were connected to all this, at least not until the police came into the post office asking a lot of questions."

"So what's happened to them? Tell me."

"You tell him," said Pearl.

"Why me?" Barrington replied. "You're the one that's gone and chopped one of 'em up." Both Jeremy and Pearl gasped at the same time.

"You've done what?" Jeremy almost screamed.

"I have not chopped anything up. I just trimmed it a little, that's all. It's not that bad really." Pearl shot an angry look at Barrington and then turned to face Jeremy. "I'll tell you what happened. Don't interrupt, Barrington."

* * *

"Well at least we've got five of the six accounted for," said Jeremy with some relief when Pearl finished her account of the day's events. "Even if a couple are damaged. I'd have to have a look at them first to decide whether they're beyond repair. They might still be okay," he said to Pearl, trying to sound encouraging. "So that leaves one still missing."

"Maybe the police have already found it," Pearl suggested. "I saw them searching the road and the field."

"Hmm. Maybe," said Jeremy, "but I searched the field before the police turned up and nothing was there, except the one I found. And I've talked to the kid, Kevin Ogden—he didn't find anything, and . . . "

"Any Tom, Dick or Harry could have picked it up," Barrington interrupted. "It could be on t'other side of the country by now," he added.

"There's always the Brigadier though. I saw him stopped by the side of the road. It's a slim chance, but you never know. Maybe he's got it," said Pearl hopefully.

"And how the 'eck are you going to get it off him? You can't just ask 'im to his face. The likes of 'im will go straight to the police if he thinks summat's up."

"Ah yes, well," said Jeremy hesitantly. "I might know the answer to that very soon." He peeked over his shoulder towards the door. Conrad was due any minute.

"Look, I've only got a few minutes left, "Jeremy whispered," so don't say anything; just listen to what I've got to say. There's someone else involved. Someone who's willing to pay a huge amount of money to get the paintings back, only I've promised him I wouldn't breathe a word about this to anybody."

"I'm not dealing with no thief," said Barrington.

"No. No, it's not like that. He's not a thief. Its, well, its complicated. Look he's going to be here any minute, so let me tell you quickly what's happened."

The three of them huddled together while Jeremy told them about Conrad and the agreement they had made about retrieving the art.

"So, there might be summat in it for us then," whispered Barrington, "if you really think you can trust 'im. That's a lot of money he's offerin' fer those paintin's."

"Maybe," said Jeremy, "although he's not going to be too pleased when he finds out I've told you about him."

"If he wants them back bad enough, he'll 'ave to play ball with us won't he," said Barrington. "I'm not givin' them up fer nothin'," he declared. "I was going to wait for the reward."

"What reward? I've heard nothing about that," said Jeremy quickly. "Who told you that?"

"George Barlow told me. He was round at my 'ouse this afternoon asking if I'd seen anything fall out of the back of yer car this mornin' as I was coming out of the post office. I told 'im nothin'."

"He might have just been saying that to get you to talk."

"But listen lad. If them paintin's are worth a bob or two, there'll be a reward out soon enough. You mark my words."

"Maybe," said Jeremy unconvinced. "But I bet it won't be much, and they'll make it really difficult to claim it. You know what they're like. You'd be better off letting me negotiate something with Rankin."

"What do you think we should do Pearl?" Barrington asked.

Pearl stood rooted to the spot, a look of deep concentration on her face. She was shocked at the amount of money the American had offered to Jeremy. If she could get just a portion of that, just a small percentage, she would be able to retire and not have to worry about being homeless without a penny to her name - she did not need much to live; she was not one for extravagances. A rush of thoughts tumbled through her mind, whirling and spinning as she grappled to put them in order so they made some sense. She had never put one foot outside the law, and yet here she was, being suckered into a scheme that she knew deep down was not honest. But what choice did she have? The question kept buzzing in and out of her head no matter how many times she tried to chase the thought away. You need the money Pearl, a little voice kept repeating; there will never be another opportunity like this one. Take it. Take it!

"Well," said Barrington impatiently. "Make yer mind up woman. This is yer chance to make a bit of money. You'll be able to treat yerself with summat you've always wanted."

"Well . . . I have always dreamed of going on a cruise. Nothing too posh. Something like the Mediterranean," she said.

"Well then?" said Barrrington.

"I . . . well . . . I don't . . . " She looked from one to the other with worried eyes. "Just tell me what I have to do."

* * *

Once he had re-positioned his chair to the right hand side of the table, Conrad could observe Jeremy without impediment from the concealment of the dimly lit dining room. He felt an immediate sense of relief when he first saw Jeremy enter the pub wearing a wrist watch; the sign that it was safe to meet at Pearl Wiggins' yard later that night to search her dustbin for the missing watercolors. But Jeremy's frenzied panic to take it off once he had reached the bar was a clear indication that something had gone terribly wrong.

Police, thought Conrad, alarmed. They must be in here. He made a swift examination of the other people at the bar, but no one stood out as particularly menacing or who looked as if they might be the police. He was about to shift position to get a clearer view across the rest of the lounge when a tall, buxom woman wearing a bright orange lipstick, in her sixties or seventies, sidled up close to Jeremy and whispered something in his ear. Conrad could tell by Jeremy's startled reaction that it was not good news. They exchanged a few hasty words and the two of them moved to the other end of the bar where they joined an elderly man sitting on the stool Conrad had vacated earlier.

"Shit!" Conrad swore under his breath. This is not good. Too much time had already passed since the Turners had fallen out of Jeremy's car. He was desperate to search the dustbin. It was the most obvious place for the paintings to be. Now he could feel the chances of getting his hands on them diminishing by the minute. He looked at his watch again—five minutes before nine. Five minutes left before he was due to make contact.

Uncertain about his next move, Conrad remained where he was. He propped his elbows on the table, interlocked the fingers of both hands and placed them under his chin. Any verbal contact with Jeremy in the pub was too risky. That left his only alternative: he would have to leave a message to meet somewhere else, under the loose stone by the stream, not something that made him entirely comfortable. "Shit," he muttered again. He formed a pyramid with his fingertips and tapped them softly against his lips as he pondered. One thing he was sure about: he would be an idiot to think that he could fully trust Jeremy. The tenuous nature of their agreement made him uneasy, but he had no other choice. The kid was his only hope of getting hold of the paintings, period. All he could do was hope to God that the money he had offered to Jeremy was sufficient enticement for the kid to fulfill his end of the bargain and keep his mouth shut.

His thoughts were interrupted by the chimes of the clock on the wall at the rear of the dining room. Nine o'clock—time to move. He gestured to the waitress for the bill and reached for one of the beer mats on the table. With the pen the waitress provided, Conrad signed for the meal and left a generous tip. He was pleasantly surprised by how good the food was, nothing fancy but certainly wholesome.

He scribbled a brief note on the back of the beer mat, pushed his chair back and put his wallet and the beer mat into his back pocket as he stood and walked slowly out of the dining area into the packed lounge. He edged around the perimeter of the room to avoid the throng of people at the bar. He glanced sideways every now and again with the hope of catching Jeremy's eye. As he approached the corridor leading to the toilets at the far end of the lounge, Conrad took one last look toward the bar. To his relief, Jeremy was looking straight back at him, eyes wide with fear, the size of two giant saucers. Conrad hesitated for a moment, raised a hand, smiled in friendly recognition, and then continued to the men's room without looking back. A middle-aged man, quite well dressed in a shirt and formal pants, followed close behind and entered one of the empty cubicles. Conrad, deep in thought, too distracted to take much notice of the man, washed his hands, cast a brief look into the mirror, swept his hair back with both hands and strode out of the bathroom. He left the pub through an inconspicuous side door that had been opened to let in some cool air.

"Was that him?" whispered Pearl. She craned her neck in the direction of the toilets. "The American?"

"Yes, but *don't* look at him! They'll see you—the police!" Jeremy hissed. "Turn around." The three of them huddled closer together and faced the bar. "You have to swear to say nothing until I've had the chance to talk to him. Both of you—right?"

"When will that be then?" asked Barrington. "How are you going to get in contact with him without the police knowing about it?"

"He's going to leave a message, tonight. It's all arranged, but I daren't risk getting it, not with the police watching me. So that means you'll have to do it, Mrs. Wiggins."

"Me!" exclaimed Pearl, taken aback.

Jeremy explained the arrangement to leave a message under the loose stone on the footbridge if they were unable to make contact in the pub.

"I'll stop by the post office first thing in the morning to get milk and some bread, at 9 o'clock. That way you'll be able to pass on the message."

"But what if they see me and, and catch me red-handed! I, I'm not sure this is a good idea, me doing it," Pearl whispered in a panic.

"It's right by the post office. You'll be passing right by it on your way home if you walk that way," implored Jeremy. If you don't do it, then it'll have to be you," he said looking at Barrington, "and that's going to look mighty suspicious, isn't it?"

"But . . . " Pearl was about to raise another objection when someone tapped Jeremy on the shoulder. Jeremy wheeled his head around and nearly fell off his stool when he saw who was standing there.

"Nigel!"

TWENTY SIX

The chill clarity of the air outside was a welcome relief after the clammy humidity of the atmosphere inside the smoky pub. Conrad paused in the doorway and assessed his surroundings. A backdrop of deep violet framed the contours of the moorland to the west as the sun melted below the horizon. He felt an immediate sense of calm as the heavy blanket of dusk settled gently upon the Village.

It was time for plan B.

Conrad turned right when he exited the pub and walked two-dozen paces uphill toward the village hall before he realized he was headed in the wrong direction. He stopped in the middle of the cobbled lane and looked about. He tried to remember where the post office was in relation to the pub and decided it was back the other way. He turned and retraced his footsteps, downhill past the pub for a few hundred meters until the street dwindled into a narrow alley. He stopped again, looked over his shoulder and then moved into the shadows. Voices from the pub floated towards him. Here and there, he could see lights pop on behind the windows of the little cottages in the village. He stood very still, his breathing barely audible, with his eyes fixed on the way he had come. A tiny movement caught his eye, a brief flicker of motion in the gathering gloom. He froze and waited. The seconds ticked by and then the minutes, when the shrill ring of his cell phone pierced the silence.

"Jesus!" he hissed under his breath. He yanked the phone out of his back pocket and held it to his ear. "Yes," he barked. "Oh, Barbara, it's you." He turned abruptly and continued down the alley at a quickened pace, his footsteps echoing off the cobblestones.

"No, no, I'm fine. Yes, it's a good time—bring me up to date."

* * *

"Sarge!" Constable Evans' voice came across the radio. "Rankin just left by the side door. Nothing went down. Spoke to a woman at the bar for a few minutes, ate dinner alone and that was it. He's walking round to the front . . . "

"Hang on . . . yeah, yeah, we've got him."

Patterson nudged Collins on the arm and stabbed a finger in the direction of the front of the pub. Conrad had just emerged from the side door and was walking slowly through the beer garden.

"Stay back out of sight," Patterson instructed Evans. "He's heading this way, walking towards the Village Hall, no wait . . . he's stopped, he's turned around . . . heading back past the pub. Do see him?"

"Yeah."

"Wait. Ten more seconds. Wait. He's just past the Green. Okay, get after him. Now. And for fuck's sake don't lose sight of him."

Patterson stabbed at the keys on his cell phone. "Fields. Listen, Rankin just left. What's Danvers doing?"

"He's still at the bar, sir. He 's with Pearl Wiggins and some old bloke," Detective Fields whispered back.

"If he moves, follow him," Patterson snapped.

"What's going on Gov.? Collins asked.

"Nothing yet. Seems our man ate dinner alone. Made no contact with Danvers. Shit." Patterson said, disappointed.

"So where's he going now?"

"Dunno, we'll soon find out if Evans can stay with him."

"Hang on a minute. Holy fuck!" Patterson peered through the windscreen.

Conrad listened as his personal assistant gave him an update on various matters relating to his estate, as well as the information he had asked for on fine art experts. He ended the conversation by thanking her, and promised to catch up with his emails later. He stopped for a moment to slide the phone back into his pocket, and took another peek over his shoulder. He squinted into the darkness behind. Nothing. Silence; except for the sound of the stream up ahead. Relieved, he set off again, picking up his pace until he reached the narrow dirt path at the end of the alley. He stopped again, pressed his back against the building and glanced behind, listening for the sound of footsteps. Still nothing. He waited a few more seconds and then slipped into the darkness. The unlit path had a creepy look about it, veiled with shadows and draped with eerie over-hanging tree limbs. Pushing aside a natural aversion for dark, forbidding places, Conrad carefully picked his way downstream, avoiding the wettest spots, until he eventually came upon the familiar landmark of the footbridge beside the post office.

He walked to the middle and stopped. He reached into his pocket for the beer mat and his phone, leaned forward against the wall with his elbows, and pretended to place a call. As he pressed the keypad with the fingers of one hand, he deftly slid the note under the loose slab of stone with the other. He held the phone to his ear for several moments and then, as if no one had picked up at the other end, he straightened, pressed a key with his thumb and dropped his hand to his side. He returned the phone to his pocket and turned back in the direction he had come.

* * *

"Jesus, is that who I think it is?" Patterson said aloud.

Collins leaned forward in his car seat and squinted through the half-light across the pub car park.

"Blimey, it's Bryce Edward's kid. Now what the fuck is he doing here?"

Patterson and Collins watched from their unmarked car as Nigel Bryce Edwards hurried, his eyes darting this way and that, with short, stabbing strides across the car park toward the pub entrance.

"The kid's looking nervous," observed Collins.

"You bet he is," said Patterson, fumbling his cell phone out of his pocket. He stabbed at the keypad again and brought the phone up to his ear. "Come on. Pick up, pick up," he snarled. "Fields! A young man, short, early twenties, dark, curly hair, has just walked in. Do you see him?"

"Sarge? Uh, just a minute . . . yeah, I see him," Detective Fields answered.

"Right. Don't take your eyes off him. It's Bryce Edwards from the gallery in Harrogate. He'll make contact with Danvers."

"Yeah—he went straight to the bar. He's with Danvers now, and Pearl Wiggins."

"Watch that bag Fields," Patterson hissed. "If that bag changes hands, or if anything in it changes hands, get your arse straight over there and you bring them in. Rankin's just left. Evans is on him. Stay on Danvers. Walker will follow Wiggins if she leaves. Got that?"

"Yeah. Got it."

Patterson hung up, leaned back and turned to Collins. "This could be it Tom. I've got a feeling something's about to go down. He went quiet for a moment while he ran an idea through his mind.

"Hmm, some of these locals are probably quite close knit and I wonder just how far some of them would go to look out for each other, like Pearl Wiggins and Danvers. What do you think?" Patterson asked.

"Barlow's the best man to ask about that," said Collins. "Although, when I questioned her this morning, she sounded as if she'd like to tan the kid's hide for reckless driving. You might have a point though. I'll talk to Barlow when I get the chance."

"Well, she is the most likely person to have found the Turners on the road and your gut told you that she wasn't telling you everything, right?"

"Right. She was definitely nervous, on edge, I'd say."

"Okay, that does it then. We'll get Walker to follow her home and see if she takes a little detour somewhere. Then we'll stop her and search the bag before she gets the chance to go inside. We've got more than enough reasonable suspicion. If she's got nothing on her, then I think it's about time we took a look through her house."

"No search warrant though Sarge, and no chance of one until, umm, probably midmorning, maybe even later. Its Saturday tomorrow."

"Shit, I'm forgetting which day it is now," Patterson complained. "I'm so tired I could sleep for a week." He locked his hands behind his head, stretched them out and yawned. "We can search the place without a warrant if she gives us permission," he said quietly.

"Yeah, right. And how the fuck are we going to persuade her to do that?" asked Collins.

"Oh, I'm sure you can use some of your boyish charm on her," Patterson snickered.

Collins let out a loud snort. "Jesus," he muttered under his breath.

"Right. Well, let's see what goes down tonight. If we haven't got our hands on those paintings by tomorrow morning, I want you to make getting that warrant top priority."

Ten minutes ticked by and then another five.

"Sarge," Collins flicked Patterson's shoulder. "Look over there." He lifted his chin to indicate a figure approaching out of the shadows from their right. Both Patterson and Collins ducked their heads and sank into their seats as Conrad walked slowly up the lane, past where they were parked and into the car park at the side of the pub.

"Evans?" Patterson spoke softly into the radio. "You got anything? What's our laddo been up to?"

"Nothing. Looks like he was out for a stroll. Got to the end of the lane, made a phone call, then followed the stream for a while. Made another phone call, then back again. That was it. Do you want me to stay with him?"

"Yes. He's heading back to his car now. Tail him. I want to make sure he heads straight back to Booth Hall, no little stops on the way."

"I'm on it Sarge."

* * *

"What are you doing here?" Jeremy nearly choked on his words.

"Jezzer!" Nigel lunged forward, ensnaring Jeremy in a tight bear hug. "Aren't you glad to see your pal? Thought you might need some cheering up, so I've come to keep you company for the weekend," he said brightly. He laughed, slapped Jeremy on the back and hailed the barman with a wave of his hand.

"Two pints of bitter over here," Nigel shouted, pointing at the bar in front of him. "Been hellishly busy today in the gallery. I'm gasping for a pint," he jabbered on, unaware of Pearl and Barrington who were staring wide -eyed, shocked by the appearance of this stranger.

Jeremy looked at Pearl and then Barrington, and shrugged helplessly.

"This is . . . er . . . a friend of mine, Nigel. We went to the same school."

"Oh," Nigel said surprised, looking from one to the other. "Sorry about that. Didn't realize you were together." He grimaced, raised his eyebrows at Jeremy and stood with a weak smile on his face.

"'Ow do," Barrington nodded at Nigel. Pearl forced the corners of her mouth into a smile.

"Ah, well they were just leaving." Jeremy threw a quick look at Pearl, opening his eyes wide, hoping she would take the hint.

"Neighbors from the village," he said aloud, as if it was the most nat-ural thing in the world to be chatting with them. "Well, nice talking to you both. Here let me help you down off that stool Mrs. Wiggins." Jeremy grasped Pearl by her arm and pulled her towards him. "I'll be round at nine when you open," he said pointedly, "for some, ah, provisions."

"Eh?" Barrington said loudly.

"Time to go," said Pearl firmly, pointing to a non-existent watch on her wrist.

"It's gone nine. Twenty past," she added.

"Cor blimey, is it that time already? Here, 'elp me down will you lad."

When his feet were firmly planted on the floor, Barrington leaned close to Jeremy and said, "Right then, I'll be over at your house tomor-row." He paused, adjusted his glasses, winked and tapped the side of his nose, "at the usual time— two o'clock. Got a nice bit of manure for the roses."

"Yeah, right, thanks. See you then," Jeremy said with a smile. His eyes flickered to Nigel and then to the table by the corridor to the toilets. The man was still there, talking on his phone, looking in the opposite direction. Jeremy kept his eyes on him for several seconds and then looked at the backs of Pearl and Barrington as they made their way to the door. As soon as they were out of earshot, Jeremy dropped his smile and spun around to face Nigel.

"I told you I wanted some time on my own," he said through clenched teeth. "The fucking police are in here watching me right now, and here you are to fuck things up even more."

"What? Oh God, shit!" Nigel shrunk against the bar with his head down. He put his lips to the pint in front of him, tilted it without lifting it from the bar and took a long draught like a camel. A line of froth remained on his upper lip when he turned his head sideways to look at Jeremy. "Jez, I'm in so much shit," he whispered. His eyes were red rimmed and watering. His bottom lip trembled. "You've got to help me man."

Jeremy stared at him, too stunned to speak. His mouth opened and closed, without emitting a sound. "Oh no, don't tell me," he finally managed to mutter. He dropped down onto his elbows next to Nigel and moved close, so their shoulders were touching. Out of the side of his mouth, he hissed, "Don't tell me you're involved in this crap. What in fuck's name have you got yourself into?"

"Tell me you've got them first. You have haven't you?" Nigel gave Jeremy a sidelong look. He sounded desperate.

Jeremy's head snapped sideways. "How many times do I have to tell you: I haven't got anything. Nothing. Parks left nothing!" he said emphatically, annunciating each syllable. He was angry.

"Then I'm dead," Nigel sniveled into his beer.

"What do mean, dead?"

"I'm done for. They want the Turners back."

"Who, what?" Jeremy said incredulously. "Look, you'd better tell me what the hell's going on." He glanced nervously into the mirror behind the bar and saw Nigel's terrified expression staring back at him. "We've got to get out of here, somewhere where we can talk. Where's your car? No, no, forget that, we'll take mine." Jeremy downed the last of his pint, tapped Nigel on the arm and slid off his stool. "Come on, we're leaving."

* * *

"Pearl Wiggins and some old bloke are leaving now," whispered Detective Fields over his cell phone. "She's still got the bag."

"Yeah, we see them," Patterson replied.

"Sir! Danvers and Bryce Edwards are getting ready to leave as well," Fields whispered urgently.

"Okay, stay with them." Patterson let his cell phone fall into his lap then grabbed the radio.

"Walker! Pearl Wiggins has just left by the front entrance. She's heading downhill towards the stream. Get on her tail and follow her home. We'll head her off before she reaches the post office and do a stop-and-search before she gets inside."

"Yep, got it," Walker replied.

Plain clothes Detective Constable Walker stepped away from the corner of the pub shortly after Pearl and Barrington emerged through the beer garden. He casually walked straight past them, then strode down the lane without a backward glance, disappearing into the darkness.

"Okay, Tom. Let's go. I'll take the front of the post office. You go round the back in case she goes in that way," said Patterson. "Let's see if our Mrs. Wiggins has got herself mixed up in all this."

* * *

"Right then, out with it. Right now, Nigel," Jeremy said as soon as they were in his car. He turned right out of the pub car park, drove alongside the Green for fifty meters, then took a left in the direction of the main road.

Nigel pressed his face against the window, slumped in his seat. "It was me Julian wanted to see when he came into the gallery," he said quietly. "He was dropping off the Turners so that I could smuggle them out of the country later on."

"What? You? Smuggle them where?" Jeremy shouted in a half scream, struggling to keep his eyes on the road.

"Switzerland, for that Rankin woman. "She's got, I mean, she had a place out there in Switzerland. She's one, she was one," he corrected himself, "one of the world's major collectors. Turner was her latest passion. She's got the *Blue Rigi* you know," he said, turning his head to look at Jeremy. "Do you remember, in December how it went to an anonymous private collector for 5.8 mill? Well, that was her, only she can't get it out of the country because of the export restriction slapped on it by the D.C.M.S. She knew the minute the *Yorkshire Collection* came onto the market, the same thing would happen to them, so . . . " he paused to formulate his words, "Julian did some kind of deal, under the table. I don't know the details about it; he never involved me in that side of things. But I was supposed to sneak them out of the country for them. Nobody's going to be watching some little nobody like me. They needed someone who was off the radar. Should have been six days ago. It was all arranged. Had a flight booked, everything, but for some reason Julian came into the gallery a day early, when I wasn't expecting him. And now they're both dead. I have no clue where the Turners are and, and," he dropped his chin to his chest, squeezed his eyes tight shut as if he were trying to drive an image from his mind, "and, I've been threatened. I don't know what to do Jez."

"What? Who? Who's threatened you? What did they say? Was it Claudia Rankin's son?" The questions came out in a torrent.

"What! No, "Nigel responded quickly. "No. I don't think he knows anything about this. He came into the gallery yesterday. You were there. You met him—the tall blond haired guy."

"So what did he want?"

"I'm not sure. I think he was after some kind of closure; retracing his mother's last footsteps, that kind of thing. It sounded as if he couldn't get his mind around her having some kind of affair with Julian, and he definitely looked shocked when my dad filled him in on what the police suspect about her. No, it wasn't him. I got a phone call later on, at the gallery, from whomever Julian got the Turners from. They want them back. He said . . . "

"Who, who said?" Jeremy interrupted.

"I don't know—I swear! I've got no idea who was talking. It was a man. Definitely English, southern, bit of an accent, Dorset maybe—sounded older."

"So how does this person know about you?"

"I don't know. I never dealt with anyone. I was just the delivery boy."

"Oh Jesus Christ!" Jeremy shouted. "Do you mean you've done this before?"

"Only once," Nigel blubbered. "I swear, only the one time before this."

"Christ," Jeremy muttered. "I can't believe I'm hearing this." He fell silent for a moment, trying to absorb what Nigel had told him. "So, what else did he say? I mean, did he ask for you by name or what?"

"Noooo," Nigel said, replaying the conversation in his mind. "I answered using my name. You know the spiel, "Good morning, Bryce-Edwards Gallery, Nigel speaking."

Jeremy cast a suspicious glance at Nigel. "And then what?"

"He said I'd got forty eight hours to get the Turners back or else I'd end up like Julian."

Jeremy gasped. "He said that, those actual words?"

Nigel nodded his head. "Yeah, those very words."

"You stupid, fucking idiot!" Jeremy shouted in disgust.

"And what if they've followed you here? Did you think about that?" Jeremy's voice rang through the car. "You only ever think of yourself, don't you? Why did you do it Nigel—eh? Why? You don't need the money. Your old man's loaded."

"I'm sorry. I'm really, really sorry," Nigel sniveled. "It, it started last year," he stammered, "when I was in Italy for five months; you know, part of my degree. Julian spends, I mean spent . . . " He squeezed his eyes shut again and sucked in a breath. "He always spent a few months every spring out there doing the rounds, soaking up the culture, a little acquisition here and there. Anyway, he took me under his wing, a favor for my old man—they go back years. He took me to the museums, the galleries, showed me the ropes, introduced me to some of his high-flying friends. You think my father's well off? Ha!" he snorted. "What he makes is peanuts compared to what I've seen. You can't imagine how much money some people have, the yachts, the mansions, the art . . . " He glanced out the window and continued. "You should see how the other half live Jez—un-fucking believable"

"Yeah, right," said Jeremy, unmoved. "So?"

"So, those bastards don't get that kind of money sitting on their asses working nine till five in some crummy office block, or slogging it out in some two-bit gallery in the backwater of bloody Harrogate, like my old man's done for the last forty years. Yeah, yeah, I know you'll say he does all right, but I don't want to be like him. I want to stand on my own. I want to make my own money, Jez. I want what Julian's got, had. Christ I still can't get used to him being dead." He shook his head and looked down at his lap. He was silent for a while and then he said, choosing his words carefully, "It was her idea, Claudia Rankin's. She's the one who pushed Julian into it. He was obsessed with her. Would have done anything for her. She had him wrapped around her little finger."

"And you didn't for one minute think that Julian might just be stringing you along, you know—using you," Jeremy said sarcastically.

"I know that, Jeremy. I'm not that stupid. Yeah, I was being used. Julian was being used. So what? I did it for the money. A few hundred thousand on the quiet—not that easy to turn down. Would you have done the same if you were in my shoes?" He turned to look at Jeremy.

Jeremy's eyes flickered to Nigel's face for a second as his mind flashed over the deal he had with Conrad. If he decided to help Nigel, it would mean betraying Conrad and abandoning any hope of getting anything other than grief from this whole affair. After what he had been through, a little monetary reward was not something he wanted to give up. Additionally, Pearl and Barrington would not get their slice of the pie. Without their co-operation, there was no guarantee he would get the Turners back anyway. It was a while before he answered.

"Maybe," he answered quietly, his voice dripping with heavy irony.

"Look, I'm sorry, Jez," Nigel repeated. "I didn't mean to get you involved in any of this."

"Don't say anything else," Jeremy snapped. "I need to think."

They drove the rest of the way in silence. When they pulled into his parent's drive he said: "Okay, you'd better stay here tonight. It would look odd if you take off now. But I want you out of here by tomorrow lunchtime, Nigel. Have you got that? If the police come poking around, asking questions, you tell them what we told Pearl and Barrington in the pub. You've come to stay with a mate, right? Nothing wrong with that, but I need some time on my own Nigel. I'm a wreck at the moment. I can't take any more drama."

"But, but what am I going to do, Jez? What if they come after me like they said?"

"You have to call their bluff don't you? Oh come on Nige, they've got nothing on you; no evidence you've helped Julian out in the past, have they? They're just trying to scare you," Jeremy said half-heartedly, trying to sound encouraging. "It's all big talk. No one's going to be stupid enough to come anywhere near you, not with the police hovering around in the background. You'll be all right." He patted the side of Nigel's knee with the back of his hand. "Come on, let's get a drink, raid my parent's drinks cabinet."

TWENTY SEVEN

Pearl hurried down the lane and into the alleyway as fast as her legs could carry her. In a panic, and distracted by the hundreds of thoughts that were swirling through her brain, she did not pay much attention to the noise her best shoes with their daring two inch heels, were making on the cobblestones as she clattered down the hill toward the stream. She was not happy about taking the dark, creepy way home. Under normal circumstances, she took the longer, well-lit route past the chip shop and bakery. She felt safer going that way. Besides, part of the route was paved, a godsend for her corns. But tonight was different. She had to locate the loose slab of stone on the footbridge and retrieve the note that was concealed underneath.

The path was a handy little short cut during the day; often used by locals if they had to pop into the post office for a quick errand, and it was also an attraction for hikers seeking a pleasant, scenic stroll into the village. At night though, because the path was narrow and unlit, it was a route few people cared to use, apart from the local teenagers who were drawn to it for those very reasons.

Pearl streaked down the path until she was about fifty feet away from the footbridge. She stopped by a thicket of overgrown bushes, and glanced over her shoulder. Satisfied there was no one behind, she stepped off the path and crept into the tangle of vegetation. She stood still for a moment to get her breath back, and then, using two fingers, prized a hole in the foliage so she could peek through.

A rustle in the undergrowth by her feet made her shrink in horror and clamp a hand across her mouth to stop from screaming. She was terrified of anything remotely rodent, but a quick flick of her shoe aimed in its direction sent whatever it was scurrying under the fence. She remained frozen for several seconds and slowly let out a breath she had not realized she was holding. She squeezed her eyes shut, swallowed, and said a silent prayer before leaning forward to take another peek along the path. She looked back up the path in the direction of the village. Nothing, only darkness and the faint outline of some overhanging tree limbs.

To her right, toward the bridge, a movement caught her eye. Horrified, Pearl dropped her hands and reeled backward, her heart hammering so loud it drowned out the sound of the stream. Oh dear Lord, have mercy upon me, she mouthed silently. Two figures, two men on the bridge, just visible in the moonlight were walking in her direction.

"She must have doubled back. She couldn't have passed me. I would have seen her," one of them whispered.

"Shit!" cursed the other man. Pearl recognized his voice at once. It was the Scotland Yard detective who had questioned her earlier. She listened as he spoke into his radio.

"Sarge, I'm with Walker. She's not here . . . nah, he didn't see her . . . she must have doubled back. We're heading back toward the pub now. We'll split and meet you outside the post office. Yep, right. Got it."

Pearl remained frozen, concealed in the shrubbery until the two men disappeared into the darkness. When she was quite sure they were gone, she shot out of the bushes, scurried onto the footbridge, located the loose stone, extracted the note, and stuffed it down the front of her blouse so it was tightly wedged between her bosom. After a quick backward glance, she hurried down the remainder of the path, slowing down to a leisurely pace as she rounded the corner post office building into the car park at the front. She was fumbling around in her bag for the front door key, when she looked up to see a stocky, grim faced man standing under the lamppost beside a parked car.

"Oh!" she exclaimed, feigning surprise when she saw him.

"Mrs. Wiggins."

"Yes."

"Detective Maurice Patterson, Scotland Yard." The man walked toward her with an ID in his outstretched hand.

He nodded toward her handbag and said, "I'm stopping you on the suspicion that you might be carrying stolen artwork. If you could just wait here a minute, Mrs. Wiggins." He indicated a spot in front of the large window of the building and then reached inside his car for a radio.

"Collins. She's here. Car park, front of the post office."

"You met Detective Collins this morning. He'll be here in a few minutes. There are some questions I need to ask you and I need to search your bag. Now we can either do it here," he said nodding towards the post office, "or we can do it down at the station. It's up to you. Wherever you'd feel most comfortable, Mrs. Wiggins." He looked at her with a steady gaze, unsmiling.

"Do you mean the police station?" Pearl whispered.

"Yes. The police station."

"Oh, well I . . . I'm not sure." Pearl's eyes widened with fear. "Am I being arrested?"

"No." Patterson said flatly. "Not yet."

The moment Collins and Walker arrived, Pearl declared she was going to faint. "Oooh, I can feel my heart racing. I've come over all lightheaded," she said, frantically fanning her face with one hand. "Oh my, I think I'm going to pass out!"

Collins and Walker rushed to her side and grabbed her under the elbows. Patterson took the key out of her hand and opened the door. All three of them guided, half carried her through to the parlor at the back of the building where they lowered her into a large chair by the fireplace.

"I can call for an ambulance if you think you need one, Mrs. Wiggins," said Collins. Patterson stood to one side, arms folded across his chest, unimpressed.

"Oh, no, no. I'll be all right in a few minutes. It's my nerves. They're not used to all this excitement. I can't take much more." She extracted a handkerchief from her blouse sleeve and blew her nose making a loud trumpeting sound. She kept her handbag clutched tightly to her chest.

"Now, now, Mrs. Wiggins," said Collins. "There's no need to get upset. You are not under arrest. We're here to have an informal chat and we need to have a quick look in that bag of yours." He sat down on the pouf in front of her and started wafting a magazine in her face. "Here, let's get a little air on your face. How about a nice cup of tea?" He looked up at Walker and motioned to the kitchen with a flick of his head. "Constable Walker will put the kettle on."

"Yes, that would be nice," Pearl sniveled. "Oh, but the shame of it; me being searched by the police like this. My Arthur, God bless his soul will be turning in his grave right now. I swear that I haven't got those paintings. I've been a law abiding citizen my whole life. I don't even cross the road at a crossin' if the little green man's not lit up. Oh, my heart . . . It's beating right out of mi chest. Ooooh, I feel faint again!"

And so it went until Patterson, mustering every ounce of willpower to keep from sounding impatient, calmly informed her that one way or another, her handbag was going to be searched. They could either do it there, or they could arrest her and do it down at the station—it was her choice. He added that it was probably better to do it in the privacy of her home. That way, fewer people were likely to find out about it.

After taking a second or two to mull over Patterson's words, Pearl slowly released her grip on the bag and held it out for Patterson to inspect.

"Thank you Mrs. Wiggins." Patterson forced a weary smile. He took the bag, handed it to Collins, and motioned with a flick of his wrist, for him to search it on the other side of the room. He pushed the pouf out of the way and pulled a chair from the other side of the room. He sat down a few feet away from her and calmly said: "There are a few more questions I'd like to ask, Mrs. Wiggins. It shouldn't take too long."

"But I've already told Inspector Collins everything I know. I told him yesterday." She looked at him with pleading eyes.

"Ah, it's Detective Collins," Patterson said with a twitch of a smile. "There are a few grey areas I'd like to get cleared up. I don't think I need to remind you of the penalties for not telling the truth, do I Mrs. Wiggins?"

"Yes, er no. I mean no!" Pearl stammered.

"Sir," Collins interrupted from across the room. He shook his head when Patterson turned to look at him.

"Hmmph!" Pearl snorted indignantly through her nose. "The only things I picked up from the road were lots of papers with writing all over them, a few newspapers, books about art, a half empty backpack and some other bits and pieces. I threw the lot into a couple of bin-liners and I gave it all to Inspec—I mean Detective Collins yesterday. If there were any paintings amongst that lot then I certainly didn't see any. You're welcome to have a good look around. You can search my bins if you like, but you won't find anything." Pearl folded her arms defensively across her bosom and added, "I don't know what else I can tell you."

"Well, perhaps you could start by telling us how well you know Jeremy Danvers."

Just for a second, a little flash of worry shot across Pearl's face. Then she shrugged her shoulders and gave a little laugh, like she was trying to cover it up. She looked down at her handkerchief as she spoke. "Well, I've known him and his family since he were a little nipper. In a village as small as this one, you soon get to know your neighbors."

"I see. So would you say you're quite close to him?"

Pearl glanced at him for a second. "Not especially. Enough to know he's not a bad lad."

Patterson leaned back in his chair and studied Pearl's face with wearied tension. When he finally spoke, his voice was hard and forbidding.

"You were seen with him in the pub tonight. What were the two of you talking about?"

"Uh . . . " Pearl's forehead creased and she did not answer right away. She twisted the handkerchief in her lap, avoiding eye contact. Then she seemed to come to a decision. "Well, I asked him what the heck he'd been up to. I told him the police were asking after him."

"And what was his reaction?"

"The poor lad was very upset, and it's no wonder, the way he's been hounded by the police. He told us, me and Barrington that is, that you think he ran off with some very valuable paintings, which is just ridiculous. I can tell you right now that you're barking up the wrong tree. He's a good boy, Jeremy Danvers." She told Patterson the story of Mrs. Hardcastle's ten-pound note. "And he's always been a great help to Barrington you know."

"Did he ask about the things that fell out of his car?"

"Yes. He was worried about his rucksack and his university papers. I told him I'd given it all to the police."

"No mention of any artwork then?"

"Huh? No. He doesn't know anything about any paintings."

"What about his American friend?"

"Who? What American friend?"

"Does the name Conrad Rankin mean anything to you?"

"Nooo," Pearl replied slowly, shaking her head. "Unless you mean the tall blond chap who was with him outside the post office this morning."

"Yes, that's him. Has Jeremy said anything about him to you?"

"Well yes, but they're not friends. He hardly knows him."

"What did Dan, er . . . Jeremy tell you?"

"He said the American fellow had come into the gallery on Friday just as he was about to leave and that he followed him to the petrol station and reached inside his jacket for a gun. The poor lad was terrified. He thought it was some criminal, a killer looking for the paintings. That's why he was driving so fast through the village. He thought he was going to be shot."

"And?"

"And he wasn't a killer at all. It was all a misunderstanding. It turns out the American chap was here to ask about his mother. She was killed you know. It was in a car accident a few weeks ago. In fact, when I think about it, I think I remember seeing it on the news. Now what was her name?" Pearl looked up at the ceiling, tapping her chin as she tried to remember. "Hmm, she was very well-to-do apparently; very wealthy, according to Jeremy."

"A misunderstanding?" Patterson prompted Pearl to continue.

"Eh? Oh yes. The American didn't have a gun at all. He apologized as soon as he caught up with Jeremy. He said he was sorry for frightening him and that he meant no harm. I watched the two of them talking. They were in the field across the road." Pearl leaned forward slightly in her chair and said confidentially, "Jeremy was one of the last people to see her alive you know—his mother." She leaned back and nodded her head sagely as if she had imparted something Patterson did not already know.

"Did you see the two of them exchange anything in the field?"

"Exchange? What do you mean?"

"Did The American, Conrad Rankin hand anything to Jeremy?"

"Nooooo, I don't think so."

"And what about Jeremy? Did he give anything to Rankin?"

"Not that I saw. They sat talking for a while."

"How long?" Patterson interrupted.

"Oh I don't know. Fifteen, maybe twenty minutes."

"And then what did they do?"

"They walked around the field looking for Jeremy's things. Then they came over here. Jeremy came in and asked me if I had picked anything up from the road. I told him I'd found a lot of papers and I'd thrown them into the bin."

"Did he ask for them back?"

"Yes, but I told him he'd have to wait. I was angry you see, about the speeding. It was only three days ago that some hoodlum came roaring through the village and nearly knocked Mrs. Wainwright clear off her feet, and it was on the crossin' as well!" I keep telling George Barlow that . . . "

"Yes, right." Patterson cut her off mid-sentence.

"So you didn't give him his belongings. Is that correct?"

"I didn't give him anything."

"I'm going to ask you this again Mrs. Wiggins. Don't answer straight away. I want you to think very carefully before you answer." Patterson straightened his back and looked Pearl in the eye. He waited a few moments before speaking again. "Have you given anything back to Jeremy Danvers?"

"I don't have to wait a single second," Pearl answered immediately. "I've already told you—I have not given anything to that boy. I swear upon my Arthur's grave."

Patterson let out a frustrated breath and swept his fingers through his hair. "Okay. So, where was Conrad Rankin while you were talking with Jeremy?"

"I'm not sure. He was outside in his car when Jeremy left."

"Did you see them leave?"

"Yes. They talked for a bit and then drove off in different directions."

"Did they meet again?" Patterson asked quickly, hoping to catch Pearl off guard.

Pearl stared at him for a few seconds like she was considering telling him more. Then she opened her eyes wide, shrugged her shoulders and said, "Well how do I know?"

Patterson exchanged a quick glance with Collins. Collins shrugged his shoulders, and with an almost imperceptible shake of his head signaled to Patterson that the interview was going nowhere.

"Right then." Patterson turned back to her with a sigh, "with your permission, we'll take a quick look around and then we'll be on our way." He stood up and turned towards the kitchen. He poked his head through the door and said, "Have you got that tea yet, Walker? You can pour us all one." As he pushed away from the door, he noticed a nail in the wall. The plaster around it was chalky and dry as if it had been hammered in recently. He scraped some loose plaster off the wall and gently rubbed it between his thumb and fingers.

"Have you been hanging some pictures Mrs. Wiggins?"

For a tiny slice of a second, a look of terror flashed across Pearl's face. She lowered her gaze and began twisting the handkerchief in her lap. When she spoke her voice was a thin, dry whisper. "I . . . it was a photograph of Arthur. I took it down seeing as I . . . well, now that me and Barrington, er, I mean, now that Mr. Smith and I are courting. I couldn't bear for him to see me happy like this . . . Arthur that is. I feel so guilty, like I'm betraying him." She choked on her words, too upset to go on.

TWENTY EIGHT

That same evening, in the quiet solitude of the library, Dickie paused to reflect upon a strange day. He was slumped in an oversized leather chair, his feet propped up on the enormous desk in front of him, cradling a glass of Famous Grouse Whisky in his lap. His head was back against the chair, eyes closed, his face a picture of perfect contentment with a wide, satisfied grin spread from ear to ear. He could never have imagined, after his beastly meeting with the bank manager this morning that the day could have turned out so splendidly. He lifted the glass to his lips, took a generous sip and opened one eye to peek at the wall to his right. He wriggled his body in smug delight at the thought of the two paintings concealed in the priest-hole behind the book-lined wall, then snapped his eye shut again, letting out a long satisfied sigh.

The little watercolor he retrieved from his car after the police left that afternoon was somewhat worse for wear, creased in the middle and a tad ragged on one side, but nonetheless, still intact. From the little information he had gleaned on Turner from his research on the Internet, in his estimation, it was still bound to be worth a pretty penny. But the real bounty of the day was the other painting he had discovered in the dining room, thanks to Millie's eagle eye. She was on her way up to the study with the leftover pastries from High Tea when she had spotted the American fellow, Conrad Rankin, poking about in the room, off limits, and immediately reported the trespass.

As soon as Millie left the study, he shoveled the pastries into his mouth and hid the plate in the top drawer of his desk, in case, heaven forbid, Olivia should awaken from her migraine and discover his illicit snack. He then shot down the hallway, past the private bedrooms, down the main staircase to the entrance foyer, down another hallway and into the dining room.

He spent a good fifteen minutes checking to see if anything was out of place, examining the contents of the glass cabinets and opening and shutting the cupboards and drawers. Seeing that he was looking for things missing rather than things added, only a remarkable stroke of good fortune could be credited for him stumbling across the watercolor hidden between the cloth napkins at the back of one of the dresser drawers.

Now the two little *beauties* were safely stashed inside the priest-hole, his own private little hide-away that no one else knew about, not even Olivia. This last thought pleased him enormously. He considered that the one great mistake he had made early on in his marriage was allowing his wife to be privy to far too much information about the running of the estate.

She was the type of woman who somehow managed to wheedle out every last detail about all things connected to the Hall, from their dire financial situation, right down to the color of his underpants. She was devilishly hard to keep secrets from. The priest-hole though, was his one last bastion of defense, the only small pocket of the Hall that she knew absolutely nothing about. It was the place where the truth about the *Grey Lady* lay hidden. The grey silk dress, the crinoline, the wig, the make-up; that's where he kept them all stashed.

Olivia would never have approved of his idea to introduce a ghost to the Hall. She would have considered it utterly ridiculous, completely out of the question, and entirely beneath them. That Baroness Montague chose to haunt the Hall of her own accord, quite out of the blue, came as a Godsend for Dickie. Olivia could not possibly hold him to account for the workings of the supernatural, and her censure was of no consequence to someone from *the other side*. It was beyond her control. Although she appreciated the extra revenue generated by such an unusual attraction, and she said nothing in public to undermine the baroness' growing reputation as being one of Yorkshire's most reliable phantoms. However, in private, behind closed doors, when all the visitors were gone, the very notion that the presence of the *Grey Lady* had any substance, Olivia dismissed as utter nonsense and superstitious claptrap.

The distant chime of the grandfather clock in the entrance hall slowly filtered into Dickie's brain, nudging him out of his reverie. He lifted his head and glanced at the carriage clock on the desk. Midnight. One hour to go before his transformation into the *Grey Lady*. He chuckled to himself. Buoyed by his fortuitous luck in finding the Turners, the timing for a little haunting could not be any better. Olivia was safely out of the way. Her migraine was likely to keep her within the confines of her bedroom until morning. Then there was Ms. Pendleton, who would without doubt, be the Hall's greatest advocate if she had the good fortune to experience a little paranormal activity.

He took another long swig from his glass and turned his thoughts back to the Turners and how he might approach Rankin about them. A meeting between the two of them had already been arranged for nine in the morning, here in the library, supposedly to discuss the sale of some of the Hall's remaining antiquities. That would of course, be the opportune time to broach the delicate subject of the paintings. But the question was: how much should he ask for them? It all depended on how far Rankin was prepared to go to get his hands on them.

"Hmm. How much, how much, how much?" Dickie repeated quietly to the empty room. It all rather depends upon the fellow's reaction when I first mention them, he thought. He settled deeper into the chair. His eyelids grew heavy, fluttered once or twice and then closed. The three large Scotches he had consumed after dinner were making him feel sleepy; that and the extra large portions he had heaped on his plate in Olivia's absence. Minutes passed. His mouth flapped open and his breathing settled into a deep rhythmic pattern. He was dangerously close to falling fast asleep, but a particularly deep nasal inhalation culminated in an earth- shattering snort and startled him back to consciousness.

"What, eh . . . what was that," he spluttered, jolting upright in his chair. He rubbed his eyes and snatched for the little clock on the desk.

"Dear God!" he exclaimed when he saw the time. He swung his legs to the floor, downed the last of his Scotch in one straight gulp and bound out of the room. He raced down the hallway until he reached the large glass display cabinet containing the 17th century muskets. After a quick check in both directions, he leaned against the wood paneled wall, located the two hidden notches, pushed backwards with his bottom, and promptly disappeared.

* * *

Up in the east wing, in the expanse of his four-poster bed, Conrad lay exhausted, unable to sleep, entangled in a thin sheet, after tossing and turning for hours. After leaving the pub car park in Tipping, he had driven back to Booth Hall with every intention of scrutinizing his mother's art inventory, but by the time he climbed up the staircase to his room, he was so weary, overcome by the time difference between Yorkshire and home, that all he had the energy for, was to take a quick shower and make a few phone calls.

At 11:00 p.m., he collapsed into bed too tired to keep his eyes open any longer. Unfortunately, in his over-tired state, his mind refused to switch off. His misgivings about Jeremy, the Turners, his mother, the police, were all mixed up, swirling unbidden in his brain, amplified by the stillness of the night. As the minutes ticked by and the hours spun away, the possibility of sleep receded even further. Finally, worn out with the battle, he turned on his back, opened his eyes and stared into the blackness. The heavy damask curtains at the window were impenetrable; not one chink of moonlight filtered through. Conrad blinked several times, willing his eyes to adjust to the dark, but the blackness was so complete he could not even make out the canopy over the bed. It was like lying at the bottom of an unfathomable abyss.

The silence was suddenly pierced by a blood-curdling scream. Conrad sat bolt upright, ears tuned to every noise. He remained frozen, trying not to breathe, when another scream sent him scrambling for the switch on his table lamp. He reached out to where he thought the bedside table was, but the constraint of the sheet wrapped around his legs made him fall off the bed. He landed awkwardly on his shoulder and let out a yelp. In a fit of anger and fear, he wrestled with the sheet, kicking out with his legs until he was free and able to rest on all fours. Panting heavily, his heart drumming, he froze again with his head cocked to one side listening for the slightest sound. After a prolonged silence, he slowly climbed onto his feet and with hands extended to feel his way around, he took a tentative step for what he hoped was the door. Four paces later, he felt something solid in front of him—the wall. He was fumbling for the light switch when he heard a scuffle in the corridor outside and the sound of a woman's voice, followed by the noise of feet thundering down the stairs. With a new urgency, he patted along the wall like a blind man. As soon as he found the door, he yanked it open and cautiously stuck his head outside to see what was happening. The lighting in the corridor was dim; the only light was provided by one small wall sconce at the far end of the landing next to the stairs. There was no sign of anyone, and not one sound.

"What the hell . . . " he whispered. He considered going right back to bed; God knows he felt bone weary, but he knew the chances of falling asleep were about nil. And those noises, the screams he heard, were just too loud to ignore.

"Shit," Conrad muttered under his breath. He decided to take a quick peek down the stairs; see if anything was amiss. If nothing was going on, he would head back to bed. Wearing only his boxers, he crept out of his room, carefully pulling the door shut behind him. On tiptoe, he made his way toward the staircase, cringing every time one of the old floorboards made a creak. He could dimly make out a large oversized urn to his right, and a large curtained window ahead on his left.

He was almost at the top of the stairs when the sound of feet thundering along a corridor on the floor below echoed up the staircase. Alarmed, he shrank back against the wall, then thought the better of it and flung himself behind the urn instead. The sound of footsteps on the stairs sent a cold stab of fear through him, making him feel as if his heart were in his throat. He remained crouched behind the urn, barely breathing until the sound of the footsteps receded and the house grew quiet again. He waited for several minutes, until his legs began to feel badly cramped, and then crept out across the landing to the top of the staircase. A low, muffled, whimpering sound off to his left made him stop dead in his tracks. The sound had come from behind the curtains. Without pausing to think, he lunged towards the window, grabbed the curtains in both hands and ripped them apart.

"Dear God, Ms. Pendleton!"

She was curled up on the window ledge, dressed in her nightgown, eyes wide with fear, brandishing a candlestick above her head, ready to strike.

"Oh, it's you Mr. Rankin! Thank God," she cried. She dropped the candlestick and collapsed into his arms.

"I–I saw her—*The Grey Lady*. I saw her," she repeated, stammering her words. "It was . . . hideous! Quite hideous. Not at all what I expected . . . Her face . . . Oh, Mr. Rankin, thank God you're here, I–I . . . " she held him tight and burrowed her head into his naked shoulder. Stunned, Conrad patted her back softly in an attempt to calm her down.

"There, there. It's okay. It's okay. Where did you see her, the uh, *Grey Lady*? What happened?"

"In–in a hallway downstairs, near the kitchen I think. I–I was on my way up here. I was going to wait you see. I–I, Oh Mr. Rankin I feel as if I'm going to faint."

"I think we need to get you back to your room. Here, come on, I'll take you back and then I'll have a look around . . . "

"No! No, I wouldn't if I were you. It . . . it was ghastly," she sniveled, clinging onto him, increasing her grip.

"Look, let me get some clothes on first." He pried her from him, and with his hand placed under her arm, steered her toward his room.

"Sit down for a minute while I find some pants." He helped her into the chair by the window.

Conrad threw on the jeans and shirt he had worn the day before, then hustled Ms. Pendleton out of his room. On tiptoe, speaking in whispers, they made their way down the staircase, through the entrance hall and into the West Wing where the other guest rooms were located. When they reached Ms. Pendleton's room, Conrad escorted her inside, poured her a glass of water, and ushered her into bed. After listening patiently to her tale of horror, finally left her quivering under the bed-covers with the reassurance that he would definitely investigate the very spot where her encounter had taken place. He promised he would report back to her in the morning over breakfast.

As he stepped out of her room, his lips curled into a smile. A ghost—what utter, ridiculous hogwash. He shook his head, laughing quietly as he made his way down the stairs to the entrance hall. He was about halfway across the foyer when a scuffling noise from somewhere deep within the building made him stop and listen. A few seconds passed, then he heard it again, only louder this time. He hesitated for a moment and decided he should investigate after all. He turned and trotted down the long hall that led past the drawing room and library.

When he reached the door to the library where the police had interviewed him, he shrank against the wall and listened, peering through the gloom in both directions. The only light was a dim swath of moonlight that filtered through a chink in the curtains at the far end of the corridor. At first, he heard nothing other than the occasional creaks and moans of an old house in its slumber, but then from some-where off to his left, he thought he could hear the sound of someone approaching. He shot across the corridor, ducked behind a tall, heavy screen and held his breath. He leaned forward to peek between the hinges, but through the darkness he saw nothing. He relaxed for a moment, but seconds later he heard the footsteps again, closer this time, and a soft rustling noise. The hairs on his arms rose and a surge of adrenaline sent his heart racing. A flicker of light from the end of the corridor made him swivel his head in that direction. He peered through the screen hinges again, trying not to make a sound. To his horror, out of the darkness, enveloped in a pool of dim light, came a shimmering apparition of silver grey, gliding, ethereal, and big. Conrad gasped, and reeled back against the wall. A floorboard creaked loudly with the shift in his weight. Holy shit! His mind screamed. This cannot be happening! He froze, rooted to the spot.

The rustling noise grew louder and then stopped abruptly. A quiet stillness descended upon the corridor; the silence punctuated by the distant ticking of a grandfather clock. Seconds passed, then a minute.

Conrad remained as still as a statue. It was so quiet he could almost hear the sound of his heart beating.

A floorboard creaked, followed by the footsteps and bustle of skirts approaching. Conrad stiffened and balled his fists, ready to face whatever was coming towards him. He squeezed his eyes shut for an instant, willing himself to remain calm and think rationally. The footsteps stopped.

Conrad's eyes snapped open to see the pool of light suspended above him. Another bolt of adrenaline surged through his body as he realized that Baroness Montague, the *Grey Lady*, the ghost of Booth Hall was hovering a few feet away from him on the other side of the screen. A jolt of fear passed through him as he noticed the screen being pulled back inch, by inch. Instinctively, he stepped to the side, away from the hand that was peeling back the screen, ready to bolt in the other direction when some inner voice spoke to him. This is ridiculous, he thought. A ghost? Oh please! A wave of disgust at his own cowardice washed over him, and that, mixed with a certain amount of genuine fear made him lunge against the screen with his shoulder, sending it crashing to the floor.

What happened next was chaos. There was a loud yelp of pain and the sound of someone badly winded as Conrad landed heavily on top of the screen. A lantern with a large candle inside smashed against the drawing room door. Conrad rolled over commando style and leaped to his feet. He swiveled around, grabbed one end of the screen and yanked it upwards at the same time as the candle flickered and died. The corridor was plunged into darkness. Caught off guard by the sudden blackness, Conrad drew back for an instant. There was a loud grunt, labored breathing, lots of rustling and scuffles. In the seconds that it took for Conrad's eyes to adjust to the dark, something burst past him; a rush of air as petticoats and silk streaked towards the end of the corridor. Startled, Conrad staggered backwards, tripped on the carpet and fell on his back. The *Grey Lady* flew around the corner, past the floor to ceiling window, illuminated for an instant by the chink of light that pierced the curtains. Without slowing, she shot a backwards glance in Conrad's direction. Their eyes met for only a split second, but it was long enough for Conrad to recognize, beyond a doubt, the face beneath the smudged white powder: It was the Brigadier, Sir Richard Cranshawe Booth.

Too stunned to move for several moments, Conrad watched, open mouthed, as the figure disappeared into the darkness. As soon as the initial shock wore off, Conrad jumped to his feet and ran in pursuit. When he rounded the corner of the hallway, he expected to see the retreating form of the Brigadier dashing ahead, but to his astonishment, the corridor was empty. There was no sign of ghost or human. The figure beneath the petticoats had vanished. Perplexed, he trotted down the entire length of the hallway looking this way and that, trying every door, searching behind every cabinet, but there was no trace of anyone.

Unwilling to accept that the Brigadier could vanish into thin air, Conrad doubled back tapping against the walls and trying each door handle again. He stopped by a large glass display cabinet and stood still. His eyes had better adjusted to the dim lighting and he could just about make out the silhouettes of the furniture and door frames. He slowly scanned the corridor and listened for any sound of movement, but there was nothing. Where in hell had Cranshawe disappeared to? There hadn't been enough time for anyone to make it to the end of the corridor without being seen, and yet, all the doors leading off were locked.

Mystified, he walked back to the window. On impulse, he whipped back one of the curtains, not really expecting to find anyone, but he was still disappointed to find the windowsill empty. He shrugged and turned to look back down the hallway again. Nothing. Baffled, he stood still a moment longer and debated lying in wait somewhere in the hope that the Brigadier might eventually emerge from his hiding place, but quickly decided against it. Too tired to face what might turn into an all night vigil, he made his way back up to the East Wing, determined to try and get at least a few hours of sleep. He would confront the Brigadier in the morning. It was going to be a long day.

* * *

On the other side of the wood paneled wall behind the glass display cabinet, concealed in the passageway that led to the priest-hole, Dickie lay panting on the floor, skirts around his ears, sweat pouring off him. His legs were bent in an awkward position, but he did not dare move so much as an inch until he was sure Rankin had disappeared. It had been a devilish night.

In the beginning, his haunting had gone according to plan. He was absolutely delighted to spot Ms. Pendleton creeping about in the hallways. He seized the opportunity to frighten her thoroughly, chasing her all the way up to the East Wing.

He crept back down to the hall outside the drawing room, close to the priest hole in case he needed to make a quick escape, hoping to spook anyone else who happened to be tiptoeing around the Hall at one in the morning, but he was sorely disappointed to find no one up. He threw in a few good noisy charges up and down the corridors for good measure and was about to turn in for the night when he stumbled upon the American fellow, Conrad Rankin poking around in the corridor outside the dining room.

Looking back on his impulse to let the American catch sight of the *Grey Lady*, he realized that it was a stupid decision. He should have turned around and disappeared into the priest-hole, but something got the better of him, pique at the fellow's obvious wealth perhaps, or maybe it was the effects of the Scotch, but he went after him, intending to scare the Armani pants off the raffish American braggart. What he had not bargained for was the young bounder's reaction, bursting out from behind the screen like that, knocking him clear to the ground, and nearly causing him to have a heart attack. He was lucky to have escaped with his wig still intact.

The incident was going to cause everything to be very tricky. He was hoping to meet Rankin in the morning with all the cards stacked in his favor, but if Rankin had recognized him beneath the white powder and wig, then the meeting was going to be awkward, very, very awkward indeed. Quite how he was going to deal it, he didn't know. God damn it.

TWENTY NINE

Conrad woke with a start sometime near dawn. It took several moments for him to get his bearings and to remember where he was. The air in the room felt chilled and still. It was early. He glanced at the clock on the bedside table and groaned when he saw the time, 5:15am. He was hoping it was later than that. He had only had a few hours sleep and was still exhausted. He rolled out of bed and padded to the window where he drew back the heavy curtains to catch the first glimmer of sunrise.

The rain had cleared overnight. It was a beautiful morning, soft and gauzy with mist. The fields close to the Hall glittered under the first pale sunshine, and he could see wisps of mist hanging from the high tops in the distance. Invigorated by the view, he unlatched the window and pushed it open. A stream of fresh air, alive with the scents of the countryside, slowly drifted into the room. He closed his eyes, inhaled deeply, and pondered going back to bed for an hour, but decided it would probably be a waste of time. He knew he wouldn't be able to sleep. He had too much on his mind. The fresh outdoor air beckoned. A brisk early morning walk before breakfast was a much better idea.

Deciding to shower later, he threw on a pair of jeans and a t-shirt and headed down the staircase, along a corridor, through the reception area and out into the courtyard where the guest cars were parked. He walked at a leisurely pace across the cobbled square, out past some derelict outbuildings until he reached a dirt road that led to the grounds at the rear of the Hall. He followed the road for a few hundred yards to a small green sign that indicated the public footpath to Nether Booth Fell. He paused for a moment to consider how long it would take him to cover the 1.8 miles to the Fell, and whether he would still have time to shower, change and grab a quick breakfast before 9:00 a.m. He glanced at his watch. It was still before six. Three hours was plenty of time. It was too lovely a morning to contemplate heading back inside. He needed to unwind and stretch his legs. Without further hesitation, he climbed over the stile that spanned the dry-stone wall, jumped down onto the narrow dirt path, and set off at a brisk clip.

The walk proved to be invigorating. Steep and uneven in places, bordered on both sides by rampant vegetation, the path gradually wound its way uphill to the Fell, a craggy outcrop that afforded a splendid view of Booth Hall and its grounds below. Exhilarated by the fresh air and exercise, Conrad could not resist the temptation to stop for a while and admire the vista below. He picked his way to the very edge, and sat on a flat boulder.

Away, off in the distance to the west, he could just about see the gentle blue swell of the Pennines. Before him stretched a patchwork of fields, sparkling and shimmering in the morning sun.

His gaze drifted to the parklands surrounding Booth Hall, and then to the building itself. The Hall that had seemed so foreboding in the gloom of yesterday's rainstorm, seemed to have a friendlier, welcoming air about it. Bathed in the warm light of dawn, despite the flaking paint and crumbling mortar, there was a timeless elegance about the place. Extensive scaffolding across the rear of the property was testament to the fact that the building was in need of restoration, but from what he had seen, the Hall did not seem beyond repair. It would be a great pity he thought, to let a place like this fall into ruin.

He considered the Hall's rich history and its touch of grandeur. It had private acreage, lush gardens, capacious courtyards and reasonable accessibility—all positives from a business standpoint. With the right kind of investment, business acumen and decent management, he could envisage a number of possibilities for the Hall's future.

Conrad stretched out on the rock and closed his eyes. He felt the sun's warmth on his face as a light breeze laden with the fragrance of moorland picked at the tufts of grass by his head. He smiled; content to embrace the peace and solitude of the moors. He pushed his worries about the Turners into the background and let his mind drift idly over less threatening thoughts.

What would it take he wondered, to buy a listed building such as Booth Hall? He tried to imagine completely renovating the Hall, preserving its historical integrity, but providing luxurious five star accommodations. He pictured the conversion of the outbuildings and stables to house some of his collections, a new set of vintage cars perhaps. What a magnificent setting for that, he thought. If the place could be made secure enough, there was no end to the possibilities. There might even be some mileage in moving some of his mother's art to the Hall. Why not bring some of her British acquisitions back to their country of origin and put them on public display? It would be a brilliant ploy to deflect the police and their suspicions of his involvement in his mother's schemes. Instead, he would be perceived as a major contributor to the arts, a generous benefactor to the cultural heritage of England. Why not, he mused? He liked it here. It could be his little hide-away, his escape from the rat race at home.

And what of the Turners? The thought popped unbidden into his mind. What was he going to do with the Turner that lay hidden in the Hall's dining room. And what if he managed to acquire all six of them? It would be madness to try and move them out of the country, so his only option, if he did not want to give them up, would be to find a safe place to conceal them for a protracted period of time; a place where he could admire them in secrecy at his leisure.

The fledgling idea of a new little business venture began to take a firmer root in his mind. He needed to make a few phone calls and assess the possibilities before setting the wheels in motion. Booth Hall piqued his interest, especially since Cranshawe Booth appeared to be in dire financial straits. No one in his right mind would dress up as a woman, fabricate and then impersonate a ghost unless they were absolutely desperate or barking mad. Conrad suspected there was an equal mix of both, but either way, for the right kind of money, he felt there was a reasonable chance that Cranshawe Booth might be enticed to giving up his ancestral home.

* * *

He arrived back at his room a little after 8:00 a.m. After taking a shower and changing into a fresh set of clothes, Conrad made his way down to the breakfast room that was situated at the rear of the Hall overlooking one of the gardens. He had worked up quite an appetite after his hike, and was looking forward to his first cup of morning coffee. He was a few feet away from the door when he heard the sound of Ms. Pendleton's loud, braying from inside the room. She was regaling the other guests in the breakfast room about her shocking encounter with the *Grey Lady* the previous night. Conrad stopped in his tracks. The last thing he wanted was to be entrapped by Ms. Pendleton and forced to endure her company over breakfast. He knew he had promised to report back to her, but he could not face listening to her entire tale again.

With a frustrated sigh, he did an about turn and beat a hasty retreat toward the library where he was scheduled to meet with Cranshawe Booth at nine. He was twenty minutes early. He briefly considered just turning up in the hope that Cranshawe might already be there, but he realized in a flash that it would be a waste of time. An ex-army Brigadier like Cranshawe Booth was bound to be fastidious about punctuality. It was probably wiser to wander around and kill some time rather than risk riling the old boy unnecessarily.

Conrad spent the next fifteen minutes wandering the sections of the Hall that were not cordoned. The Hall did not open to the public until eleven, so he was able, despite the complaints of an empty stomach, to enjoy his tour alone. At 8:55 a.m. he meandered back to the library and at 8:59 precisely, he rapped on the door with one knuckle.

"Enter!" A loud voice bellowed from within. "Ah, Mr. Rankin, come in, come in. Please have a seat," said Cranshawe Booth, straightening from behind his reading desk and gesturing towards a cozy seating area by one of the windows. He was dressed in an opulent velvet smoking jacket. "It's a little more comfortable over here by the window. Affords a rather nice view over the gardens don't you think?"

"Yes, Thank you," Conrad replied, somewhat taken aback by Cranshawe Booth's conviviality.

"Can I get you anything? A coffee, biscuits perhaps?" Cranshawe Booth waved towards the large cocktail table where a coffee pot and tray of biscuits were already set out. "Freshly brewed," he added.

"Coffee would be just fine thank you."

"Pour away old boy. I'll be with you in a tic." He turned to the bookcase behind the desk, opened a small cabinet concealed behind a row of books and extracted a bottle of Scotch.

"Secret stash." He waved the bottle in the air. "Care for a little tipple in your coffee? No? Well don't mind if I do. Start the day on the right foot, eh?" He flashed Conrad a beaming smile.

They drank their coffee, exchanged opinions on the weather and engaged in a few moments of good-natured pre-ambling before eventually getting to the point of the meeting.

"Right then," Cranshawe Booth said, placing his empty cup on its saucer. "Let's get down to business, shall we?" He leaned back in his chair, clasped his hands together, and waited for Conrad to open the conversation.

Conrad poured himself a second cup of coffee. When he spoke, he chose his words carefully.

"About last night . . . " He paused and looked into Cranshawe Booth's eyes for a reaction. The Brigadier stiffened noticeably, but remained silent.

"Well, we can't just pretend it never happened can we," Conrad laughed. "If you and I are going to discuss any business, it's something we need to get cleared up."

Cranshawe Booth shifted uncomfortably in his seat and answered with a cautious, "Yes. Well, I'm not all together sure what you're talking about old boy, but I'm fascinated. Do carry on."

"Oh come on," Conrad scoffed, with a hint of exasperation. "You and I both know exactly what I'm talking about—last night in the corridor outside of this very room. You know damned well that I saw you last night," Conrad laughed again. "You . . . impersonating the *Grey Lady* for God's sake. I mean, what's that all about?" Conrad leaned back in his chair with an amused smile on his face.

Cranshawe Booth maintained eye contact for a second and then looked away towards the window.

"Ah. So the game is finally up. It was only a matter of time I suppose." His words were one long sigh. He turned to face Conrad before speaking again.

"I can only hope you are a man of discretion, Mr. Rankin. If this Hall is to survive until the end of the year, then it is imperative that you do not let 'the cat out of the bag,' so to speak." He hung his head and looked at his hands.

"In times of dire circumstance," he continued, "one has to resort to desperate means. These last few, well no, I shall rephrase that: these last thirty years have not been easy, far from it." He lifted his head and swept an agonized glance about the room. "Some might say that my loyalty to this place has been misplaced, but it is everything I have. It's a Grade 1 listed building you know, ruinously expensive to maintain.

"It's swallowed every penny. It pains me to tell you this, but I'm in beyond my means I'm afraid. The coffers are empty." He shook his head solemnly. "I had rather hoped I could have kept this grand old place going until I popped my clogs, but well," he paused and took a deep breath, "I'm rapidly running out of options. Booth Hall has been in my family for generations, Mr. Rankin. It permeates the very core of my being. Without it, I . . . well . . . I don't quite know what will become of us. Believe me, I have not left one stone unturned to try and raise the necessary funds." He spent the next ten minutes describing to Conrad some of the commercial ventures he had introduced in his attempts to save the Hall.

"So there you have it," Dickie concluded. "I have done absolutely everything humanly possible to keep this place standing, and yes, that even includes assuming the identity of a fabricated phantom in a last ditch effort to draw business in, and," he drew himself up and lifted his chin, "and I will not apologize for it."

Taken aback by the Brigadier's lengthy confession, Conrad did not respond immediately. He leaned back in his chair and pondered an appropriate reply. A small part of him felt sorry for the man sitting in front of him. He was well aware of how humiliating it must have been for a pompous snob like Cranshawe Booth to share the details of his financial situation.

The awkward silence was broken when Conrad expressed his commiseration over the Hall's decline. He was about to touch upon the subject of his interest in the place when Cranshawe Booth cut him off.

"Faced with ruin, I will close off my conscience completely to what I am about to do next. I am not proud of what I am about to say, but I have reached rock bottom."

Conrad stared back at him, a number of explanations flashing through his brain.

"I have the Turner. The one you hid at the back of the dresser drawer in the dining room."

Conrad's jaw dropped open. A spark of alarm flickered across his face.

"I also have another one. A nice little watercolor I picked up from the road yesterday. They're both safely hidden away in a place known only to myself. As you know, the police were here yesterday. They knew I had driven through the village in the morning, and they asked if I saw anything—the paintings in particular. I lied to them. They have no idea that I have them. Please don't insult me by denying that you know what I'm taking about."

He lifted his chin and continued. "If you want the paintings as much as I think you do, then I expect we can come to some arrangement, conducted of course, with the utmost discretion. For a handsome amount, I am prepared to relinquish the art, and I will swear upon the ground this Hall is built upon, that I will not utter one word of our agreement until the day arrives when I am no longer on this Earth."

Caught off guard, wrong-footed by such frankness, Conrad felt his composure slip for a second. With considerable effort, he forced a look of calm to his face, but inside he was reeling from Cranshawe Booth's shocking revelation about the Turners. He realized that he was going to have to recalibrate his tactics, and quickly. He dragged a hand over his mouth and chin, casually repositioned himself in his chair, and then said as calmly as he could:

"Well, that's quite a speech. I admire your candidness, but your suggestion for an *agreement* is based upon two assumptions: one, that the art you are referring to is in fact worth a significant amount of money, and two; that I'm interested, and possibly reckless enough to put myself at risk by breaking the law. I could go straight to the police with what you've told me."

"You could, but you won't. I would deny everything. There is no proof that I have them, and I can assure you that if the police came looking, the Turners would never be found."

"They're still here, in the Hall?" Conrad asked.

"I'd be a fool to tell you where they are. You can rest assured that they are in a safe place. No one will find them."

Conrad sat still, his eyes trained on Dickie's face. A minute of silence passed between them.

"And what if I have no interest in them?"

"Ah well, then that leaves me in a rather awkward position doesn't it? A few pieces of art that I can't display or sell on the open market are worth bugger all to me. I might as well rip them to shreds, throw the lot into the River Ouse and dispose of the evidence. Unless . . . " Dickie paused. His hands were clasped across the front of his stomach. They tensed and relaxed repeatedly as he fought some inner battle. He remained silent for several seconds, trying to find the appropriate words to convey the fact that he was prepared to use blackmail if necessary. His eyes flickered to the window for a brief moment. When he returned his gaze to Conrad, his face was cold and unsmiling. A veil of moisture had formed on his upper lip.

"Your fingerprints are all over the Turners Mr. Rankin, "he said bluntly. "I'm sure Scotland Yard would be interested to hear your explanation."

"What?" Are you trying to blackmail me?" asked Conrad, taken aback. He felt a momentary surge of rage.

"Yes, Mr. Rankin, I am. I'd rather hoped we could have avoided visiting that premise. Blackmail is a dirty word, one that does not resonate well with my moral fiber, but I'm backed into a corner. If I can't raise a decent amount of money and very soon, then I'm going to lose this place and everything in it. I've tried all manner of desperate schemes to save it and I've stooped to the depths of humiliation. I have been forced to compromise both my dignity and my integrity. My wife is barely speaking to me. She feels she can no longer hold her head up in public. I am at my wits end. So you see Mr. Rankin, I really have nothing left to lose, do I?"

Conrad leaned back in his chair keeping his gaze fixed on Cranshawe Booth's face. Seconds ticked by before he answered.

"Nobody blackmails me," Conrad answered. "You can turn them in, but you'll gain nothing other than the satisfaction of putting me in an awkward situation." He paused for a moment, his face creased into a look of deep concentration as if he were trying to come to an important decision. When he spoke again, it was in a more conciliatory tone.

"I am interested in the Turners, very interested, but right now I don't know what they're worth and I'm not sure who is the rightful owner. I want to believe that my mother acquired them by legal means, in which case they will legitimately belong to me, but if she didn't . . . well, it would be a great pity to let something so rare slip through our fingers before we know more about them, wouldn't it? There could be a lot more to be gained if we sit tight for a while.

I'm not sure how much the police told you, but there are four other pieces missing in the village. If I'm able to get hold of them, then I'm going to need some help. They would have to be concealed in a safe place for an indeterminate time until I know what I'm dealing with. Now, if you are prepared to wait and work with me, then I think we can come to a suitable financial agreement." It was the Brigadier's turn to be taken aback. His eyes widened in surprise.

"Another four, eh? And you know who has them?"

"I'm going to find that out this morning."

"But I don't quite understand. If it turns out that your mother has done nothing wrong and you inherit the Turners, then what will be in it for me?"

"You'll be adequately reimbursed."

"And if they're stolen . . . " He paused to pat the sweat from his upper lip with a napkin. "What then?"

"Ah, well. That brings me to something else I want to discuss with you—a business proposition." Conrad checked the time on his watch.

"I've got just under an hour before I have to leave. We can also talk about this later if we're both free."

"Right. Go on old boy," Cranshawe Booth replied with heightened interest.

"Well, this is all mere speculation at the moment. I haven't had the chance to look into it yet," said Conrad, glancing about the room. "I have a few ideas that might just save this place. They might not be feasible, but I'm prepared to have my people look into it."

"Uh, I'm not sure that I understand," said Cranshawe Booth, flabbergasted.

"You said you hosted a Range Rover convention here at one time?"

"What? Yes, back in 1998. I believe. Raised a few pounds, enough to keep us ticking over that summer. Why do you ask?"

"Know anything about vintage cars, Sir Richard?"

"Yes. A little," Cranshawe Booth answered uncertainly. "Not quite sure I catch your drift old boy."

THIRTY

Jeremy pulled up outside the post office a few minutes before nine. He did not get out of the car immediately, but sat still, eyes squeezed shut, hands placed on either side of the steering wheel. He felt a wave of nausea, and made a silent vow to never touch another drop of alcohol. His only solace was the knowledge that he had managed, very easily, to ply Nigel with so much booze that he would be sofa- bound and safely out of the way for the whole morning.

He got out of the car and made his way to the entrance. The sound of the bell tinkling above the door sent a shard of pain through his head. His tongue felt like sandpaper.

"Oh, thank goodness. There you are. You're late," Pearl's voice rang out from behind the cash register. She beckoned him over. "Quickly, before someone comes in."

"Morning," said Jeremy as he made his way to the counter. His eyes felt like two black holes in his head. It hurt to talk. "Did you get the note?"

"That Detective Patterson from Scotland Yard was waiting in the car park when I got back. The other one, Detective Collins and some other constable, came later. They came in here asking more questions and they searched my bag," Pearl said hurriedly.

"What? They came in? Did they have a search warrant?"

"No, but I told them to go ahead and have a look around, all innocent like."

"You didn't tell them anything, did you?" asked Jeremy cautiously.

"No, I did not, but they know something's going on. It's a good thing the paintings aren't here. I was shaking in my shoes. I don't care for those Scotland Yard detectives. They made me feel very uncomfortable, very uncomfortable, like their eyes were burning straight through me." Pearl's words poured out in a torrent.

"But did you get the note?" Jeremy asked again, interrupting her.

"What? Oh, yes. It's here." She reached inside her blouse and withdrew the damp, crumpled remnants of the beer mat. She handed it over the counter to Jeremy and whispered, "It says you're to meet him in the library in Wickham at eleven."

Jeremy unfolded the note and read the brief message: Library. Wickham. 11:00 a.m.

"You've plenty of time," Pearl said, "but I'm very worried about all this. We'll be going to jail if the police find out, and for a long time too. Detective Patterson said I'd go to jail for aiding and abetting; that's what he called it." She fished around in her apron pocket and pulled out a handkerchief. She dabbed her nose and sniffed loudly. "I don't know what my Arthur would think about all this if he were still here; I really don't. I'm not sure we're doing the right thing. It's been eating away at my conscience." She leaned across the counter and whispered. "Maybe we should just give the paintings back to the police and be done with it."

"You know we can't do that. It's too late to back out now," said Jeremy. "We're up to our ears in this. If we stick together and keep our mouths shut, we'll be all right. Really." He gave her an encouraging smile. "Where has Barrington put the paintings? They are in a safe place, right?"

"I'm not sure where he's put them. He won't tell me. You don't think the police will search his cottage do you?"

"I doubt it. I can't see how they'd link him to all this, but you never know . . . "A broad smile creased his face. "I've just had an idea, Mrs. Wiggins, a very good one. Now listen. I want you to hold tight. Do not do anything you wouldn't normally do. You don't want to make the police any more suspicious. You don't have the paintings anymore, so if they come back, you don't have a thing to worry about. You're going to have to be patient and wait for me to get in touch with you again."

"I know, I know," she nodded. "I can't afford any trouble Jeremy, not at my age. I've no family left and I've got my retirement to think of. I've not got much." She looked at Jeremy with sad eyes. All she would have to live on after she retired was a small pension and her secret cache under the loose floorboard in the corner of her bedroom. She had no hope of paying off her mortgage. "I'll have to leave this place you know. I won't be able to afford to stay."

"You don't own this place?" he asked, surprised.

Pearl shook her head and sighed. "No. I don't. It's a long story."

"Oh," said Jeremy, unsure of what to say. He gave her a weak smile and glanced at his watch.

"Look, I should be going. I think I've been followed here, so I'd better walk out with some bread and milk. Make it look like an innocent visit for some provisions. Oh, and have you got anything for a headache? My head's killing me."

On the drive back to his parent's house, Jeremy placed several calls on his cell phone to Barrington. After the third unsuccessful attempt, he was about to give up when Barrington finally answered.

"Hello?" Barrington answered uncertainly. He didn't get many calls.

"Barrington, it's me, Jeremy. Don't say anything, just listen."

"Eh? Who is it?"

"It's Jeremy. Jeremy Danvers," Jeremy shouted into the phone.

"Oh. Hello Lad. How are you keeping?"

"Good. Good. Listen, I need you to do something for me. I want you to drive to the house. Can you come now? It's very important."

"Eh? But I'm not due until this afternoon."

"Yes, I know that," Jeremy replied, trying not to sound frustrated, "but I need your help with something. Can you come now instead of this afternoon?"

"Right. Yes. I think I understand," Barrington answered slowly. "Am I to bring something with me?"

"No! Do not bring anything," Jeremy answered emphatically. "Just bring yourself okay?"

"What about the pa . . . ?"

"Don't say anything else!" Jeremy cut Barrington off mid-sentence. "We'll talk when you get here, okay? Drive around to the back of the house and pull up as close as you can to the back door."

"Oh, right. Got it. I understand. Right you are. Back of the 'ouse. I'll be over in a jiffy."

* * *

As soon as Jeremy heard the crunch of Barrington's tires on the gravel drive, he shot to the kitchen door at the back of the house and opened it a crack.

"Psssst!" he hissed. He gestured at Barrington with his hand. "Come in. Hurry!"

"Did you see a car parked in the lay-by down the lane?" Jeremy asked the moment Barrington stepped inside the kitchen.

"Can't say that I did, but then again, I wasn't payin' much attention," said Barrington. "Why?"

"Shhhush!" Jeremy brought a finger to his lips and jabbed an index finger in the air pointing toward the next room. "We've got to keep our voices down. Remember Nigel, the friend who turned up in the pub last night? He hasn't left. He's asleep on the sofa. Here . . . sit down for a minute." Jeremy walked over to the kitchen table and pulled out a few chairs.

"I'm being watched," Jeremy said. "There's been a car parked there since yesterday. It followed me this morning when I went to the post office, which is why I need your help."

"Ah, so you saw Pearl Wiggins then? Did she find the note the American chap left on the bridge?" Barrington asked.

"Yes. He wants to meet in the Wickham Library at eleven."

"The library? All the way over in Wickham, eh? Why there?"

300

"Well, he knows we're being watched. There's nowhere to meet in secret in Tipping. The place is just too small. My guess is he's chosen Wickham because it's bigger. There'll be less chance of being spotted, and it'll be easier to lose the police."

"I can see the logic in that. Now do you think you can trust this fellow? An American. You 'ardly know him."

"I have to trust him and so do you. We don't have any other choice," Jeremy whispered. He lifted his head and pointed at the kitchen clock. "Look. I've got an hour before I meet him. This is what we need to do: I want you to drive me there in your car. I'm going to hide on the back seat so the police won't know I'm with you. They'll think I'm still here in the house. That way I won't be followed. You're going to drop me off right outside the library and I'll call you when I need picking up, right?"

"Right. That sounds like a half decent plan. But maybe I should be there when you meet this bloke. I might be getting' on in years, but I've 'ad a lot of experience lad. I'm a good judge of character. I'll know straight up if he's playing yer for a fool."

"No, I'd better meet him on my own. He doesn't know there's anyone else involved yet. It might scare him off if he sees me with you."

"Hmmm, all right then. Maybe you should be on yer own at first," Barrington said slowly, "but . . . " he paused and looked Jeremy in the eye, "I'm the one who has the paintin's now aren't I?" He let the question hang for a few seconds before continuing. Jeremy remained silent, a feeling of worry rising in his belly.

"I want to meet 'im fer miself."

"Er . . . well, I'm not sure," Jeremy began to say half heartedly, but Barrington cut him off immediately.

"Wait a minute. Like I said lad: You 'aven't got the paintin's and I have. I hold the trump cards if yer get my meanin'." He winked at Jeremy and smiled. "I'm in charge now."

Jeremy pressed his lips together and nodded slowly. You wily old bugger, he thought.

"Right then," said Barrington. "Now we've got that cleared up, I'll get the tomato plants I've got for yer mother out of the car. I'll take 'em round the front. That way if anyone's lookin' they won't get suspicious about why I'm here."

Wickham's library was a modest structure built from the same locally quarried stone as most of the other buildings in the town. It had no distinguishing features other than the sign outside that read, *Wickham Public Library*. Its location next to a park with a children's playground made it a popular venue for young families.

Conrad drove by without stopping. He took note of the full car park and the number of cars parked on either side of the narrow street outside. He had not expected a small market town library to be this busy. He followed the street to the end and took the right fork back onto the main street. A quick glance in his rearview mirror confirmed the presence of a blue Ford one car back that had been on his tail since leaving Booth Hall.

"Shit," he muttered. He had to lose the blue Ford before meeting Jeremy in the library. He also needed to find somewhere to park. It was already eleven. He was going to be late.

"Shit," he said again. He made a quick left turn off the main thoroughfare into a small cobbled side street. A large sign indicated no parking.

"Dammit," he cursed.

He drove to the end of the street and made another left into a narrow lane where cars were parked down one side. To his relief, a number of spaces were available. He crept forward until he reached a gap that was big enough, pulled alongside and backed in. The blue Ford entered the street behind him. It drove past slowly, the driver's face obscured by a pair of dark sunglasses. Conrad waited until it reached the end of the lane, then pulled forward out of the parking space, slammed his car into reverse and backed up in the opposite direction, tires screeching until he was back in the cobbled side street again. He spun the car around, shot to the end of the street and swung into the traffic on the high street. He drove for several minutes, blending into the long line of cars as they snaked their way through town. When he was sure he was no longer being followed, he turned off the high street at a Lloyds bank. He drove into its small car park at the rear and slipped into a space reserved for customers only. After a final check in his mirrors, he got out and set off for the library, a good quarter of a mile away. By the time he walked through the library's double entry doors, it was close to 11:20.

"I was beginning to think you weren't coming," Jeremy whispered as Conrad dropped into the chair beside him. He was sitting in the comfy chair section next to the periodicals. Its location on the ground floor across from the checkout desk offered a good view of the entrance and exit. The seats were arranged in a rectangle around a large, low table. Six of the ten seats were occupied. A young mother with a toddler in her lap looked up as Conrad arrived. He smiled at her; she smiled back and then averted her eyes. The woman on the other side of Jeremy was dozing over her magazine; her head nodding close to her chest as she gradually lost her battle with sleep. Barrington, wearing an old faded tweed cap, sat on a chair across the table, pretending to read the Daily Telegraph.

"I know I'm late. I'm sorry. I was being followed and had to lose them. Then I couldn't find a place to park," Conrad said, a little out of breath. "I had no idea this place was going to be so busy." He glanced around the library, his eyes eventually settling on the children's section in the far corner. "Jeez, it's noisy in here."

"It's better than upstairs in the reference section. It's too quiet up there. At least we can talk here," said Jeremy.

"Christ, you look awful. What have you been doing?"

"Nothing – just too much to drink last night."

Conrad studied Jeremy's face with concern. "Are you sure nobody followed you here?"

"Yes, I'm positive."

"Good, so what happened last night? Have you found them?"

"Four of them. I know who's got them." Jeremy whispered out of the side of his mouth.

"Really?" Conrad gasped. He leaned closer to Jeremy. "Who?"

"This is where it gets complicated," said Jeremy. He looked away and fiddled with the end of his T-shirt. He looked uncomfortable. "We can get them back, but . . . " he hesitated.

"What? Tell me," Conrad said, intrigued.

Jeremy swallowed. "There are two more people involved."

"What? Oh shit!" Conrad stiffened in his seat. "Who's got them?" he asked again. He looked Jeremy in the face waiting for an answer. "You've not told them about me, have you?"

"I didn't have any choice," Jeremy answered quickly. His eyes flickered to Barrington. "They want to make a deal."

Conrad pressed his lips together, his eyes locked on Jeremy's face. Seconds ticked by. "Oh Jesus," the words came out in one long sigh. He relaxed his shoulders and sank into the chair. "You'd better tell me everything. What happened after I left you outside the post office?"

"I went back to my parent's house. Patterson from Scotland Yard and this other copper were waiting for me in an unmarked car."

"Do you think you were followed from Harrogate? I mean, how did they know you were going to show up here?"

"No, I wasn't followed. They went back to the gallery after I left. Bryce Edwards told them I was coming back here."

"Right. So what happened?"

"They searched me. They searched the car. Asked a load of questions. Threw a few warnings at me about theft, concealing evidence, all that kind of stuff, and that was it."

"They didn't search the house?"

"Nah. They probably didn't have a search warrant, and there'd be no point. They knew I hadn't been inside."

"Then what?"

Jeremy looked down at his hands. "I, well, I . . . " he hesitated. "I sneaked out the back of the house on my bike and came straight here to the library."

"You did what? I thought I told you to stay put, out of the way until it was time to go to the disco. What the hell did you come here for?"

"Don't worry. I used the back lanes. There's no way they could have followed me," Jeremy said quickly. "I couldn't just sit in the house all day. I had too much on my mind. I needed to find out about the Turners."

"Jesus. I hope you weren't seen. They can easily find out what you've been looking at you know," said Conrad.

"I know. That's why I came here to the library. I didn't want to use the computer at home," Jeremy explained.

Conrad shook his head disapprovingly. "You took a big risk." He sighed heavily. "All right then, what did you find out?"

"Not much. They're part of his 'Yorkshire Collection". Turner's hot at the moment. You'd have to have them appraised by an expert, but I'm guessing they're worth a lot.

"How much do you think?"

"I dunno, but going off what some of his stuff has sold for recently . . . " Jeremy thought for a few seconds. "Have you heard of the Rigi Collection?"

"Yeah, vaguely. It sold for millions, didn't it?'

"That's right. *The Blue Rigi* - it went for 5.8 million pounds.

"Really?" Conrad's eyes widened.

"Yeah. Your mother bought it."

"What!" Conrad said louder than he had intended. He looked genuinely shocked. "My mother. Really? How do you know?"

"I'll get to that in a minute. I've got a lot to tell you."

"Okay, I'm sorry," said Conrad. "Carry on."

"Well, I managed to speak to Kevin Ogden, the kid who was seen outside the post office. We don't need to worry about him. He hasn't got anything, but he did say he saw Pearl Wiggins from the post office picking stuff up from the road. He also told me there was a reward out for the paintings."

Conrad raised his eyebrows. "A reward? The police didn't mention anything about that to me."

"Ah, so they've spoken to you? They didn't say anything about a reward to me either. The kid said it was the local constable who told him."

"Do you think the kid was telling the truth?"

"I'm not sure. Probably. The person who has them thinks the same thing." Jeremy's eyes flashed to Barrington for a second.

"Oh shit," Conrad said slowly. "This complicates things."

"I know," Jeremy agreed. "Anyway, after talking to the kid, I went to the pub where you saw me last night. There was no way I could talk. The

police were there —in plain clothes. They were watching me and . . . "
He took a deep breath and looked down at his lap. "And I got cornered."

Conrad stared at him. "What do mean?"

"The two people you saw me with at the bar, Pearl Wiggins and the old guy, Barrington Smith. He was the old guy who was coming out of the post office car park when the stuff fell out of my car."

"Right . . . go on," Conrad said slowly.

Jeremy shifted uncomfortably in his chair. He clasped and unclasped his hands on his lap. He looked nervous and ill at ease. He swallowed several times before he whispered, "They've got four of them. They're thinking of holding onto them until they know for sure there's a reward out for them. If you want them back now, they want fifty thousand pounds. That's about . . . "

"Seventy thousand dollars," Conrad finished the sentence for him.

"But there's something else I've got to tell you first. You're not going to like this." Jeremy lifted his head and looked Conrad in the eye. "Nigel Bryce Edwards turned up last night—in the pub just after you left. He told me everything. He was the one Julian Parks was looking for when he came into the gallery with the Turners. He was meant to smuggle them out of the country, to Switzerland. He and Parks were working for your mother."

Conrad's jaw dropped. "Wait a minute. Are you telling me that my mother was behind this whole thing?"

"Ssshhh!" Jeremy brought a finger up to his lips. "People are looking at us."

A few heads swiveled in their direction. Barrington lowered his newspaper and peered at them over the top of his glasses. Jeremy widened his eyes and shot a warning glance at Barrington not to interfere.

"Yes, but I only know what Nigel's told me," Jeremy said quickly. "I don't know for sure. He could be lying but," he paused, "I think he's telling the truth."

Conrad propped an elbow on the armrest of his chair, covered his jaw with one hand and closed his eyes. "I can't believe I'm hearing this," he said through his fingers. He remained silent for several seconds. When he spoke again, he was quiet and despondent. "Tell me then. Tell me everything you know."

Jeremy repeated what Nigel had told him. By the look on Conrad's face, it was obvious that he had no clue about his mother's activities.

"That's why she never involved my father, and why she kept her collections secret from me," Conrad whispered, more to himself than to Jeremy. "She'd been operating outside of the law. She knew I'd be drawn in; that I wouldn't be able to resist. She wanted to protect me from myself."

"Yeah. It seems that way. I'm sorry," Jeremy said. He fell silent. "What do we do now, then?"

Conrad gave Jeremy a wry smile. "Well, there are only two choices: give them up or keep them. I should really turn the lot of you in and walk away with a clean conscience. I should wash my hands of it all." He looked Jeremy in the eye. "Shouldn't I?"

Jeremy held his breath and said nothing.

"Shouldn't I?" Conrad repeated, unable to conceal his anger and disappointment. He held Jeremy's gaze for a few seconds and then turned away. He raked both hands through his hair and breathed a loud sigh.

"Cranshawe Booth's got the other two," he said shortly.

"What?" It was Jeremy's turn to be surprised.

"Yep, both of them. He picked one up from the road, and he's got the one we found in the field as well."

"What? How did that happen?"

"It's a long story," Conrad began. "Not everything is as it seems at Booth Hall."

Conrad told Jeremy an edited version of what had happened since they last met. He made no mention of his ghostly encounter with the *Grey Lady,* and he did not divulge the more personal details of Cranshawe Booth's confession, but he let Jeremy know that Booth Hall was fast approaching financial ruin.

"The Hall is falling apart and Cranshawe Booth hasn't got a penny left to his name. He's desperate enough to do anything to save it, including threatening me about the Turners. He said he'd hand them over to the police if I didn't pay him a significant amount of money."

"Oh crap—Blackmail? Jesus!"

"Yes, but it was a desperate attempt on his part. It won't come to that," Conrad assured him. "We talked for nearly an hour. Let's just say I have something up my sleeve—business. You don't need to worry about him."

Jeremy looked at him open mouthed. "But even if you get them from him and get hold of the other four, what are going to do with them? I mean you can't just pack them in with your luggage can you? There's no way you're going to get them out of the country."

"I know that. They'll have to stay here, hidden in a safe place until I can make some arrangements. Cranshawe Booth is adamant that the two he has are in a safe place, so that leaves the other four."

"And where are you thinking of hiding them?"

"I don't know yet. We'll cross that bridge when we come to it. We have to get hold of the Turners first. Then we'll need to move quickly because I'm leaving the day after tomorrow. I'm running out of time."

"Right."

"So where are they now? Who's got them—Pearl Wiggins or the old guy?"

"Uh, right, well," Jeremy hesitated. He looked down at his hands and then cast a quick glance across the room before finally meeting Conrad's eye. He puffed out his cheeks and nodded in the direction of the chairs facing them across the table.

"Him. He's got them. That's Barrington Smith."

Conrad's head swiveled around. Barrington was staring at them with his arms folded across his chest. The paper he was reading lay discarded, on the empty seat next to him.

"About time," he grumbled loudly.

Conrad flashed Jeremy a look of disbelief. "What's going on?" he asked angrily.

Jeremy stood up and lifted his hands in helpless defeat.

"I'm sorry. He gave me no other choice. He wants to talk to you." He glanced at Barrington who was having difficulty getting out of his seat.

"Look, I'd better go and help him."

Jeremy offered Barrington his arm and helped pull him to his feet.

"I've had a word with him," Jeremy whispered. "He knows you've got the paintings."

"Eh? What was that? These bloody chairs are too low," Barrington complained loudly. He straightened up, nodded in Conrad's direction and lifted a forefinger to the peak of his cap.

Conrad got up, smiled uncertainly and extended a hand to Barrington. "Hello Mr. Smith. I'm Conrad. Conrad Rankin."

"Ow do," Barrington replied. He wrapped his bony fingers around Conrad's hand in a firm grip and pulled him closer. "You and me 'ave got some serious talking to do." He studied Conrad's face with suspicious eyes. "If yer want them paintin's back, you'd better listen to what I 'ave to say. We'll go over 'ere," he said, dropping Conrad's hand and pointing to a row of computers along the back wall. "I need a desk to sit down at so I can read through my conditions. I've got 'em all written down on a piece of paper." He slapped the side of his trousers. "It's 'ere in mi pocket."

Conrad gave Jeremy a look of wide-eyed dismay.

Jeremy shrugged his shoulders. "I had no idea he was going to do this," Jeremy hissed.

"Right then," Barrington said, when they were all gathered around one of the small desks. He reached into his trouser pocket and pulled out a crumpled piece of paper. He held one corner on the table and began to smooth the rest out with his palm.

"I've 'ad all night to think about this. Before I go through what I've written, there's summat I want to say."

He lifted his eyes to Conrad's face. "I don't know much about you, other than what Jeremy 'ere 'as told me. He seems to trust you, but I've not 'ad the chance to form mi own opinion. What you say to me this mornin' will determine whether you'll ever see the paintin's again," he said flatly. "Jeremy 'ere 'as looked out for me these past years, and now I'm going to do the same fer 'im. I don't forget who mi friends are. So, you've got some convincin' to do Mr. Rankin. You'd best start by tellin' me about yerself and why it is you want them paintin's so bad."

Conrad didn't answer immediately. Caught off guard by Barrington's frankness and still upset by what he had just learned from Jeremy about his mother, he took a few moments to think.

"I know this might be difficult for you to believe, but I didn't even know of the paintings existence until two days ago. I flew here from the U.S. to get some closure about my mother's death." He paused and looked at Jeremy for a second. "I don't know how much Jeremy has told you, but in case you don't know, she was killed two weeks ago in a car crash just outside of Knaresborough."

Barrington looked on steadily, giving nothing away.

"It would seem," Conrad continued, "that she'd been involved in acquiring art by illegal means; at least that's what the police seem to think and . . . " He stopped and cast a quick look at Jeremy. " . . . that's what Jeremy has learned from another source. I knew nothing about this, I swear." He looked Barrington square in the eye and said, "I knew she had a fondness for art, and I knew she had some nice pieces, but I had no idea, absolutely none, that she would stoop low enough to steal what she couldn't buy." He turned his head and addressed Jeremy. "I'm still shocked by what you've told me; I really am."

Barrington nodded his head, a look of deep concentration written across his face. "But you've known all along that she might have stolen these, these what-you –call-it, these Turners. So if you knew she might have done wrong, then why have yer been so keen to get yer 'ands on 'em? I mean, why haven't you kept yer 'ands clean and given 'em straight back to the police?"

"Ah. That's a good question to ask and one that I want to answer honestly, Mr. Smith. I don't know how much time you've got; it might take me some time for me to explain."

"You can take as much time as you like," said Barrington firmly. "I've got all day."

During the next ten minutes, Conrad offered a convincing, clear version of himself, making it difficult for Barrington not to feel a little warmth toward him. Barrington studied Conrad's face for a good half minute in silence before speaking.

"I'm sorry about yer mam. I lost mine years ago," he said sadly. "I've never 'ad much. I fought for mi country when I were nothin' more than a lad, and then I came back home to look after mi old mam. Took her years to die. It was an 'orrible death. Wouldn't wish it on my worst enemy—cancer of the throat. Never 'ad the money to get her taken care of properly. She was forty-six years old." He shook his head solemnly.

"I inherited the 'ouse from her, God bless her 'art, and the ninety quid she'd saved and kept 'idden in a tea caddy. That were a lot of money to us back then you know. She worked her fingers to the bone and never once complained. She was in service to a posh family in London and then one up 'ere. That's how I got this grand name of mine," he said with a broad grin. 'I gave you a handsome name to make up fer the plain one of 'Smith,' she used to say. People will always remember it. It'll help you make something of yerrself." He shook his head and laughed quietly at the memory. "Toiled away and lived in 'ardship all her life. She did it fer me you know," he said quietly. "Never knew mi dad." He fell silent and looked down at the piece of paper under his hand. He lifted it from the table and looked at it for a moment. "Anyway, I 'ad no job to come home to after the War. Most of mi mates were dead, killed in the fighting. I've worked odd jobs all mi life. Good honest ones, mind." He lifted a gnarled finger to make his point, "and I've never asked fer nothin' from nobody. I'm not a greedy man, Mr. Rankin. I want you to know that." He paused and looked Conrad in the eye. "Now if them paintin's are worth millions, like some seem to think they are, then what I'm goin' to ask for is nothin'. Right then, let's get on with it."

He adjusted his reading glasses and held out the list out in front of him. He cleared his throat and began reading.

"Number one: Give Jeremy Danvers a job. Something to do with art."

He peered over the top of the piece of paper and said to Conrad, "I'm sure you've got plenty of fancy contacts Mr. Rankin, and as you've just said, you've got your mam's art collection to look after. You'll be needin' some 'elp won't you?" He looked at Jeremy with raised eyebrows. "What do yer think, lad? Would that suit yer?"

Jeremy stared back speechless.

"It's all right," said Barrington, holding up a hand for quiet. "No need to say anything yet. Let me finish first."

"Number two: 25,000 pounds for Pearl Wiggins and a cruise to the Mediterranean, all expenses paid. That's summat she's always dreamed of," he added.

"Number three: 25,000 pounds for Barrington Smith and a trip, all expenses paid, to France. I've been a few times since the War," he said looking up over the top of his glasses, "but I'd like to go to the war memorials one last time before I pop mi clogs. There's a special grave I need to visit." He squeezed his eyes shut for a moment. He thought of Ernie, his best buddy.

"And that brings me to the last thing on mi list." He opened his eyes and looked at Jeremy. "This last 'un concerns you, lad. I want you to make me a promise. Let me read it out." He laid the paper on the desk, smoothed it flat and began reading.

"Number four: Jeremy Danvers must look after Ernie if anything 'appens to Barrington Smith. There, that's it," said Barrington. "I want you to make that promise to me right now, lad. I'm not getting' any younger and its been preying on mi mind about what'll 'appen to Ernie if anything 'appens to me. I'll not be able to go to mi' grave quietly, if I 'aven't got this settled."

"I, well, yes," Jeremy stuttered. "Of course. I promise I'll look after him."

"Ernie?" asked Conrad puzzled.

"His cat," Jeremy explained.

"Aye. Mi cat, bless 'im," said Barrington. "So, them's mi terms: take 'em or leave 'em; it's up to you Mr. Rankin," he said folding the piece of paper and shoving it into his back pocket.

"Well, you've taken me by surprise," said Conrad, taken aback. There's a lot to consider. I'm going to need a few minutes to think about this."

He looked at Jeremy and said, "Jeremy, can I have a quick word?" He indicated the other side of the library with a flick of his head.

"I'm sorry Mr. Smith. If you'll just give us a minute, I need a quick word with Jeremy."

Barrington touched the peak of his cap and said, "You go right ahead. I'm not goin' anywhere. I'll be waitin' ere fer you."

The two of them walked to the children's section and disappeared behind a tall bookshelf.

"Well, what do you think?" Conrad asked. "Is he serious?"

"Oh yes. He's serious all right," Jeremy began. He gave Conrad a brief summary of his relationship with Barrington. Once they were finished talking, they strolled back to the desk where Barrington was waiting.

"Okay," said Conrad. "Jeremy's told me a little about you and he's convinced me that this might work, but," he emphasized the last word, "I'm putting myself in a vulnerable position if we go ahead with this, so I'm going to have to make a few conditions of my own."

Barrington raised his eyebrows in surprise. "Oh, right. Spell 'em out then."

"First of all, I need to know that you've got the work in a safe place; somewhere the police won't find them if they get a search warrant."

"Oh, there's no need to worry about that: they'll not be found." Barrington said confidently.

"And they're out of the sun; somewhere dark and no damp, right," Jeremy interjected.

"They're in the dark all right. I've 'idden em amongst a stack of newspapers in the throne room." Barrington winked at Conrad, pleased with himself.

Jeremy laughed when he saw the puzzled look on Conrad's face.

"He means the toilet."

"What?"

"It's separate from the bathroom, so there's no damp, and it's the newest part of the 'ouse," Barrington informed him. "It used to be outside you know. That whole row of cottages 'ad outside lavs until just after the war."

"Really?"

"That's right—in the back yard. Eeh by eck, it were freezin' in the winter," Barrington chuckled.

"Do you think they'll be safe enough there?" Conrad asked, turning to Jeremy.

"Hmm. I don't know," said Jeremy dubiously. "I doubt they'll search there. I can't think how they'd connect him to any of this."

"Well just in case, I think you ought to come up with a better place to hide them."

"Oh, I'm already on to it," said Barrington with a throaty laugh. "I know the perfect place for 'em. There's not a soul will look fer 'em where I've got in mind." He tapped the side of his nose and winked at them both.

"Where?" Jeremy asked.

"Leave it with me, lad. Leave it with me."

"Right, well that's something I'm going to have to leave with you. I'm flying back to the States the day after tomorrow, so I haven't got much time. That brings me to another condition."

He looked first at Jeremy and then at Barrington. "It goes without saying that the two of you will swear to secrecy. Not one word to anybody, right?"

"Right," Jeremy and Barrington answered simultaneously.

"I can't meet your terms straight away," Conrad said to Barrington. "I have one or two ideas floating in my head right now, but I need time to get things sorted. You're both going to have to wait for . . . "

"How long?" Jeremy interrupted. "I've got my graduation in a few weeks. It'll all come out in the open then about my art degree. My parents will go ballistic when they find out I've been lying to them for years. My mother will never forgive me for the humiliation in front of the rest of the family, and then there's this whole business with the police." He shook his head and looked down at his feet. "I'm done for. They'll kick me out of the house."

"You'll have to sit tight for at least a few weeks. If I hang around any longer, the police will be even more suspicious. I need to get back to the States and work out how we're going to do this. I need to get an expert opinion on the possible value of the Turners, and there's other stuff I need to look into. You'll have to be patient."

"A few weeks is a long time to be sittin' around waitin' and doing nothing," said Barrington unhappily. "I might be better off just waitin' fer the reward."

"Look, I can't just take a wad of cash out of the bank and hand it to you, can I? Not without drawing the attention of the police. It might be that I have to give it to you in installments or something like that. I need time to think about it."

"You've got a week and a half and not a day longer. I want this settled before 'is graduation," said Barrington with a nod in Jeremy's direction. "He needs a job before his mam and dad get wind of what he's been up to at university, so you'd better get yer skates on and get summat sorted."

"But I . . . "

"A week and a half," Barrington said firmly. "That's yer lot. What date does that bring us to? If I don't 'ear from you by then, I'm going to claim the reward if there is one, and if there isn't, then I'll be switchin' to Plan C."

Jeremy and Conrad stared at Barrington in stunned silence.

"Okay, okay," Conrad eventually said. "You drive a hard bargain, Mr. Smith. He looked at Jeremy. "I'll be in touch with you within the week. It'll be a job offer. Curator, something like that. We can work out the details later."

"And make sure it's a decent wage. This 'ere's a clever lad and he's no slacker either," Barrington interrupted.

"Yes, yes. Don't worry about that. Look, I'm not going to be able to speak to you for a while," Conrad said to Barrington. "Not until all this blows over. For now though, I can give you a little incentive to keep your side of the bargain." He reached into his back pocket for his wallet and pulled out a wad of bills. He flicked through the money. "Here's a couple of thousand. It's all I've got on me."

"By gum, that's a lot of dosh to be carryin' round with yer," said Barrington shocked. "What've yer done, robbed a bank already?"

Conrad looked at him surprised. "No, I usually keep plenty of cash on me." He gave an embarrassed laugh. "Here, take it."

Barrington stared at the money. "It'll be the first time I've ever 'eld so much," he said with a huge smile. He held out a hand to Conrad, "You've got a deal Mr. Rankin."

THIRTY ONE

Fifteen months later, in the shade of an olive tree on the terrace of a quaint little restaurant overlooking the Mediterranean, Maurice Patterson closed his eyes and took a long sip of Rioja. A light breeze, laden with the sound of slapping waves against the hulls of fishing boats in the harbor, rustled the leaves above his head. A mid-afternoon glass of wine was one of his new pleasures.

He had been in Nadaques, a sleepy fishing village in northeastern Spain for nearly a month, part of an eight week hiatus between his retirement from the police force and taking up his new appointment as general manager of a fine arts security group in the private sector. Days and weeks of idling his time away doing nothing in particular, stretched like a delicious banquet before him. The security of a decent pension, a healthy lump sum deposited in the bank, and a new job in the pipeline gave him a warm, comfortable, feeling. His smile stretched from ear to ear; the smile of a cat with its cream—satisfied, happy, and smug.

He opened his eyes, took another sip of wine and looked idly at the boats tugging on their moorings. The deep azure water glittered and sparkled, shimmers of light and dark as the warm breeze danced across its surface. Patterson tilted his head to look at the harbor from a slightly different angle. He compared the image in his mind to the postcard he bought earlier that morning. He glanced to his right beyond the wall to a path that led to an olive grove and looked back again to the water. He figured the photographer must have been close to the wall when the picture was taken.

He smiled and let his gaze drift to the fringe of whitewashed houses on the slope beyond the harbor. They were blanched, baking in the heat, their wrought iron terraces overflowing with geraniums, vibrant against the lavender blue sky. Thank God, this one little sanctuary had managed to survive the high-rise invasion of concrete that had consumed much of the coastline. It was nothing short of a miracle.

A swift movement on the wall next to him caught his eye, making him turn in that direction. A lizard skittered across the stones only a few feet from his table. It shot down the side of the wall, disappeared into a crevice near the ground, and re-emerged several seconds later. It was cautious at first, advancing a few feet at a time, before darting across the terrace toward a table occupied by two young women.

They sat at one of the tables in the shade under the awning, talking loudly and laughing, both English. Mid-twenties Patterson guessed. The slimmer, blonder of the two glanced in his direction and caught him looking at her. She had an intelligent, serious face. Attractive. He held her gaze for a split second, startled by the blueness of her eyes and quickly looked away. In that tiniest moment, in the blink of an eye, he felt a spark of recognition. He was certain he had met her somewhere, but he couldn't remember where or when. He reached for the menu and pretended to study it. He sneaked another furtive glance at her and felt that same flicker of perception. It hovered for a split second, tantalizingly close, like a butterfly just out of reach, and then it fluttered away again. He squeezed his eyes shut as if this act might somehow force the memory into the open, but it remained hidden, stubborn, unwilling to reveal itself.

Damn it, he cursed. It doesn't matter. Forget it. He turned his chair aside, away from her, and tried to contemplate his itinerary for the evening. He thought about his usual leisurely stroll through the village, down its white labyrinth of alleys lined with little gift shops, followed by a restful meal at one of the many delightful restaurants. His only dilemma was which restaurant to choose. Shall it be a meat dish this evening, or shall I have seafood, he pondered, or perhaps paella? So many choices. He sank down lower in his chair, swirled the wine in his glass and inhaled its fruity bouquet. Berries, he thought, definitely raspberry with a hint of spice. He emptied his glass, signaled to the waiter for another, and returned to his daydream about supper. He was busy salivating about an imaginary array of tapas when a loud shriek startled him out of his reverie.

"Oh my God, it's a reptile!" She was on her feet, the girl with the blue eyes, a chair held in front of her like a lion tamer. "It's there, under the table!"

Her friend, a shorter woman wearing a large hat with an over-sized floppy rim, screamed and leaped out of her seat, fanning a napkin like a matador, in the lizard's direction. The two women clung to each other, squealing and flapping their hands in panic as the lizard made a frantic dash to the low lying wall on the other side of the terrace.

Two of the waiters shot out from inside the restaurant to investigate the commotion. "Oh, it's nothing, only a leetle leezard," said one of them laughing, holding his palms in the air. "It's gone now, see? No problem eh?" His face was a mixture of relief and mild amusement. "For you, I make sure." He walked over to the wall, stamped his foot and waited a few seconds. "See, it's gone now. It no come back. Evertheeeng is okay. Please," he beckoned with his hands for the women to sit. He walked back to their table and pulled out a chair. He swept a hand across his chest, made a mock bow and announced, "Ladies, my name is Manolo. I will protect you."

"Oh, thank you, thank you," the two women chorused. They sat down, giggling, embarrassed by their outburst.

"I'm so sorry. I thought it was a snake at first," the tall blond apologized. "I bent down to get my napkin and there it was, right by my hand." She shivered and then swept her long hair on to the top of her head, securing it with a clasp. She fanned her face with one hand and laughed. "I think we could do with another drink after that."

"Good idea, yes," her friend readily agreed. She looked up at Manolo and pointed to their empty glasses. "Two more please."

The moment she lifted her hair from her face, Patterson knew why he thought he knew her. It came to him in a flash, a tiny second of clarity. It was her resemblance to Claudia Rankin, albeit a much younger version, that was now quite obvious to him. It bothered him that he had not been able to recognize it immediately; he was not one to easily forget faces. Perhaps it was his mind's attempt at some kind of unconscious self defense mechanism, a futile effort to preserve the sanctity of his first real vacation in years, because right now, Claudia Rankin was one of the last people he wanted to think about. He had come here for one thing—solitude. He wanted peace and quiet and an escape from anything remotely connected with his former life.

"Shit," he muttered. He felt a hot surge of anger well up in his chest. It just wasn't fair. Here he was, tucked away in a little hideaway, hundreds of miles from England, and still he could not bloody well escape from his sour memories of the Turner case.

It was the last case he had worked on before leaving the force. It had turned out to be a debacle, a humiliating failure, and no matter how far from home he traveled, the reminders of it seemed to be everywhere. They were in the accent of a stranger, in the smell of the air or in the nuance of a sound. Today, it was in the eyes of the woman.

He stared at her, disappointment and disgust written on his face. He knew he was being ridiculously unjust, blaming her for ruining his afternoon, but he could not help himself. The puzzled, surprised look on her face when she saw him scowling at her gave him a good measure of satisfaction. He waved at the waiter and asked for the bill.

"What, no more Rioja today? You all feeneeshed?" The waiter affected a disappointed voice. "Perhaps you come again tomorrow?"

"Perhaps," Patterson answered tersely.

He left the restaurant in a hurry. With a silent resolution to banish all thoughts of Claudia Rankin and her son from his mind, he repositioned his sunglasses, tilted his hat against the sun and stepped off the terrace into the blazing afternoon heat. He set off at a fast clip along the harbor path towards the village, determined to find a quiet corner in a bar where he could continue his afternoon sojourn without any further distraction.

Lord knows, he had spent the last year sifting through the files, re-examining old cases, trying to find a reason, any manner of indiscretion to warrant the arrest of Conrad Rankin. But all he had found were whiffs of rumor, hints of suspicion, and a handful of false leads. There was no solid evidence, nothing concrete. The bastard had gotten away with it.

It frustrated the hell out of Patterson to know, deep down in his gut, that Rankin was guilty. Call it intuition or a sixth sense. He knew beyond a doubt that Rankin had the Turners; that he had been in collusion with the kid, Jeremy Danvers, and that somehow, the two of them had out-smarted the police and engineered a plan to squirrel the art away. To this day, he still puzzled about how they had done it. He never did unearth the connection between the two of them.

He strode faster, making his way uphill through the myriad of meandering alleyways to a small tapas bar tucked away in one corner of the plaza. He flopped into a seat under a large umbrella and promptly ordered a cold beer. He took off his hat, placed it on the table and wiped the sweat from his brow with a paper napkin. The bar was mercifully quiet. Only a few of the tables were occupied. Beside the open door-way, three old men with deeply tanned wrinkled faces, wearing cardi-gans despite the heat, were crouched over a game of dominoes. Locals, Patterson guessed.

A peel of laughter from the center of the plaza caught his attention. A group of four young students were lolling about by the fountain. One of them, a short pudgy youth with dark curly hair, was flicking water at the others. Their backpacks were heaped against the steps of the church on the far side.

"Oh Christ," Patterson cursed into his beer. "Here we go again." This time there was no mistaking who the kid by the fountain reminded him of—Nigel Bryce-Edwards, the spoiled, fat little runt who eventually confessed to his part in the Turner case. Patterson looked up at the sky and addressed the heavens with his thoughts. When are you going to give me a break? Huh? He threw up his hands in a helpless gesture and made a quiet, resigned laugh. I give up. I bloody well give up. He took a long swig of beer, raked a hand through his hair and thought back to the day he arrested Nigel Bryce Edwards. The recollection brought a smirk to his face.

* * *

Bryce Edwards had turned up unexpectedly at the Three Bees pub in Tipping on the first night of their investigation in the village. He left not long afterwards with Jeremy Danvers, one of the main suspects in the case. The two of them went back to Danver's parent's house and spent the night.

Until then, there had been nothing to point the finger at Bryce Edwards other than a suspicion deep in Patterson's gut that the kid was somehow involved. Patterson recalled quite clearly, his feeling of elation when information came through later that night that implicated Nigel Bryce Edwards beyond any reasonable doubt. A check of the airlines revealed that Bryce Edwards had been booked onto a flight for Geneva for the week following the death of Parks. The booking had been made a month earlier. Patterson immediately made the connection between this flight and another flight taken by Bryce Edwards back in 2003.

In the spring of 2003, one of Patterson's moles hinted that a major piece by impressionist painter Alfred Sisley, was about to be smuggled out of the country. It had been missing for more than ten years after being stolen from a museum in Scotland. Nigel Bryce Edwards' flight to Geneva had been one week after Patterson's informant came forward. Patterson also discovered that Parks and Claudia Rankin were both in Switzerland around that time.

A check of auction house records revealed that Claudia Rankin had been a major bidder for impressionist landscapes, particularly those executed in the UK. Alfred Sisley's work would have been near the top of her list of desires. Given Bryce Edwards's connection to Parks and Claudia Rankin, the coincidence was too much for Patterson to ignore. It was the breakthrough he had been waiting for.

They caught Nigel Bryce Edwards unaware early the following afternoon, sleeping off a hangover on the sofa in the living room at Jeremy Danver's parents' house.

Patterson laughed when he thought about the look of horror on Bryce Edwards' face when they burst in and read him his rights. Danvers too, had been stunned. He looked as if a bolt of lightning had struck him when they produced a search warrant for the house.

Bryce Edwards swore his innocence, demanded a lawyer and refused to say anything. They let him stew in the local constabulary for twenty-four hours. Then he was transferred to headquarters in Harrogate where he was interviewed again and asked to make a statement. Patterson recalled that it had not taken long for Bryce Edwards to fall apart.

Confronted with the evidence of his trip to Switzerland in 2003, and documentation of occasions over the last three years when he, Parks and Claudia Rankin had all been in the same vicinity, his resolve to keep his mouth shut soon began to evaporate. The prospect of having his bank accounts scrutinized finally persuaded him to make a full confession.

In a lengthy statement, Nigel Bryce Edwards told about his relationship with Parks and their *arrangements* to move certain pieces of art out of the country. He admitted to receiving a payment of 200,000 pounds for transporting the Alfred Sisley out of the UK to Geneva in 2003, but insisted that he had no idea it had been stolen. He also confessed that he and Parks had planned to move six paintings from Turner's Yorkshire Collection to Switzerland in the third week of June 2005. According to Bryce Edwards, Claudia Rankin had been the driving force behind these schemes. There was no tangible evidence he could offer to substantiate this claim, but he believed that Parks had been obsessed with her and would have done anything to stay in her favor. Bryce Edwards admitted that he had never once met Claudia Rankin face to face; all communication had been through Julian Parks.

For Patterson, Nigel Bryce Edwards's confession was a crushing disappointment. Not only was Bryce Edwards unable to shed any light on the whereabouts of the Turners, he also failed to reveal any damaging information on Conrad Rankin and Jeremy Danvers. Bryce Edwards remained steadfast in his defense of Danvers, stating repeatedly that every time he questioned Danvers about the Turners, Danvers vehemently denied any knowledge of them.

As for Conrad Rankin, Bryce Edwards insisted that he had never seen nor heard of him before the death of Claudia Rankin and Parks. The first time he had ever come into contact with Conrad Rankin was in the gallery in Harrogate, shortly after returning from Parks' funeral. According to him, Rankin called in at the gallery to ask questions and gain some closure on his mother's death. When told of the suspicion surrounding his mother and Parks and their alleged involvement in the disappearance of the Turners, his reaction, according to Bryce Edwards, had been one of genuine surprise, shock even. There was nothing to implicate Conrad Rankin. Not one shred of evidence.

The only piece of information Bryce Edwards was eager to divulge was his story of an anonymous phone call threatening his life if he failed to come up with the Turners, but Patterson did not believe one word of it. He dismissed the phone call as a piece of fabrication; a ruse thought up by Bryce Edwards in an attempt to make Jeremy Danvers confess he had taken the Turners. And to divert the police's attention and have them barking in the wrong direction.

It gave Patterson enormous pleasure to nail Bryce Edwards, but he was gutted by the lack of evidence on his other suspects. He never doubted that Danvers and Rankin were heavily involved in the whole affair. He always suspected that Parks had left the paintings at the gallery; that Danvers had bolted with them and had somehow managed to lose them in Tipping. The story the two of them told about their car chase across Yorkshire was ridiculous enough to be almost believable, but how they were able to establish an alliance was the one thing Patterson was unable to fathom. Both of them were under constant surveillance. Rankin had been tailed since he set foot on English soil, and Danvers had been watched from the moment Patterson arrived in Tipping. There appeared to have been no window of opportunity for them to forge any kind of friendship. The only occasion when Rankin was off their radar was in Wickham, on the Saturday morning when they lost him for a couple of hours. Danvers though, had not left his parents house that morning apart from a brief trip to the post office around 9:00 a.m. Surveillance reported that he was out of the house for about twenty minutes, nowhere near long enough to get to Wickham and back. Other than the old man employed by the Danvers for a few odd jobs and a spot of gardening, no one was seen entering or leaving the house.

Danvers was taken to the local constabulary at the same time as Bryce Edwards, leaving Walker and Fields to search the house. Unfortunately, they were forced to release Danvers after twenty-four hours. There simply wasn't sufficient evidence to bring charges. Nothing was found at the house and Danvers stuck unwaveringly to his original story, adamant that he was innocent and knew absolutely nothing about the Turners. The kid came across as a gullible, hapless youth, essentially harmless with an endearing, almost comical presence. Patterson recalled that Danvers was unable to sit still in his seat, wringing his hands constantly and casting worried glances toward the door. He reminded Patterson of a startled deer in the headlights, wide-eyed with fear and ready to take flight at any moment. There were moments early on in the questioning, when Patterson felt a small measure of pity for the kid, but that sympathy quickly turned into frustration. After hours of questioning, Patterson was forced to concede, reluctantly, that Danvers was probably telling the truth when he said that he had no idea about what Nigel Bryce Edwards and Parks had been up to. It pained Patterson to let him go, but he had no choice. There were too many grey areas in Danvers's statement that Patterson was not happy about; too many loose ends. He was unable to throw off a growing sense of unease, as doubts kept niggling away in the back of his mind. He was missing something, but he was never quite able to put his finger on it.

While Bryce Edwards and Danvers were being questioned, Patterson had his three men on loan from Yorkshire poke around the village hoping that someone might come forward with information on the Turners. They spread out across the village, visited the local stores, and spoke with as many locals as they could, but they came up with nothing, not even a whisper. George Barlow, the local constable, kept his ear to the ground, but he also failed to generate any new leads.

Patterson reluctantly agreed to let Barlow spread the rumor that a reward might be on offer, but instead of flushing out the Turners, by four o'clock that afternoon, a long line of villagers were snaked outside the constabulary building under the impression that the "Antiques Road-show" was in town. Barlow was then forced to spend the rest of the day trying to explain to the disgruntled old dears who had spent hours rummaging through their attics for what they hoped were priceless antiques, to turn around and go back home again.

The only information of any interest that George Barlow was able to report was the hot gossip about a new courtship between Pearl Wiggins and the old chap, Barrington Smith. They had been spotted together in the pub the previous evening and the news spread like wildfire. At least it explained to Patterson, in part, why Mrs. Wiggins was so agitated when they attempted to search her handbag. He found it astounding how this one piece of information could have generated such a huge amount of interest in such a short time. The villager's concern about a few missing paintings was pale by comparison.

By the time Sunday morning rolled around, an ominous feeling of defeat began to settle on Patterson's shoulders like a cast iron weight. His mood matched the dark bank of thunderclouds that were steadily building to the east, made all the worse by the departure of Fields, Evans and Walker. His appeal for extended manpower fell on deaf ears. Scotland Yard was in the process of downgrading art crime on its list of priorities. Major cutbacks were on the horizon.

Under pressure to wrap up the investigation, Patterson's time was running out. With no new leads to follow, and a mountain of paperwork building on his desk in London, he was unable to justify staying in Tipping any longer. Over a gloomy breakfast that Sunday morning, he and Collins made their preparations to leave.

"We'll swing by Booth Hall on our way out and see if Rankin's willing to talk some more," said Patterson.

"I don't think he will," replied Collins, "not without some fancy lawyer."

"Nah, neither do I, but I'm not leaving here without giving it another shot. He's a smug bastard, so you never know. His kind like to think they're above the law. He might just see us for his own amusement—a little light entertainment. That's the time when they slip up," said Patterson slyly.

"Yeah. Well, let's hope he does because we've got piss all on him."

THIRTY TWO

The memory of their last meeting with Conrad Rankin was so clearly etched in Patterson's mind that it still pained him to think about it, even now, after more than a year had passed. The recollection of Rankin's swaggering smugness caused Patterson to choke on his beer. It spilled down the front of his shirt and into his crotch.

"Jesus!" He swore loudly. He sprang to his feet and grabbed a napkin off the table. The chair made a loud scraping noise against the cobbles. A couple sitting a few tables away raised their eyebrows and threw him a strange look.

After several minutes of frantic dabbing, Patterson slumped back into his chair, sweating heavily from the sudden burst of activity. A bead of perspiration trickled down the side of his face. He could feel his shirt sticking to his back. Bloody Rankin, he thought bitterly. Some of the poisonous hatred he had been nurturing over the last fifteen months welled up in his chest.

He flashed an apologetic smile at the couple and beckoned to the waiter for a fresh beer. He sat waiting with a grim smile welded to his face. He squinted through his eyelashes at the church across the square as his thoughts drifted back to that depressing morning at Booth Hall.

* * *

The village was overcast and gloomy when he and Collins set out. By the time they reached the gravel parking area at the rear of the Hall, a steady drizzle was falling.

Collins turned off the ignition. The two men peered through the windscreen, reluctant to face the walk to the entrance. "We're going to get soaked," Collins said.

"You don't say," Patterson bristled. His mood had deteriorated further. He opened his door a crack and looked up at the sky. "Shit. It looks like it's in for the day. We're going to have to make a run for it."

They sprinted from the car to the entrance foyer. After waiting for what seemed like hours at the reception desk, a grey-haired, elderly woman dressed in a pink ruffled housecoat shuffled into view. It took them several minutes to convince her that they were genuine policemen.

"I'll call his room then, shall I?" asked the old woman.

"No, no. If you give us directions, I'm sure we can find it," said Patterson sternly. He was fast running out of patience. "We don't have a lot of time."

"Oooh no! I can't do that. Her Ladyship would have my guts for garters if she found out I let visitors wander round the Hall unsupervised. Besides, you don't want to be getting lost in the East Wing," the old woman cackled. "It's 'aunted you know."

"I'm sorry, what was that you said?"

"It's 'aunted by the Baroness Montague. Hung 'erself with her own pearls after being jilted by the gardener. Mr. Rankin's sleeping in the very room where it 'appened." She narrowed her eyes and studied their reaction.

Patterson flashed a quick look at Collins, who stared at the old woman with a poker face. Only the merest flicker of amusement in his eyes betrayed his real thoughts.

Patterson's face creased into a look of scorn. "Well, I doubt the Baroness will be up this early," he said sarcastically "We're here as part of a police investigation. I do not want Mr. Rankin to know that we're on our way. Is that clear? Now, what's his room number?"

"Well!" She held a hand to her chest, clearly offended. "He's up in the East Wing." She pointed a gnarled finger to a corridor leading off the reception area.

"Straight down past the portraits and then left up the staircase. It's the room right at the end. If that will be all gentleman, I have important things to attend to." She lifted her chin in indignation, gave a snort, and turned to leave. "Well, I never," she mumbled as she left. "These young 'uns 'ave got no manners these days."

"A fucking ghost, my arse," scoffed Patterson from the side of his mouth as they paced down the portrait corridor.

"Yeah right," Collins laughed. "The Headless Phantom of Booth Hall—as if."

They spoke in hushed tones, snickering, sharing a number of dismissive comments, until they reached the top of the creaking staircase. Then they stopped talking and crept along the hallway to the door at the end. With a nod of his head, Patterson gave Collins the signal to knock on the door. They didn't have to wait long. The door swept open after the second knock.

"Ah, Detective Sergeant Patterson and Detective Collins. You're back again." Rankin greeted them brightly. "What can I do for you?"

"We'd like to ask you a few more questions, if you don't mind," said Patterson.

Rankin stepped back from the door and beckoned them into the room with a wave of his hand. Apart from the tiniest flicker of surprise on his face, there was no obvious sign that he was alarmed to see them. It was as if they were expected.

"Come in. There are a couple of chairs over there by the window if you'd prefer to sit. I'm in the middle of packing, so if you don't mind me putting a few things into my case while we talk . . . " He paused and glanced at his watch. "I've got a little time." He smiled and nodded at the open suitcase on the bed. "But please, can I get you gentlemen anything—water, or tea perhaps? I can call room service, although I have to warn you, things can be a little slow around here," he said, laughing lightly.

"No, thank you. This shouldn't take too long. Where are you heading?" Patterson inquired politely. He stood casually in the middle of the room, one hand in the pocket of his trousers. Collins took a chair by the window. He extracted a small notebook from his jacket and began flicking through its pages, giving the appearance of being a little bored and uninterested. Rankin spoke as he lifted a folded shirt from the bed and placed it in the case.

"I'll be checking out at eleven and then I'm driving down to London. My flight's out of Heathrow tomorrow evening, as I'm sure you already know." He glanced at Patterson and smiled. "I'm staying at the Savoy. A little shopping and some business to attend to," he added. He seemed at ease and in good spirits.

Collins raised his head with sudden interest. "Business. What kind of business?"

Rankin hesitated over his suitcase for a second. When he looked up his face was serious. "You know, I really don't have to tell you any of this. I'm assuming that you're going to get to the point of this visit. I can give you five minutes and no more than that."

A muscle worked in Patterson's jaw. He looked at Rankin with thinly disguised dislike. "I didn't realize you were here on business. You didn't mention it the last time we spoke."

Rankin didn't respond immediately. He straightened and turned to face Patterson. When he eventually spoke, the corners of his lips again curled into a smile. "Real estate," he stated matter-of-factly. "Excuse me, I need to get some things from the bathroom." He walked across the room with a languid, slow, satisfied gait. He disappeared for a few seconds and then re-emerged with a handful of toiletries. "I have an appointment with Harvey Felton, a real estate solicitor in Knightsbridge tomorrow at ten. He specializes in unique properties."

Collins scribbled the name down in his notebook and shot a glance at Patterson. "Really?" Collins said. "You're buying a property here in the U.K?"

"I'm considering it." Rankin dropped the toiletries into a wash-bag, and turned to face Patterson. He shrugged his shoulders, cast a quick look around the room and said, "This place actually."

Both Patterson's and Collins's jaws dropped open.

"What? Booth Hall?" Patterson said, taken aback. "This is all a bit sudden isn't it?"

"Yes, I suppose it is, but I'm only looking into it at this stage. Nothing is written in stone, but I rather like the idea of being lord of my own manor," he quipped light heartedly. Patterson exchanged a look with Collins.

"Why now?" he asked.

"Oh, this whole missing Turner thing has set me thinking about my mother's art. I haven't had the chance to run through it all yet, but, as I'm sure you already know, it seems I've inherited an extensive collection, including a good many British works." He leaned against the end of the bed and folded his arms across his chest. "I've made a few phone calls, gathering information." He motioned to the cell phone on the bedside table. "Most of the art is in the States—New York and Boston. All of it's behind closed doors, not on public display." He lifted his eyes to Patterson's face. "I'm thinking of changing that. I've got to speak to my people first and I've got a great deal of homework to do, but I have an idea to bring some of the art back to its country of origin, create a museum, and have it on display here. There are some major pieces you know."

"Yes, I'm well aware of that," said Patterson, nodding his head, still trying to process what he had just heard. He narrowed his eyes in concentration, his thoughts racing. "Hmm, well that's putting yourself to a lot of trouble though, isn't it? I mean why not just keep the art where it is, view it at leisure in the privacy of your own homes, or create a museum over there? Or is it the philanthropist in you Mr. Rankin, a need to extend your benevolence to this community for some reason? I mean Yorkshire is a long way from home, isn't it?" he asked suspiciously. Rankin laughed and flashed a beguiling smile.

"Like I said, I have a few ideas up my sleeve. It's not just about the art. There are a number of possibilities for a place like this, but . . . " He paused and looked at his watch. "I'm afraid it would take up too much of your valuable time for me to explain. Now if you're finished, I really do need to get a move on." He moved to the wardrobe and took a jacket off a hanger.

"Uh no, not quite," said Patterson with a forced smile on his face. "Just a couple more questions. Where were you between 11:00 a.m. and 1:00 p.m. yesterday?" He walked over to the table where Collins sat. "Don't mind if I sit do you? I need to take the weight off my feet."

"I was in Wickham," Rankin answered with a hint of irritation.

"What for?"

"Because I wanted to have a look around the place. It's as simple as that."

"And where did you go exactly? I'm just curious."

"Down by the river, the park and a few stores. Look, I'm running late. I need to leave soon if I'm going to avoid the rush hour traffic around London. I want to stop for lunch on the way down."

"Did you meet anyone?"

"Where?"

"In Wickham." Patterson kept his eyes locked on Rankin's face.

"What? No." Patterson noted the flicker of a look in Rankin's eyes and the split second of indecision when he answered, little telltale signs of someone not telling the truth.

"So you were alone the whole time?"

"Yes," Rankin answered immediately this time. "What I did or where I went is none of your business Sergeant. Now what is it you really want?"

"Oh, but it is my business if you were handling or conspiring to conceal stolen art Mr. Rankin."

Rankin stiffened. A flash of anger shot across his face. "Gentlemen, I think it's time our *little chat* was over," he said abruptly. "I've got nothing else to say to you. If you're accusing me of something, then I'll pick up that phone right now and call the embassy." He paused and looked Patterson in the face. "Now, if you don't mind . . ." He indicated the door with an open palm. "It's time you left."

* * *

"Hmm. He was lying about Wickham," Collins said quietly as they re-traced their steps along the portrait corridor.

"Yep. The slippery bastard's lying through his teeth, but we've got nothing on him and he knows it. We'll know by the phone records if he's been in contact with anyone, but I think we're too late. If, and I mean *if* he had hold of the paintings and made the drop in Wickham, they'll be long gone by now."

"Yeah, but he wouldn't be so stupid to have them in the car would he? He'd have taken one hell of a risk to pass them on right under our noses."

"I agree. I think our boy was in Wickham to talk to the person who's got his or her hands on them, to make a deal. We've ruled out Pearl Wiggins. I would have put my money on Danvers, but he was in his house all morning."

"Hmm . . . apart from the trip he made to the post office earlier on, around 9:00 a.m. . . . unless . . . " Collins pondered out loud. "Unless he sneaked out the back."

Patterson stopped in his tracks. "Fields said he was watching the house the whole time. "

"Yeah, Fields said he didn't see Danvers leave, but he was at the front of the house. Who's to say Danvers didn't sneak out the back?"

"But how could he get to Wickham and back if he wasn't in the car? He only had a couple of hours. He couldn't have had enough time if he went by bike." Patterson rubbed his chin and thought for a moment.

"Hang on a minute." He stopped walking. "The old guy, the odd job man—what's his name?"

"Barrington Smith?"

"Yeah, that's him—Pearl Wiggins's new beau. What time did he call at the house?"

"Around 10:30 wasn't it?'

"Right, and he called again later on, about thirty minutes before we arrived to execute the warrant and pick up Bryce Edwards. That would have been at 1:30 p.m."

"So three hours in between, the same time that Rankin went missing. Danvers could have used the old guy to sneak him to Wickham and back."

"Shit!" Patterson broke into a fast walk. "We'd better get back to the village. Get Barlow on the phone. I want to know everything about Barrington Smith. Get his address and find out what kind of relationship he has with Danvers."

They strode quickly down the portrait corridor, across the reception room, and out through the heavy wooden entrance doors. They paused briefly in the doorway, pulled their jackets tight against the rain, and dashed across the drenched car park.

"What about Rankin," Collins panted as he fell into the car. "We let him walk?"

"Yeah, for now." Patterson sank heavily into the passenger seat. A look of disappointment hung from his face. "He'll be a good boy at first. He's got his mother's collection to keep him busy for a while, and then when he gets bored, he'll do the rounds at the auction houses making bids on pretty much everything that takes his fancy. He'll flash his money around, make his name as an art collector, and build up his own little cache. But his type is all the same. He's an obsessed collector just like his mother—insatiable, never satisfied. So it's only a matter of time before he starts coveting stuff that he can't get his hands on legitimately. He'll slip up eventually, and when he does, I'm going to be right there waiting. The name of the game, Tom, is patience. It might take two, three, maybe five years, but I will nail that bastard."

* * *

Collins pressed his cell phone to his chest and whispered to Patterson, "Barlow's in church, Sarge. He'll be done in about forty-five minutes. Do you want me to ask him to leave?"

"Nah—leave him. Tell him to meet us at the constabulary when he's finished."

"Right." Collins lifted the phone to his cheek and repeated Patterson's instructions.

"Did you get the address?"

"Yeah, 16 Cherry Lane, left off the main road a few hundred yards from the post office. We're lucky Smith doesn't go to church." Patterson nodded his head in agreement.

"You'd better step on the gas. I want to catch the old bugger at home."

* * *

Fifteen minutes later, they rolled up outside Barrington Smith's cottage.

"All the curtains are shut," Collins observed from the car. "It looks like he's still here."

"Good. Come on, let's see what he's got to say," said Patterson, unbuckling his seatbelt. Patterson waited until Collins was by his side, then rapped on the front door. A minute passed without a response. Patterson knocked again, louder this time. Collins took a step to his right and peered through a gap in the curtains in the front window.

"Can't see anything," he said.

"Shit," muttered Patterson. He banged on the door with the side of his fist. "He's probably deaf as a post." He was about to knock a third time when a rattling noise that sounded like the sliding of a bolt and chain could be heard behind the door.

"Psst," Patterson beckoned to Collins. "He's here."

Collins straightened and stepped quickly to Patterson's side as the door opened an inch.

"Who is it?"

"It's the police," Patterson addressed the door. "Detective Sergeant Patterson and Detective Collins. We'd like to have a word with you."

"Who?"

Patterson rolled his eyes at Collins. He leaned forward and shouted through the crack, "It's the police. We need to talk with you, Mr. Smith!"

"Show me yer identification through the window," a voice shouted back. The door slammed shut.

"Dear God," Patterson grumbled. "Come on," he motioned to Collins. They stepped away from the door and pressed their ID's against the dirty windowpane. Patterson breathed a loud frustrated sigh, "This is going to take all bloody day."

Inside, the curtain was pulled to one side. A spindly grey-haired old man leaned forward and squinted through the pane. He looked as if he had just got out of bed.

"'Ang on!" he shouted. "I need to get mi specs!"

"Oh for Christ's sake!" Patterson's blood was beginning to boil.

"Let me see what he's doing," said Collins. He cupped his hands to the window and peered inside. "Looks like he's left the room. Oh wait, he's coming back." He grabbed Patterson's ID and held it up next to his own.

"I can't see 'em properly. You'll have to pass 'em through the door so I can get a proper look." Seconds later there was the rattling of the door chain again and the door opened a little wider. "Pass 'em through 'ere!" Patterson snatched Collins's ID and pushed both of them through the door.

"We're from Scotland Yard Mr. Smith. It's important we talk with you. Open the door now," he said. He began tapping his foot on the step. Silence. "Mr. Smith, are you still there?" A minute passed, and then another. "Mr. Smith!"

After what seemed like an eternity, the door opened a tad more and out shot a gnarled hand holding the ID's. "'Ere you can 'ave 'em back. 'Ow the 'eck do I know if they're the real thing or not? I've seen 'ont news about 'ow these burglars trick old folk like me into letting them into their 'omes. You'll 'ave to fetch George Barlow, the local constable if I'm to let yer in." The door slammed shut again.

"Jesus Christ," Patterson cursed through clenched teeth. He raked his fingers through his hair and turned to Collins. "Get Barlow over here, now."

* * *

Twenty minutes later, George Barlow pulled into the lane.

"What's kept you?" asked Patterson impatiently when Barlow met them.

"Oh, what a morning! I've had to fend off Audrey Ormerod and her ramblers. They ambushed me as I was leaving the church. Asking all sorts of questions, they were. Now, if there's someone you might want to talk to, it's Audrey Ormerod. There's nothing that goes on in this village that she doesn't know about, but you do so at your own risk. A conversation with that woman is a perilous undertaking, not to be taken lightly." He flashed them a beaming smile. "Now then, what seems to be the problem here? Is old Barrington giving you a spot of bother?" he chuckled. "He's a wily old bugger you know."

"Yes, we know. Just get us in there will you?" Patterson snapped. He nodded toward the front door. "The old sod won't let us in."

"Leave it with me," said Constable Barlow. Patterson and Collins stood behind him. Barlow rapped on the door and shouted, "Barrington, it's me, George. You can open up now!" A minute passed. The door chain rattled. The door opened an inch.

"Is that you George?"

"Yes, it's me," Barlow answered. "These gentlemen want to ask you a few questions."

"What about?"

"They're from Scotland Yard. Remember the other day when I told you about those missing paintings? Now, open the door. We don't want to be having this conversation out on the street, Barrington. We're getting wet out here," Barlow coaxed patiently.

"Let me put mi teeth in first," came Barrington's surly reply.

Several more minutes passed before they heard the sound of bolts being pulled back and the rattling of the door chain. The door opened slowly to reveal Barrington standing in his pajamas. A length of string tied around his waist held up the bottoms.

"You'd best come in then," he said, grudgingly.

"Mr. Smith," Patterson nodded to Barrington as he walked into the tiny front living room. He took a quick look around the disheveled room and then perched on the end of the battered sofa.

"Detective Collins." Collins introduced himself with a half hearted smile and took a seat next to Patterson.

Constable Barlow closed the door behind him and sat in the shabby armchair by the fireplace. Barrington remained on his feet by the door with his hands folded against his chest.

"Now what the 'eck is all this about? It had better be important, getting me out of bed like this."

"We'll be as quick as we can," said Collins.

"Right then. Can you tell us where you were yesterday between 11:30 a.m. and 1:30 p.m.?"

"On mi allotment."

"Allotment?" Collins flashed a look at Constable Barlow.

"Oh, er a number of villagers have their own small allotments – a small plot of land where they grow their own vegetables. They're located round the back of Moss Lane," Barlow answered.

"They were given out durin' the War," said Barrington.

"Right, "said Collins."And you grow your own vegetables?"

"Aye. Tomaters, courgettes, cauliflowers, lettuce, taters, the lot— 'cept turnips. I've always 'ad a problem with mi turnips."

"And were you on your allotment all morning?"

"No. I 'ad to nip out on a few errands."

"What errands were those?" Collins asked casually.

"Well, I dropped some tomaters off at Mrs. Danvers 'ouse, and then I went to the bakery for mi usual pasty. I treat miself to a pasty every Saturday fer mi lunch. Meat and 'tater's mi favorite."

"Look, why don't you sit down for a moment Barrington," Barlow interrupted. "You must be getting tired standing there by the door. Here." He got up and pointed the armchair he had vacated. "Come and sit here."

"I thought you said it wouldn't take but a minute. Sounds to me like it's goin' to take a lot longer than that," Barrington grumbled. "I haven't even ad the chance to feed Ernie yet."

"The cat," Barlow explained.

"Ah." Collins lifted his chin.

"Are you them fellas from London?" Barrington asked.

"Yes, that's right," said Collins.

"Oh, well then. Why didn't yer say so?" Barrington's face lit up. "'Ang on a minute, I've something to show yer." He shuffled out of the room. Moments later, after a lot of muffled banging and scuffling, Barrington reappeared holding a large object covered in brown paper and wrapped with string. "It were mi mam's," he said proudly as he carried the item over to a tall set of narrow drawers squashed next to the settee. He swept a pile of newspapers and other bits and pieces to the floor with his elbow and carefully placed it in the middle. "'Ere we are then. Can yer 'elp me the string George? I can't undo the knots."

The Constable shot an apologetic glance at Patterson and Collins, and strode over to help Barrington. "Now what have you got in here Barrington? I don't think this is quite what the detectives had in mind."

"'Ere—get 'old of this corner and peel it back carefully," Barrington instructed, "And I'll pull it back from this end. There we are. It's a beauty 'int it?" He stood back and viewed the gilt rimmed, decorative vase with deference for a few seconds before turning to Patterson and Collins with a look of delight on his face.

"What do yer think? I'll bet it's worth a few bob. It were given to mi mam by the last family she worked for: The Browns, a posh family from London. It were a parting gift fer her services. She 'ad to leave when she got sick. She died in 1947 did mi mam. She were just forty-six," he said sadly. He fell silent for a few seconds. "Ah well, she left me this." He nodded at the vase. "And ninety pounds she'd saved up in a tea caddy. That were a lot of money in them days yer know."

Constable Barlow gave an embarrassed little cough and widened his eyes at Patterson and Collins. "We're sorry about your mother Barrington." He pressed his lips together and turned to look at the vase. He bent down for a closer look. "Very nice Barrington. A very nice piece indeed, but the detectives here," he nodded in Patterson and Collins's direction, "are here to investigate the disappearance of some paintings."

"Eh? Paintin's? What paintin's?" Barrington's head swiveled round. "I know nowt about any paintin's. Yer not here from The Antiques Road Show then?"

Patterson squeezed his eyes shut for a second and took a deep breath. When he spoke, his voice was noticeably strained. "No, we are not. I am Detective Sergeant Maurice Patterson from Scotland Yard and I am in the village to investigate the disappearance of some very valuable paintings by an artist called Turner. He's a famous watercolorist."

"Who?" Barrington interrupted. "I don't care much for water colors. I prefer oil miself. They look grander in my opinion. Disappeared eh? Stolen? 'Ow the 'eck did they get 'ere in Tipping? And what's it got to do with me?"

"We're talking to as many people from the village as we can Mr. Smith," interjected Collins.

"Is there a reward fer 'em?" Barrington narrowed his eyes.

"Ah, no. Not yet," said Collins.

"Hmmph," Barrington snorted. He pressed his lips together in disappointment. "So when will there be one?"

"We're not quite sure," said Collins uncertainly.

"Meanin' there int goin' to be one!" Barrington shouted angrily.

"How well do you know Jeremy Danvers?" Patterson asked firmly, changing the subject.

"Well enough. Why do yer ask?"

"When did you last see him?"

"Int pub Friday night. He's 'ome from university."

"Did you see him yesterday?"

"No."

"How about when you dropped off . . . uh, what was it you dropped off at the Danver's house?"

"Tomater plants, and no I didn't see 'im."

"You were there for about ten minutes. What else did you do besides drop the tomato plants off?"

"Eh?" Barrington paused to think. "I went round the back and filled the bird feeder. Then I dropped the plants off round the front, under the porch."

"Was that the only time you went to the Danver's house yesterday?"

"No, I called round again with the manure fer the roses. I keep it wrapped in plastic bags until I've enough to take round. I've not spread it yet. I'm doin' that today if the weather clears. She likes me to spread it when they're away. She doesn't care fer the smell of it – Mrs. Danvers, that is. I've been workin' fer 'em fer years 'aven't I, George?"

"Did you see Jeremy the second time?"

"No, I weren't there fer long. Just forked a bit in a pile near the compost heap. Now listen to me, if you've got any madcap idea that Jeremy's done summat wrong, then you're barkin' up wrong tree, I'm telling yer right now that lad hasn't got a bad bone in his body. He's 'elped me over the years. Got me a cell-u-lar phone you know, and he 'elps me with mi video. If it weren't fer im, I'd still be int stone ages." Barrington waved an arthritic finger at them. "I'll 'ave none of it," he said sternly.

"Has he mentioned anything about any paintings to you?" Patterson asked unsmiling. "And I have to warn you that it is a serious offence to lie to the police." He looked Barrington squarely in the face.

"No he bloody well 'asn't!" Barrington shouted. "Only that the police 'ave got wrong end of the stick. Instead of harrassin' poor innocent kids like 'im who've done nowt wrong all their lives, you lot should be out roundin' up the real criminals like them rapists and murderers who are runnin' free. I don't know what this country's comin' to anymore. Bloody police do nothin' to keep honest folk like me safe in our own 'omes. It's ever since the Conservatives got in. The country's gone downhill ever since. And another thing while you're 'ere George: when are you goin' to do summat about Charlie Batham's two youngsters? Them two scallywags have been on my wall again, nickin' mi apples from mi tree!"

"Jesus Christ get us out of here!" Patterson exclaimed as he climbed back into the car.

Collins laughed, "Could you imagine working in this place? I pity poor Barlow."

Patterson stared through the windscreen at the drenched grey landscape and shook his head. "It would be my idea of a living Hell. Let's get out of this Godforsaken hole. I need some decent urban grime."

* * *

"You like another beer?" A voice rang in the distance. "Sir, you want another, or you want the beeel?" The voice persisted, interrupting Patterson's daydream. Patterson straightened in his chair and looked up at the waiter by his table.

"Huh? Oh, yes, right." He rubbed his face with both hands, reached for his wallet and left several notes on the table. He glanced at his wrist-watch. Four-thirty. Time to wander back to his room, have a nap and then change for the evening. He paused at the edge of the square for a moment and debated which direction to take. He finally settled on the slightly longer, but shadier route, which wound its way through the olive groves above the town. He dashed across the baking square to get out of the sun and then made his way up a steep little backstreet. He walked with his head down, deep in thought.

Before leaving the shade of the olive grove, Patterson stopped to admire the view. Out of breath, he stood panting with both hands on his hips as he gazed out across the harbor to the dazzling azure of the Mediterranean. Apart from one or two sailboats speckled against the horizon, and a few small fishing boats closer to shore, the vast expanse of blue was virtually empty. He tilted his head to the sun and felt it's rays dapple across his face as it filtered through the olive branches. He closed his eyes for a moment and considered his favorite proverb, 'All things come to he who waits'. The corners of his lips curled into a satis-fied grin. He had retired from the police force, but he was by no means severed from the art world. On the contrary, in his new position as Head of Dalton's Art Security, he would be involved at an intimate level. He still had his contacts, his moles. It was only a matter of time before Rankin made a mistake, and when he did—he, Maurice Patterson, would be coiled like a cobra, ready to strike. He gave a little snort of laughter and continued on his way.

THIRTY THREE

Less than a thousand miles away, nine hundred and twenty-six to be exact, Conrad was working on his laptop behind a voluminous desk in the private drawing room of the newly renovated West Wing of Booth Hall. He glanced up as Jeremy walked into the room.

"Hi, Jeremy. Is everything in place for the new exhibition?"

"Pretty much. We're still working on the lighting and there are a few issues with the extra staffing we're going to need, but nothing that can't be taken care of."

"And security?"

"It's airtight," said Jeremy with confidence. "Our new Head of Security seems to know what he's doing. He's running checks on the alarm system, and all the major pieces are wired."

"Good. It still amazes me, how lax security is at most small museums. No wonder art theft is rife."

"Yeah well, it's mainly lack of funding," Jeremy sighed. "No worries here though," he added brightly.

"Nope." Conrad got up and walked around the desk to a large bookcase by the window. "Here, look at these," he said, grabbing a stack of colorful, glossy brochures. He placed them on the desk and offered one to Jeremy. "They just came in. What do you think?"

"Oh, very nice," said Jeremy. He read parts of the brochure out loud: "'Born from the magnificent private collection of Claudia Rankin, Booth Hall is now home to an astounding number of high profile works by

British Masters such as J.M.W. Turner, George Stubbs, Joshua Reynolds and Thomas Gainsborough."' He nodded his head approvingly.

"'An intimate space set within the elegant confines of a 17th century manor house . . . a peaceful, meditative experience . . . a quintessential art haven . . . a bold collection.'"

"And look at the quotes," said Conrad, pointing to them with his finger.

"'For an intimate look at some of the world's great art, Britain's smaller, lesser known museums, such as Booth Hall, provide the ideal setting.'" Conrad smiled. "And this one by the curator of art at the Cleveland museum: "'Booth Hall is the one museum where I really feel at one with the artist. Perhaps its because the environment complements his work so well. We tend to think we know Turner's work, as the images have become so enmeshed with our psyche, but this collection allows us to see the whole range of his creative output.'"

Jeremy placed the brochure back on top of the pile. "It's amazing what you've managed to do with this place. I never thought you'd be able to pull it off."

"Yeah, well, it hasn't been easy," said Conrad. He stood by the window and looked out. "It's taken a lot longer than I thought. There's been so much red tape to get through, and Cranshawe Booth . . . " He shook his head and laughed. "Boy, he took some persuading." He waved Jeremy over to the window and pointed outside.

"Look at the stables. The renovations are nearly finished. We should have the Equestrian Center up and running in a month or so"

"Do you think it's enough to keep the Cranshawe Booths happy?" Jeremy asked.

Conrad thought for a moment, a serious look on his face. "Not entirely," he answered. "They'll never get over the fact that Booth Hall is no longer theirs, but deep down I think they know that things could have been a lot worse."

"She barely acknowledges me," Jeremy complained.

Conrad laughed and gave Jeremy a friendly slap on the shoulder. "That doesn't surprise me. Olivia Cranshawe Booth barely tolerates me either. We have an *understanding*, but her kind will always look down their noses at us, no matter what. It's the way they've been brought up. You'll never change it. But, I do think they're particularly well suited to running the Equestrian Centre and organizing the shooting parties, don't you?"

"Oh yeah," Jeremy agreed. "It's right up their alley."

"And they're free of debt. They've got a nice little nest egg in the bank now. It wasn't easy getting Cranshawe Booth to sign over all owner-ship and rights to me, but I eventually managed to persuade him that he wasn't going to get a better deal than the one I was putting on the table. I've let them stay on at the Hall. They've got the whole of the East Wing, the conservatory and a private garden; a damned sight better than he'd have got if he'd have signed everything over to the National Trust.

"That's true," Jeremy agreed. He fell silent for a moment. Then he whispered, "And the Turners, are they still here?"

Conrad didn't answer immediately. After a prolonged silence, he turned to look Jeremy in the eye. "It's better that you don't know where they are. That way if you're questioned again, you won't be lying any more. They're in a safe place. That's all you need to know."

"But they're still in this country, right?"

"Yes. I had to move them. I couldn't have it where Cranshawe Booth could get his hands on them. He has no clue where they are now. I'm the only one that knows. Their secret is safe with me."

"It's a pity they've got to stay hidden. At least two of them are worth a fortune."

"I know, but there's no other choice. One day, perhaps they'll resur-face again. Who knows? Now, how are you getting on with Jason?" Conrad asked, quickly changing the subject. "He knows his stuff inside and out. He'll be a great mentor for you."

"I know. I don't know how to thank you for everything you've done. Working with someone like him, one of the world's best authorities on fine art, well, its . . . its beyond anything I could ever have dreamed of."

"I'm happy for you," Conrad said, smiling. "And what about your parents? Have they forgiven you yet?"

"Oh God, no. They'll never get over he fact that I lied to them for over three years, but at least they haven't cut me off completely. The initial embarrassment when it all came out nearly killed them, particularly my mother, but we're talking again—just."

"They'll come round in time," said Conrad. "When they see this place and what you've done here, they'll be proud of you. Just wait and see."

"Maybe," said Jeremy doubtfully. "Art isn't their thing, but if they understand that I'm making a half decent living out of it, then they might change their minds. We'll see."

"Oh they'll change their minds when this place is finished. This," Conrad said, indicating the Estate with a sweep of his hand, "is only the beginning. I'm waiting for Listed Building Consent and planning permission from the local authority and The English Heritage. I'm keeping the historical integrity of the Hall and all the outbuildings, so it shouldn't be an issue, but I want to expand at the back, and add more galleries to showcase some of my own collections. I've got arms, armor, porcelain, furniture, and all sorts of treasures. I really want to make a name for myself, in my own right, as a great collector and to do that we need to separate specific works of art from the millions of pieces already in existence, and assemble and order them in such a way that increases or advances our understanding of that art in particular. That's where you come in. I need your help to do this. I want to put Booth Hall on the map as one of the best, if not *the* best small museum and art gallery in the country. That means we'll also need to have a changing program of special exhibitions designed to complement our permanent collections. It's quite an enterprise." A radiant smile spread across his face.

"Wow, it's a lot of work, but I'm excited," said Jeremy. "Who would have thought," he chuckled. "Ah well, I'd better get back to the gallery. He started for the doorway, then stopped. "Oh, I nearly forgot why I came in here. I wanted to show you this." He reached into the folder he was carrying and handed a small card to Conrad. "I got a post card from Mrs. Wiggins. It's from Barcelona, one of the stops on her cruise. I thought you might like to see it."

Conrad gave a quiet laugh and took it from him. He read the brief message on the back and then handed it to Jeremy.

"She's certainly a character isn't she?"

"That is something of an understatement," Jeremy laughed. "Did you know she's retired from the post office now? She rents a small cottage at the end of Potters Lane. She helps out in the bakery every now and then. I think it gives her something to do."

"I take it she's remained *discreet* about our little arrangement?"

"Oh yes. She's still terrified the paintings are going to turn up and her fingerprints will be all over them. I don't think she'll ever say anything. She's too frightened, and besides, she's got a nice little nest egg now, just like the Cranshawe Booths. No, she'll keep her mouth shut."

"And what about old Barrington? I think I've seen him puttering about in the gardens. How's he doing?"

"He's not changed one bit, still grumbling about everything. He still does odd jobs for my parents, but I think he spends more time here helping Wilfred out. The two of them make a good team." Jeremy shook his head and laughed. "They're both as decrepit as each other, but at least they're in keeping with the character of this place. You should hear them reminiscing about the War together: You'd think it was still 1945. Do you remember how he brought the paintings over here? I still can't get over that."

"How can I forget?" said Conrad with amusement. "Rolled up in brown paper, sealed in plastic grocery bags, and then hidden in a sack full of manure. Unbelievable."

"It worked though. No one would ever have thought about looking in a pile of manure. Could you imagine the look on Patterson's face if he knew?" He looked at Conrad and they both burst out laughing.

"But can you still trust him?" said Conrad once he stopped laughing. He's a sly old dog."

"I don't think anyone would believe him, do you? No, but seriously, he's happy now he's got his "little inheritance" left to him by a long forgotten second cousin in America. And he's been back to the Battlefields in France, which, I think, was what he wanted more than anything. He never mentions anything to me. He gives me a knowing wink every once in a while, a little reminder. I wouldn't worry about him though. He's hasn't got the time or the energy to cause you any trouble. He's far too busy trying to fend off the attentions of Mrs. Wiggins."

"Oh Jeez. Can you imagine the two of them together?" said Conrad. They fell about laughing again.

Alone again, Conrad flipped open his laptop and retrieved the page he had been looking at before Jeremy walked into the room. It was an image of Manet's "Le Repos". Conrad stared at it, transfixed. "An homage to love and to the intimacy between painter and subject," he whispered. There were so many levels of desire captured in his eyes at that moment. After spending more than a year admiring and learning about his mother's art collections, he now wanted, more than anything else, to add to them with his own acquisitions. His favorites, by far, were the Impressionists. He had, without any doubt, inherited a fabulous collection, but one more Manet? What would it take, he wondered, to acquire a painting like this? He had learned that it was on permanent display in the Rhode Island School of Design, bequeathed by Mrs. Edith Stuyvesant Vanderbilt Gerry. He scrolled down the page and studied the photograph taken of the exterior of the RISD. It was a modern rectangular building, aesthetically displeasing in his opinion. It was the wrong setting entirely for a painting of such beauty. Such a pity, he thought.

With a loud sigh, he snapped the lid of the laptop shut, straightened from his desk and wandered into the hallway outside. He strode past the line of portraits until he reached the one he was seeking. The cold, ugly, disapproving face of Mrs. Prendergast stared back at him. He stepped back a little, tilted his head this way and that, and then leaned in more closely to get a better look. His lips curled up into a self-satisfied smile. Now that Mrs. Prendergast had been placed into a much grander, ornate frame, there really was no way of telling that one of the Turners was concealed behind her hideous portrait. The five remaining Turners were concealed in similar fashion behind five more canvasses on the wall. He laughed quietly to himself then moved on to the end of the hallway. He rounded the corner then stopped before two portraits that were set apart from the others, claiming an entire wall.

The first was of his father: a cold, flat rendition, devoid of expression and emotion. It was much as Conrad remembered him. He peered at the painting for a good minute, hoping to feel some kind of communion with it, but he turned away, disappointed as always.

He much preferred the portrait on the right. On each of his visits to Booth Hall, he would take the time to come here, to stand and look and wonder. The face of the woman was elegant, poised, refined and beautiful. She was the feminine version of himself: his mother, Claudia.

I never knew you, and you never took the time to know me, he thought sadly. You and I are not the same. I am not selfish like you. He stared into her ice-blue eyes for a second more, then turned to leave. In the very instant that he lowered his gaze, something out of the corner of his eye caught his attention. He turned to face the painting again. He could have sworn that he had seen a movement, the tiniest flicker of something in her face. He could feel his heart beating in his chest. You are being ridiculous, he told himself. Very tentatively, holding his breath, he stepped closer to the canvas. The corners of her lips were still curled into the faintest of smiles and her eyes shone with a trace of amusement. Nothing had changed.

"Jeez," he said aloud. I've been working too hard. I should take a break.

He turned away and strode back to his office. He slumped into his chair behind the desk and gazed out the window to the rim of moorland in the distance. Where should I go? He wondered. Somewhere new, I think.

A small voice from within his psyche whispered back to him. He squeezed his eyes shut and tried to push it away, but it was persistent and grew louder.

"No!" he banged a fist on the desk. "I am not like you. I'm not listening." The image of the portrait of his mother floated through his mind, her eyes twinkling with amusement. Her soft voice whispered: "The Manet, Conrad. It's in Rhode Island."

THE END